O9-AHS-882

Dear Reader,

I'm delighted to welcome you to a very special Bestselling Author Collection for 2024! In celebration of Harlequin's 75 years in publishing, this collection features fan-favorite stories from some of our readers' most cherished authors. Each book also includes a free full-length story by an exciting writer from one of our current programs.

Our company has grown and changed since its inception 75 years ago. Today, Harlequin publishes more than 100 titles a month in 30 countries and 15 languages, with stories for a diverse readership across a range of genres and formats, including hardcover, trade paperback, mass market paperback, ebook and audiobook.

But our commitment to you, our romance reader, remains the same: in every Harlequin romance, a guaranteed happily-ever-after!

Thank you for coming on this journey with us. And happy reading as we embark on the next 75 years of bringing joy to readers around the world!

Dianne Moggy

Vice-President, Editorial

Harlequin

RaeAnne Thayne finds inspiration in the beautiful northern Utah mountains, where the *New York Times* and *USA TODAY* bestselling author lives with her husband and three children. Her books have won numerous honors, including RITA® Award nominations from Romance Writers of America and a Career Achievement Award from *RT Book Reviews*. RaeAnne loves to hear from readers and can be contacted through her website, raeannethayne.com.

Mona Shroff is obsessed with everything romantic, so she writes romantic stories by night, even though she's an optometrist by day. If she's not writing, she's making chocolate truffles, riding her bike or reading and she's just as likely to be drinking wine or gin and tonic with friends and family. She's blessed with an amazing daughter and loving son who have both gone to college. Mona lives in Maryland with her romance-loving husband.

New York Times **Bestselling Author**

RaeAnne Thayne

SHELTER FROM THE STORM

**HARLEQUIN
BESTSELLING
AUTHOR
COLLECTION**

**HARLEQUIN®
BESTSELLING
AUTHOR
COLLECTION**

Recycling programs
for this product may
not exist in your area.

ISBN-13: 978-1-335-00855-8

Shelter from the Storm
First published in 2007. This edition published in 2024.
Copyright © 2007 by RaeAnne Thayne

Matched by Masala
First published in 2022. This edition published in 2024.
Copyright © 2022 by Mona Shroff

For questions and comments about the quality of this book, please contact us at CustomerService@Harlequin.com.

Harlequin Enterprises ULC
22 Adelaide St. West, 41st Floor
Toronto, Ontario M5H 4E3, Canada
www.Harlequin.com

Printed in U.S.A.

CONTENTS

SHELTER FROM THE STORM

RaeAnne Thayne

To Darcy Rhodes, for sharing your singing and your smiles, for changing diapers and telling jokes and helping us take unforgettable journeys we once thought were impossible. You'll always be part of our family!

Chapter 1

"Would you take your shirt off, please?"

Under other circumstances—and from just about any other woman—Daniel Galvez might have been tempted to take those words as a rather enticing request.

From Dr. Lauren Maxwell, he knew all too well she meant nothing suggestive—as much as he might wish otherwise.

He sighed, detesting this whole ordeal, even as he knew he had no choice but to comply. His right hand went to the buttons of his uniform and he wrestled them free, uncomfortably aware of her watching him out of those intense blue eyes that seemed to miss nothing.

He had to work hard to hide a wince as he shrugged out of his shirt, mentally bracing himself for the moment she would touch him with those cool fingers.

The pain didn't worry him. He had coped with much

worse than a little scratch on the arm. Handling Lauren and the feelings she always stirred up in him was another matter entirely.

She watched him take off his shirt, her eyes veiled as they always seemed to be in his presence, and he wondered what she saw. The dirt-poor Mexican kid on the school bus in the fraying, too-small jeans and the threadbare coat? Or the harsh, hard-as-nails cop she must hate?

Those cool, lovely features didn't reveal even a hint of whatever she might think of him. Just as well, he thought. He had a feeling he was better off not knowing.

"Sorry to come in so late," he said as he pulled his blood-soaked shirt away. "I wouldn't have stopped if I hadn't seen the lights on as I was driving past."

She raised an eyebrow, though her attention remained fixed on his reason for being in her examination room of the Moose Springs Medical Clinic. "That's quite a nasty laceration you've got there, Sheriff. What were you going to do about it, if you weren't going to stop here? Stitch it up yourself?"

If he were capable of such a feat, he probably would have tried rather than finding himself in this uncomfortable position. "I figured I would catch a minute to run into the emergency clinic in Park City later."

That was still his preferred option. But since he was missing two deputies this weekend in a department that was already understaffed, he didn't have that luxury.

This was his third night of double shifts and he just couldn't spare the personal leave to drive the half hour to Park City, sit in the emergency clinic there while he waited his turn for a couple hours among all the banged-up skiers and tourists with altitude sickness, then drive a half hour back to Moose Springs.

With the ski season in full swing, Park City in January was crazy anyway—throw in an independent film festival that drew thousands of Hollywood types and their entourages, and he would just about rather chew tire spikes than spend time there if he didn't have to.

Even if that meant baring his chest for Lauren Maxwell.

"You know I'm always on call for you and your deputies if you need me," she said. Though her voice was low and polite, he still felt a pinch of reprimand.

She stepped forward, close enough that he could smell the subtle, intoxicating scent of jasmine and vanilla that always seemed to cling to her. She didn't touch him yet, just continued to study the jagged three-inch cut on his upper arm that was beginning to throb like hell.

"How did you say you were injured?"

"Bar fight down at Mickey's. Some joker from out of town got mad when Johnny Baldwin kept playing 'Achy Breaky Heart' on the jukebox."

"Uh-oh. He and Carol are fighting again?"

"Apparently. By about the sixth go-around, the tourist had had enough of Billy Ray and tried to physically prevent Johnny from putting in another quarter."

"I hope you didn't arrest him for that. Sounds like justifiable assault to me."

A muscle twitched in his cheek at her dry tone, though it was taking most of his concentration to keep his mind on the story and away from how incredible it felt to have Lauren Maxwell's hands on him, even in a clinical setting.

"Most of the bar probably would have backed the guy up at first. But of course he had to go and push his luck. He went just a bit too far and insulted both Johnny and any woman stupid enough to go out with him in the first place. And of course three of Carol's brothers happened to be sitting at the other end of the bar and they didn't take too kindly to that. By the time I got there, everybody in the place was having a good old time throwing punches and smashing chairs. I was trying to take the tourist into custody, mostly for his own protection, when his buddy came after me with the business end of a broken beer bottle."

"I'm sorry."

He lifted his uninjured shoulder. "Hazard of the job."

"Should I be expecting more casualties?"

"From what I could tell, the damage seemed to be mostly bloody noses and a couple of black eyes. The paramedics showed up just in case but I appeared to get the worst of it."

"I imagine Mickey's not too crazy about having his bar ripped apart."

"You know Mickey. He was right in the middle of it all."

She probed the edge of his wound and he couldn't hide a grimace.

"Sorry," she murmured, stepping away. "I'm going to have to clean it up a little before I can put in any stitches. Sit tight while I grab a suture kit and some antiseptic."

"No problem."

The moment she left the room, he huffed out the breath he hadn't realized he'd been holding. Okay, so this hadn't been one of his better ideas. He should have just accepted his fate and driven into Park City, to hell with the jam it would put in his schedule.

Being here alone in the medical clinic with Lauren

after hours was far too intimate, much too dangerous for his peace of mind.

He sighed, frustrated once again at this tension that always simmered between them.

It hadn't always been this way, but the events of five years earlier had changed everything. Lauren was still cordial, unfailingly polite, but she didn't treat him with the same warmth she gave everyone else. Every interaction between them seemed awkward and tense.

Though they grew up a few blocks away from each other, they may as well have been on different planets when they were kids. For one thing, she was three years younger. At thirty and thirty-three, now that didn't seem to make much difference. But when he was thirteen and trying his best to find his place in the world, a ten-year-old girl held about as much interest to him as learning the fox-trot.

Beyond that, they had been worlds apart demographically. She had been the smart and beautiful daughter of the town mayor—his dad's boss—and he had been the son of Mexican immigrants who never had enough of anything to go around but love.

He had tried to cross that social divide only once, the year he finished out his football scholarship and graduated from college. He had come home to work construction at her father's company for the summer before starting his police-officer training in the fall and he suddenly couldn't help noticing smart, pretty little Lauren Maxwell had grown into a beautiful college freshman, home for the summer between terms.

One night she had stopped by her father's office at the same time he dropped in after a job to pick up his paycheck. They had talked a little, flirted a little—though in retrospect, that had been one-sided on his part—and he had ended up asking her to dinner.

She had refused him firmly and decisively, almost horror-stricken, leaving him no room at all to maneuver around his abruptly deflated ego.

He could survive a little rejection. Hell, it had probably been good for him, a college jock far too full of himself.

If that had been the end of it, he imagined they could have salvaged at least a casual friendship over the years, especially after they both returned to settle in Moose Springs. She was the town's only doctor and he was the sheriff, so they were bound to interact sometimes.

But what came after had effectively destroyed any chance he had of claiming even that.

There was too much history between them, too many secrets, for anything but this awkwardness.

He wasn't sure how much she knew. Enough, obviously, for her to simmer about it. If she knew the whole truth, she would despise him even more. Somehow that knowledge did nothing to squash the attraction that always seethed under his skin, the edginess he couldn't seem to shake.

The door opened suddenly and she returned carrying a tray of bandages and suture supplies. He must have done a credible job of hiding his thoughts. She gave him a smile that almost looked genuine—until he saw the murkiness in her blue eyes.

"You'll have to sit down so I can reach your arm. You can rest it on this table."

He hesitated only a moment before he sat down where she indicated and thrust out his arm. The cut was jagged and ugly and still stung like hell, but he knew it looked worse than it really was.

Still, he winced when she pulled out a needle to numb the area. He would far rather face a dozen broken beer bottles than a needle. She caught his expression and gave him a reassuring smile. "It will only sting for a minute, I promise."

Feeling foolish and itchy at her nearness, he stoically endured the shot, then the gentle brush of her hands as she washed off the blood with Betadine and went to work stitching him up. He finally had to focus on a painting on the wall of two children on a beach eating ice cream and couldn't help wishing for a little cold refreshment to offset the heat of her fingers touching his skin.

"You're very good at that."

She didn't look up from her careful suturing. "Thanks. I considered a surgical specialty when I was in med school but I decided I wanted to see more of my patients than their insides."

"Lucky for us, I guess."

She didn't answer and the silence stretched between them. He scrambled around for another topic of conversation and grabbed the first one that came to him. "How's your mother?"

This time her gaze did flash to his, her expression unreadable. "Good. The warm St. George climate agrees with her. She's become quite a rabid golfer now that she can play all year."

He tried to picture soft and prim Janine Maxwell ripping up the golf course and couldn't quite get a handle on it. But then he never would have pictured Lauren Maxwell choosing to practice in quiet Moose Springs, when she could have gone anywhere else in the world.

Oddly, she seemed to follow his train of thought.

"Mom wants me to sell the clinic and open up another one in southern Utah."

He didn't like the sudden panic spurting through him at the thought of her leaving. "Will you?"

Her hair brushed his arm as she shook her head. "Not a chance," she said firmly. "Moose Springs is my home and I'm not going anywhere."

He didn't miss the defiance in her voice and he fully understood the reason for it. Things couldn't always be easy for her here—he knew there were some in town who would rather drive the thirty-five minutes to Park City for their medical care than walk through the doors of any clinic run by the daughter of the town's biggest crook.

The good people of Moose Springs hadn't taken R. J. Maxwell's embezzlement of more than a million dollars of their hard-earned money very kindly. Even five years after his death, there were those who still carried a pretty hefty grudge.

Most people in town didn't blame the daughter for the father's sins, but he had heard enough whispers and veiled innuendos to know *most* didn't mean *all*. A certain percentage of the population wasn't as fair-minded.

If the full story ever emerged, he knew that percentage would probably increase dramatically.

Lauren's own mother had been quick to escape Moose Springs after the scandal broke. He couldn't understand why Lauren seemed determined to remain in town despite the ugly blotches on her family's laundry.

"That should do it," she said after a moment, affixing a bandage to the spot. "I'll write you a prescription for a painkiller and an antibiotic, just to be on the safe side."

"Just the antibiotic," he said, shrugging back into his ruined uniform shirt.

"That's a nasty laceration. You might be surprised at the residual pain tomorrow."

"I'll take an aspirin if it gets too bad."

She rolled her eyes but before she could speak, his communicator buzzed with static and a moment later he heard his dispatcher's voice.

"Chief, I've got Dale Richins on the line," Peggy Wardell said. "Says he was driving home from his sister's in Park City and blew a tire."

"He need help with it?"

"Not with the tire. But when he went in the back to get the spare, he found a girl hiding in the camper shell of his pickup."

He blinked at that unexpected bit of information. "A girl?"

"Right. She's beat up pretty good, Dale says, and tried to escape when he found her but she collapsed before she could get far. She only *hablas* the *español,* apparently. Thought I'd better let you know."

He grabbed for his blood-soaked coat, sudden dread congealing in his gut. One of the hazards of working in a small town was the fear every time a call like this came in, he didn't know who he might find at the scene.

He knew just about everyone in the growing Latino community around Moose Springs and hated the possibility that someone he knew—someone's *hija* or *hermana*—might have been attacked.

"Thanks, Peg. Tell Dale I can be there in five minutes or so."

"Right."

He headed for the door, then stopped short when he realized Lauren was right on his heels, passing a medical kit from hand to hand as she shoved the opposite hand into her parka.

"What do you think you're doing?" he asked.

"I'm coming with you," she said, that Lauren stubbornness in her voice. "Sounds like you've got a victim who will need medical care and if I go with you, I can be on scene faster than the volunteer paramedics."

He didn't want to take the time to argue with her—not when a few seconds consideration convinced him the idea was a good one. Lauren was more qualified to offer better medical care than anything the volunteer medics could provide.

"Let's go then," he said, leading the way out into the drizzling snow.

Daniel drove through the slushy roads with his lights flashing but his siren quiet, at a speed that had her hanging on to her medical kit with both hands.

She gritted her teeth as he hit one of the town's famous potholes and her head slammed against the headrest.

"Sorry," he said, though he barely looked at her.

Nothing new there. Daniel seldom looked at her, not if he could help himself. She was glad for it, she told herself. She didn't want him looking too closely at her. He already knew too much about her, more than just about anyone else in town—she didn't want him aiming those piercing brown eyes too far into her psyche.

She gripped her bag more tightly as he drove toward the scene, trying not to notice how big and hard and dangerous he seemed under these conditions.

Sheriff Daniel Galvez was not a man any sane person would want to mess with. He was six feet three inches and two hundred and ten pounds of pure muscle. Not that she made note of his vital statistics during the rare times she had treated him or anything—it was just hard to miss a man so big who was still as tough and physically imposing as the college football player he'd been a decade earlier.

Beside him, she always felt small and fragile, a feeling she wasn't particularly crazy about. She *wasn't* small, she was a respectable five feet six inches tall and a healthy one hundred and fifteen pounds. It was only his size that dwarfed her. And she wasn't fragile, either. She had survived med school, a grueling residency and, just a few months later, crippling shock and disbelief at the chaos her father left in his wake.

She shoved away thoughts of her father as Daniel pulled the department's Tahoe to a stop behind a battered old pickup she recognized as belonging to Dale Richins. The old rancher stood behind his camper shell, all but wringing his hands.

He hurried to them the moment Daniel shut off the engine. "The little girl is inside the camper shell of my truck. I had a horse blanket in there. I guess that's what she was hiding under. Looks like you brought medical help. Good. From what I can see, she's beat up something terrible."

He looked at Lauren with a little less suspicion than normal, but she didn't have time to be grateful as she headed for the back of the pickup. Daniel was right behind her and he didn't wait for her to ask for help—he just lifted her up and over the tailgate and into the truck bed.

He aimed the heavy beam of his flashlight inside as she made her careful way to the still form lying motionless under a grimy blanket that smelled of livestock and heaven knows what else.

She pulled out her flashlight, barely able to make out the battered features of a Latina girl.

"She's so young," Lauren exclaimed as she immediately went to work examining her. Though it was hard to be sure with all the damage, she didn't think the girl was much older than fourteen or fifteen.

"Do you know her?" Daniel asked, leaning in and taking a closer look.

"I don't think so. You?"

"She doesn't look familiar. I don't think she's from around here."

"Whoever she is, she's going to need transport to the hospital. This is beyond what I can handle at the clinic."

"How urgent?" Daniel asked from outside the pickup. "Ambulance or LifeFlight to the University of Utah?"

She considered the situation. "Her vitals are stable and nothing seems life-threatening at this point. Send for an ambulance," she decided.

She lifted the girl's thin T-shirt, trying to look for anything unusual in the dim light. She certainly found it.

"Sheriff, she's pregnant," she exclaimed.

He leaned inside, his expression clearly shocked. "Pregnant?"

"I'd guess about five or six months along."

She moved her stethoscope and was relieved to hear a steady fetal heartbeat. She started to palpate the girl's abdomen when suddenly her patient's eyes flickered open. Even in the dim light inside the camper shell, Lauren could see panic chase across those battered features. The girl cried out and flailed at Lauren as she tried to scramble up and away from her.

"Easy, sweetheart. Easy," Lauren murmured. Her skills at Spanish were limited but she tried her best.

"I'm not going to hurt you. I'm here to help you and your baby."

The girl's breathing was harsh and labored, but her frantic efforts to fight Lauren off seemed to ease and she watched her warily.

"I'm Lauren. I'm a doctor," she repeated in Spanish, holding up her stethoscope. "What's your name?"

Through swollen, discolored eyes, the girl looked disoriented and suspicious, and didn't answer for several seconds.

"Rosa," she finally said, her voice raspy and strained. "Rosa Vallejo."

Lauren smiled as calmly as if they were meeting for brunch. It was a skill she'd learned early in medical school—pretend you were calm and in control and your patients will assume you are. "Hello, Rosa Vallejo. I'm sorry you're hurt but an ambulance is on the way for you, okay? We're going to get you to the hospital."

"No! No hospital. Please!"

The fear in the girl's voice seemed to hitch up a notch and she tried to sit up again. Lauren touched her arm, for comfort and reassurance as much as to hold her in place. "You've been hurt. You need help. You need to make sure your baby is all right."

"No. No. I'm fine. I must go."

She lunged to climb out of the truck bed but Daniel stood blocking the way, looking huge and imposing, his badge glinting in the dim light. The girl froze, a whimper in her throat and a look of abject terror in her eyes. *"No policía. No policía!"*

She seemed incoherent with fear, struggling hysterically to break free of Lauren's hold. Daniel finally reached in to help, which only seemed to upset the girl more.

"Hold her while I find something in my kit to calm her," Lauren ordered. "She's going to injure herself more if I don't."

A moment later, she found what she was looking for. Daniel held the girl while Lauren injected her with a sedative safe for pregnant women. A moment later, the medicine started to work its calming effect on her panicked patient and she sagged back against the horse blankets just as the wail of the ambulance sounded outside.

Lauren let out a sigh of relief and started to climb out of the truck bed. When Daniel reached to lift her out, she suddenly remembered his injury. She ignored his help and climbed out on her own.

"You're going to break open all those lovely stitches if you don't take it easy."

"I'm fine," he said firmly, just as the volunteer paramedics hurried over, medical bags slung over their shoulders.

"Hey, Mike, Pete," Lauren greeted them with a smile.

"You trying to take over our business now, Doc?" Pete asked her with a wink.

"No way. You guys are the experts at triage here. I happened to be stitching up the sheriff at the clinic after the big brawl at Mickey's bar. When he received this call, I rode along to see if I could help."

"Busy night for all of us. What have we got?"

Daniel stepped closer to hear her report and Lauren tried not to react to his overwhelming physical presence.

She gave them Rosa's vitals. "I have a young patient who appears to be approximately twenty weeks pregnant. It was tough to do a full assessment under these conditions, but she looks like she's suffering multiple contusions and lacerations, probably the result of a beating.

She appears to be suffering from exposure. I have no idea how long she's been in the back of Dale's pickup. Maybe an hour, maybe more. Whether that contributed to her hysteria, I can't say, but I do know she's not very crazy about authority figures right now. Seeing the sheriff set her off, so we may have to use restraints in the ambulance on our way to Salt Lake City."

"You riding along?" Mike Halling asked.

"If I won't be in the way."

"You know we've always got room for you, Doc."

She stood back while he and Pete Zabrisky quickly transferred the girl to the stretcher then lifted it into the ambulance.

"I'm guessing she must have climbed in the back of the truck in Park City, or wherever Dale might have stopped on the way. Though I'm pretty sure the attack didn't happen here, I'm going to put one of my deputies to work processing the scene," Daniel told her while they waited in the stinging sleet for the paramedics to finish loading Rosa into the bus.

"All right," she answered.

"I won't be far behind you. I'd like to question her once she's been treated." He paused. "I can give you a ride back to town when we're done, if you need it."

She nodded and climbed in after Mike and Pete. Maybe she had a problem with authority figures, too. That must be why her stomach fluttered and her heartbeat accelerated at the prospect of more time in the company of the unnerving Daniel Galvez.

Chapter 2

Watching Dr. Lauren Maxwell in action was more fascinating to him than the Final Four, the World Series and the Super Bowl combined. As long as she wasn't working on him and he didn't have to endure having her hands on him, Daniel wouldn't mind watching her all day.

As he stepped back to let the ambulance pull past him, with its lights flashing through the drizzle of snow, he could see Lauren through the back windows as she talked to the paramedics in what he imagined was that brisk, efficient voice she used when directing patient care.

In trauma situations, Lauren always seemed completely in control. He never would have guessed back in the day that she would make such a wonderful physician.

He still found it amazing that the prim little girl on the school bus with her pink backpacks and her fake-fur-trimmed coats and her perfectly curled blond ringlets seemed to have no problem wading through blood and guts and could handle herself with such quiet but confident expertise, no matter the situation.

She loved her work. It was obvious every time Daniel had the chance to see her in action. Medicine wasn't a job with Lauren Renee Maxwell, it was more like a sacred calling.

In the five years since she'd come back to Moose Springs and opened her clinic, he had watched her carefully. Like many others, at first he had expected her to fail. She was the spoiled, pampered daughter of the man who had been the town's wealthiest citizen. How could she possibly have the stamina to cope with all the gritty realities of small-town doctoring?

Like almost everyone else, he had quickly figured out that there was more to Lauren than anybody might have guessed. Over the years, her clinic had become a strong, vital thread in the community fabric.

They were all lucky to have her—and so was that young girl in the back of the ambulance.

"What am I supposed to do now?" Dale Richins asked, his wide, grizzled features concerned.

"We're going to need a statement from you. The address of your sister's house in Park City, any place you might have stopped between there and here. That kind of thing."

"I can tell you where LouAnn lives. She's on the edge of town, the only part the old-timers can afford anymore, with all the developers trying to buy everybody out. But I can tell you right now, I didn't stop a single place after I left her house. Headed straight home. I don't know if I even would have known that girl was back there if

I hadn't stopped to fix the flat. She would have likely froze to death."

"You did the right thing, trying to help her."

"What else was I supposed to do? Little thing like that." He shook his head. "Just makes me sick, someone could hurt her and leave her to find her own way in the cold. Especially if she's pregnant like the doc said. It's got to be only eight or nine degrees out here. I can't imagine how cold it was in the back of that drafty old camper shell while I was going sixty-five miles an hour on the interstate. It's a wonder that little girl didn't freeze solid before I found her."

"Yeah, it was lucky you found her when you did."

"Who do you figure might have done this to her?"

"I couldn't guess right now until I have a chance to talk to her. I imagine she was probably looking for some way to escape when she stumbled onto your truck and camper shell. The lock's broken, I see."

"That old thing's been busted since before you quit your fancy job in the city and came home. But yeah, that makes sense that she was looking for a way out."

"So either she was injured somewhere near your sister's house or she stumbled on your truck sometime after the beating. I'll know better after I can interview her."

Dale cleared his throat. "You let me know if she needs anything, won't you? I can't afford much, but I could help some with her doctor bills and whatnot."

He couldn't help being touched at the crusty old rancher's obvious concern for his stowaway. Most of the time, Dale was hard-edged and irascible, cranky to everyone. Maybe Rosa reminded him of his three granddaughters or something.

"Thanks," he answered. "That's real decent of you."

"Least I can do."

"There's Deputy Hendricks," Daniel said as another department SUV approached. "She'll take a statement from you with the particulars of your sister's address and all, and then she can drive you home when you're finished."

"What the hell for? I can drive myself home."

"I'm sorry, Dale, but we're going to have to take your truck to the garage down at the station to see if we can find any evidence in the back. It's standard procedure in cases like this."

The rancher didn't look too thrilled with that piece of information. "Don't I have any kind of choice here?"

"You want us to do everything we can to find out who hurt that girl, don't you?"

"I suppose…"

"You'll have it back by morning, I promise."

That didn't seem to ease Dale's sour look, but the rancher seemed to accept the inevitable.

"You heading to the hospital now?" he asked.

At Daniel's nod, he pointed a gnarled finger at him. "You make sure R.J.'s daughter treats that girl right."

Though he knew it was a foolish reflex, Daniel couldn't help but stiffen at the renewed animosity in the rancher's voice. How did Lauren deal with it, day after day? he wondered. Dale wasn't the only old-timer around here who carried a grudge as wide and strong as the Weber River. She must face this kind of thing on a daily basis.

It pissed him off and made him want to shake the other man. Instead, he pasted on a calm smile. "Dale, if you weren't so stubborn, you would admit Lauren is a fine doctor. She'll take care of the girl. You can bet your ranch on it."

The other man made a harrumphing kind of sound but didn't comment as Teresa Hendricks approached. Daniel turned his attention from defending Lauren—something she would probably neither appreciate nor understand—and focused on the business at hand.

"Thanks for coming in on your first night off in a week," he said to his deputy. "Sorry to do this to you."

"Not a problem. Sounds like you had some excitement."

He spent five minutes briefing her on the case, then suggested she drive the rancher home and take his statement there, where they both could be warm and dry.

"I'm going to follow the ambulance to the hospital and try to interview the vic," he said. "If anything breaks here, you know how to reach me."

The snow seemed to fall heavier and faster as he drove through Parley's Canyon to the Salt Lake Valley. It was more crowded than he would have expected at eleven at night, until he remembered the film festival. This whole part of the state was insane when all the celebs were in town.

By the time he reached the University of Utah Medical Center, his shoulders ached with tension and he was definitely in need of a beer.

At the hospital, he went immediately to the emergency room and was directed down a hallway, where he quickly spotted Lauren talking to a man Daniel assumed was another doctor, at least judging by the stethoscope around his neck.

The guy was leaning down, and appeared to be hanging on every word Lauren said. He was blond and lean and as chiseled as those movie stars in their two-thousand-dollar ski jackets up the canyon, trying to see and be seen around town.

Daniel immediately hated him.

He took a step down the hallway and knew immediately when Lauren caught sight of him. She straightened abruptly and something flashed in her blue eyes, something murky and confusing. She quickly veiled her expression and it became a mask of stiff politeness.

Just once, he would love the chance to talk to her without the prickly shell she always seemed to whip out from somewhere and put on whenever he was near.

"Sheriff Galvez," she greeted him, her delicate features solemn. "Have you met Kendall Fox? He's the E.R. attending tonight. Kendall, this is Daniel Galvez."

The doctor stuck out his hand and Daniel shook it, though he couldn't escape the impression they were both circling around each other, sizing up the enemy like a couple of hound dogs sniffing after the same bone.

He didn't miss the dismissal in the doctor's eyes and for the second time that night, he had to fight the urge to kick somebody's ass. He wouldn't waste his energy, he thought. Lauren was too smart to go for the type of smooth player who couldn't remember the name of the woman he was with unless she had it tattooed somewhere on a conveniently accessible portion of her anatomy.

"How's our victim?" he asked.

"She's gone to Radiology for some X-rays," Lauren spoke up. "The tech should be bringing her back in a moment. Kendall… Dr. Fox…and I were just discussing the best course of action. We think—"

Dr. Jerk cut her off. "She has a little frostbite on a

couple of her toes, an apparent broken wrist and some cracked ribs."

"How's the baby?" Daniel pointedly directed his question back to Lauren, ignoring the other man.

She frowned, looking worried. "She's started having some mild contractions right now. We've given her medication to stop them, but she's definitely going to need to be closely observed for the next few days."

"She give any indication who put her here?"

Lauren shook her head. She had discarded her parka somewhere, he observed with his keen detective eye, and had put surgical scrubs on over the pale blue turtleneck she had worn when she treated his shoulder. Her hair was slipping from its braid and he had to fight a ridiculous urge to tuck it back.

"She clams up every time we ask."

"I was afraid of that. She's got to be frightened. It would sure make my job easier if she could just give me the name, age and last-known address of the son of a bitch who put her here. Of course we have to do this the hard way. Can I talk to her?"

"You cops. Can't you even wait until the girl gets out of X-ray?" Fox asked.

Daniel slid his fists into his pockets and pasted on that same damn calm smile that sometimes felt about as genuine as fool's gold.

He really hated being made to feel like a big, dumb Mexican.

"I didn't mean this instant," he murmured. "But I would like to talk to her as soon as possible, while the details are still fresh in her mind."

The doctor looked like he wanted to get in a pissing match right there in the hallway, but before he could unzip, a nurse in pink scrubs stuck her head out of one of the examination rooms.

She didn't look pleased to find the E.R. doctor still standing close to Lauren, a sentiment with which Daniel heartily concurred. Her reaction made him wonder if the good doctor was the sort who left a swath of broken hearts through the staff.

"Dr. Fox, can you come in here for a minute?" the nurse asked. "I've got a question on your orders."

The doctor's handsome features twisted with annoyance but he hid it well. "Be right there."

After he walked down the hall, a tight, awkward silence stretched between Daniel and Lauren. He found it both sad and frustrating, and wondered how he could ever bridge the chasm between them.

He wasn't exactly sure how much Lauren knew about the events that led up to her father's exposure and subsequent fall from grace. If she knew all of it, she must blame him for what happened next.

He sure as hell blamed himself.

"How's your arm?" she asked.

The blasted thing throbbed like the devil, but he wasn't about to admit that to her.

"Fine," he assured her. "Sorry I wasted your time on that. If I'd known I would have to make a trip down here to the city, I could have just had them fix me up here while I was waiting to interview our beating victim. But then, I doubt anybody on staff here can claim such nice handiwork."

She blinked at the compliment and he watched a light sprinkle of color wash over her cheekbones. "I...thank you," she murmured.

"You're welcome."

They lapsed into silence again.

"How's Anna these days?" Lauren asked after an awkward moment. "I heard she was in the Northwest now."

Grateful for the conversation starter, he smiled at the thought of his baby sister. "She loves Oregon. She runs a little gift shop and gallery in Cannon Beach that seems to be doing well. I took a few days and drove up there last year and she seems happy."

"She's not married?"

Some of the tension between them seemed to ease as they talked and he wanted to prolong the moment indefinitely. "No. Marc's the only one of us to bite the bullet so far. He and his wife live in Cache Valley. They have twin boys we all spoil like crazy."

"And Ren is still in Central America?"

"Right. We can't get him away from his sea turtles."

She opened her mouth to answer, but cut off the words as a hospital worker pushed a gurney around the corner.

"Here's Rosa," she said.

The beating victim looked even younger here in the harsh glare of the hospital lights and her bruises showed up in stark relief against the white linens. Daniel studied her features, trying hard to find any hint of familiarity, but he was certain he didn't know her.

He helped push the gurney through the door into the examination room, earning a censorious look from Lauren for the mild exertion. He returned it with a bland smile, though he had to fight down a spurt of warmth. He liked her worrying about him far too much.

"How did it go, Riley?" she asked the kid, who looked young for an X-ray technician, as his hospital ID identified him.

"Good. She fell asleep while I was waiting for the films and I didn't have the heart to wake her. Poor thing."

"She's been through a terrible ordeal. She must be exhausted."

Lauren took the films from him and slid the first of several into the light box hanging on the wall. She studied it, then exchanged it for another and finally a third, a frown of concentration on her lovely features.

"Just as we suspected," she said after a moment. "She's got three broken ribs, a fractured ulna and a broken nose."

"Somebody did a real number on her." He was angry all over again at the viciousness behind the attack. "How's the baby?"

Lauren studied tape spitting out from a machine that was attached to a belt around Rosa's abdomen. "The contractions have stopped. That's a good sign. We did an ultrasound earlier and the fetus seemed healthy. It's a miracle. She's a dozen different shades of black and blue on her abdomen. My guess is somebody kicked her hard at least two or three times in an effort to induce abortion."

Daniel had a feeling this was one of those cases that would grab on to him with rottweiler jaws and not let go until he solved it. "Can I talk to her?" he asked.

Lauren pursed her lips. "My instincts say to let her sleep for a while, but I understand your urgency. You likely have to return to Moose Springs as soon as possible."

"I do. I'm sorry. We're shorthanded tonight." He paused and met Lauren's gaze. "It's not just that, though. I want her to tell me what happened. The quicker she identifies whoever did this to her, the quicker I can lock the bastard up."

* * *

Though he spoke with a hard determination that didn't bode well for the perpetrator, Lauren didn't feel so much as a twinge of sympathy for whoever had done this. They deserved to feel the full wrath of Daniel Galvez, a terrible thing indeed.

"I'm right there with you on that sentiment," she told him. "In fact, if you gave me half a chance, I'd like to be the one twisting the key in the lock."

"I've got to catch him first and I can't do that until I talk to Rosa."

Lauren sighed. "All right. Why don't you wait in the hall while I wake her, though. She might panic if you're the first thing she sees when she opens her eyes."

He raised an eyebrow. "Am I really that scary?"

She felt her face heat and regretted her fair coloring that showed every emotion to the world like a big neon billboard. "I meant your uniform," she answered stiffly, though she had to admit, she found the man absolutely terrifying.

Could he tell? she wondered, hoping it wasn't as obvious as her blush. She wasn't afraid he would physically hurt her, though he was big and powerful and all large men tended to make her uncomfortable on some instinctive level.

With Daniel, though, she was more wary of her own reaction to him and all the feelings he sparked in her, emotions she would rather not be experiencing for someone with whom she had such a tangled, complicated relationship.

To her relief, he let the matter drop. "Yell when it's safe for me to come in, then," he murmured, slipping out of the room with far more grace than a man his size should possess.

The room immediately felt about three times bigger without his overwhelming presence filling it. Lauren let out the breath she always seemed to hold around him and moved to her patient's bedside.

"Rosa? *Niña,* I need you to wake up."

When she didn't respond immediately, Lauren gently shook her shoulder. "Rosa?"

The girl's eyes blinked open and she looked around in wild confusion, panic blooming in her dark eyes. Her gaze shifted to Lauren and a light of recognition sparked there. "*Doctora.*" She covered her abdomen with her hands. "*El bebé. Está bien?*"

"*Sí. Sí. Está bien.*" She smiled, wishing she had a little better command of Spanish. If things weren't so tensely uncomfortable with Daniel, she might ask for private lessons. But of course, that was impossible, so for now she would have to muddle through.

"Rosa, the sheriff is here to talk to you about who hurt you."

The panic returned to her features. "*No. No policía.*"

Lauren sighed. The physician in her wanted to urge her patient to rest, to promise her she could have this difficult interview later when her body had a chance to begin the healing process.

She couldn't, though. Daniel had a job to do—a job she very much wanted to see him conclude with an arrest. She just had to trust that he would handle a frightened girl with both tact and compassion.

"I'm sorry, Rosa," she answered in Spanish. "But you must tell him what happened."

The girl shook her head, her hands clasped protectively around her abdomen as if she feared Daniel would snatch the child from her womb. Lauren gave her a reassuring pat. "It will all be all right. You'll see. Sheriff Galvez only wants to help you."

Rosa said something in Spanish too rapid for Lauren to pick up on. She had a feeling she was better off not knowing.

She went to the door and opened it for Daniel. "She's upset and doesn't want to talk to you," she said in an undertone. "I honestly don't know how much she'll tell you. I'm sorry. I can give you a few moments but if I think you're upsetting her too much, I'll have to kick you out."

"All right."

When he entered the room, Rosa shrank against the bed linens, her fine-boned features tight with tension. Daniel pulled out one of the guest chairs and sat on the edge of it. He moved slowly, like someone trying to coax a meadowlark to eat birdseed from his hand.

He spoke Spanish in a low, calm voice. She couldn't understand him well, both because he pitched his voice low and because he spoke too quickly for her limited comprehension skills.

After a moment, Rosa answered him quickly, reluctance in every line of her body.

Lauren found it a surreal experience trying to follow their conversation when she only understood about one word in five. Even without a perfect command of the language, she could hear the compassion ringing through his voice.

He genuinely cared about Rosa, Lauren thought. The girl might be just a stowaway he had never seen until an hour ago, but he wanted to get to the bottom of things. She suddenly knew Daniel would go to any lengths to protect the girl. Fate had dropped her into Moose Springs, and she had become one of his charges.

She had a feeling his sincerity wasn't translating for Rosa. She shook her head vehemently several times, and Lauren could at least understand the most frequent word the girl employed. "No" sounded the same in English and in Spanish.

After several moments of this, Rosa turned her head against the wall, a clear message that she was done talking to him. Daniel said something, his voice low and intense, but Rosa didn't turn around.

At last Daniel stood with a sigh, his big handsome features tight with frustration. He tucked a business card in Rosa's hand. The girl closed her fingers around it, but didn't even look at either the card or at Daniel. With another sigh, Daniel nodded to Lauren and left the room.

She followed him. "She won't talk?" she asked when the door closed behind them.

"She claims she doesn't remember what happened to her."

Lauren frowned. "She has no head injury that might account for a loss of memory. I suppose it might be some self-protective psychological reaction to the trauma…"

"There *is* no loss of memory. She remembers perfectly. She's just not telling."

"Doesn't she understand her safety and that of her baby is at stake here?"

"I think that's exactly what she's thinking about. I think she just wants to pretend none of it happened. 'I'm fine, the baby's fine. That's all that matters,' she just kept saying over and over."

"I'll talk to her. She'll be under my care and the attending's here for at least the next two or three days. I want to consult with the high-risk ob-gyns on staff here and make sure we monitor her closely to ensure no lasting harm to the fetus from her injuries. I don't know that it will do any good, but I'll try to persuade her she has to talk to you, or whoever did this to her will get away with a double attempted murder."

"Thanks, Lauren. I'll try to stop back in first thing in the morning. Maybe she'll change her mind about talking to me by then."

"You put in long hours, Sheriff."

He smiled and the sight of those white teeth flashing in that darkly handsome face sent her stomach trembling. "I could say the same for you, Doc."

She gazed at him for far longer than was probably polite, until he finally cleared his throat.

"You still need a ride back to Moose Springs?"

Chill, she chided herself. This was Daniel Galvez, the one man in town who shouldn't rev her motor. She would be better off with a player like Kendall Fox. At least he just annoyed her. Being with Dr. Fox never left her feeling like she had just stood in a wind tunnel for two or three days.

"If it's not too much trouble."

"No trouble," he assured her, though she couldn't help feeling he wasn't being completely truthful.

"Just give me a few more moments to wrap things up with Kendall and I should be ready."

"Here comes the good doctor now."

She turned and found Kendall walking purposefully down the hallway.

"The sheriff is my ride back to Moose Springs since I came in the ambulance," she said quickly, hoping to deflect any more flirtation. "Do you mind if I leave my patient in your care?"

"We'll take good care of her until they can find a bed for her on the medical floor."

"I'll be back first thing in the morning to check on her," she said. "I want a phone call in the night if her condition changes at all. Make sure the nurses know that when they admit her upstairs. Any change at all, I want to hear about it."

"I'll take care of her, I promise." Kendall gave her the full wattage of his lady-killer smile. "I'm on until seven in the morning and I expect doughnuts and some decent coffee out of the deal."

"Done."

As her interactions with Dr. Fox went, this one was fairly innocuous. She could only hope she would get through the hour-long drive with Daniel Galvez as painlessly.

Chapter 3

The slushy snow of earlier in the evening had given way to giant, soft flakes as the temperature dropped. Daniel drove away from the U. toward the canyon that would take them back to Moose Springs through the feeder streets along the foothills. Roads here were mostly clear, though he knew the canyon would probably be dicey.

He was painfully aware of Lauren sitting beside him and wondered if they had ever been alone like this. He was so conscious of her that it took all his powers of concentration to keep his attention on driving as he took the exit to I-80 through the canyon.

Still, he was aware of every movement from her side of the SUV. When he caught her covering a yawn, he risked a look at her. "Go ahead and sleep if you need to. I've got a pillow in the back."

"I'm all right. It's been a rather long day. I imagine you know all about those."

"This week, I certainly do." He signaled to change lanes around a car with out-of-state plates going at a crawl through what was just a light layer of snow.

The scanner crackled with static suddenly and he heard radio traffic of somebody in Park City reporting a drunk-and-disorderly patron at one of the popular restaurants on Main Street.

"I'm sure that's not the first one of those they've had this week," Lauren said.

"Yeah, and it won't be the last until Sundance is over. The detective I spoke to tonight on the way here sounded just a little frazzled."

"Things are busy enough in Park City in the winter with all the skiers. Throw in the film festival and it's a nightmare."

"Have you been to any screenings this year?"

She shrugged. "I don't have a lot of free hours to go to movies. You?"

"No. I caught a few screenings last year but I'm afraid this one is going to pass me by. Too much work."

"We're pathetic, aren't we? Sounds like we both need to get a life outside our jobs."

"I'd love to," he deadpanned, "but who has the time?"

She laughed out loud at that, the low, musical sound filling all the cold corners of his Tahoe. "*We* are pathetic. I was thinking the exact same thing. By the time I finish a twelve-hour shift at the clinic, I'm lucky to find the energy to drive home."

"You need a vacation." He pushed away the image of her on a white sand beach somewhere, a soft sea breeze ruffling her hair and her muscles loose and relaxed.

"Funny, that seems to be the consensus," she said. "You'll be surprised to find, I'm sure, that I'm actually taking one next week. Coralee and Bruce Jenkins are going on a cruise. Rather than hire a temp to be the office manager for a week, I decided to close the whole clinic and just give everyone the time off. My staff needed a break."

"Good for you!"

"The town got along without any doctor at all for a long time. I'm sure a few days without me will be bearable."

"What are you doing with yourself?"

"I haven't decided yet. Mom's bugging me to come down and visit for a few days. I might. Or I might just stick close to home, try out some new cross-country ski trails, maybe take in a movie or two in Park City."

"I'm sure Dr. Fox would be happy to take you to a screening if you just said the word."

He immediately wished he had just kept that little statement to himself. Out of the corner of his eye, he saw Lauren's eyes widen with surprise. Even from here, he could see color flare on her delicate cheekbones. "Kendall? I don't think so."

He knew he should let it rest but he just couldn't seem to make himself shut up. "Why?" he pressed. "He's good-looking, successful, probably loaded. Seems like a good catch."

"Maybe *you* should date him," she said tartly.

"I'm not the one the good doctor couldn't take his eyes off."

"You're delusional. I'd be happy to refer you to a doctor who can prescribe something for that."

He laughed, but figured he should probably change

the subject before he revealed too much, like the attraction he had done his best to hide for more than a decade. Before he could come up with a conversational detour, she beat him to the punch.

"What about you?" she asked. "I heard rumors of wedding bells a few summers ago when you were dating little Cheryl White."

"She wasn't little," he muttered.

"Not in physical assets, anyway. But wasn't she barely out of high school?"

He had to admit, he was a little stung by her implication that he might be interested in jailbait. At the same time, he had to wonder why she noticed who he dated. "Cheryl was twenty-one when I started dating her. She didn't even have to use fake ID to get into Mickey's."

"That must have been a relief for you. It probably would have been a little awkward to have to arrest your own girlfriend."

It must be late, if she could tease him like this. The tension usually simmering between them was nowhere in sight as they drove through the snowy night. He savored the moment, though he was fairly certain it wouldn't last.

"For the record, Cheryl was never my girlfriend. We only dated a few times and we never discussed wedding bells or anything else matrimony-related. You ought to know better than to listen to the Moose Springs gossips."

Even without looking at her, he could feel her light mood trickle away like the snow melting on the windshield.

"You're right. Absolutely right." Her voice cooled several degrees in just a few seconds. "Who gossips *to* you will gossip *of* you, isn't that what they say? And I certainly don't need to be the subject of any more whispers in Moose Springs."

The ghost of her father loomed between them and all the usual tension suddenly returned. He would have given anything to take his heedless words back, but like those snippets of gossip spreading around town, they couldn't be recalled.

His hands tightened on the steering wheel and he made some innocuous comment about the weather. She responded in a quiet, polite voice, as if those shared moments of intimacy had never been.

It was nearly midnight when he pulled up in front of the clinic. Three or four inches of snow had fallen while they had been in the city and her aging Volvo was buried.

He reached across the space between them to his jockey box for his window scraper. The movement brought him closer to her and he was surrounded by jasmine and vanilla.

His mouth watered and his insides gave one big sigh, but he did his best to ignore his automatic reaction. He pulled out the scraper and returned to the safe side of the vehicle—but not before he heard a quick, indrawn breath from Lauren.

He chanced a look at her. The SUV was parked under a lamppost and in the pool of light, he found her blue eyes wide and her lovely features slightly pink.

He wasn't quite sure what to think about that so decided to put it from his mind. "Wait here where it's warm," he ordered.

Her forehead furrowed with her frown and now any flush that might be on her features turned to annoyance. "Are you kidding? I just put seven stitches in your arm, Daniel. *You* wait here where it's warm. Better yet, go on home and rest. I don't need a police escort to scrape the snow off my car."

"Wait here," he repeated, in the same no-nonsense voice he used with the prisoners at the jail.

Her sigh sounded exasperated, but he didn't let that stop him as he stepped out into the blowing cold that soaked through the layers of his coat to settle in his bones.

Nights like this made him feel all his thirty-three years—and more—and he couldn't help but remember every single hit he took as a running back at Wyoming. He ignored the aches, especially the throb and pull of the stitches in his arm, as he brushed the snow off her car then scraped the thick ice underneath.

He wasn't particularly surprised—just annoyed— when she joined him in the cold. She slid into the driver's seat of her vehicle and turned over the engine. After a chugging kind of start, the motor engaged. A moment later, she emerged with another window scraper and went to work on the other side of the vehicle.

When the windows were clear, she stood back. "Thank you for your help," she murmured. "And for the ride."

He didn't want it to end, he realized, as tense and uncomfortable as things became at the end there.

How pathetic was that?

"Don't you have any gloves?" he asked. "Your hands are going to be freezing by the time you get home."

"They're around somewhere. I keep buying pairs and losing them between here and my house."

He reached into the pocket of his parka. "Here. Take mine. I've got an extra pair in the squad vehicle."

Her mouth lifted slightly. "No offense, Sheriff, but your hands are a little bigger than mine." She waggled delicate fingers that would be dwarfed by his gloves and he felt huge and awkward. "Thank you for the offer but it's only half a mile. I should be fine."

"Good night, then," he said. "Thanks again for your help earlier stitching me up."

"You're welcome. Be careful of those sutures."

She smiled a little and it took all his willpower to keep from reaching between them, tucking her into his warmth and kissing the tired corner of that mouth.

She climbed into the Volvo and he returned to his Tahoe as she slowly pulled out of the parking lot into the deserted streets, her tires crunching on snow.

He pulled out behind her and they seemed to be the only fools out on the road on a cold January night. Everybody else must be snuggled together at home.

Okay, he didn't need that image in his head. Suddenly the only thing he could think about was cuddling under a big quilt with Lauren in front of a crackling fire while the snow pelted the windows, her soft body wrapped around him and jasmine and vanilla seducing his senses.

Reality was light-years away from fantasy—so far it would have been amusing if he didn't find it so damn depressing as he followed her through the snowy streets.

She lived on the outskirts of town, in a trim little clapboard house set away from her neighbors, the last house before the mountains. When they reached it, Lauren pulled into her garage and slid from her Volvo. In the dim garage light, he could clearly see her exasperated look as she waved him on.

He shook his head and gestured to the house. He waited until the lights came on inside and the garage door closed completely before he drove off into the snowy night.

She stood at her living room window watching Daniel's big SUV cruise slowly down the street.

How very like him to follow her home simply to ensure she made it in safely. It wasn't necessary. The distance between the clinic and her house wasn't far. Even if her ancient car sputtered and gave out on the way, she could easily walk home—in good weather, she walked to and from work all the time.

Yet Daniel had been concerned enough to take time out of his busy schedule to follow her home. A slow, steady warmth spread out from her core as she watched his taillights disappear in the snow.

She shouldn't feel so warm and comforted by his simple gesture, as if those big, strong arms were wrapped around her. It was foolish to be so touched, but she couldn't remember the last time someone had fussed over her with such concern.

Just his nature, she reminded herself. Daniel was a caretaker. He always had been. She could remember watching him on the bus with his three younger siblings, how he had always stood between them and anybody who might want to bully them. He wouldn't let anybody push them around, and nobody dared. Not if they had to run the risk of incurring the wrath of big Danny Galvez.

Oh, she had envied them. His sister had been in her grade and Lauren used to be so jealous that Anna had an older brother to watch out for her. Two of them, since Ren was just a year younger than Daniel.

She had longed for a noisy, happy family like the Galvezes. For siblings to fight and bicker and share with.

Siblings. Her mouth tightened and she let the curtain fall, hating the word. She shouldn't feel this anger at her father all over again but she couldn't seem to help herself.

She had siblings as well. Three younger brothers from her father's second family, the one she and her mother had known nothing about until after R.J.'s suicide and all her father's dark secrets came to light.

A few years ago she had met them and their mother— a woman who had been as much in the dark about her husband's other life and Lauren and her mother as they had been about her. They had all seemed perfectly nice. Children who had adored R.J. as much as she had and a widow who had still seemed shell-shocked.

They hadn't wanted any further relationship. Just as well, because Lauren didn't know if she quite had the stomach to continue being polite to the innocent children who had been the cause of R.J.'s relentless need for cash. Maintaining two households couldn't have been cheap and her father's way of augmenting his income was dipping into the public till.

She sighed and pushed thoughts of her half siblings away, focusing instead on Daniel Galvez and his caretaking of the world.

She shouldn't feel singled out simply because he followed her home to make sure she arrived safely. This wasn't any kind of special treatment, just Daniel's way with everyone.

Imagining it meant anything other than politeness would be a dangerous mistake.

She turned away from the window and the dark night. Returning to her empty house late at night always depressed her, highlighting the lonely corners of her life. She needed a dog, a big friendly mutt to lick her chin and rub against her legs and curl up at her feet on the rare evenings she was home.

With her insane hours, she knew that wouldn't be fair to any living creature, though perhaps she should get a fish or something, just for the company.

She turned on the television for noise and headed for the bathroom. A good, long soak in hot water would chase away the tension of the day and perhaps lift her spirits.

She had no reason to be depressed. She was doing the job she loved, the one she had dreamed of since she was a young girl in junior high biology class. If she had no one to share it all with, that was her own fault.

She was lonely. That was the long and short of it. She longed for someone to talk to at the end of the day, for a warm body to hold on a winter's night.

Too bad her options were so limited here—eligible single males weren't exactly thick on the ground in a small town like Moose Springs—but she was determined to stay here, come hell or high water.

What other choice did she have? She owed the town a debt she could never fully repay, though she tried her best. She couldn't in good conscience move away somewhere more lucrative and leave behind the mess her father had created.

The best cure for loneliness was hard work and she had never shied away from that. And perhaps she ought to stay away from Daniel, since spending any time at all with him only seemed to accentuate all the things missing in her life.

Her gray mood had blown away with the storm as she drove through the predawn darkness the next day through town. Her clinic hours started at nine but she figured if she left early enough, she could make it to see Rosa at the hospital in Salt Lake City and be back before the first patient walked through the door.

She felt energized for the day ahead as she listened

to *Morning Edition* on NPR. The morning was cold and still, the snow of the night before muffling every sound. She waved at a few early-morning snow-shovelers trying to clear their driveways before heading to work.

Most of them waved back as she passed, but a few quite noticeably turned their backs on her. She sighed but decided not to let it ruin her good mood.

This area was settled by pioneer farmers and ranchers and for years they had made up the bedrock of the rural economy. But for the last decade or so Moose Springs had become more of a bedroom community to workers in Park City and Salt Lake City who were looking for a quiet, mostly safe place to raise their families.

She was glad to see newcomers in town and figured an infusion of fresh blood couldn't hurt. Still, she hoped this area was able to hang on to all the small-town things she had always loved about it.

The interstate through the canyon was busy with morning commuters heading into the city, but the snow had been cleared in the night so the drive was pleasant.

As she had promised, she stopped at her favorite bakery not far from the hospital to pick up a dozen doughnuts and several cups of coffee for Kendall and the floor nurses.

Juggling the bag, the cup holder and her laptop, she hurried inside the hospital and went straight for the E.R., hoping she could catch the nurses who had helped with Rosa before their shift changed in a half hour. She had learned early in her career that nurses were the heart and soul of a hospital and she always tried to go out of her way to let them know how much she appreciated their hard work.

She found several nurses gathered at the station. They greeted her with friendly smiles.

"No sexy sheriff with you this morning?" Janie Carpenter, one of the nurses she had worked with before, asked her.

If only. She shook her head. "Sorry. I'm on my own. But I brought goodies, if that helps."

"I don't know." A round, middle-aged nurse grinned. "Between doughnuts or a hottie like that, I'd choose the sheriff every time. I was thinking I just might have to drive to Moose Springs and rob a bank or something. I certainly wouldn't mind that man putting me under arrest."

"Or under anything else," Janie purred. "Think he might use handcuffs?"

Lauren could feel herself blush. She wanted to tell them Daniel was far more than just chiseled features and strong, athletic shoulders. But maybe he enjoyed being drooled over. She pulled one of the doughnuts out and grabbed the last cup of coffee in the drink holder.

"I owe this to Dr. Fox. Is he around?"

Janie rolled her eyes. "Haven't seen him for a while. He's probably flirting with the nurses on the surgical floor. I'll be happy to set it aside for him, though."

She handed over the stash, not believing her for a second. Oh, well, she tried. It was Kendall's own fault for being such a player.

She waved goodbye to the nurses and headed up to Rosa's floor. Nobody was in sight at the nurse's station on this floor except a dour-looking maintenance man haphazardly swirling a mop around.

Served her right for coming just as the nurses were

giving report. She could hear them in the lounge as the night shift caught the fresh blood up on their caseload.

She smiled at the janitor but he still didn't meet her eye so she gave up trying to be nice and began looking for Rosa's chart. Probably in with the nurses, she realized, and went to the lounge to ask if they were done with it.

"Here it is. She had a very quiet night," a tired-looking nurse said, handing over the chart. "No more contractions and I peeked in on her about an hour ago and she was sleeping soundly."

"Thank you."

When Lauren returned to the desk, the janitor was gone. She spent a moment flipping through the chart, pleased with what she saw there. Her vitals were stable and her pain level seemed to be under control. The few times she had awakened, she had seemed calm and at ease.

Lauren didn't want to wake her patient, but she also didn't want to leave after coming all this way without at least checking on her.

As she paused outside the door to her room, a strange whimpering noise sounded from inside and her heart sank. Despite what the night nurse had charted, maybe the mild painkillers Rosa had been treated with weren't quite cutting it.

She pushed open the door to check on the girl, then gasped.

The horrific sight inside registered for only about half a second before Lauren started screaming for security and rushed inside to attack the man who was trying to smother her patient.

Chapter 4

After that first instant of disoriented, stunned panic, everything else seemed a blur. She rushed the man, almost tripping over the mop and bucket on her way toward him as she yelled for him to stop and for security at equal turns.

With no coherent plan, she slammed into him to knock him away from her patient. The force of her movement knocked them both off balance and they toppled against the rolling bedside table, sending it crashing to the floor and the two of them after it.

The man scrambled to his feet to get away and Lauren lunged after him, barely registering the coarse fabric of his janitor's uniform as she grabbed hold of it. For some wild reason she was intent only on keeping him there until security arrived, but he was just as intent on escape.

He shoved her to get her away from him, hissing

curses at her in Spanish as he fought her off. Finally he just swung his other beefy fist out and slugged her, the blow connecting to the cheekbone and knocking her to the ground.

White-hot pain exploded in her skull. In an instant he was gone. She couldn't have stopped him, even if she hadn't been forced to release him when she fell.

Lauren's vision grayed and her stomach twisted and heaved from the pain. She wanted to curl up right there on the floor, but Rosa was clutching her throat and still gasping for air. Lauren forced herself to keep it together for her patient's sake. Using the bed for support, she pulled herself to her feet and hurried as fast as possible to the terrified girl's side.

"Come on, sweetheart," Lauren urged, grabbing the oxygen mask from the wall above the bed and placing it as gently as possible over Rosa's mouth at the same time she hit the emergency call button.

"Take deep breaths. That's the way. You're fine now. Nobody's going to hurt you."

Though she forgot all about the language barrier and spoke in English, Rosa seemed to understand her. The shaken girl made a ragged, gravelly sound deep in her throat and Lauren handed her the water glass by the side of her bed just as the first nurses rushed in.

"What is it? What happened?" the first one asked. "Are you okay?"

Lauren was shaking, she realized, and her head throbbed like it had been crushed by a wrecking ball. "No. I'm not okay. A man just attacked my patient. Call security. Have them block all the exits and entrances. They need to look for a Latino male in his mid-twenties.

He was wearing a maintenance worker's uniform but it was too short for him so I'm guessing it wasn't real."

"You're bleeding!" the nurse exclaimed.

"Forget about me," she said harshly. "Just call security!"

The nurse rushed out and Rosa gave a strangled whimper. Lauren saw she was inches away from hysteria. She slid onto the bed and gathered the girl to her, as much to comfort her as to find a safe place to sit for a moment before her legs gave out.

"You're okay. You're safe now."

"Mi bebé. Mi bebé."

"Okay, okay. We'll check everything out but I'm sure your baby is all right."

As the adrenaline spike crested, Lauren had to fight to hold on to her meager breakfast. It wasn't easy.

She had been physically attacked only once before in her life and finding herself in this situation again brought back all those long-dormant feelings of shock and invasion she thought she had worked through years ago.

She didn't know what was stronger, the urge to vomit or the urge to crawl into a corner and sob.

"Rosa. Is that the same man who hurt you?"

The girl hesitated, though Lauren could tell she understood her fractured Spanish.

"The only way you can be safe is to report what happened so he can be arrested."

The gross hypocrisy of her words struck her, but she couldn't worry about that now. Not when her patient's life was at stake.

"Rosa, you're going to have to tell someone what happened. You have no choice anymore. Will you talk to Sheriff Galvez?"

Rosa let out a sob and curved both hands over her abdomen. After a moment, she gave a long, slow nod.

He was bone-tired, so tired all he wanted to do was pull over somewhere, put his hat over his face and doze off for a few decades.

A smart man would be home in bed right about now dreaming soft, pleasant dreams that had nothing to do with crimes or accident reports or people in need.

He, on the other hand, had decided on a wild hair to drive into the big city after his shift ended to check on their assault victim. He could only hope a night in the hospital had changed her mind about talking to him about what had happened to her.

He worked out the kinks in his neck as he parked his SUV and headed for the front entrance of the hospital. Four security guards and a Salt Lake City police officer stood just inside, a pretty heavy security force. Maybe they had beefed up security for some kind of high-profile patient. His guess was that some kind of A-list movie star from the film festival had broken a leg on the slopes or something.

He recognized the city cop as Eddie Marin, an old friend from police training. "Hey, Eddie. What's going on?"

The officer greeted him with familiar backslapping. "Galvez, long time no see."

"What's with all the uniforms?"

"Incident up on the medical unit. Some dude tried to off a patient. We've sealed off the entrances but the guy seems to be in the wind. We can't find any trace of him." He gave Daniel a considering look. "Not saying we don't appreciate all the help we can get, but isn't this one a little far out of your jurisdiction?"

"I'm off duty, just following up on an assault victim dumped in my neck of the woods. What does your suspect look like? I'll keep an eye out for him on my way up."

"We had an eyewitness who caught him in the attack and was hurt trying to fight him off. She was pretty shaken up but Dr. Maxwell described a Latino male in a janitor uniform, five feet eleven inches, one hundred ninety pounds, half his left eyebrow missing from a scar. Only problem is, we can't find the bastard anywhere in the hospital."

Daniel registered none of the description, too caught up in the words preceding it. "Did you say Dr. Maxwell? Lauren Maxwell?"

"I think that's her name. You know her?"

"She was injured?"

Eddie blinked at his urgent tone. "Perp punched her and knocked her to the floor. She's pretty banged up and needs a couple stitches but she won't leave her patient."

"What room?"

Eddie gave him a careful look. "You okay, man?"

"What the hell room are they in?"

The officer told him and Daniel didn't bother waiting for the elevator, he just raced for the stairs, his heart pounding.

He wouldn't say he was intimately familiar with the sprawling hospital but he had been here many times on other cases. He knew his way enough to find the room Eddie had indicated, and in moments he reached the medical wing.

Even if the officer hadn't given him the room number,

he would have known it instantly by the crowd of people milling around. His own uniform seemed to smooth the way as he fought his way through until he made it to the room.

He found Lauren just outside the doorway, gesturing to another Salt Lake police officer he didn't recognize.

She was holding a blood-soaked bandage to her cheek and her face was pale and drawn. Rage burned through him at whatever bastard might have hurt her and he wanted to fold her against him and keep her safe from the world.

She cut off her words the moment she saw him.

"Daniel!" she exclaimed, shock and relief mingling in her voice. Before he quite knew how it happened, she seemed to slide into his arms, pressing her uninjured cheek against the fabric of his uniform and holding on tight.

She felt delicate and fragile against him and despite the layers of his coat, he could feel the tiny shudders that shook her frame.

She sagged against him for only a moment, just long enough for him to want to tighten his arms and hold on forever. After entirely too short a time, she pulled away, a rosy flush replacing the pale, washed-out look she had worn when he first saw her.

He wanted to pull her back into his arms but he knew they didn't have that kind of relationship. The only reason she had turned to him in the first place was likely because he represented a familiar face, comfort and security amid her trauma.

Already, he could see her replacing the defenses between them and once more becoming the cool, controlled physician who could handle anything.

"What happened?" he asked.

She let out a breath. "It was terrible. Absolutely awful. I walked into the room to check on Rosa about half an hour ago and found a janitor with his hands around her neck, choking the life out of her. Only he obviously wasn't really a janitor. She says he was the same one who attacked her."

"How is she?"

Her eyes softened and he had the impression that had been exactly the right thing to say, though he wasn't quite sure why.

"Petrified and shocked. She keeps saying *mi bebé* over and over. Physically, I don't think she was injured by the latest attack but she's severely traumatized by it."

"And you?"

"I'm all right. He got in a good punch. I tried to hold him until security got here but he…he was bigger and stronger than I was."

Her shoulders trembled again. To hell with this, he thought, and pulled her back into his arms, whether she wanted to be there or not. He didn't know if the move was for her comfort or his own, he only knew he couldn't let her stand inches away from him and suffer.

This time she stayed a little longer before she slid away from him. "I'm okay. I am. A little shaky but I'll be fine. I'm glad you're here."

He knew she meant on a professional level, but the words warmed him anyway. He was grateful to be there, too, and had to wonder what higher power had inspired him to drive to the hospital this morning, exactly when he would be needed.

If he hadn't stopped for coffee on the way, though,

he might have made it in time to stop the bastard. The thought haunted him.

"Do you think after this latest attack, Rosa might be ready to tell us what's going on?"

Lauren sighed heavily. "I think she's realizing she doesn't have any other choice if she wants to stay alive. I asked her and she agreed she would talk to you."

He didn't want to leave Lauren, but a nurse approached them. "Dr. Maxwell, the surgeon is ready for you."

"Surgeon?" he exclaimed.

She made a face, then winced at the motion. "Plastic surgeon. It's stupid but the hospital insisted he be the one to stitch up my cheek."

"Careful of the needles. I hate those things."

She gave him a half smile, which was all she seemed to be able to manage with her battle scars. "How can a man who played football against three-hundred-pound linebackers be afraid of a tiny needle?"

"What can I say? I'm a wimp."

She smiled again, looking noticeably more calm than she had when he arrived.

"Go take care of your face," he urged. "I'll go see if I can persuade Rosa to talk to me."

When he walked into the hospital room this time, Rosa didn't look surprised or frightened to see him, only re-signed. Such fatalism in features as young and battered as hers was disconcerting.

He greeted her in Spanish. "How are you feeling?" he asked.

"Like I've been kicked by twenty donkeys," she answered quietly.

He met her gaze intently. "You have to tell me what is going on, Rosa. You know that, don't you?"

One hand was in a cast, but the other fingers tightened on the blanket and she suddenly seemed painfully young. "I am afraid."

"I understand that. Anyone in your position would be. But we can't help you unless we know who is trying to hurt you and your baby."

She closed her eyes, one hand resting on her abdomen. When she opened her eyes again, the raw fear in them twisted his heart.

"Rosa?" he prompted.

She sighed as if the entire weight of the world rested on her narrow shoulders. "His name is Gilberto Mata."

"Is he your baby's father?"

She looked down at the tiny mound beneath the covers. A spasm of emotion that almost looked like shame tightened her mouth. "I don't know. Maybe. It could be him or...others."

Her lip trembled and she wouldn't meet his gaze. He had to wonder if she might feel more comfortable with a female investigator, but he didn't want to interrupt the flow of her story by asking her, not when she seemed willing to tell him what had happened.

"Is that why he hurt you?" Daniel asked. "Because you had been with other men?"

She gave a harsh laugh and this time she did look at him, a deep, horrible bitterness in her eyes. "No. He was there when I was with the other men. He stood by laughing while all three of them, they raped me. And then he took his turn."

Madre de Dios. What the hell kind of trouble was this little girl mixed up with? He fought the urge to squeeze her hand and tell her everything would be all right.

"I am so sorry, Rosa," he finally said, abashed at the

inadequacy of the words. "Maybe you had better start at the beginning."

She wiped away a single tear. "The beginning seems another lifetime ago. Six months ago I was working in Tegucigalpa. My mama, she died two years ago. I tried to stay in our village but there was no work and I had no money. I went to the city with my friend Consuela and we found work in a factory sewing clothes."

"How old are you?"

"I will be sixteen years on July sixth," she said, looking a little surprised by the question.

Daniel tried to put the years together. If her mother had died two years ago, she would have been about fourteen when she took a factory job.

"Consuela and I, we did not make much money but it was good, honest work. One day some men came to the factory. They talked to some of the girls and said we could find work in America and they would help us. They filled our stupid heads with stories of the riches we would find here and the good life we would have, like in the movies we see. I did not believe them, but Consuela, she wanted to try. The men flattered her, told her she was beautiful, that she would find good work. I tried to talk her out of it but she would not listen. She begged me to go with her and I finally agreed. I just wanted to protect her, and without her I had no one left in my country."

She bunched the blanket in her uncasted hand. "For five days Consuela and I and a dozen other girls rode in the back of a closed truck, with no food and only a little water. It was so hot and we thought we would die. At last we arrived in Texas but for some of us, our journey was not done. They told us they had good work for us in Utah. Stupid fools, we believed them."

Another tear trickled down her cheek and he handed her a tissue from a box by the bed. "What happened when you got here?"

"I soon realized what kind of work we were to do. Prostitutes. Whores. They told us if we did not do what they wanted, we would be killed. I would not do it. I was a good girl in Honduras. So the bosses, the men who brought us here…they forced me. Gilberto, he is the worst. We were all afraid of him."

Daniel clamped down his fury, doing his best to hide it so he wouldn't frighten Rosa. He couldn't conceive the kind of animals who would force young, innocent girls into a dark, ugly world of prostitution. That such things were happening only miles from his safe, quiet town seemed an abomination.

"I was lucky. Because I cried so much when…when they made me do those things, I only had to wash the dishes, do the laundry and scrub the floors."

"Do you know where this all happened?"

"Six of us work above a bar in the town of Park City. The Lucky Strike. The others, including my friend Consuela, are in Salt Lake City somewhere. I do not know where."

"What happened to make Gilberto want to hurt you?"

"It was my fault. A few months ago I discovered I was pregnant from…from that first week. I was angry at first and hated what was inside me as much as I hated whatever man had put the baby inside me. But after some time, I knew I couldn't blame the baby, that nothing was her fault. I tried to hide it and find a way to escape. They watch us carefully and lock us in at night but I thought I might be able to sneak out the window. I didn't know where I would go after that but I knew I must get away.

They would kill my baby. They had made one of the other girls have an abortion and I knew they would do the same to me."

She shivered. "Last night I tried to escape but Gilberto, he found me. He…he beat me and was going to rape me again. Then he saw I was pregnant and he started calling me names, hitting and kicking me, trying to make me lose the baby, too. I fought him and knocked him down the stairs, then ran as fast as I could. It was a big crowd on the street and somehow I got away from him. I ran and ran until I had no more breath. I thought I would die, I hurt so much. I didn't know what to do, then I saw a truck parked in front of me. I could see a blanket inside, and the back, it was unlocked. I climbed inside and pulled the blanket over my head to hide from Gilberto. The next I remember, the man with the white hair opened the truck and found me there. And that is all."

An understatement if he ever heard one. Human smuggling, rape, forced prostitution, attempted murder. There were more class-A felonies in this girl's story than he sometimes dealt with in six months.

"I thought I was safe now, until I woke up in the hospital and found Gilberto in my hospital room. Again, I expected to die and then the pretty doctor, she came rushing in and fought him off."

She sniffled a little and he handed her another tissue. "I am sorry she was hurt. I did not believe Gilberto would find me here."

"That's a good point. How *did* he find you? Did you call someone and tell them you were in the hospital?"

"No. No one. Who would I call? I told you, my friend Consuela, I do not know how to reach her now. They separated us and she is working in Salt Lake City. The other girls at the bar, we did not talk much. They kept us apart most of the time. I know no one else."

It didn't make sense. He supposed they could have been monitoring police traffic on a scanner when they had called for an ambulance to transport her here. It was the only explanation he could come up with, though it seemed a stretch.

"Why does Gilberto want you dead badly enough to come here and try to finish the job?"

"Because I am a fool." She wiped at her eyes again. "Do you know what it is like to be afraid and filled with anger at the same time? When Gilberto was hurting me and…and trying to hurt the baby, I… I told him to stop, that if he did not, I would go to the police, I would tell them everything that had happened to us here since we left Honduras. I had more freedom than the other girls because I cleaned the rooms. I do not snoop, but I see things and I knew the names of the men who hurt me and who made the other girls do those things."

"Everyone?"

"Except the big boss. I do not know his name and I have not seen him, I only know he is Anglo. But I lied. I told Gilberto I did. I should not have said that but I only wanted him to stop hitting me. I thought if he was afraid of being arrested he would let me go."

She covered her face. "I was stupid. An imbecile. He only hit me harder and I knew he would kill me."

"You can't blame yourself, *niña*. None of this is your fault."

She started to weep then, huge, wrenching sobs, and Daniel leaned forward and squeezed her shoulder. The next moment, she threw herself against him, sniffling against his uniform in much the same place Lauren had done.

He patted her hair awkwardly, wishing he had some words that might make this miserable situation all better. Before he could come up with anything, the door opened and Lauren came in. She paused in the doorway, a soft, arrested look in her eyes he didn't quite understand.

She had a stark white bandage on her cheek, but the color had returned to her features, he was grateful to see.

"I'm sorry to interrupt, but Rosa is overdue for pain medication and I don't want her to get behind. How are you?" The last words were in Spanish, directed at the girl.

"Better," Rosa said shyly. She laid back against the pillow, her gaze on Lauren's bandage. "I am sorry you were hurt by Gilberto Mata. He is a bad, bad man and would have killed me if not for you. You saved my life."

Lauren blinked a little at her gratitude, then smiled. "Daniel, will you tell her I didn't go to all the trouble to fix her up only to lose her again to this Mata character?"

Daniel complied.

"How long will I stay here?" Rosa asked.

"I can't answer that right now," Lauren said, and Daniel translated for her. "At least tonight, I'm thinking. They're going to move you to a more secure location in the hospital."

"Are you leaving?" Daniel asked.

"My clinic is supposed to be opening—" she checked her watch "—right now. I can reschedule some of my patients but not all of them. Tell Rosa I'll be back later this afternoon after I'm through at the clinic."

Rosa yawned suddenly and Daniel thought she must be exhausted after her ordeal of the morning and by the retelling of her story.

Lauren picked up on it as well. "Get some rest. They should be moving you sometime this morning, but rest until then." She paused. "Sheriff Galvez, may I have a word with you?"

Curious, he nodded and followed her from the room.

"Did she tell you what this is all about?"

He nodded. "She and several other girls have been smuggled out of Central America to be used as prostitutes and unpaid labor."

"Slavery?" She looked appalled.

"It's alive and well in the underground," he said. "And a much bigger problem than many people realize. Rosa tried to escape when she realized she was pregnant as a result of rape in her early days in the country. She was caught and beaten because of what she knows and because she threatened to go to the police. I don't think they'll stop with one attempt on her life, especially now that they know for sure she's here."

"We can't leave her here unprotected with some maniac on the loose. I've talked to the hospital and they're going to put full-time security outside her room but I'm not sure some rent-a-cop will be enough. What else can be done?"

"I'll make sure there is adequate protection. You do realize, this is bigger than the Moose Springs Sheriff Department can handle. I'm going to have to call in the FBI on this one and I'm sure they'll set up a multijurisdictional task force."

"Good. I hope they find the bastards who did this to her and string them up by their *cojones*."

He blinked at such fierceness coming from the cool, collected Dr. Maxwell. But then he looked at the bandage marring the soft loveliness of her features and couldn't help but agree.

Chapter 5

Lauren was an hour and a half late for her first appointment of the day and spent most of the morning trying her best to catch up without sacrificing the personalized time she liked to spend with each patient—all while her mind seemed stuck on a courageous young girl recovering in a hospital miles away.

One of the things she enjoyed most about being a small-town doctor was the sheer variety of patients she saw, everything from prenatal visits to setting broken arms to pulling slivers out of tiny fingers. Every day was different, full of new challenges to test her abilities.

Just now she was seeing one of her favorite patients, Cameron Vance. Cam had epilepsy and though he regularly saw a neurologist at the children's hospital in Salt Lake City, she was still his primary care provider and saw him for routine visits.

Just now he was suffering from a case of the sniffles that had lasted for ten days.

"Besides the gross runny nose, how's everything else going with my favorite climber dude?" she asked him.

Cameron grinned. "Awesome. Me and Cale are gonna go to Jackson Hole and climb the Grand Teton this summer. We're in training."

At that surprising bit of information, Lauren raised an eyebrow to his mother, Megan, one of her good friends.

Megan shrugged. "What can I do?" she said. "Cale assures me Cameron has the climbing skills to handle it. He'll be ten by then and is certainly experienced enough for it. I can't really say no, especially since he hasn't had a seizure since the big one last summer."

Lauren knew just which *big one* Megan referred to. In August, Cameron had been lost in an abandoned mine in the foothills above Moose Springs and had gone without his seizure medication for more than thirty-six hours. He had been rescued in the middle of a prolonged grand mal seizure by Cale Davis, one of the FBI agents assigned to his case, just seconds before a mine cave-in would have trapped them all.

At Christmastime, Megan had married the man who had rescued her son and Lauren was thrilled to see them all so happy.

"Cale will take care of him," she assured Megan now. "He won't take Cameron anywhere it's not safe. He's a great stepdad."

"He is, isn't he?" Megan glowed when she talked about her husband and, as happy as she was for her friend, Lauren couldn't help the little spurt of envy.

It was small of her, she knew. Megan hadn't had an easy time of things. Cam and his sister, Hailey, had lost their father a few years ago when he was killed fighting in Afghanistan. Megan had raised her children alone, dealing with all the emotional and physical strain of Cameron's epilepsy. She deserved every slice of happiness she could find and Caleb Davis was a great guy who was obviously crazy about her.

Lauren was thrilled for her. But in comparison to Megan's newfound joy, her own personal life fell somewhere between dry and excruciatingly dull.

"What do you recommend for Cam?" Megan asked now and Lauren jerked her mind away from her own private pity party and focused on her patient, as she should have been doing all along.

"I'm guessing with the duration of his symptoms, we're looking at a sinus infection here."

"That's what I thought, too."

"You don't need me, do you?" She smiled at Megan.

"Yes, I do," Megan said firmly. "I don't know what we would do without you and your clinic so close."

She might not have a personal life, but she did have a pretty darn good professional one, Lauren reminded herself. "I'm going to write Mr. Monkey here a prescription for an antibiotic that should be fine with his other medications. As to the cold symptoms, I know you're leery about giving him some of the over-the-counter decongestants because of the chance they may trigger a seizure. The best thing I can recommend is some good old-fashioned chicken noodle soup. If you want, I can email my favorite recipe with plenty of garlic and onions. That should help clear him out."

"Definitely. I'm always looking for soup recipes."

She made a note reminding herself to send it as soon as they finished. "If his symptoms don't improve in a couple of days, call me back and we'll try to figure something else out."

"More garlic, maybe?"

Lauren smiled. "It couldn't hurt."

She turned to Cam. "Let me know when you and Cale head off for the big climb. I'm going to want pictures of you on top of the Grand to hang in my office. And let's hope your nose has stopped running by then, because that would just be gross at high altitude."

They shared a grin as Megan took the scribbled prescription from her and stuck it in her purse.

"Thanks, Lauren," she said on her way out the door.

As they were her last appointment before lunch, Lauren walked them out to the waiting room.

Her office manager held up a hand to stop them. "You're probably getting a bit on the old side for a sticker," Coralee said to Cameron. "But can I interest you in a sour ball?"

"Heck, yeah," he exclaimed. At a chiding look from his mother he rolled his eyes. "Yes, ma'am," he corrected. "Thank you."

Coralee grinned and was pulling out her secret stash of candy when the low chime on the door rang. Lauren looked up and was startled to find Daniel standing in the doorway, looking big and tough and intimidating.

To her dismay, her pulse quickened and everything inside her seemed to sigh in welcome.

He looked exhausted, she thought. His eyes were bleary and he needed a shave, and she had to wonder when he had slept last.

"Sheriff Galvez!" Cameron exclaimed and bounded over to Daniel. At the sight of the boy, he straightened and seemed to lock away his exhaustion. The two of them greeted each other with a series of high fives and handshakes that looked as complicated as it was well choreographed.

"Hey, Cam. Megan. Two of my favorite people. How's everything at the Vance-Davis compound?"

Megan hugged him. "Good. When are you coming to dinner again? You owe us, since you bailed the last time."

"Sorry." He made a rueful face. "That was the night we had that bad accident out on Barrow Road, wasn't it?"

"That time. Before that, it was the structure fire at James Woolstenhume's barn and the time before that was a traffic stop that turned into a drug bust, I think. The next time we invite you to dinner, do me a favor and try to keep the emergencies to a minimum, won't you?"

He smiled with affection at her teasing. "I'll do my best. Can't make any promises."

"That's the trouble with you law enforcement types." Megan nudged his shoulder. His good one, Lauren was relieved to see. "Next week, okay? Which night works for you, Friday or Saturday?"

"Uh, I'll have to check my schedule and get back to you."

"Lauren, you should come, too. I've been meaning to have you out again. We'll make it a party."

Megan gave her a guileless smile, but Lauren could swear she felt the tug of a matchmaking web.

She flushed and didn't dare look at Daniel. "I'm supposed to be on vacation next week."

"Good, then you'll have plenty of time to get ready." Megan didn't wait for an answer as she herded Cameron toward the door. "I'll call you both in a day or two to work out the details. Thanks again for the prescription. Let's hope it takes care of this kiddo's runny nose."

"I...you're welcome."

After the door closed behind him, the room seemed to steady as if they had all just been caught in the eye of a cyclone. She finally risked a look at Daniel and found him looking as nonplussed as she felt. She was about to ask him about Rosa when he turned away from her and headed for the reception desk.

"What's this I hear about you heading out on a cruise, Coralee? When do you sail?"

Lauren's office manager was always eager to talk about her trip. "Next week. I've already got my bags all packed, waiting by the door."

"You'll have to forgive me," Daniel drawled, "but I'm having a real tough time picturing Bruce on the beaches of Tahiti, soaking up the sun in a Speedo."

"Oh, heaven forbid!" Coralee made a face. "He says he's just coming along for the food and the fishing. Though I'm sure he won't mind seeing the island girls in their hula skirts."

"How's Sherry?" he asked, launching Coralee into her second favorite topic after her upcoming vacation—her grandchildren. Lauren stood back and watched them, marveling that he could make small talk with all the heavy matters that must be weighing on his mind.

This was part of the ebb and flow of a small community, stopping and talking and asking after loved ones.

Daniel seemed comfortable talking to everyone in town, which was one of the things that made him such a good sheriff. He was respected and well liked by all segments of Moose Springs, from kids like Cameron to the low-income families to the town leaders.

He appeared to get along with everybody in town— except her.

She sighed, wishing that thought didn't depress her so much. Watching his easy rapport with Megan and Cameron and Coralee only reinforced how stiff and uncomfortable he always seemed with her.

"Sorry to drop in like this without an appointment," he said, and she realized with a start he was talking to her. "I was wondering if there's any chance you could take a look at my arm? Something doesn't quite feel right about it."

He wanted *her* to look at his arm? This, from the man who had endured her ministrations the night before like she was shoving bamboo shoots under his fingernails?

He had just come from a morning spent at the University of Utah Medical Center. If his arm was bothering him so much, why didn't he just have someone there check it out?

"Of course," she managed through her shock. "I can do it now. We were just about to go to lunch."

"Do you want me to stick around?" Coralee asked.

"No, that's all right. I know you're meeting your sister for lunch at the diner. Go ahead."

Lauren led Daniel to an exam room. "Uh, do you want to unbutton your shirt?" She could feel her face flush at the question and prayed he didn't notice.

He leaned against the exam table and folded his arms across his chest—including the injured one in question. "No. I just used that as an excuse so I could talk to you without Coralee overhearing our conversation. I didn't realize she would be leaving anyway or I wouldn't have had to come up with a good story."

"Right. Coralee is harder to lie to than my mother."

"You lie to your mother, Dr. Maxwell? I'm shocked."

"I know. I'm a terrible person."

A muscle twitched in his cheek but he didn't give in to a full-fledged smile. "What did you tell Coralee about the bandage?" he asked.

"The truth. Or mostly the truth. I told her I had an accident at the hospital while checking on a patient."

"I think that's wise. I know she can be discreet, but the fewer people who know what's going on, the better."

"It wasn't really that. I just didn't want to worry her. Coralee is a bit of a mother hen, especially with my own mother living six hours away now." She paused. "While you're here, you might as well let me take a look at your shoulder."

He looked less than enthralled at the idea. "That's really not necessary. I'm fine."

"Humor me. I want to make sure you're not starting with any infection. You can tell me what happened this morning at the hospital while I check you out. Your injury, I mean."

She wanted to bite her tongue for adding that last part so quickly, especially when he gave her a long, measuring look. She geared up for an argument about her demand, but either he was too tired to put up much of a fuss or his arm really *was* bothering him.

After a moment, his fingers went to the buttons of his uniform shirt and he started working them free. Lauren refused to acknowledge the ripple of her insides as he started baring all that smooth skin and hard muscles. He was a patient, for heaven's sake. She had to treat him with all the professionalism and courtesy she showed all her other patients.

She pulled the bandage away to find a little redness and swelling around the wound site.

He flinched when she touched it and she chewed her

lip. If she needed a reminder to keep her mind away from him as a very attractive man, there it was. He obviously didn't like her touching him, even in a professional capacity.

She needed to remember that and forget about how her hands itched to smooth over him.

By the time she finally stepped away from him and shoved her hands into the pockets of her plum-colored sweater, Daniel was sweating and light-headed from holding his breath the whole time she had her hands on him.

He tried to hide his deep inhale behind a cough.

"Everything looks fine," she said. "A little red and swollen, but that's not out of the ordinary. If you notice any of that starting to spread at all, make sure you let me know."

Her voice was cool and brisk and he did his best to match it.

"I'll do that," he said. He fumbled with his buttons with fingers that felt big and awkward, as if they were bandaged, too.

He sure as hell hoped his arm healed soon because he couldn't endure her touching him again.

Okay, there was a lie he knew he couldn't sneak past either Lauren's mother or Coralee Jenkins. The barebones truth was just the opposite. He *did* want her hands on him, just not in any kind of medical setting.

"Now tell me how Rosa is doing?"

He cleared his throat, shifting gears back to what he knew he should be focusing on. "She was fine when I left an hour ago. Exhausted, since she didn't get much sleep before Cale and Gage McKinnon showed up and she had to go through it all again."

"Cale and his partner are handling the case?" Lauren asked. "That's a relief."

"Her imprisonment, rape and attempted murder definitely fall under their jurisdiction in the Crimes Against Children Unit," he answered. "We don't know if all the possible victims are under the legal age, but since Rosa will be the star witness and she's only fifteen, CAC will be spearheading the investigation."

"Great. With you or Cale both on the case, whoever did this will be behind bars in no time."

"I hope so, but I'm afraid it's not going to be that easy. The real reason I stopped by was to let you know she's been moved to a more secure location in the hospital. Even though you're the physician on record, you're going to need the access information before the guards will let you in. Assuming you're still planning to stop by, anyway."

"Of course."

He nodded, not at all surprised. Lauren was a dedicated doctor, completely committed to her patients. He would have been surprised if she *hadn't* been planning to drive to the city again that night.

"It's still not the ideal situation. I don't believe this Mata or the people he's working with will just give up trying to shut her mouth, but for now this is the best we can do, moving her to a more secure location and keeping security posted at her room at all times."

"I hope it's enough. What about when she's released?"

"We're still trying to work that out." He fought back a yawn. "The FBI is trying to find a good placement for her. She'll have to stick around to testify to the grand jury while the FBI gathers enough evidence to break up the smuggling and prostitution ring so they can make arrests. How much longer do you think Rosa will need to stay in the hospital?"

"Under normal circumstances, I would probably keep her at least a few more days, probably through the weekend. She hasn't had prenatal care throughout the pregnancy. That complicates things. I would recommend careful monitoring for the rest of her pregnancy, especially given the nature of the assault and the fact that she's already had some early contractions."

"I'll give the FBI a call and let them know they should plan on having a new placement for her by the day after tomorrow, at the latest."

"Will you let me know how things are going?" she asked.

"Of course."

He shrugged into his coat and was putting on his hat to leave when she touched his arm. "Daniel, how long since you slept last?"

As if her words finally pierced whatever force of will was keeping him functioning, he was suddenly so tired he wanted to lean his forehead against her and fall asleep right there.

"Yesterday morning, six a.m.," he admitted.

"You need some rest. I'm sure you don't need me to tell you that. You've been an athlete and you know it's not at all healthy for you to burn yourself out like this."

He hadn't had anyone fuss over him for a long time. He wasn't quite sure how to handle it. "There have been a few unusual circumstances the last twenty-four hours keeping me awake. But I'm heading home now. I have high hopes I'll be able to fall into my big, warm bed and not wake up again until my shift tonight."

She still look worried but she managed a smile. "Do that. We need you strong and healthy."

He wasn't at all sure why color rose on her delicate cheekbones, but he found it fascinating.

"The town, I mean," she said quickly. "If you wear yourself out, you're bound to compromise your immune system and leave yourself open to all kinds of infections."

"Right. We wouldn't want that, would we? Don't worry about me. You've got enough on your plate taking care of the whole town. I'll be fine."

Did she have any kind of drugs he could take that would give him a stronger immune system when it came to her? he wondered as he finally left her clinic and drove toward home. Something that would keep her from invading his thoughts and completely taking over?

He had told her these last twenty-four hours had been full of unusual circumstances. Right at the top of that list was the fact that he had spent more time in her company since he walked into her clinic yesterday evening than he ever had. Even when he hadn't been with her physically, she hadn't been far from his mind.

Was it wishful thinking on his part to think perhaps she wasn't completely immune to him, either? He had sensed several times last night and again this morning that she might be softening toward him. Things between them seemed easier, somehow. Slightly more comfortable.

He liked it. More than liked it.

He drove past her massive childhood home, the biggest house in town, all wrought iron and elegant cornices and perfectly groomed grounds. She had sold the place after her father's death to a young couple from Utah County. Nice people. The husband commuted to Orem every day to work in the state's own version of Silicon Valley and the wife volunteered in the little Moose Springs library.

A few blocks later, he reached his own house, the same four-room clapboard house where his parents had raised their family. He had fixed it up before his mom lost her fight with cancer, added a family room off the back and another bathroom, but it was still a small house on a tiny lot.

Daniel sighed. Here was the hard reminder he needed. Lauren had been raised in luxury and comfort, the pampered only child of two doting parents. He had grown up fighting for one minuscule bathroom with two brothers and a sister.

The biggest obstacle between them wasn't really his humble upbringing or her socially elevated one. He might see that as a glaring difference, but he had a feeling Lauren really wouldn't care about that.

She *would,* however, care about his role in her father's downfall and subsequent suicide.

No amount of wishing on his part could change that.

Chapter 6

She was ready for a vacation.

Friday morning dawned stormy and cold as she drove the busy canyon from Moose Springs to the hospital in Salt Lake City. Her wipers worked steadily but they couldn't keep the big, juicy flakes off the window and she was grateful for the all-wheel-drive of her car.

Lauren had grown up driving in snow but she still wasn't crazy about it. She always found it stressful and demanding. Winter driving wasn't so bad in tiny Moose Springs, where she never encountered more than a few other cars on the road, but the early-morning commute into the city was another story altogether.

By the time she pulled her Volvo into the parking lot at the hospital, her shoulders were tight and her fingers ached from gripping the steering wheel. She climbed out of her vehicle and stepped into four inches of snow that hadn't been scraped off the parking lot yet.

Maybe later in the week when things were settled with Rosa, she ought to give in to her mother's pressure tactics and head to southern Utah for a few days. Soaking up the sun in St. George seemed like a lovely idea right about now.

A week of leisure time would be a decadent luxury. She hadn't had a break longer than a quick weekend in five years and the grim truth was, she wouldn't be taking this one if not for Coralee and her anniversary cruise.

A little respite would be good for her, a chance to recharge and remember why she started in medicine in the first place. And some sunshine right about now might lift her spirits out of this funk.

She walked through the door, stomping snow off her boots. The first person she saw in the lobby was Kendall Fox, talking to a couple of women in scrubs. He looked ruggedly handsome, with that sun-streaked blond hair and skier's tan, and she had to admit her ego enjoyed a nice little boost when his eyes lit up with pleasure at the sight of her.

He excused himself from the other nurses and headed toward her. "Lauren! I was hoping I would bump into you today."

"Oh?" Why couldn't she summon a little attraction for vivid blue eyes and a man who knew just what to do with them? Instead, all she could think about were Daniel's eyes, dark and warm and solemn.

"Yeah. Don't ask me how I did it but I scored an invite for one of the huge after-screening parties up at Deer Valley tonight. I need to find a gorgeous woman to escort, and of course I thought of you. What time can I pick you up?"

She had to admit to a flicker of temptation. When he

wasn't hitting on anything that moved, Kendall could be funny and charming and attentive. She was tired of living like a nun. Was it wrong to want a little diversion from the solitude of her life?

A moment's reflection was all she needed to reinforce what a lousy idea that would be. She wasn't at all interested in a player like Kendall, who probably had the cell phone numbers of every available female at the hospital and a few unavailable ones as well.

If she went out with him and had to spend the evening fighting off his inevitable moves, she would be left more depressed than ever.

"Sorry. I've got plans tonight," she lied.

"Break them. Come on. How often do you get to mix with the Hollywood glitterati in your little Podunk Cow Springs?"

"*Moose* Springs. You're right, almost never. And yet somehow I still manage to lead a rewarding, fulfilling life."

"You want fulfillment, I can provide it beyond your wildest dreams," he murmured in her ear.

She barely restrained from rolling her eyes. Okay, forget lousy idea. Going out with Kendall Fox, even for the sake of a little conversation, would be a nightmare of epic proportions. She would spend the whole night fighting off his wandering hands and wishing she were somewhere else. Or at least that *he* was *someone* else.

She started to answer—or at least tell him to back off and give her a little room to breathe here—but the words died in her throat. Some instinct had her looking up and she was horrified to find Daniel standing ten feet away from them, watching her out of those dark eyes of his that suddenly didn't look remotely warm.

"Daniel!" she exclaimed. She had no reason to feel so absurdly guilty but that didn't keep hot water from washing over her cheekbones.

She quickly stepped away from Kendall.

"Lauren. Dr. Fox." She couldn't tell if that reserve in his voice was politeness or disdain.

She forced a cheerful smile. On the one hand, she was grateful to have a ready excuse to escape Kendall's persistence. On the other, she would have preferred anyone other than Daniel be the one to ride to her social rescue.

"I imagine we're here to see the same person," she said brightly. "I'll walk up with you."

An instant of surprise registered in his eyes, but he quickly veiled it. "All right."

Kendall's features tightened with annoyance. He opened his mouth but she cut him off. The last thing she needed right now was for Daniel to be standing nearby when she told Kendall she wasn't interested in ever going out with him.

"Have a good time at your party," she said, hoping her refusal was firm and clear, then led the way through the hospital lobby toward the bank of elevators.

She and Daniel were the only two people taking the elevator. In such close quarters she was acutely aware of his size and how small and fragile she always felt next to him.

He look rested, she thought. Or at least not quite as exhausted as he had two days earlier in her office, when she had seen him last.

"We need to talk," he said abruptly, when the doors glided closed. He smelled of soap and clean male and he was freshly shaved. It was all she could do not to run her hand along that strong, hard jawline.

She blinked. "Okay."

"Are you planning to write discharge orders today?"

Right. Rosa's case. What else would they have to talk about? "I can't know that yet until I have a chance to look at the chart and see how her pain level was during the night and whether she's had any repeat contractions. If she had a quiet night, I don't really have any reason to keep her longer. Unless you think she's safer in the hospital."

"I don't," he said as the elevator lurched to a stop on Rosa's floor. The doors opened and Lauren was vastly relieved to step out into the hall, where she could breathe without inhaling his delicious scent.

"I got a call from hospital security this morning that there was a suspicious man lurking around here last night just as visiting hours were closing," he went on. "He walked down the hall, saw the security guard outside Rosa's room, then backtracked. They tried to detain him for questioning but he disappeared. I have to believe they'll try again."

Her hands tightened on her laptop case. "Does Rosa know?"

"Not unless security or the FBI told her. Cale is meeting me here this morning to talk about a safe house situation for her."

"It's good of them to keep you in the loop."

"I'm making sure they do on this one. She trusted me enough to tell me what was happening and I won't betray that trust by just turning her over to the FBI without making sure they have a good placement for her."

When they reached the secured unit, they found Cale and his partner Gage McKinnon standing at the nurse's station. Lauren had met Gage the summer before during the search for Cameron Vance. She smiled a greeting and asked after his wife, Allie, and his daughters and infant son, whom she had met at Megan and Cale's wedding.

They exchanged small talk for a moment, then Lauren excused herself. "I need to check in on my patient," she said.

Rosa was sitting up eating breakfast and watching Spanish soap operas when she walked in. The girl smiled at her. Three days after her attack, the bruises and swelling were beginning to fade and Lauren could see the fragile loveliness begin to emerge.

She greeted the girl in her painfully precise Spanish and asked how she was feeling.

"Good. Better," Rosa said with a shy smile.

"I see that. You're looking good," Lauren said. "Did you sleep well?"

Rosa shrugged and said something quickly in Spanish that she didn't quite catch.

"Sorry. Slower, please," Lauren begged.

Rosa repeated her statement and this time Lauren caught the key word. *Nightmare.*

"I'm sorry," she said softly. "Those will fade in time, I promise."

This, she knew from experience. Her own had faded some time ago, though once in a while they still reared their ugly head. Two nights before—the night after she had caught the man in Rosa's hospital room smothering the life out of her and he had struck her—Lauren's own nightmare had returned for the first time in a long time.

In her dream she had been eighteen again, trapped and helpless and frightened.

This time she had fought back, as she hadn't dared do

then, and had kicked and clawed and finally stabbed her attacker with a conveniently placed scalpel.

If she had the right words in Spanish, she would have told Rosa that nightmares could sometimes be empowering, could sometimes alert a woman to the amazing truth that she had grown past her fears into a capable, strong woman.

She didn't have that kind of command of the language, though, so she only squeezed her shoulder. "It will get better," she promised again.

She finished her exam of the girl and then returned to the hallway, where Daniel stood talking to the FBI agents.

"What's the verdict?" Cale asked. "Do you think she's in any condition to be released?"

Daniel wasn't the only one who felt protective toward the girl. She folded her arms across her chest. "Before I'm prepared to answer that, I need to know if you have a safe place for her to go."

"You sound just like Dan. I'll give you the same answer I gave him. Not yet, I'm afraid. At least not any option I'm all that crazy about. Our best possibility is a safe house we use down in the Avenues, close enough that we can get her to the hospital in just a few minutes if we need to."

"Sounds perfect," Daniel said.

"Only trouble is, it's not available right now and it won't be for another few days," McKinnon said.

"What's behind Door Number Two?" Lauren asked.

"You won't like it," Cale predicted.

"Try me."

"We thought maybe we could check her into a hotel near the hospital until she testifies to the grand jury next week."

Lauren narrowed her eyes. "No way. You can't possibly be considering dumping a frightened, pregnant girl who doesn't speak English into a cold, impersonal hotel somewhere."

"I know that. That's the dilemma we're facing. We have agents and safe houses in other states where we could send her, but we need Rosa close for her grand jury testimony. Are you sure she's ready to be discharged?"

She wanted to tell him no, that Rosa should stay right where she was, but she couldn't lie in good conscience, not when the bed should be used for someone who really needed it.

"There's no medical reason for her to stay," she admitted. "Her condition is stable and she is recovering nicely from her injuries. But I'm telling you right now that if you plan to abandon this girl in some seedy motel somewhere, I will damn well make something up to keep her here!"

Daniel had to smile as Lauren's impassioned words rang through the hallway, drawing the attention of several nurses at the desk. He knew she was a good doctor, but this was the first time he realized how committed she was to the welfare of her patients.

No, he didn't want to cheer. He wanted to pull her into his arms and kiss her until they were both breathless.

"Do you have any other suggestions?" McKinnon asked.

"Yes," Lauren said firmly. "She can stay with me."

"What?!" Daniel and both of the FBI agents exclaimed the word at the same time.

"I'll take her to my place in Moose Springs until your safe house is ready. After today, I'm off for a week and I can stay with her and watch over her, keep her company, monitor her for more contractions. I can give her one-on-one attention."

"Absolutely not," Daniel snapped.

Lauren lifted her chin, apparently not at all intimidated by three menacing males. "Why not? It's a perfect solution. She'll be absolutely safe at my house. Who would ever think to look for her there? And I can care for her far better than any FBI agent stuck in a safe house with her!"

"It's completely out of the question. Isn't that right?" he demanded of the FBI agents.

He was stunned when he glanced at Cale and found his lips pursed as if he were giving the idea serious consideration. "I don't know. It's certainly an option."

"It is *not* an option." He wanted to shake Lauren and Cale both. And maybe McKinnon for good measure, even though the other FBI agent hadn't said a word. "How can you even consider putting a civilian in that kind of danger?"

"What danger?" Cale asked. "It makes a lot of sense. Rosa needs a safe place where her medical condition can be closely monitored. This seems like a good solution and if we handle this right, the smuggling ring would have no way to connect Rosa with Lauren."

"Other than the minor little fact that Lauren is her *doctor,* for hell's sake!"

He was apparently talking to himself. Lauren ignored his objections—and so did the FBI agents, whom he had always considered reasonable men before this.

"We would need to figure out a way to sneak her out of the hospital in case they're watching the entrances and exits," McKinnon said. "Your address isn't in public record, is it?"

"No," Lauren said. "I use a PO Box for all my personal correspondence and everything else comes to the clinic."

"This could work," Cale said. "We'll have to run it past the brass to get their input but I think this could definitely work as a temporary option for only a few days until our safe house is available and our staffing issues resolve a little. What do you think, Gage?"

"It can't hurt that your house is just a mile away from Dr. Maxwell's, for additional support if it's needed."

"True."

Before he could say anything else, a cell phone rang suddenly. The two agents exchanged looks and Mc-Kinnon answered his phone in a low voice. A moment later, he hung up.

"Sorry, we've got to run," he said, heading toward the door. "We just got a break in another case we're working."

"What about Rosa?" Daniel asked. "We need to settle this!"

"We'll make a few phone calls and see if we can put the wheels in motion," Cale said. "We'll get back to you later today."

To his intense frustration, they both hurried toward the elevator before Daniel could raise the whole host of objections crowding through his mind. He and Lauren were left standing alone.

"You don't have to stand there glaring at me like I just ran over your foot or something," Lauren said. "I think it's a good idea."

"I think you're insane. And I think Davis and Mc-Kinnon are right there with you in Crazy Town."

"I didn't see *you* coming up with anything else! You know they can't just toss her into a hotel somewhere. She's been raped and abused and nearly strangled. She's frightened and alone and she needs friends more than anything else. Right now, we're the only people she knows and trusts in the entire country!"

"What if they figure out where she is somehow and follow you to Moose Springs?"

"They won't."

"What if they do?" he pressed, his attention on the stark white bandage on her cheek. "You've already been hurt once watching out for her. You have no idea what kind of resources these people might have. They found her here, didn't they? I sure as hell don't need that kind of trouble in my town."

He could see the temperature in her eyes drop well below freezing. "Since when is Moose Springs *your* town? I don't believe I need your permission to invite a guest to my home."

"In this case, you do," he snapped. "Despite their misguided enthusiasm for the idea, Cale and Gage and the others at the FBI will never agree unless I give the final okay. I'm the local law, I get the last word. That's the way it works. I can make all kinds of trouble for them until they decide maybe it's not such a great plan after all."

"You would do that? Put up a fuss, just so you can keep your town clear of the riffraff?"

He didn't think he had ever seen her so angry. Hurt, yes. Devastated, definitely. When he and the chief of police had shown up at her big, ornate childhood home to tell her and her mother about R.J.'s suicide in jail, she had been desolate with grief.

Now, she was just pissed. He couldn't quite understand it.

"Why is this so important to you?" he asked. "You've treated other crime victims, plenty of them. I've brought more than my share to your clinic myself. You always treat them with compassion and professionalism, but not to the point where you want to take them home with you. Why are you so invested in Rosa's situation?"

He thought he saw something flicker in her eyes, something murky and dark, but she quickly veiled it.

"She's my patient," Lauren said briskly. "Beyond that, Rosa is a courageous young girl who has survived a terrible ordeal. I want to help her. Right now, this seems like the best way I can do that. With the clinic closing next week, I have plenty of time to spend with her. It works out all the way around."

Daniel knew Lauren was devoted to her patients, the kind of rare doctor who was available in case of emergencies 24/7.

This was the perfect example of her dedication, that she wanted to go so far, possibly put herself in harm's way for the second time in a week, to help a young girl she had only met a few days earlier.

"You should be taking a vacation, not babysitting a patient. What were you planning to do before this came up?"

Lauren shrugged. "I thought about following the sun and going to southern Utah for a few days to visit my mother," she admitted. "But I can do that anytime, really. Over a long weekend, even. I couldn't go right now and have a good time, knowing that I left Rosa huddled in some cold, impersonal hotel room with strangers who probably don't care what she's been through or how much strength it took for her to come forward and report what happened to her."

She tempered her tone. "You're the one who said you wouldn't turn her over to the FBI unless they had a good placement for her. They don't and so I'm coming up with my own."

In a twisted kind of way, the idea *did* make sense. Moose Springs was completely off the beaten track, a quiet little town no one would ever suspect as the safe haven for a key federal witness in a human smuggling case.

He had to admit, Rosa would probably do better if she spent her first few days out of the hospital with someone who could watch her carefully for any signs she might be overdoing things—and she would definitely do better with people who cared about her than distant FBI agents more concerned about their case than a young girl's bruised psyche.

He sighed heavily, already regretting what he was about to do.

"All right. If you want to go ahead with this crazy idea, I won't stand in your way. On one condition."

"What condition?" she asked, her voice wary.

"I'm part of the deal."

She stared at him, shock widening her eyes. "You what?"

"You can call it chauvinism, you can call it machismo, you can call it whatever the hell you want. But I'm not letting the two of you stay out at your place alone when Rosa has already twice been targeted for murder and you've been injured. You want to take her home with you, fine. But I'm coming, too."

Chapter 7

Several hours later, Lauren stood just inside her storm door, watching in the light cast from her porch light as Daniel helped Rosa out of the backseat of a nondescript sedan she didn't recognize.

It wasn't his, she knew. On his personal time, Daniel drove a big white pickup truck that only served to make him seem more darkly gorgeous behind the wheel.

Maybe it belonged to the sheriff's department. Or perhaps the FBI had provided transportation, since they weren't able to provide much else in the way of support.

What had she done? Daniel Galvez was coming to stay at her house for at least a day or two, possibly longer. He would eat at her table, he would use her shower, he would fill every corner of her little house with that huge presence.

She hadn't really planned out her impulsive offer for

Rosa to stay at her house back at the hospital this morning. The words had escaped her mouth before she had fully considered the ramifications.

If she had taken the time to think it through, she might have anticipated that Daniel would insist on stepping forward to provide protection for Rosa—and for *her*.

If the thought had even crossed her mind, she probably would have rescinded her suggestion and consigned poor Rosa to a hotel.

No, she thought as she watched them make their careful way up the walk she had just finished shoveling. She still would have demanded Rosa stay here. She just would have been better prepared to tell Daniel all the reasons his presence was not required—not required and certainly not at all good for her sense of self-preservation.

She watched him lift Rosa over a rough section of sidewalk, the solid bulk of his shoulders not even flexing at the effort, and her insides ached.

She held the door open for them, giving Rosa a wide, welcoming smile. She did her best to keep that welcome on her features when she faced Daniel, but she guessed some of her reservations must have filtered through when his mouth tightened and his dark eyes grew cool.

"Come in," she said in Spanish. "I'm so pleased you are here." Lauren tried to include both of them in that statement, even though that self-protective part of her nature wanted to shove Daniel back onto the porch and lock the door behind him.

"Gracias," Rosa said quietly. She looked tired, Lauren thought with concern.

"Come. Sit," she urged, and led them both to the open living area off the kitchen. In the rare hours she was home, this was the space she tended to utilize the most.

A fire crackled in the fireplace and the room was several degrees warmer than the rest of the house. She settled Rosa in her own favorite chair by the fire and tucked a blanket around her.

"How was your drive?" she asked Daniel.

"Long. We traded vehicles three times in case anybody followed us and we took the most complicated route possible."

"Did you see anyone?"

"I never saw a tail, except Gage and Cale. They followed us to Park City and then turned around. I don't think anyone saw us leave. We borrowed an ambulance for the first leg of the journey and sneaked her out in that."

Worry creased his features. "Just because we made it here safely doesn't mean we're out of the woods yet, though. This whole situation makes me itchy."

"I know." The gravity of his expression gave her pause. She prayed she wasn't putting Daniel in harm's way. She couldn't back out of this now, no matter how much she dreaded several days of enforced intimacy with him.

She turned her attention to her patient. "Rosa, how are you feeling?" she asked in Spanish.

The girl tried to smile, but Lauren could see the circles under her eyes and the strained exhaustion tugging down the corners of her mouth. She murmured something in a low voice that Lauren didn't quite catch and pointed to her head, but the doctor in her didn't need the words to know what her patient was communicating.

"Your head hurts? I can give you something for it, something safe for the baby. I've made some dinner for you, but I think you should rest first until you feel better."

"Sí." Relief flickered in her dark eyes. *"Gracias."*

Lauren helped her from the chair and showed her to the small guest room she kept ready for her mother's visits.

Since Janine had plenty of reason to hate coming back to Moose Springs and usually avoided the place as if everyone in it had a highly contagious form of leprosy, the room had rarely been used. As a result, it was rather sparsely decorated, just a bed with a pale lavender floral bedspread, a plain dresser and a bedside table.

Rosa gazed around wide-eyed, as if she were walking into the posh suite of a four-star hotel. Tears formed in her eyes and she whispered her thanks in Spanish several times.

Lauren's heart twisted for what this poor girl had endured. Impulsively, she hugged her. "I'm happy you're here," she murmured again in Spanish. "Rest. I will bring you something for your headache. The soup will wait until you're feeling better."

With a relieved sigh, Rosa nodded and sat on the edge of the bed. Knowing it would be a difficult task with the cast on her arm and the pain of her cracked ribs, Lauren knelt and helped her out of her shoes. She wore shiny white tennis shoes with pink stripes and Lauren wondered where they had come from.

All her clothes—even her parka—looked new and Lauren was embarrassed she hadn't thought about what Rosa would wear from the hospital since the girl's own ragged clothes had been ripped and bloody after the attack.

She wondered if the FBI agents had the foresight to provide them, but some instinct told her exactly who had been thoughtful enough to remember such an important detail.

Daniel.

Her stomach gave a funny little flip when she pictured him in a shoe department somewhere picking out white tennis shoes with pink stripes on the sides.

Pushing away her silly reaction, she settled Rosa into bed, drawing the fluffy comforter around her, then went in search of her medicine.

When she returned from giving it to Rosa, she found Daniel in the entryway stamping snow off his boots and carrying a large dark duffel in one hand and a small blue suitcase in the other.

"This is the rest of Rosa's stuff." He handed over the suitcase.

"Did you buy it for her?" she asked, though she already knew the answer.

He shrugged. "There's not much in there but I tried to think of everything she might need. Toothbrush, a night-gown, socks, that kind of thing. One of the nurses helped me guess the sizes."

She imagined the nurses would help him with anything he might ask when he looked at them out of those sexy dark eyes that seemed to see inside a woman's deepest desires...

"Where do you want me to stow my gear?" he said.

"Oh. Right." Flustered, she drew herself back to the conversation. "I have a small room I use as an office, right next to Rosa's. It has a couch that folds out. It's not the most comfortable bed in the world but I'm not really set up for a lot of houseguests. I'm afraid I don't have anything else."

Except for my bed.

The thought whispered through her mind with an insidious appeal she found both horrifying and seductive.

She was in serious trouble here if she couldn't go ten seconds without entertaining completely inappropriate thoughts about the man.

"I'm sure I've slept in worse places," he answered. "It will be fine, don't worry."

Easy for *him* to say. He wasn't the one who couldn't seem to focus on anything else but the way his broad shoulders filled her small entry, how his size and strength seemed to dwarf all the perfectly normal-sized furnishings in her house.

"You'll have to point the way."

She blinked. "The way?"

"To the foldout couch."

"Oh, yes. Of course. The office is the second door on the right. The first one is Rosa's room. Mine is across the hall and there's a guest bathroom next to that. I'll show you."

She led the way down the short hallway and opened her office door. He set his bag inside and she showed him the bathroom across the hall.

"It's a little small," she apologized, wondering if he would even fit in the shower.

As soon as the thought entered her mind, she shoved it away quickly. She did *not* need to go there.

"I'm sure it will be fine."

"There's room in the medicine cabinet for anything you need to put there. Razors, your toothbrush, whatever."

For some ridiculous reason, her face heated at that. It seemed terribly intimate to have a man here. How pathetic must her love life be if she could blush at having a man in her bathroom?

"Thanks," he murmured, and she had the oddest feeling he didn't find this whole situation any easier to handle.

"I, uh, fixed some soup earlier if you're hungry," she said after a moment. "It's all ready. Chicken and black bean."

"Sounds great. Thanks."

They returned to the kitchen and Lauren quickly went to the stove to stir the soup, then reached into the cupboard for a bowl.

"There is silverware already on the table. Just sit wherever you would like and I'll dish it for you."

He stood in the doorway. "You don't have to wait on me, Lauren. That wasn't part of the deal."

"You're a guest in my home," she said. "You might be an uninvited one, but you're still a guest."

He laughed a little abruptly at her tartness. "I guess that's plain enough."

"Sit down, Daniel. You can have some soup, even if you are on guard-dog duty."

A muscle twitched in his cheek. "Well, if you want the truth, I haven't had time to eat all day and whatever you're cooking smells delicious."

"I'm not much of a cook," she confessed, "but I do have a few good soup recipes."

He finally complied, though he didn't look happy about it, and she filled two bowls with the steaming soup, flavored with cilantro, lime and jalapeño peppers.

"Here you go," she said, setting both bowls on the plates she had already set earlier. She gestured to the garnishes already on the table—shredded cheese, tortilla strips, sour cream, more jalapeños and cilantro. "You can put whatever garnishes you want in it. It's kind of a flavor-your-own deal."

"It looks great. I'm sorry you went to so much trouble."

"It wasn't any trouble."

It did look delicious, she had to admit. Just the thing for a snowy Friday night. She put a little grated cheddar in hers and a few baked tortilla strips, but she wasn't at all surprised when he piled on the jalapeños.

He seemed so close here at her small square table, huge and overpowering. She was acutely aware of the broadness of his shoulders and the blunt strength in his arms and the scent of him, leathery and male.

So much for enjoying the soup. She couldn't taste anything, she was far too twitchy just being this close to him.

This certainly wasn't the first meal they had ever shared. Moose Springs was a small town with very little in the way of entertainment except the annual Fourth of July breakfast and the August Moosemania celebration. Everybody turned out for those, and over the years she and Daniel had almost certainly shared a table.

They had many of the same friends in common—Mason and Jane Keller, Cale and Megan Davis. But even those times they had attended the same dinner parties or barbecues, there had always been others around to provide a buffer.

She couldn't remember ever sharing a meal with him alone like this. For some reason, it had all the awkwardness of a blind date—something she made it a practice to avoid at all costs.

"I was wrong," he said after a moment. "Your soup isn't delicious. It's divine."

She mustered a smile. "Thank you."

"This is the perfect thing to warm the blood on a cold winter night," he said, then winced at the inanity of his conversation. Not only was it a banal thing to say, it was patently untrue.

His blood didn't need any more temperature spikes. He only had to sit within a few feet of Lauren to be plenty warm. Before the evening was done, he was very much afraid he would be sweltering.

He was doing his best to focus on the meal in front of him and not on Lauren, with her soft blond hair pulled back in a loose ponytail and her slim feet in fuzzy socks and her skin rosy and flushed in the warm kitchen.

It was an impossible task. Even with the bandage on her cheek, she was so lovely here in her house, sexy and soft, and with every taste of soup she took, he wanted to whip the spoon out of her mouth, throw it against the wall and devour those lips.

His body ached just breathing the same air. How ridiculous was that? He had always known he had a thing for her, but these last few days had just demonstrated it was far more than a little unrequited crush.

He was powerfully attracted to her. He couldn't remember ever reacting this way to a woman, this wild heat in his gut. Every nerve cell in his body seemed to quiver when she was anywhere around and he couldn't seem to focus on a thing but her.

She sipped her water, and when she returned the water goblet to the table, a tiny drop clung to her bottom lip. He couldn't seem to stop staring at it, wondering what she would do if he reached across the table and licked it off.

"What do you usually eat?" she asked.

He blinked away the unbidden fantasy, harshly reminding himself he was here to do a job, to protect Lauren and her houseguest, not to indulge himself by wishing for the impossible.

He forgot what she had asked. "Sorry?" he managed.

"We keep the same kind of hours and I know you don't have much more time than I do. I just wondered if you eat every meal on the run or if you take time to cook a decent meal once in a while."

"I'm not a great cook but I do try to fix a few things on my days off. Whenever I can, I cook extra so I have things to warm up during the week. I think my deputies and Peggy and the other dispatchers think I live on nothing but cold cereal and frozen dinners. They must feel sorry for me, because it seems like somebody is always inviting me over for dinner."

"Like the department stray dog?"

He smiled. "Something like that."

She returned his smile. Daniel stared at the way it lightened her features, made her look not much older than Rosa. His breath seemed to catch in his throat and he did his best to remind himself of all the reasons he couldn't kiss that soft mouth.

"While Rosa and I are here, I really don't expect you to wait on me. I'll do my share of the cooking. Why don't I take breakfast?"

"Since cold cereal is your specialty?" she teased.

"I can fix more than cold cereal," he protested. "For your information, Miss Doubter, I'm great at toast and can usually manage to boil water for oatmeal, too, without burning the house down."

"I hope so. I'm fairly fond of my house," she said.

The conversation reminded him of something he meant to bring up with her earlier. "If the FBI doesn't make the offer, my department will pick up the tab for the groceries Rosa and I use while we're here. Just keep a tally and send the bill to my office when this is over."

Her spoon froze halfway to her mouth, then she returned it to her soup bowl with a clatter. "Absolutely not!" she exclaimed.

He wasn't quite prepared for her vehemence. "Why not? Rosa is ultimately my responsibility. You're not obligated to pay for her room and board, my office should be taking care of that."

"Forget it, Daniel. I'm the one who insisted she stay here. She is a guest in my house and I will take care of feeding her."

"You didn't want me as part of the package."

"No. I didn't," she snapped, and though he knew it was crazy, he couldn't help feeling a little hurt. How could he burn for her so hotly when she didn't even want him around?

"Fine, we'll compromise," he said. "You can pay for Rosa's food and I'll pay my own."

"This is stupid. I've already bought enough groceries to last a week or more for all three of us. Just take your share out of the huge collective mental ledger everyone seems to be keeping, the one marked 'Maxwell family debt' and clearly labeled 'unpaid.'"

She clamped her teeth together as soon as the bitter words were out and looked as if she regretted saying anything.

Was that what she thought? That everyone believed she owed her heart and soul to Moose Springs, just because her father was a crook?

"There is no collective ledger, huge or otherwise."

"Right." She rose, her usually fluid movements suddenly jerky and abrupt as she started clearing away the dishes. He had been considering asking for a second helping, but he forgot all about it now, struck that she could entertain such a misguided notion.

"Everyone knows you're not responsible for what your father did, Lauren."

"Do they?"

He frowned at her pointed question. Okay, he had to admit there might be some validity in her bitterness. The other day with Dale Richins, he had experienced just a taste of what she might encounter in certain circles. The scorn, the disdain.

It suddenly bugged the hell out of him that anybody could blame an innocent girl for her father's crimes.

"In their hearts, everyone knows that. But some people in town are just more stubborn and pigheaded on this issue than they ought to be. How can it be your fault? You were only a girl when he first, uh..."

His voice trailed off and he wasn't quite sure how to couch his words in polite terms.

"Go ahead and finish it, Daniel. When R.J. first starting dipping his fingers into the city's meager financial well."

"Right. You were just a child. Anybody who can blame you for what R.J. did is being mean and stupid."

"Intellectually, I know that. It doesn't make the digs and slurs in the grocery store any easier to deal with it. My father paid for my medical school tuition out of stolen money—which means, in effect, that the people of this town paid for my education. Do you think I'm not aware of that every time I look at my diploma?"

He had no idea she tied the two things together, her father's embezzlement and her own medical school bills. Guilt spasmed through him at his own role in this whole thing. If she knew the truth, she probably would have added rat poison to the soup.

"Lauren—"

"This town owns me, body and soul. My father made sure of that. I can never leave here, no matter all the slights and slurs and whispers I have to endure. They paid for my education and I am obligated to damn well give them their money's worth."

She shoved a dish in the dishwasher with a clatter. "But you know, it doesn't matter what I do, how much I give. I can pour out my soul here in my practice, work twenty hours a day, treat anybody who walks through the door whether they have any intention of paying me or not. But I'll still always be crooked R. J. Maxwell's daughter."

"You can't change where you came from, Lauren, no matter how hard you try."

He should know. He had spent way too much time during his teenage years wishing he could belong to any other family in town except the dirt-poor Galvez family, with a mother who scrubbed toilets and a father who did every miserable grunt job that came along at R. J. Maxwell's construction company, for usually half as much as anybody else on the crew, just because he didn't have a green card.

Now, it shamed him deeply that he had ever considered his family inferior to anyone else.

He used to ride his bike past Lauren's grand house on Center Street and want everything inside there—furniture that matched and didn't come from Goodwill, a soft, pretty mother who smelled like flowers instead of disinfectant, his own bedroom instead of the crowded, chronically messy one he had to share with two annoying younger brothers.

He used to think Lauren's life was perfect. She had everything—money, brains, beauty. He wanted the kingdom, and in his deepest heart, he had wanted the beautiful golden princess who came along with it.

Over the years, he had learned that the kingdom was built on sand, the king was a fraud and a cheat, and the castle had been sold long ago to pay his bills.

But the princess.

Oh, yeah, he still wanted the princess.

"I know I can't change what my father did," she said quietly. "I live with it every day."

"You've done more to make things right than anyone could ever expect of you, Lauren. Anyone who doesn't see that, who doesn't admire and respect the hell out of you for what you've done here, is someone who doesn't deserve even a moment of your time."

At his words, something about her seemed to crumble. One moment she was looking at him with defiance and bitterness and the next, her soft mouth trembled and she stared at him out of luminous blue eyes welling with tears.

"Ah, hell. I'm sorry. Don't cry, Lauren. Please don't cry."

He rose and pulled her into his arms. He couldn't help himself.

She sagged against his chest and her arms slid around him. To his vast and eternal relief, she sniffled a few times but she didn't let the tears loose. He held her close, burying his face in hair that smelled of jasmine and vanilla. After a moment, she stirred and lifted her face to his.

"I'm sorry. I try not to indulge in pity parties more

than once or twice a month. You just caught me on a bad day."

"Don't mention it," he murmured, and then he couldn't help himself. He took what he had been fantasizing about since he walked into her house earlier.

Chapter 8

Her mouth was soft, delicious, like sinking into the best dream he had ever had. After one raw instant, his body revved into overdrive and he could focus on nothing but how incredibly right she felt in his arms.

He wanted to devour her, right there in her kitchen, just wrap his arms around her, drag her to the floor and consume every inch of her. Even as the wild need raged through him, ravaging his control, he forced himself to take things slow and easy, to hide his wild hunger behind a facade of soft, steady calm.

He hadn't been with a woman in a long time, but he knew that wasn't the reason why his vision dimmed and he suddenly couldn't seem to keep hold of a coherent thought.

That reason was simple, really. Lauren.

He couldn't quite believe she was here in his arms, the

girl who had been affecting him in a strange, baffling way since he was a kid.

Even when he had been sixteen and big for his age, the toughest kid in school, he had dreamed of sweet Lauren Maxwell. The mayor's little girl, with her shiny blond ponytail and her soft, pretty hands and her wide, generous smile.

It had mortified him, this fascination with her, and even then he had known anything between them was an impossibility.

The taste of her seemed to soak through his bones and he couldn't seem to get enough. This was stupid, he knew. Monumentally stupid. Playing chicken with an express train kind of stupid.

He had to reign in his hunger. If he didn't, if he gave in to it, how could he ever return to the stiff politeness that had marked their relationship since her father's death?

He drew in a ragged breath and did his best to clamp down on the wild need raging through him.

He might have even succeeded if he hadn't heard the soft, seductive sound of his name on her lips, against his mouth, and felt her hands tremble over the muscles of his chest.

They had come this far. One more kiss wouldn't hurt anything. That's what he told himself, anyway.

And a tiny portion of his mind even believed it.

She was sliding into an endless canyon of sensation, surrounded by the heat and strength and leashed power of Daniel Galvez.

Somehow, she wouldn't have expected his kiss to be so slow, so easy and gentle. Though she couldn't say she spent a great deal of time fantasizing about men and their kissing styles, if she had to guess Daniel's, she would have expected him to kiss a woman like the athlete he had been, fast and fierce and passionate.

Instead, he seduced her with softness, teasing and tasting and exploring. He nibbled her lips, he traced light designs on the bare skin of her neck with his fingertips, he rubbed his cheek against hers—and she found that light rasp of evening stubble against her skin far more evocative and sensual than a full-body massage.

He kissed her until every nerve ending inside her seemed to quiver, until she wanted to melt into him, to wrap her arms around his strong neck, press her body against his muscles and lose herself in him.

When she was young, she used to love it when Moose Springs held its annual celebration and the town paid for a small carnival for the children with giant inflatable slides and a Tilt-o-Whirl and enough cotton candy to power the midway lights on juiced-up kid power alone.

Her favorite was the pony ride. Once, when she was probably seven or eight, her father had slipped the carnival workers a few extra dollars to let her just keep riding that little horse around and around. She probably rode for half an hour and she had never forgotten the magic of that night, with the lights flashing and the screams of children braving the more terrifying rides and the smell of popcorn and spun sugar and spilled sodas.

This was far more exhilarating than any long-ago pony ride. She didn't want the kiss to end, she just wanted to lock the cold, snowy world outside her kitchen and stay right here in his arms forever with this wild heat churning through her insides and this fragile tenderness settling in her heart like a tiny bird finding a nest.

The only sounds in the kitchen were the soft soughs of

their breathing and the low crackle of the fire in the other room. Finally, when she was very much afraid her legs weren't going to support her much longer, Daniel made a sound deep in his throat, something raw and aroused, and deepened the kiss.

She sighed an enthusiastic welcome and returned the kiss. He pulled her closer and she molded her body to his. This time she relished how small and delicate he made her feel next to his size and strength.

They kissed until she couldn't breathe, couldn't think, until she was lost to everything but Daniel, his taste and his scent and his touch.

Suddenly, over the sound of their harsh breathing, she heard something else. The rather prosaic sound of a toilet flushing somewhere in the house. Rosa.

Lauren froze as if she had stepped naked into that storm outside the windows. Jarred back into her senses, she scrambled away from him, her heart beating wildly.

What, in heaven's name, just happened here? Had she really just been wrapped around *Daniel Galvez?*

Her face flamed and it was all she could do not to press her hands to her cheeks. What must he think of her? She had responded to him like some wild, sex-starved coed. She had all but dragged him to the floor and had her way with him.

She was fairly certain she had even moaned his name a time or two. How could she ever look him in the eye again?

"Rosa must be awake," she said, keeping her gaze firmly in the vicinity of his chest, until she realized that probably wasn't the greatest idea since it only made her want to smooth her hands over those hard muscles once more.

"Sounds like," he said. Did his voice sound more hoarse than usual? she wondered.

She finally risked a look at him and could have sworn he had a dazed kind of look in his eyes—the same baffled, disoriented expression she saw in patients with mild concussions.

Had Daniel been as affected as she had by that shattering kiss? How was it possible? He disliked her. Okay, *dislike* might be a bit harsh. But he certainly never seemed interested in her on that kind of level.

Except once, she reminded herself—so long ago, it seemed another lifetime. More than a decade ago, he had asked her out and she turned him down. Quite firmly, if she recalled.

He had been the first guy to show any interest in her since the grim events of that spring and she had been far too raw and messed-up to even consider it. The very idea had terrified her. The details were a little hazy but she was fairly certain she hadn't been very subtle with her refusal, either.

In all those years, Daniel had never given her any indication he might be interested in her. Things between them were always strained, always slightly uncomfortable, though both of them did their best to be polite.

That kiss, though.

That was certainly not the way an uninterested man kissed a woman.

Her stomach muscles fluttered and she didn't know what to think. She suddenly was desperate for a little space to figure out what had just happened between them.

Distance from the man was not something she would likely find in the next few days, she realized with considerable dismay. Her house was small but had always seemed more cozy than confining to her. With Daniel here—six feet three inches of him and all that muscle—she suddenly felt like the walls were squeezing in, sucking away every particle of oxygen.

"Uh, Lauren—" Daniel began, but whatever he started to say was cut off as Rosa came into the kitchen, looking much more rested than she had when they arrived.

She greeted them with a shy smile, apparently oblivious to the tense undercurrents zinging through the kitchen like hummingbirds on crack cocaine.

"How are you?" Lauren asked in Spanish.

"Better," Rosa answered.

"Sit. I'll get you something to eat. Would you eat some soup?"

She dipped her cheek to her shoulder, looking hesitant to put anyone to more trouble.

Daniel said something in rapid Spanish, too fast for Lauren to understand, and pulled a chair out for her at the table. Rosa's shyness lifted and she giggled a little and nodded, then obediently sat down.

"What did you say?" Lauren asked.

"I told her she had to have some of your delicious soup or I would end up eating it all and end up too fat to wear my uniform."

He gave an embarrassed smile and Lauren stared at it, an odd emotion tugging at her chest.

She was in trouble here, she thought as she hurried to the stove to dish Rosa a bowl of soup. Panic spurted through her and it was all she could do not to drop the soup all over the floor.

Oh, she was in serious trouble.

She could probably handle the physical attraction. But she suddenly realized she had no defenses against a man who had the wisdom to cajole and tease and look after a frightened young girl like she was his own little sister.

The evening that followed had to live on in her memory as one of the most surreal of Lauren's life. While Rosa picked at her bowl of soup, the storm that had been toying with this part of the state all day let loose with a vengeance. The wind lashed snow against the window and moaned under the eaves of her little house.

Daniel threw on his coat and made several trips to the woodpile out back so they had a good supply of split logs close to the house. Lauren gathered lanterns and flashlights just in case the power went out, as it often did during big storms like this that brought heavy, wet snow to knock out power lines.

While she cleaned the kitchen and loaded the dishwasher, Daniel checked in with his department.

She listened to his strong, confident voice as he reviewed emergency storm protocol with his lieutenant and she thought again how lucky the people of Moose Springs were to have him as their sheriff. He was wonderful at his job and truly cared about the people he served.

She knew her reasons for setting up her practice in her hometown but why did *he* stay here? He could be working anywhere. He had spent his first few years in law enforcement as a Salt Lake City police officer and many had expected him to stay there and make a promising career for himself. Then his mother had fallen ill, his father was killed and he had returned home.

His mother had lost her battle with cancer shortly after Lauren returned to town. So why did Daniel stay all these years?

She enjoyed listening to him. It was silly, she knew, but she loved hearing him in action. Oh, she had it bad.

He ended the phone conversation just as she finished wiping down the countertops.

"If you need to go on a call or something during the night, I'm sure we'll be fine here," Lauren offered.

"I've got good people working for me and I'm sure they have everything under control. But if something comes up that nobody else can handle, one of my deputies can come here and relieve me for a while."

"Does everyone know you're staying at my house?"

His mouth tightened and his expression cooled. It took her a moment to figure out how her question must have sounded, as if she worried about her reputation.

He answered before she could correct the assumption. "No. Only Kurt Banning, my second-in-command, knows the entire story. As far as everybody else is concerned, I'm taking some personal leave. That should set your mind at ease."

"My mind is not at all unsettled."

Not about her reputation, at any rate. She was afraid she had none in Moose Springs.

She could have an entire orgy of sexy law enforcement officers camping at her house and people would just shake their heads and ask what else could they expect of R.J.'s daughter?

"Is there a free plug for my cell phone somewhere?" Daniel asked. "I want to make sure I've got a full charge while I can in case the power goes out on us."

"Yes. Of course. Good idea." She showed him an open plug, then spent a few moments digging out her own cell phone to charge in case she was needed on a medical emergency.

What if they were both called out on a crisis at the same time? she wondered, then decided to set her mind at ease, at least on that score. It was certainly possible, but she had no doubts Daniel would have thought of every eventuality.

The wind lashed the windows as Lauren went to join Rosa in the living area. The girl was curled up on the couch with a blanket over her, watching a comedy on the Spanish language channel. Lauren could only pick out half the words and she was just reaching for her latest lousy attempt at knitting when Daniel joined them and settled in the recliner.

He watched TV with Rosa for ten minutes until the show ended, though she had the feeling he was only pretending to pay attention.

Was he as off balance as she was by that kiss? she wondered. Even a half hour later, she could still taste him on her mouth.

She was wondering if she had any DVDs with Spanish subtitles, for the sake of distraction if nothing else, when Daniel suddenly jumped up from the recliner.

"Let's play a game or something."

"Okay," she said slowly. "What did you have in mind?"

"I don't know. What have you got? You have a deck of cards?"

"I'm sure I do somewhere."

"What about a card table?"

"In the garage against the north wall."

While he went in search of it, she finally unearthed a deck in her kitchen junk drawer that was probably left over from medical school study breaks. While she was searching, Daniel had found the card table and had set it up near the fireplace.

"What did you have in mind?" she asked after the three of them settled into the chairs he brought in from the dining room and he shuffled the deck.

"I don't know. I was trying to come up with some game that would transcend the language thing. What about Crazy Eights?"

She didn't believe she had played that game since she was about ten years old in summer camp. But she was willing to try anything that might keep her mind off that stunning kiss.

For the next hour, they played Crazy Eights and War and SlapJack, and a new one to her called Burro Castigado, similar to draw poker. Daniel must have been inspired with the cards, Lauren thought. As they played, Rosa giggled and smiled and seemed much more like a girl than a young woman who had survived a horrendous ordeal.

After a while, she moved to the kitchen to make some popcorn and she could overhear Daniel and Rosa speaking in Spanish. Daniel's low laugh drew her gaze.

She watched them together for a moment, a funny pang in her chest. He was so kind to the girl, just as he used to be to his own younger sister. She used to be filled with envy that Anna had three big, strong brothers to watch out for her. It had hardly seemed fair to Lauren, when she had none.

He turned suddenly and caught her watching him. Something flared in his dark eyes, something hot and intense. In her mind, she was in his arms again, savoring that strength around her and the flutter of nerves as her body seemed to awaken from a long, cold sleep.

Their gazes caught for a long moment, until the microwave dinged and yanked Lauren back to reality. She pulled the popcorn bag out and took her time shaking it into a bowl while she tried to force her pulse to slow again. She was never going to make it through the next few days if she didn't get a grip over herself here.

At last she felt in control enough to return to the card table, and pasted on a bright smile.

They played for another half hour, until she caught Rosa trying to cover a yawn. It was nearly eleven, Lauren realized with some surprise.

"You need to sleep," she said to the girl. "Come on, let's get you settled for the night."

Daniel had picked out a warm, roomy nightgown for her and Lauren showed her the toothpaste, washcloths and towels. Rosa bid her good-night with a smile that was growing more relaxed and comfortable.

When she returned to the other room, she found Daniel shrugging into his heavy coat once more.

She frowned. "I'm quite certain you brought in enough wood earlier to last for at least a week. There is no reason for you to go out into the storm again."

"I figured I'd shovel your walk before I turn in."

She was about to argue the sidewalk could wait until morning but some restless light in his eyes tangled the words in her throat. He looked like a man with energy to burn.

She could think of other ways to exhaust that energy, but she wasn't about to suggest them to him.

"Thank you," she said instead.

She picked up her pitiful knitting again while he was outside and tried to focus on the news, but it was a losing battle. All she could think about was the man out there braving the elements to shovel her sidewalk.

When he returned twenty minutes later, snowflakes

were melting in the silky darkness of his hair and his cheeks were flush with cold, but he seemed far easier in his skin.

"It's a b-witch out there," he said, stomping snow off his boots and shaking it from his coat. "That wind chill coming from the north has got to be at least minus ten. I bet we get a foot or more."

She nodded. "Nights like this make me grateful to be home in front of the fire instead of driving through the snow on my way to an emergency somewhere."

"Makes me glad for insulated windows," he said, shrugging out of his coat. "When I was a kid, we used to stick blankets over all the windows in our house. They were all single-paned. I imagine they probably let in more cold than they kept out."

He laughed suddenly at a memory. "Ren used to put cups of water in front of them so we could measure how long it took for ice to form. He was always doing crazy things like that. First thing I did after I moved back was to replace them all with energy-efficient windows and blow better insulation into the walls. Made a hell of a mess and cost a fortune, but the house stayed about thirty degrees warmer in the winter."

Lauren couldn't help thinking of her own home, where her mother insisted on keeping the thermostat at seventy-three degrees and invariably had a fire going as well. R.J. used to complain about the heat bill, but never enough to make her mother turn down the thermostat.

Of course, her mother didn't know R.J. was heating another house somewhere.

"Would you like something warm?" she asked. "I've got several kinds of cocoa."

His raised eyebrow lifted even higher when she

opened a cupboard to show the wide, varied selection inside. Orange chocolate, chocolate raspberry, chocolate mint, chocolate cinnamon, chocolate amaretto and plain old delicious milk chocolate. She had about every flavor of hot chocolate ever invented.

"I'm something of a cocoa junkie in the winter," she admitted ruefully. "Even in the summer sometimes, if I've had a bad day. Nothing comforts quite like it."

He watched her, a strange, unreadable light in his eyes. She didn't know what it meant, she only knew it made those blasted stomach flutters start all over again. After a moment, he shook his head. "Maybe tomorrow night I'll take you up on that."

She let out a breath. However would she endure so much time trapped here in his company, especially when she couldn't stop thinking about that kiss?

"I can help you pull out the couch in the office if you'd like."

"I was just thinking I would stretch out over there, if that's okay with you."

She gazed at the short couch near the fire, then at his long, muscled body. The two things seemed a definite mismatch.

"Are you sure?" she asked. "It's no problem at all to make the couch into a bed."

"This is fine. That way I can be close to keep the fire going, just in case the storm knocks out the power in the night."

"I'll bring you some blankets and a pillow, then."

She pulled them out of her small linen closet, certain as she returned to the living room that she shouldn't find the idea of him watching over her and Rosa such a comfort.

She was a strong, independent woman. She certainly didn't need a man to take care of her, to bring in her wood and shovel her walks and tend the fire through the night.

She didn't need it, perhaps. But she couldn't deny that she found it very appealing to share the everyday burdens of life with someone else once in a while.

When she returned with the linens, she found him sitting on the recliner, gazing into the fire. He looked up at her entrance, and again she was surprised at the odd, glittery expression in his eyes.

"Here you go. Good night, then. If you need anything else in the night, let me know," she said.

"I'll do that," he murmured, and she could feel the heat of his gaze on her all the way through the kitchen and down the hall to her bedroom.

Chapter 9

Something woke him in the early-morning hours.

He instantly sat up, alert and on edge. The house was quiet, the only sound the low murmur of the fire flickering low, reduced now to just a log burned almost all the way through and a few red embers glowing in the dark.

His instincts humming, he looked around, trying to figure out what had awakened him.

The house was *too* dark. *Too* quiet.

It only took a moment for him to figure out why. As he and Lauren had both feared, the power must have gone out in the storm. The fire provided the only light in the house and the usual subtle sounds of a juiced-up house were nowhere in evidence. No buzz of a refrigerator, no whirr of a furnace kicking on. Nothing.

The only thing he could hear now besides the fire was the wind hurling snow at the windows. He slid off

the couch and threw another log from the pile onto the
glowing embers. It crackled for a moment, but he had no
doubt the coals were hot enough that it would soon catch.

Moving with slow caution, he eased to the window
and peered out into the storm. He looked up and down
her isolated road, but could see no other lights out there,
not even the ambient glow from the concentrated lights
of town he might have expected.

Though he knew from experience that any power outage was a major pain in the neck for law enforcement of-
ficials, the pitch-black set his mind at ease.

If the whole town had lost power, obviously Lauren's
house hadn't been targeted specifically by someone cutting her juice for nefarious reasons.

He didn't know what kind of threat might lurk out
there for Rosa, but he wasn't about to take any chances.
Someone wanted her dead because of all that she knew.
Melodramatic as it seemed, it wasn't wholly out of the
realm of possibility that someone might cut Lauren's
power to have better access to her house.

They had tried to kill Rosa in her own hospital bed.
He had a feeling these bastards would certainly have no
qualms about killing anybody else who got in their way.

He hated this whole damn situation. A pretty young
girl like Rosa should be dreaming about her *quincea-
ñera*, should be trying out makeup and giggling with
her friends and discovering the vast world of possibilities awaiting her. Instead, she was battered and bruised
and five months pregnant from a brutal gang rape, doing
her best to stay alive.

And Lauren had put herself right in the middle of Rosa's troubles by bringing the girl home to recover.

He sighed, his mind on the woman asleep in her room

just a few yards away. What a mess this assignment was turning into. In the first eight hours after bringing Rosa here, he had hurt Lauren's feelings, dredged up memories she didn't want and kissed her until he managed to forget his own name.

He could only wonder, with a strange mix of dread and anticipation, what the morning would bring.

In the soft glow of the fire, he could read the face on his watch. It was 2:30 a.m., which meant he had probably slept a grand total of maybe an hour and a half all night. And though he had slept, he couldn't say those had been the most restful ninety minutes he'd ever enjoyed.

He should have expected it. Lauren's house wasn't exactly conducive to a good night's rest. How could it be, with her subtle scent of jasmine and vanilla surrounding him and the knowledge that she was only a few footsteps away burning in his gut?

He couldn't stop thinking about that kiss, those incredible moments in the kitchen when she had been in his arms, all soft and warm and delicious. After all these years of wondering what it might be like to kiss her, to touch that skin and taste her soft mouth, he had to admit the reality had far surpassed any fantasy.

And reliving the moment over and over again sure as hell wasn't going to help him get any sleep.

He reached for his cell phone and dialed his dispatcher. Tonight, Jay Welch was on duty and as Daniel greeted him, he pitched his voice low so he didn't wake up Lauren or Rosa.

"Hey, Sheriff," Jay said. "I thought you were taking a few nights off, squeezing in a little R&R."

Rest and recreation. Right. There was absolutely nothing remotely restful about staying in Lauren's house, having to fight like hell to keep his hands off her.

And the only recreation he could seem to wrap his brain around was exactly the activity he knew he wouldn't be engaging in anytime soon.

"I'm still around," he murmured. "Just checking on the situation there with the power out."

"So far, so good. The backup generator kicked in right away. We're starting to get a few anxious calls from people wondering what's going on. The power company says a tree came down north of town and knocked out the power line. They expect to be back in business no later than an hour."

Without electricity, most furnaces couldn't turn on, even if they were natural gas- or oil-fueled. A house could get mighty cold during a January blizzard without heat for an hour. He thought of those single-paned windows in his childhood home and couldn't help a shiver, despite the little fire now burning cheerfully in the grate.

Most people around here had secondary heat sources like fireplaces or wood or pellet stoves, but he didn't want to take any chances with the health and safety of the people of his town. "I'll check in with you in an hour for an update. If it's not back up and running by the time the sun comes up, we're going to want to start welfare checks on some of the senior citizens who live alone."

"Okay."

He hung up and sat on the couch gazing at the dancing flames and wondering what he was supposed to do with all this restlessness burning through him.

Suddenly, he heard a noise somewhere in the house. He reached for his 9mm, thumbed off the safety and rose, alert and ready. An instant later Lauren's bedroom door opened.

She stood just outside the rim of light from the fireplace, but he didn't need illumination to know the sound he heard was her.

He slid the safety on and tucked the gun back under his pillow on the couch. "I hope I didn't wake you while I was on the phone," he said.

"You didn't. I think I woke when the power went out. That sounds silly, doesn't it?"

"Not *that* silly. I did the same thing."

They lapsed into silence and he wondered why she was out here instead of tucked into her warm bed.

"Everything okay?" he asked.

She stepped farther into the fire's glow and he could see the rueful expression on her face. "I just realized that even after I went to all that trouble to round up secondary light sources for a possible outage, I forgot to take a flashlight into my room when I went to bed. I was lying in bed wondering how I could sneak out here in the dark and grab one without waking you, then I heard you on the phone."

"I was just checking in with dispatch," he said. "Jay Welch has already talked to the power company and we're looking at about an hour before it's back online."

"It's good you had the foresight to keep the fire going," she said, grabbing a flashlight from the table where she had assembled them earlier in the night. "What about Rosa? I wondered if I should let her sleep or wake her to let her know the power is out. I wouldn't want her to wake up in the middle of the night in the pitch-dark and be frightened."

"I can listen for her. If I hear sounds of stirring, I'll explain to her what's going on. Those bedrooms are going to get mighty cold without the furnace if the power company's estimate is wrong and it takes them longer than they figure to fix the problem. I'll have to wake you both up so you can come out here and bunk by the fire where it's warm."

"You don't have to stay up all night to watch over us, Daniel."

"I don't mind."

She tilted her head and studied him and he wondered again what she saw when she looked at him. "I know you don't. You watch over everyone, don't you?"

Was that how she saw him? He shrugged, uncomfortable. "It's my job to keep the people of Moose Springs safe. Go back to bed, try to get some sleep. I'll wake you if the power doesn't come back up in an hour or so."

"I couldn't sleep now anyway."

He should keep his distance from her. One of them should have a little good sense here. If he were smart, he would insist that she march right back into her bedroom and stay away from him.

Too bad he didn't feel very smart around the delectable Dr. Maxwell.

He sighed. "You might as well come in and sit down out here by the fire, then. We can keep each other company until the lights come back on."

She hesitated, just long enough for him to wonder if the tug and pull between them unnerved her as much as it did him. He couldn't have said which he would prefer: that she go back to bed and leave him alone or that she come in and sit beside him so he could indulge his unwilling fascination a little longer.

She chose the second, pausing only long enough to

turn on the light switch so they would know when the power was back on, then she sat in the armchair.

In the fire's glow, he could see she wore soft, lace-edged cotton pajamas the color of spring leaves. He did his best not to think about how they would feel under his fingers.

When she pulled her knees up and wrapped her arms around them as if she were cold, he lifted one of the extra blankets she had brought him from the end of the couch and tossed it to her.

"Thanks," she murmured. She snuggled into it, tucking the edges around her feet. They sat for a moment, accompanied only by the low rumble of the fire, their own breathing and the distant wind.

"When I was a kid, I used to love storms like this when the power would go out," she said into the stillness. "That sounds crazy, doesn't it?"

"I guess it depends why you liked it."

"My dad would make it all seem like a big adventure. When the power went out in the middle of the night like this, he would pull out the sleeping bags from the garage and start a fire in the big fireplace in the great room and the three of us would roast marshmallows and pop popcorn and tell stories just like we were camping out."

He had to admit that even after all these years, he didn't like hearing anything positive about R.J. Maxwell. He had never quite understood how a woman like Lauren could come from such a bastard.

"Sounds great," he said politely.

"It was. Even when I was in high school, Dad would still drag us down there. When he was home, anyway. He was always so busy, off on his *business trips*."

The resentment in those last two words left him

acutely uncomfortable. He knew the real reason her father spent so much time away from him, but he wasn't sure if *she* knew he was one of the few who were aware of all the facts. They had never talked about this before, about the motives behind R.J.'s embezzlement and everything that went along with it. He wasn't sure he wanted to talk about it now, in the hushed peace of the night.

Before he could come up with a response, she shook her head slightly; and even in the darkened room, he could see regret flitter across her lovely features.

"Sorry. I didn't mean to sound embittered. I really do try not to be, but sometimes it slips through."

"You have a right to be angry, Lauren."

She had a right to be angry at *Daniel,* he thought. She just didn't know it—and he didn't know if he had the courage to tell her.

"Most of the time the whole situation just makes me sad." She gazed into the fire, avoiding Daniel's gaze. "If R.J. hadn't taken a coward's way out of the mess he created, the first question I would ask would have been why my mother and I weren't enough for him."

"He loved you, Lauren. He was always proud of his daughter."

"Right." After a moment she smiled, though it looked strained. "Let's talk about something else, can we? I'm really not in the mood to dredge up any more of the past tonight."

What are you in the mood for? he wanted to ask. The question almost spilled out as images flashed through his mind of those heated moments in her kitchen earlier.

He forced his mind away from that dangerous line of thought. As much as he yearned to taste her and touch her again, he knew it was impossible.

"You want to pick the topic or should I?" he asked after a moment.

Her teeth flashed white in the dark as she smiled. "I will. I was wondering this earlier. What are you doing here, Daniel?"

"W-e-e-ll," he drew out. "It's a little cold sleeping out in my truck on a night like tonight. Your couch is much more comfortable for guard-dog duty."

"I don't mean here, right now. I mean, why did you stick around in Moose Springs? I know you came back to help your mother when she was sick. But after she died, why did you stay here when you could have gone anywhere?"

He hadn't been expecting the question and it took him a moment to formulate a reply. "I don't think there's any one answer to that. This is my home and I love it here. That's one reason, probably the easiest, most obvious one."

"What else?"

"I don't know." He shrugged. "Maybe I felt like I had something to prove."

Her eyes widened with surprise. "Why would you think that?"

"We grew up in different worlds, Lauren."

"Not that different. You lived three blocks away."

"In a shack that R.J. probably wouldn't have considered a fit place to store his riding mower."

In the glow from the fire, she looked flushed. "Your parents were wonderful people. Your mother was always so sweet. Every kid in town would save their allowance for weeks to buy those cherry empanadas she sold at Moosemania Days. And I don't think I ever saw your father when he wasn't smiling."

"I agree. They were great people. That didn't change the fact in a lot of people's minds that we were dirt-poor Mexicans."

As soon as the words were out, he heartily wished he hadn't said them. He didn't need to emphasize the differences between them. They were obvious enough.

"And so you wanted to show people you were more than that. That's why you worked so hard in school, why you pushed yourself at football, why you worked to become an indispensable deputy in the sheriff's office?"

"It started out that way, anyhow. Pretty pathetic, isn't it?"

"You had nothing to prove, Daniel. Absolutely nothing! Look at all you've achieved! Not only did you have a full-on football scholarship, but you were the high school valedictorian, as I recall, and Ren was the year after you. Anna would have had the same honor in our grade but, uh, someone else beat her to it. She had to settle for salutatorian."

"Don't worry. She doesn't hold a grudge against you. At least not much of one."

She laughed, as he had hoped she would. It echoed softly through the room and warmed him at least a dozen degrees.

"I don't know about Marcos, since he was a few years behind Anna and me. How were his grades?"

"He was third in the class."

"What a slacker!"

"We think it's because he was the baby and Mom and Dad took it easier on him than the rest of us."

She smiled, then tilted her head to study him. "You're a good sheriff, Daniel. Maybe the best Moose Springs has ever had."

He fought the urge to rub an embarrassed hand to the burn at the back of his neck. "I don't know about that. I can say, I never expected to enjoy it as much as I do. Being here, being home, feels right."

"Think you'll ever move away?"

"I don't know. I get offers once in a while. But it all comes back to me asking myself if I could really be happy anywhere else. I don't have a good answer to that so for now I'm staying."

"Good." She spoke barely above a whisper and the sound of her low voice strummed down his spine like a soft caress. His gaze met hers and she didn't look away.

Again, the memory of that kiss seemed to shimmer between them and he could think of nothing else, the sound of her murmuring his name when he kissed her, the taste of her as she opened for him, warm and welcoming, how perfectly *right* she had seemed in his arms.

He wanted more. Much, much more.

He could kiss her again. He knew it wouldn't take much for him to lean forward and close the distance between them. The ache to touch her again was a physical burn in his gut.

Even as he started to lean forward, to take what he so desperately wanted, reality came rushing in like that cold wind out there and froze his muscles.

Things were tense enough between them. Was he willing to throw in another kiss that could never lead anywhere?

Yeah.

Hell, yeah.

But he wasn't sure where things stood between them. Though she responded the last time in the heat of the moment, she had looked stunned afterward and he was certain he had caught more than a glimmer of dismay in her gaze.

He let out a breath and the sound of it seemed to echo in the still room. "Lauren—" he began, not sure what he intended to say. *Kiss me before I die on the spot,* maybe.

Whatever it might have been was driven from his mind when the power came back on suddenly, an abrupt, jarring shift from dim to full, bright light.

He blinked a few times to adjust his vision. When he could see through the glare, he saw that in those brief moments she had drawn her arms tighter around her knees and all her defenses were firmly in place.

Just as well. The seductive intimacy of those few moments alone in the dark with her could never survive the harsh glare of light.

She was relieved, Lauren told herself firmly. The power switching back on at just that moment when he had been gearing up to kiss her—and she had so desperately wanted him to—must have been some kind of an omen, a karmic warning that she was messing in dangerous things she damn well ought to stay clear of.

She might be able to sell that argument to her intellect. Her body was another matter entirely, and all she seemed able to focus on now was the deep well of disappointment inside her.

The furnace kicked in and she knew it would be blowing its warmth through the house any moment now.

"Looks like we're back in business," she murmured, mostly to fill the sudden awkward void between them.

"For now. Let's hope it stays on."

She shouldn't regret the loss of that quiet intimacy between them. She knew it was dangerous, knew it filled her mind with all sorts of treacherous thoughts, but she couldn't help feeling as if she had lost something rare, something precious.

"I suppose I'll say good night, then."

"Try to get some rest."

"Same to you."

She rose, self-conscious now about her favorite thread-bare pajamas. She hadn't given them a thought when the power was out, but now she wished she'd thrown a robe on before wandering out.

In her bedroom, she closed the door behind her and leaned against it, just for a moment.

It was foolish, she knew, but she wanted the electricity to blink out again. She wanted to be sitting out there with Daniel in the dim firelight, to be listening to his deep voice and feeling the strength and heat of him. A few more moments. Was that too much to ask?

Too bad she had learned the bitter lesson long ago that a girl couldn't always have everything she wanted.

Chapter 10

Two days later, Lauren was just about ready to climb out of her skin. She was beginning to understand the frustrated restlessness of a mouse in a cage.

After forty-eight hours in her house with only Daniel and Rosa, she was edgy and out of sorts and needed some sort of physical outlet. If the snow wasn't still howling out there, she would suit up and jog around the block. The idea tempted her, despite the blizzard, but she decided she really wasn't in the mood for the inevitable argument with Daniel about it.

She had to settle for the mild but distracting exertion of cooking dinner for the three of them.

Not wanting to bother Rosa and Daniel in the adjoining room, she tried her best not to bang pots and pans around as she pulled out the frying pan she needed to sauté chicken.

They didn't even look up from their movie as she set it on the stove and added olive oil to begin heating.

They were watching a DVD of a comedy with Spanish subtitles and every once in a while she could hear their laughter echo through the little house. She was pleased to hear Rosa relaxing, but each time she heard Daniel's bass laugh, she felt as if he had reached across the distance between them to stroke her neck with strong fingers.

Outside, the wind continued to lash snow against the window, as it had much of the day. The blizzard had continued on and off for two days and Daniel had been on the phone a great deal, coordinating his department's response to the storm.

She didn't find much consolation that this enforced isolation was tough on him as well, especially in the midst of a weather crisis. Some time ago, she tried to convince him she and Rosa would be fine here alone for a few hours if he needed to get out in the middle of the action with his deputies.

She thought it had been a reasonable enough suggestion. Daniel just raised one of those expressive eyebrows of his and assured her he wasn't going anywhere.

More's the pity. She sighed as she finished cutting up a chicken breast and slid it into the olive oil in the frying pan, filling the kitchen with sizzling heat.

Maybe he would let *her* go somewhere and help his department with the storm cleanup. True, she didn't know a blasted thing about directing traffic or cleaning up weather-caused accidents. But at this point, she was just about willing to do anything that would get her out of the house for a moment or two so she could regain a little psychic equilibrium.

She filled her large stockpot with water for the pasta,

then set it on to boil while she tackled the fresh vegetables for another of her few specialties. She was slicing red and yellow peppers when Daniel laughed again at something on the show.

A shiver slid through her and she almost chopped her finger off. Oh, this was ridiculous. Still, she couldn't resist a quick peek into the other room. Rosa was stretched out on the couch while Daniel had taken over Lauren's favorite easy chair. He sprawled in it, wearing jeans and a rust-colored sweater. He looked rugged and masculine and so gorgeous, he made her insides ache.

She was in serious trouble here.

She grabbed the onion and started slicing it fiercely. Her eyes started watering profusely, but she didn't care. Damn him, anyway. For two days, she had done her best to ignore the thick tension between them, but she wasn't making any progress whatsoever.

He was just so...*there.* He seemed to fill every corner of her small house with the potent force of his personality.

She found everything about him fascinating. She enjoyed listening to him talk to his deputies with a firm voice that managed to convey authority and respect at the same time. She liked watching him with Rosa. He treated the bruised and battered girl with a gentle kindness that touched her deeply.

She also admired his deep reservoir of patience, this further proof that he was often quite literally the quiet spot in a storm to those around him. For a man with such an overwhelming personality, Daniel had an almost Zen-like calmness to him in the middle of a crisis.

Calm did not mean *detached.* Not in the least. Even now, when he appeared relaxed and at ease watching a movie, he never seemed to shed that subtle air of alertness about him, like some kind of predator constantly sniffing the air for prey.

Throughout the last two days, he had put on his winter gear several times to brave the storm, ostensibly to shovel the driveway or for more firewood, but she had the feeling he also used the opportunity to case her house and its surroundings, looking for anything unusual.

He was a dangerous man, she thought as she stirred the chicken. More so, she imagined, because it would be easy—and disastrous—for an opponent to mistake his outward calm for inward placidity. Anyone foolish enough to err so badly would have to overlook those sharp dark eyes that never seemed to miss anything.

She could only hope they didn't see *everything*. She would die of mortification if he guessed her attraction.

Oh, she had it bad. Now that it was out in the open in her psyche, she couldn't believe she had missed it all these years, all the reasons she was tense and uncomfortable around him.

Her attraction had always been this undefined thing in her mind, this awareness of him that was somehow lost in her frustration and sadness over the past.

How would their relationship change after this time with Rosa was over? How on earth could things ever return to the way they were before, that wary but polite accord?

She was checking the cookie sheet of breadsticks baking in the oven, their yeasty smell mingling with the spices in the chicken, when some sixth sense warned her Daniel had entered the kitchen behind her.

Even without turning around, she knew he was there by a sudden subtle vibration in the air, a stirring of the molecules, an alertness in her nerve endings.

Her pulse kicked up a notch, as it seemed to do whenever he was within five feet of her, but she pasted on a smile and turned around, only to find him watching her with an odd expression on his face, something dark and intense and unsettling.

He hid it quickly and moved to the coffeepot to refill his cup. "Smells delicious," he said, gesturing to the sizzling chicken. Did he sound more gruff than usual? she wondered, then dismissed the thought.

"Thanks," she murmured.

"You don't have to do all the cooking. I know we've talked about this but I should have been more proactive. Sorry to dump the burden on you. Things have been a little crazy, with the storm and all. To be honest, I forgot all about it, but I promise, I'll cook breakfast and dinner tomorrow."

"I really don't mind cooking," she assured him.

"It's only fair. And I don't mind it, either."

"Do you expect you and Rosa will still be here by dinnertime tomorrow?" she asked.

"I'm still waiting to hear from Cale on the status of their safe house situation. We'll know better after he checks in." He paused. "Whenever we get out of here, I imagine you'll be happy to have us out of your way."

"You're not in my way."

Much.

She was a lousy liar and his rueful half smile indicated he didn't believe her any more than she believed herself.

Not that she would be completely thrilled to have them gone. On the one hand, she would be vastly relieved when her life returned to normal and her clinic reopened. On the other, she was terribly afraid she would be lonely when this was all over.

She had a good life, she reminded herself as she added the pasta to the boiling water. Every day she tried to make a difference in the world, to help the people of her community live healthier, happier lives. She had no reason at all for this discontent simmering under her skin.

"You know," he said after a moment, "if Cale and McKinnon do find another placement for Rosa in the next day or two, you would still have time left of your vacation to go visit your mom in southern Utah."

"Maybe. I don't want to make any definite plans until things are figured out here."

The timer went off, indicating the breadsticks were done. She slid them out, aware of him watching her the whole time.

"Anything I can do in here?"

She wanted him out of the kitchen. How could she possibly concentrate on cooking with him crowding her psyche this way? "No. I just need to toss it all together. Go back to your movie. Everything should be ready in ten minutes or so."

"I can set the table, at least."

"All right."

For the next few moments, they worked together in silence, Daniel setting out plates and silverware while Lauren brushed melted butter on the breadsticks and finished sautéing the vegetables.

She was concentrating so fiercely on trying to ignore him that she nearly caused a disaster. When she determined the pasta was done, she carried the stockpot to the sink to drain and almost collided with Daniel, who must have gone to the cupboard by the sink for glasses.

He caught her and steadied her, but a tiny amount of hot liquid spilled over onto the front of his sweater.

"I'm sorry!" she exclaimed. "Are you all right?"

"Fine. It's a thick sweater."

This time she was certain his voice sounded rough. She lifted her gaze from his shirtfront to his face and that jumpy, fluttery feeling twirled through her insides at the raw hunger she surprised in his expression.

"I... Good," she said breathlessly. They froze there in an awkward tableau, then he stepped away.

"You'd better drain that before you get burned."

The pasta. Right. She hurried to the sink, hoping he would attribute her sudden flush to the cloud of steam curling around her.

The doorbell rang just as the three of them were clearing the dinner dishes. The change in Daniel was rapid and disconcerting. One moment he was teasing Rosa in Spanish, the next he became alert, predatory.

"Stay here," he ordered, his voice hard and flat.

He headed toward the door, reaching for something under his sweater. He had a gun. Good Lord. She should have realized he would be armed. He was here for protection, for heaven's sake, she reminded herself. He couldn't very well face down Gilberto Mata with nothing but his fists, no matter how powerful they were.

Still, the sight of that stark, black weapon in his hand drove home the precariousness of the situation—and the dangerous edge to Daniel's nature he usually managed to cloak from view.

From the angle of the kitchen cabinets, she only had a sliver of a view into the entryway. She watched Daniel ease to the front window and barely twitch the curtains to look out on to the porch, just like a gunfighter in the Wild West.

She held her breath, but whatever he saw there must have set his mind at ease. He quickly holstered his weapon again and worked the locks on the door.

"It's okay. Everything's okay." She gave a Rosa a reassuring smile when she heard Daniel greeting Cale Davis.

A moment later, both men entered her kitchen, and the cozy room instantly seemed to shrink. Though Lauren knew Rosa had met the FBI agent when she was in the hospital, the girl seemed tense and anxious in his presence.

Seeing her reaction only reinforced to Lauren how very comfortable Rosa had become with Daniel. That thought was further validated when Daniel smiled at Rosa and she visibly relaxed.

"We've just finished eating," Lauren said. "There's plenty left. Are you hungry?"

He shook his head. "I'm fine, thanks. Megan's holding dinner for me at home so I can't stay long. Since your place is on my way home, I figured I would stop and see how things have been going."

"Quiet," Daniel answered.

"That's good. Just the way we like it. Sorry I haven't checked in with you before now. We've been in the middle of a big bust on another case. I think we've finally tied up all those loose ends and are ready to put all our energies into this case."

"Has there been any progress?" Lauren asked.

Cale glanced quickly at Rosa, who was hovering close to Daniel. "Some," he said. "We're closing in on the smuggling ring. With the information Rosa gave us, we've been able to find Gilberto Mata. We know who he is and we've got a tail on him."

"Have you arrested him?"

Cale shook his head. "Not yet. We're trying to track his movements, his known associates, that kind of thing, to see if we can figure out who else might be involved and find the other girls Rosa talked about. Her friend and the others. That's going to take some time. We know from her statement that she knows at least four other men were involved besides Mata, the three other men who raped her and who handled the day-to-day operations and another one who seemed to be calling the shots. There have got to be more than that if they're keeping the other girls somewhere—"

Rosa said something quickly in Spanish to Daniel, a questioning look on her fragile, half-healed features. She must have been asking him to translate the conversation. Since Lauren had spent the last two days trying in vain to follow the rapid conversations between Rosa and Daniel, she thought she understood how Rosa felt.

"Can I tell her what you said? She deserves to know what's going on," Daniel said.

Cale pursed his lips. "You're right. She does."

Daniel quickly explained what the agent had said and Rosa nodded. Lauren actually understood her response as she asked him in Spanish why they hadn't already arrested the man who hurt her.

Cale apparently understood some Spanish as well. "Explain to her that we can't move too quickly on this and risk blowing the whole investigation by sending them all running back over the border. As I said, we're still trying to find the other girls she talked about. We need a few more days to make sure we can get them out safely when this all goes down."

Daniel translated his words to Rosa, who nodded solemnly.

"Federal prosecutors want to convene a grand jury by Tuesday or Wednesday so we can get some indictments. We would like to prep Rosa to testify as early as the day after that."

He looked at Lauren. "Do you think she'll be up to that?"

"Are you asking me as her doctor or as her friend?" she asked, and couldn't help the ridiculous little glow that blossomed inside her when Daniel gave her a wide smile of approval.

"Both, I suppose," Cale answered.

"I think you're going to need to ask her that. Medically, there's no reason she can't testify. She's rebounding remarkably well from a horrific beating. She still has pain and will for some time, but both she and the baby seem to be fine. Emotionally, she's suffered months of trauma and she's going to be healing from that for a long time."

Cale turned to the girl and asked her in Spanish if she would be willing to testify about what happened to her so the men who hurt her could be arrested.

She shook her head vehemently, her eyes wide and her expression taut with fear. Lauren instinctively went to her. But Daniel moved first. He squeezed her shoulder gently and spoke in a soft, reassuring voice.

At first, Lauren couldn't understand what he said. Only after she translated the words in her mind did his meaning become clear. He told Rosa she was strong and beautiful, courageous enough to handle this task they put before her, as hard as it would be, and he swore he would be with her the entire way.

Rosa swallowed hard, her fingers trembling as she twisted them together. She looked as if she wanted to run out the door and escape this whole situation, but after a moment she seemed to straighten her shoulders.

"If it will help the other girls to be safe and away from those bad men, then yes, I will tell what I know."

Daniel smiled at her with pride and affection. As Lauren gazed at those strong, handsome features, the terrifying truth poured over her like someone had just rushed into the kitchen and dumped a bucket full of snow over her head.

She was in love with him.

Instinctively, she fought to deny it. She couldn't be. It wasn't possible.

Yes, she was attracted to him. That was a normal physiological reaction to a powerful, gorgeous man. Yes, she admired his dedication and his commitment to his job and his town, his kindness and his compassion.

But *love*.

That was something else entirely.

Even as her mind tried to rationalize, to frantically search for some escape, the inevitable truth seemed to settle into her chest, seeping into her soul.

She was in love with Daniel Galvez.

How could she have missed it all these years? They had definitely been there, these feelings growing inside her. Looking back, she could see clear signs. She had always had a bit of a crush on him as a girl—just like all the other girls at school.

Daniel had been tall, dark, gorgeous, athletic—and slightly rough around the edges. All the things that twittered the hearts of silly teenage girls, and she had been no different.

She had put it out of her mind over the years, but since they both returned to Moose Springs as adults and she watched the kind of man that boy had grown into, these tender feelings had been growing inside her—untended and wild, but still somehow finding root.

Through her dismay, she realized Cale and Daniel were still talking about the case.

"What about the safe house situation?" Daniel asked.

"We should have everything set by tomorrow afternoon. We've got a couple female agents standing ready to stay with her. One of them is fluent in Spanish, too."

"That's good," Daniel said, relief in his voice. "I'll feel better if she has someone to talk to."

"Things will be easier with her in our place by the U. This way the prosecutors will have easier access to prep her for her testimony." Cale paused. "You two okay here one more night?"

"I'm good," Daniel said. "Lauren?"

No. She was *not* good. Didn't anybody else notice the sane order of her life crumbling around her feet?

"She can stay here as long as necessary," she managed.

"Thanks. Tomorrow should be sufficient."

Could she make it through one more day? she wondered as Daniel showed Cale to the door and she and Rosa resumed clearing the dishes from the kitchen table.

Oh, this was a complete disaster, she thought as she stood filling the sink with soapy water for the dishes that weren't dishwasher-safe. She was destined for heartache here.

She thought of the tension that was always there just below the surface when she was with Daniel. He didn't share her feelings. She had never picked up any kind of vibe like that.

Maybe she just missed it. She had been too stupid to realize her own feelings. But he had kissed her.

A fluke, she assured herself, a temporary aberration brought on by the heat and intensity of the moment.

Who would have guessed when she stepped up to offer a wounded patient a sanctuary for a few days that she would discover a grim truth about herself that would rock her to the core?

"Everything okay?"

She looked up from the sink to find Daniel had returned to the kitchen and was watching her with concern in his eyes.

"Much harder and you're going to scrub the nonstick coating right out of that pan," he said.

She stilled her movements, hoping the truth wasn't painfully obvious in her features.

"Yes. Of course. Everything's fine," she lied. "Just fine. Why wouldn't it be?"

Chapter 11

Something was wrong.

Daniel covertly studied Lauren throughout the remainder of the evening, trying to figure out exactly what had happened at dinnertime to make her so jumpy and out of sorts.

She tried to hide it, but he could see some kind of turmoil seething in her blue eyes. Though she went through the motions of watching another DVD with them, he didn't think she caught any of it. Half the time she wasn't even looking at the screen, she was gazing into the flickering fire or out the window at the snow. She seemed the proverbial million miles away.

Maybe this situation was harder on her than she let on. *He* sure as hell found it a nightmare.

Being this close to Lauren—living in her house, surrounded by her things, by her scent, by her sheer presence—was just about the hardest assignment he had ever endured.

He had gone undercover as a scumbag drug dealer for five months back on the job in Salt Lake City and had seen—and done—things that still made his gut burn. All for the greater good of busting up a crime ring that focused exclusively on hooking junior high and high school kids on methamphetamines.

The whole thing had been a miserable, soul-sucking time in his life. While the two dozen resulting arrests hadn't completely washed away the stink of it from his skin, they had certainly helped.

Sitting in Lauren's house, pretending a casualness he was far from feeling, seemed much harder than those five months.

He ached to touch her again. Every time he came within a few feet of her, he had to shove his hands in his pockets to keep from reaching for her.

Maybe that's why she was so twitchy, because she feared he was going to jump her again any minute now.

She didn't need to worry. He could have reassured her on that score. He had vowed to himself the night before that he would keep his hands off her for the duration of this assignment and he would damn well keep that oath, no matter how impossible it seemed at times.

The music on the movie swelled and he realized the closing credits were rolling. He hadn't paid much more attention than Lauren. He only hoped Rosa had enjoyed it.

"Do you want to watch another one?" Lauren asked in Spanish.

Rosa shook her head. "I'm tired," she said softly, her hand resting on her abdomen.

Lauren studied her with concern. "You're hurting, aren't you?"

Rosa started to deny it, then finally she shrugged.

Lauren turned to him. "Can you ask her if it would be all right for me to check her temperature and blood pressure? I'm afraid I don't quite have the language skills."

He repeated her question to Rosa, who shrugged again. She *did* look achy and upset and he admired Lauren's powers of observation.

She rose with her usual grace and left the room. When she returned, she carried her medical bag. She flipped up the lights they had dimmed for the movie and sat down next to Rosa on the couch.

As usual, he found watching Dr. Maxwell in action far more absorbing than anything on the silver screen. Despite her halting Spanish, she made Rosa completely comfortable with her quiet skill. After a quick check of temperature and blood pressure, she pulled out a small sensor from her bag, the same one she had used during her initial exam of Rosa.

"I'm going to check the baby's heartbeat, okay?" She patted her chest to pantomime a heart beating and pointed at Rosa's abdomen.

"Do you want me to leave?" Daniel asked.

"That's up to Rosa."

He repeated the question to the girl, who shook her head. "Just turn around," Rosa ordered.

He had to smile at the peremptory tone—something she was using more and more as she became more comfortable with them both. He complied, then was astonished a moment later to hear a rapid, steady heartbeat filling the room.

"Is that the baby?" he asked, amazed at the strength of it.

"That's her," Lauren said. "She's a fighter. That's a strong, normal heartbeat."

A moment later, the miraculous sound stopped. "You can turn around now," Lauren said.

When he shifted his gaze, he saw she was putting the monitor thingie away while Rosa pulled her shirt back down. Instead of looking thrilled to hear the heartbeat, she was looking increasingly distressed.

Lauren must have picked up on it, too. "What is it?"

Rosa shrugged but her chin gave an ominous quiver and her big dark eyes started to fill up with tears.

Daniel's first instinct—like that of any sane man—was to shove his chair back and run like hell. Lauren could handle it. She must know exactly how to deal with a young girl's tears.

She'd been one, after all.

He started to shift his weight forward to escape, but Lauren caught the movement. She impaled him in place with a glare.

"What is it? Everything is fine. Good. Are you hurting somewhere else?" she asked in her stilted Spanish.

He sighed. As much as he desperately wanted to escape any emotional outburst, he couldn't leave, not with the language barrier between Lauren and her patient.

Rosa pressed a hand to her chest. "Here," she said.

"You're having chest pains?" In her dismay, Lauren forgot herself and asked the question in English, then looked helplessly at him. He repeated the question in Spanish.

Rosa sniffled once, and then unleashed the floodgates. "My heart," she sobbed. "It aches inside me. I worry so much. What will happen to my baby? She did nothing wrong and I do not want her to die. I am glad she is a fighter, as Dr. Lauren says, that Gilberto Mata did not kill her. But I cannot love her. Who will take care of her?"

Daniel couldn't begin to imagine what she must be going through, pregnant as a result of rape, afraid for her life in a country where she didn't speak the language.

"What did she say?" Lauren demanded, frustration at the language barrier obvious in her features.

"She's worried about the baby."

"Her heartbeat was fine. Better than fine. It's great," Lauren said, clearly baffled.

"Not the baby's physical well-being. More about what will happen to her." He translated the rest of what Rosa had said and watched the anxiety in Lauren's eyes turn to soft compassion.

"Oh, Rosa," she said, and hugged the girl. *Big help there,* he thought, panicking more. Rosa only seemed to sob harder.

After a tense moment, she seemed to calm down and Lauren produced a tissue.

"The other day in the hospital, you said you wanted to give the baby up for adoption, remember? Rosa, there are wonderful couples with so much love to give a child. If that's what you decide, we will find the perfect home for your baby, I promise you. I'll help you. You can choose exactly where the baby goes."

He translated for Lauren, though he had the impression the girl understood the gist.

She twisted the tissue in her hands until it was mangled. "But what if my baby hates me for giving her away?"

"She won't. I promise." She squeezed the girl's hands,

tissue and all. "I can tell you that from experience. I was adopted and I have never been anything but grateful to the woman who gave me life."

He stared at her, struck dumb at that unexpected bit of information. How had he never known that about her, in all his months of investigating R.J.? Or maybe he had learned it, he had just been so consumed with vengeance he hadn't internalized the information.

He suddenly remembered his translator duties and relayed what she had said to Rosa. Her words seemed to ease much of the girl's worries. Lauren spent a few more moments reassuring her, until the tears appeared to have dried up, to his vast relief.

"Come on," Lauren said. "The best thing for you right now is rest. You will feel much better about everything in the morning."

"Thank you," Rosa whispered. "Thank you for everything. You have both been so kind to me."

Lauren hugged her once more, then went with her to help settle her for the night.

She returned just as Daniel was throwing another log on the fire. She paused inside the room and again he caught the wild edge of restlessness in her stance.

"I don't believe I ever knew you were adopted," he said.

She blinked as if she hadn't quite been expecting his statement. "It wasn't some big dark secret," she said. "I don't think about it much, it's just part of who I am."

"What were the circumstances?"

"The usual, I guess. My parents were married for five years and found out they couldn't conceive. This was in the early days of in vitro. They tried everything, apparently, without success. Finally they went the private adoption route."

"Do you know anything about your birth mother?"

"Only that she was young and pregnant and alone, like Rosa," she said. "That's all."

Was this the reason Rosa's situation seemed to affect Lauren so strongly? She had sympathized with the girl from the very beginning. He had asked her why she had insisted on bringing Rosa home with her to Moose Springs to heal. Perhaps this helped explain her actions somewhat.

"She chose my parents before the birth," Lauren continued, "but stipulated there be no contact between them. My mother and father never met her. I don't know anything more about her than that."

"Have you ever wanted to look for her?"

"When I was in high school, I was curious. I guess I grew out of it, right around the time I figured out only fools go borrowing trouble."

"How do you know it would be trouble?" he asked. "Maybe you would be friends."

"Maybe. I just figured she could find me if she wanted. She knew my parents' names and where they lived. She would only have to Google R.J.'s name to know the whole ugly story. It wouldn't be hard to find mention of his only surviving child in those stories. His only legal one, anyway."

Again, he heard the bitterness in her voice. He knew the reason for it and he ached for her. Before he could respond, she spoke again.

"We don't need to dance around this, Daniel. You must know all the gory details. You worked in the sheriff's department at the time everything happened so I'm sure you were privy to all the juicy details that never made it into the papers."

If she only knew.

Before he could respond, Lauren forced a smile. "I'm sure you're wondering if my mother's inability to conceive had anything to do with the choices R.J. made later. The other family he kept in Salt Lake City. His three bouncing baby boys from another woman who thought she was happily married to a man who merely traveled more than she liked. I've certainly wondered the same thing. My mother was unable to give him a son and apparently he found someone who could."

Though she tried to hide it, he heard the raw pain in her voice and would have given anything to have the right words to ease it, as she had comforted Rosa.

"I do know the truth," he said carefully. "But you can be sure I'm one of only a few who do."

"I figured as much, otherwise everyone in town would know by now."

"Have you met them?"

She gave a humorless laugh. "Still more trouble I didn't want to go borrowing. My family tree is quite a wild tangle, isn't it? But yes, I have met my half brothers. Ian, Jamie and Kevin. And their mother. She's a very sweet woman who didn't deserve a betrayal like this."

"Neither did you or your mother."

"No, we didn't." She sighed. "I'm sorry. You must think I brood about the past constantly. I've talked about this more the last few days than I have since it all happened. I'm not sure why that is, but I would really like to put it behind me."

This was the perfect opening for him to tell her the

truth he had been running from, the guilt that burned through him whenever they talked about the grim ghosts of the past.

He hesitated. If he told her, everything between them would be ruined, this fragile friendship that had begun to take flight the last few days. If he told her, she would loathe him. How could she not?

Perhaps he would be better to just let things stay as they were. No. He couldn't take the coward's way out, not about this.

He sighed. He had to come clean, and damn the consequences.

"Lauren, there's something I should tell you."

She studied him across the room, his darkly handsome features suddenly solemn, and her stomach jumped with nerves.

"Whatever it is, I don't want to hear it," she said immediately, jumping up from her chair. "Not tonight."

"Lauren—"

She cut him off. "I need to do something physical. If you need anything, I'll be in my room on my yoga mat in the downward-facing dog."

He studied her intently, until she flushed under the weight of it. She could only hope he couldn't see the wild chaos of emotions she was doing her best to hide from him.

"Why are you running away?" he asked.

"Who's running away?" she retorted, then sighed at his raised eyebrow. "Okay," she admitted. "I'm running away."

"Why?"

She gave a short laugh. "I'm a physician, Daniel. In

my world *we need to talk* is just about the most terrible thing I can say to a patient. The only time I ever use those words, I invariably follow them up with something really awful. Whatever it is you want to tell me about my father or anything else, I don't want to hear it. Not tonight. I don't care if that makes me some kind of an ostrich up to my eyeballs in sand. I just… I can't take any more right now."

Though she knew it was rude to a guest in her home, she left without waiting for an answer and retreated to her bedroom, where she quickly changed into workout clothes.

At first, she pushed herself through her asanas, but after ten minutes or so her body and mind relaxed and she could feel the long days of tension begin to seep out of her.

Thirty-five minutes later, she finished her usual poses and was asking herself why she hadn't tried this days ago to still the turmoil inside her, when she heard the outside door open and close.

Daniel must be outside shoveling snow, she assumed. This would probably be the perfect time for her to grab a bottled water from the refrigerator, something she had neglected earlier in her haste to escape from him.

For the first time in days, her mind wasn't churning and her muscles felt pleasantly loose as she went to the kitchen and opened the refrigerator. She found a bottle and was taking a long, refreshing drink when that sixth sense warned her she wasn't alone.

She turned and found Daniel standing in the doorway, his eyes shadowed.

Her relaxed feeling disappeared. Acutely conscious of her yoga clothes—a midriff-baring tank and stretchy capris—she swallowed hard, sincerely wishing she had never left her mat.

"Snow's stopped."

Her nerves tingled at the hoarse note in his voice.

"I… Good. That's good."

"I'd say we got at least a foot out of the storm. Maybe eighteen inches."

How could he possibly talk about the weather, with all the currents zinging between them? She couldn't even manage to string together a coherent thought.

"How'd the, er, low-down dog go?"

That strange note in his voice caught her attention again and she took a closer look at his expression. She finally saw the hunger there—hot desire with an edge of desperation.

She continued to stare at him, hypnotized by the twitch of muscle in his jaw. He was so big, so dangerously male, and all she could think about was how easy it would be to tug him into her bedroom right now and get her hands on all that hard strength.

He wanted her. She couldn't quite believe it, but she couldn't deny the evidence in his eyes.

"It's the, um, downward-facing dog." Her voice sounded hoarse as well. "I feel much better—all loose and relaxed. You should try it."

She took another swallow from the bottled water. When she lowered it, she found him staring at her mouth. Had she left a water droplet or two there? she wondered, sweeping her tongue across her bottom lip to be sure.

Daniel made a strangled sound. "You're killing me here, Lauren."

"I'm…what?"

"I have to kiss you again. I'm sorry."

She had only half a second to wonder why he seemed compelled to apologize for something she wanted with a fierce ache, and then she was in his arms.

His lips were cold from being outside and he tasted of mint. She shivered as he pressed her against the cabinet, his mouth hard and possessive. Oh, my. She wrapped her arms around his neck, relishing the strength of him against her curves. Raising her arms lifted her exercise tank another few inches, baring more of her midriff and she could feel the nubby texture of his sweater against her skin.

When he slid a hand to her bare back, under the cotton of her tank, and pulled her closer, she forgot all about it—forgot to breathe or think or do anything but exist in the heat of his arms. Raw sensation glittered through at the touch of his fingers on her bare skin, at his tongue stroking hers.

Oh, my.

He was so big and solid, like those mountains outside the window, and she wanted to melt into him.

Where their kiss two days before had been slow, easy as a sluggish creek on a hot summer day, this one was a raging, churning whirlpool. She feared if she wasn't careful, the urgent force of it would suck her down and carry her away.

Clinging wildly to the spinning edges of her sanity, she summoned every ounce of willpower and managed to wrench her mouth away from his long enough to come up for air.

She could feel his chest's rapid rise and fall, see the dazed desire in his eyes.

Had she really done that to him? It didn't seem possible that she could have that effect on someone who was usually so calm and unruffled under any circumstances.

"You taste just like I always imagined you would," he murmured.

It took a moment for his words to sink in. When they did, she raised disbelieving eyes to his. "You…imagined kissing me?"

He still held her, his hands on the bare skin of her back, and his low laugh rumbled against her chest. "Not much. Only just about every time I saw you for the last decade or so. Possibly more."

She managed, barely, to keep her jaw from completely sagging open. She swallowed hard. "You have not."

His expression suddenly guarded, as if he wished he hadn't said anything, he dropped his arms and stepped back. She instantly felt about a dozen degrees colder in her skimpy yoga clothes.

"I don't mean to argue with you, Dr. Maxwell, but I know my own fantasies, thanks very much."

Here was twice in one day she felt she had just entered some kind of alternate universe. He had fantasized about *her?*

She rubbed her chilled arms. "I… Why didn't you ever do anything about it?"

"Tried that once and you shot me down. Quite brutally, in fact. I didn't see the need to embarrass both of us by a repeat performance."

Disoriented and more off balance than she was in her most challenging yoga pose, she didn't know what he meant at first. It took her a moment to realize he must be referring to the time she had turned him down for a date, that terrible summer she had returned to Moose Springs between her freshman and sophomore year of college.

She would have felt threatened by any male who showed interest in her that summer. She was jumpy, skittish. Someone as athletic and virile and *overpowering* as Daniel would have sent her spiraling into panic.

But that had been years ago, another lifetime. All this time he had wondered about kissing her and he had given her absolutely no indication of it until now.

She couldn't quite fathom it—at the same time, she realized she probably hadn't exactly given him any encouragement to do more than wonder.

"I'm sorry. It wasn't you," she said lamely. "I...that was a crazy summer."

He leaned a hip against the counter. "It doesn't matter."

It did, she realized. She could tell by the studied casualness in his eyes. Somehow her rejection had bothered him very much.

All these years, she thought the subtle tension that always seemed to simmer between them stemmed from what her father had done. How foolish of her, especially when Daniel had made it clear many times that he didn't believe her responsible for her father's sins.

She didn't know whether to be relieved or dismayed that his discomfort might have more to do with her blunt rejection, that he thought she disliked him all these years, when she had been fighting her own attraction.

She let out a breath. How could she ever explain how messed up she had been that summer, what a blur those weeks had seemed?

She had to, though. She loved him. He deserved the truth, no matter how hard the telling of it might be for her.

"Daniel, I promise. It wasn't you. I had...reasons."

"Yeah?"

She sighed. She did *not* want to have this discussion

in her workout clothes, probably smelling like that low-down dog he talked about.

"Give me a minute to change and I'll explain. Okay?"

She didn't wait for an answer, just made her escape.

Fifteen minutes later, he sat back on his heels after tossing another log into the fire and watched the flames consume it, trying fiercely to remind himself he was working here. He needed to keep his senses alert and vigilant to guard against any possible danger to the women under his care.

He couldn't risk losing control with Lauren, not with so much at stake. Maybe he would be better off if she just decided to stay in her room for the night. Temptation was far easier to resist when it wasn't gazing at him out of columbine-blue eyes.

But he had to admit, he wanted to hear what she had to say. More, he wanted to know if the desire he had seen in her eyes had been real or just a reaction to the heat of the moment.

He gave a heavy sigh. He had it bad. No surprise there. He just needed to try like hell not to let her see how he burned for her. He still yearned for the pink-and-white princess in the castle.

No. He didn't want that fairy-tale dream. He wanted Lauren. The smart, dedicated doctor who poured her heart and soul into healing her patients, the one who showed such kindness and compassion to a frightened young girl, the courageous woman who faced down an entire town's whispers.

She came out a few moments later, her hair damp and curling at the ends. She must have taken time to shower before changing into soft jeans and a white blouse.

She looked beautiful, soft and warm and delicious.

As he gazed at her in the fire's glow, the truth seemed to kick him in the gut like a pissed-off mule.

He was in love with her. Not because she took away his breath, but because of all those things he had thought about earlier. Her courage, her strength, her compassion.

Her heart.

His own chest ached and he fought the urge to rub his hand across it. He was in love with her and probably had been since those days he used to ride his bike by her house.

What the hell was he supposed to do with that?

"I'm going to make some hot chocolate," she said. "Do you want some?"

He wanted things to go back to the way before, when he thought he was just a stupid kid craving the pretty blonde princess who represented everything he didn't have.

"Sure," he mumbled.

"What flavor?"

As if he cared about that right now. "Anything."

She spent a few more moments in the kitchen. His mind churning with shock and dismay, he tried his best to keep his eyes off her as she bustled around boiling water, pulling out mugs, pouring, measuring, stirring.

Was Lauren the reason he was still thirty-three and single? He had come close to changing that a few times, but had backed away before things reached the sticking point. Those other relationships never felt quite right, no matter how hard he tried to make them so.

What a mess. He was in love with a woman who would despise him if she knew the truth about what he had done. He finally gave in and rubbed the ache in his heart.

When she returned, she handed him a blue mug with

intricate silver snowflakes on the side. "It's cinnamon. I didn't know which one to pick for you but, um, I know you like cinnamon mints."

A rosy blush crept over her cheekbones and for the life of him, he couldn't figure out why. Was it because she had noticed the kind of Altoids he preferred?

"Thanks," he murmured.

She perched in the chair opposite him and sipped at her cocoa. He obediently tried his. Though he usually preferred the liquid jolt of coffee, he had to admit there *was* something comforting about sitting here in the night by a flickering fire sipping cocoa, despite the tension in his gut and the turmoil in his heart.

After a moment, she let out a sigh. "I don't know where to begin."

He set his mug down on a coaster on the coffee table. "You don't have to say anything, Lauren. The past is done. Let's forget it."

She went on as if she didn't hear him, as if she had a script in her head and was going to get through it, no matter what.

"I'm very sorry I rejected you that summer. The truth is, I would have turned down any man who asked me out. But especially an athlete like you, someone big and tough and...overwhelming. It wasn't anything personal, I swear."

"It doesn't matter," he said again. "I just figured you weren't interested. No big deal."

"Any other time, I would have been."

He watched color rise in her cheeks again. She cast him a sidelong glance, then quickly looked away.

"Any other time except that summer I would have *definitely* been interested."

Chapter 12

At her words, he swallowed hard, a hundred different thoughts racing through his mind. He finally focused on the words that preceded her stunning declaration.

"What was different about that summer?"

"Everything. *Everything.*"

She paused, both hands wrapped around her cocoa mug. "You have to remember, I was young, barely seventeen, when I started college. Young enough and stupid enough to think I could handle any situation. I was wrong. Seriously wrong."

He knew with sudden certainty he didn't want to hear this.

"Near the end of my second semester, I had an...incident that threw me off. Oh, this is harder than I thought it would be."

Grim premonition in his gut, he wanted to tell her to

stop right there. But if she could be tough enough to talk about it, he damn well could hear her out.

She sighed. "I was attacked. Date-raped. He was an athlete, the captain of the rugby team and I can remember feeling so flattered when he asked me out. He walked me back to my dorm and my roommate was gone for the weekend. I let him in. I knew it was stupid, but I did it anyway. So we were talking and before I knew it, he was pushing me to do things I didn't want to do. He was bigger than I was, stronger than I was, and…wouldn't take no for an answer."

His hand fisted around his mug so tightly, it was a wonder the thing didn't explode into shards.

"Did you file charges?" the cop in him compelled himself to ask.

She shook her head. "I told you, I was young and stupid. I was so embarrassed that I'd allowed him in when my roommate wasn't home, that I had been stupid enough to think I was worldly enough to handle anything. I just wanted to come home to Moose Springs, to my mama. I thought everything would be okay if I could only come home. Somehow I made it through the last few weeks of the term and came back for the summer to work for my dad and try to get my head back to normal."

She blew out a breath. "And then I missed my period."

He jerked his gaze to her and found her cheeks pink and her eyes determinedly fixed on the fire. "As you can guess, it was a pretty terrible time. I was terrified to tell my parents, terrified of anybody with a Y chromosome who dared to talk to me. I couldn't believe this was happening to me and I just wanted it all to go away."

His throat tightened, imagining her as an eighteen-year-old girl, traumatized and frightened and alone. Like Rosa, he realized, with only a few more years under her belt.

Suddenly everything made sense. Her compassion for the girl, her insistence on bringing her home and caring for her, as Lauren probably wished someone had done for her.

That summer when he had burned with embarrassment at her blunt rejection, he convinced himself she was just some rich bitch, a country-club baby who didn't want to dirty her hands by being seen with somebody like him.

Now he was ashamed that he had even entertained the thought for a moment.

"What happened?" he asked gruffly.

"I had a miscarriage. Less than seven weeks gestation. In retrospect, it was a blessing but I felt terribly guilty at the time, as if I had somehow wished the pregnancy away. I ended up having to tell my mother and she got me help—a good doctor and a good therapist."

He didn't know what to say, what to do. What man would, after finding out some bastard had done such a thing to the woman he loved? His first instinct was to demand the man's name so he could find him and mete out some long overdue justice.

Finally, he said the only words he could. "I'm so sorry, Lauren," he murmured.

"I'm not a victim. Please don't treat me like one. I promise, I don't even think about it much anymore."

She paused. "That's not quite true. Last week after I was attacked in the hospital, I dreamed about it again. About him." She smiled a little. "This time was different. In my dream, I stabbed him with a scalpel and, it felt great. I suppose that makes me sound vicious and bloodthirsty, doesn't it?"

"I'd like to do that to the bastard and more," he said quietly.

She stared at him for a moment and then she took a deep breath. "He *was* a bastard but I refuse to let a few moments out of my life a dozen years ago define me. I'm not a victim," she repeated. "I've had years to deal with what happened and I'm fine now. I wouldn't have even mentioned it except I wanted you to know why I was messed up that summer and why I treated you so coldly. It honestly wasn't you, Daniel."

"Good to know. I guess I can spend the next decade or so trying to heal my battered ego."

Her eyes widened with distress.

"Kidding, Lauren. I was kidding. I was a college jock way too full of myself back then. My ego could certainly stand being knocked down a peg or five or ten."

She smiled, then shifted her gaze back to the fire. "I don't know if this helps the healing process at all, but I should tell you that if you had asked me out any other time—before that summer or after I came back to Moose Springs—I would have jumped at the chance."

"You don't have to pretend anything, Lauren."

"Who's pretending? Why do you think I stutter and stammer and generally act like an idiot around you most of the time?"

"What are you talking about? You're never anything but professional and courteous."

"Is that what you call it when I all but jumped you in my kitchen?"

"Hey, I'm a big fan of professional courtesy."

She laughed, then rubbed her hands on her jeans. "So now that I've spilled all my secrets, where do we go from here?" she asked.

She might have spilled all hers, but he still had a few to go. He knew this would be another good opening to tell her about the investigation, but he couldn't seem to form the words. Not yet. He had to give her the truth but he couldn't bear the idea of that trust and affection in her eyes changing to hurt and anger.

"Uh, where would you like this to go?" he asked instead.

"That's up to you. If you asked me out again, I promise, I wouldn't say no this time."

"I'm afraid I wasn't very original back in the day. I think my master plan probably would have been pretty boring—to take you to dinner and a show and hopefully sit in the back row during the movie and neck."

She swallowed and that adorable pink flush crept over her cheekbones. "We've already had dinner. But I suppose we could watch a DVD."

His heart pounding like crazy, he stepped forward. "Or we could skip the movie and just head right on to the good stuff."

She smiled a little tremulously. "I was really hoping you would say that."

She sighed his name when he kissed her and he found it the most erotic sound he had ever heard.

Her mouth was soft and warm, and tasted like raspberries and chocolate, rich and sweet and addicting. He couldn't seem to get enough, especially when she sighed again and wrapped her arms around his waist.

This was as close to heaven as he had ever imagined, Lauren in his arms, the fire popping and hissing in the background, this seductive heat swirling around them.

He kissed her until his blood jumped wildly through his veins, until they were both breathing hard and it was all he could do not to press her against the couch and rip her clothes off.

He pulled away to give himself a little room to catch his breath, but she wasn't having any of it.

"Don't stop," she murmured. What man could resist an invitation like that? Certainly not him. With a strangled groan, he kissed her again, lost in a haze of desire.

He wasn't aware of any conscious movement but before he quite realized how it happened, they were in her bedroom.

She had left a lamp on in her room and it illuminated a wide bed covered in plump, luxurious pillows and a downy comforter in salmon and pale green. Like the rest of her house, this room was warm and comfortable, a haven from the stress and tension outside her doors.

Her room smelled like her, that subtle scent of jasmine and vanilla that made him think of warm, moonlit nights. He kissed her again just inside the door, intensely aware of the bed just a few steps away, how easy it would be to carry her there and do everything he had ever dreamed of, and more.

"I like the necking part of your dating strategy," she murmured against his mouth, sending heat shooting straight to his groin.

"I'm pretty crazy about it, too, right about now. A guy's got to go with what works."

He felt her smile against his skin and his heart swelled. He wasn't just crazy about the kissing. He was crazy about *her*.

"What comes next?" she asked. "I hope you're not going to tell me this is the part where you drop me off with a kiss at my door."

He loved this playful side of her, especially because

he had the feeling she didn't show it to many people. He was about to answer when she pressed her mouth to the curve of his jaw and he had to lean against the door just to keep from falling over at her feet.

"Are you kidding?" he said hoarsely. "I don't think I could go anywhere right now, even if your house caught on fire."

"Good," she murmured. "I want you right here."

She pulled him closer and he surrendered to the heat and the hunger. He didn't know if she led him to the bed or if he guided them both there. He only knew he wanted to be closer to her.

He wanted everything.

Her mouth was warm, welcoming. He slid a hand to her skin just above the waistband of her jeans. She had the most incredibly soft skin and he couldn't seem to get enough.

He dragged his mouth away from hers and trailed kisses down her neck, pausing just above the first closed button of her shirt, just a breath away from the slope of her breast. He could hear the rapid beat of her heart as he cupped her through the material and she arched against his fingers. He pressed his mouth to the exposed skin as he worked a button free and she shivered.

He paused, surrounded by her softness and the delectable scent of her and tried to catch hold of his wildly scrambling thoughts. "Everything okay?"

"Yes. Oh, *yes*."

She kissed him fiercely and his fingers fumbled with the rest of her buttons like some stupid, awkward kid in the backseat of his dad's car.

She wore nothing beneath her shirt but skin, a discovery he found as surprising as it was incredibly sexy.

He didn't pull her shirt off, just unfastened it, then

eased back so he could see her. He didn't think he had ever seen a more arousing sight than her soft, pale curves against the dark comforter.

"Touch me," she begged. "Please, Daniel."

The entreaty in her voice seemed to wake him from a dream, some hazy wonderland where reality didn't exist, just the joy and peace he found in her arms.

A few more moments and they would both be naked, bodies entwined as they tangled up her pretty bed. That's exactly where this was headed. He wanted it, she wanted it.

But he couldn't do it.

He swallowed and felt like he had just taken a mouthful of glass shards.

He should have told her long before now about her father and his. Though he wanted to make love to her as he had never wanted anything in his life—with a hot, heavy ache in his gut, with every iota of his heart, body and soul—he knew it would be wrong.

Before they took this most beautifully intimate of steps together, his damn conscience demanded he had to give her the truth, no matter how painful the consequences.

It was the right thing to do. The decent thing. But right now he had to admit he wouldn't mind having a little more ruthlessness and a whole lot less conscience.

It seemed a Herculean task but he slid his hand away from her skin and rolled over on the bed, gazing up at the ceiling fixture.

"We can't do this, Lauren. We have to stop."

With her shirt undone and her breasts full and achy from his touch, Lauren gazed at him in the glow from her bedside lamp, baffled and disoriented.

Why had he stopped? Had she done something wrong? He was as aroused as she was. She could see it in the slight unfocused look to his eyes, in the rapid, ragged edge to his inhalations.

She sat up, pulling the edges of her shirt closed and wishing she could pull her composure around her so easily. She didn't exactly have a lot of experience with this sort of thing.

"Is this because of what I told you? About what happened to me in college? I swear, I'm absolutely fine in that department. No lingering hang-ups whatsoever. Daniel, I want you to make love to me." She gave a rueful smile and held up a hand. "Look, I'm trembling with it."

An odd, pained expression twitched across his features, and then he stood up. "I want you, too, Lauren. More than I have ever wanted anything in my life. More than I want to breathe. You are the sexiest, the most incredible woman I know."

He sighed. "This has nothing to do with what happened to you. Or not what happened to you in college, anyway. That you had to endure such a thing makes me furious and sad and sorry. But it doesn't make me want you any less."

"I'm sorry. I missed something here, then. We both are obviously on the same page, so why did you stop? Are you worried about Rosa?"

He blinked as if he had forgotten all about her houseguest and the reason for his presence here.

"Not until you said that," he admitted. "That should tell you a little of what you do to me. I've never forgotten the job before. It's not Rosa. It's…there are things you should know before we take this any further."

He sighed and took her hand and a vague premonition

curled through her. "Lauren, I care about you. The last thing in the world I want to do is hurt you."

Her hand trembled in his. "But?"

"Earlier tonight I tried to tell you something. Something important. You said you didn't want to hear it. And while I can understand your reluctance, I can't in good conscience kiss you like this, touch you, until you know the truth."

More than a little nervous now, she worked the last few buttons of her shirt, wondering what this was all about. "So tell me."

He sighed. "I can't do this in here. You and a bed are too potent a combination in my mind. Do you mind if we go back in the other room?"

She shrugged and walked out into the living area. The fire had burned down while they had been in the bedroom and Daniel paused to toss another log on and stir the coals. She had the feeling he was trying to find the right words, and her nervousness ratcheted up a level.

Finally he turned to face her, his beautiful features shuttered, and their intimate embrace seemed miles away.

"I read a quote somewhere once, something about how the past lies upon the present like a giant's dead body. That's what I feel like right now, that I can't even move until I try to pry free of this heavy deadweight of the past."

She didn't have any idea what he was talking about, but she could see by the solemn set to his features that this was serious.

He sighed. "I need to tell you what happened five years ago, things you have every right to know before this goes any further. Once you have the information, you may very well decide you don't want to see me again. I hope to God that doesn't happen. But whatever you decide, I have no choice but to deal, just as I've had to live with the consequences of the wheels I set into motion."

Five years ago. She didn't have to do the math to know what he referred to and a grim unease started in her stomach and spread. "I assume this has something to do with my father, then."

"Everything." He let out a breath. "It has *everything* to do with R.J."

To her surprise, he sat down on the sofa beside her and took her hand, absently holding her fingers as he spoke. "I have to start the story with my own father. You said you remembered that he was always smiling. He was. My father was a good man—a great man—who came to this country with nothing but a dream of making a better life for his family. That might be a cliché but it was absolutely true for Roberto Galvez. He was the most humble, hardest-working man I've ever known. He could find the good in anyone, no matter how poorly they might have treated him."

"I always liked him," Lauren said. "I was sorry to hear he died."

His fingers tightened on hers. "He was killed the summer before I came back to Moose Springs. I think you were starting your residency. How much do you know about what happened to him?"

She frowned, trying to remember. Those had been hectic days and she had been two thousand miles away in Chicago. "Not much. It was some kind of accident, wasn't it?"

"Right. An *accident*." He turned the last word into something harsh and ugly.

"What happened?"

"He was killed on one of R.J.'s construction sites in

Park City, when the substandard materials Maxwell Construction was in the habit of using to cut corners collapsed. He fell eight stories. He was conscious the whole time until he died an hour later on the way to the hospital."

Nausea churned in her stomach and she pressed a hand there. She had seen construction fall injuries during her E.R. rotation. She knew exactly what kind of excruciating pain Roberto Galvez must have endured in that last hour of his life.

"I'm so sorry," she said, the most inadequate words in the English language. Here was one more truth about her father she had been sheltered from, another illusion laid to rest.

"My mother was lost without him," Daniel went on. "She was already sick herself with the cancer and she just couldn't function. My brothers and Anna and I knew one of us would have to come home and stay with her. They were all still in college and I couldn't ask them to walk away from their educations. Since I already had my degree and was working as a cop in Salt Lake—something I could do anywhere, including Moose Springs—I decided to come home."

This was only the setup to whatever he wanted to tell her. She knew it, could feel the tension rolling off him as he continued holding her hand.

"I was so angry when I came back. I had a million reasons to hate R.J. already. I blamed him for my father's death, for the decades of substandard wages he paid him, for the subtle but pervasive humiliation he heaped on a man just trying to support his family."

He let out a breath. "Then Maxwell Construction used my father's illegal resident status to somehow wiggle out of paying my mother any kind of financial settlement for his wrongful death or even paying his pension. When they cut off her insurance benefits—a widow fighting breast cancer—my anger turned to rage."

Oh, she hated this. She wanted her daddy back, the man who sat her on his lap and read her stories, who loved to tickle her with his whiskers, who roasted marshmallows with her in the fireplace when the power went out. She didn't want to know how ruthless and amoral he had been in his business dealings.

"Anyone would be furious," she managed through a throat that felt raw and bruised. "What happened was wrong."

"I knew the score in Moose Springs. I always had. Your father called the shots in town and everybody jumped to do what he wanted. I came back home with one overriding goal, besides taking care of my mother. To bring your father down."

At last he pulled his hand away as he rose and stood by the fire. "I became obsessed with finding dirt on R.J. It sounds melodramatic now, five years later, but I spent every waking moment of my off-duty time digging through garbage. I followed paper trails, I studied budgets, I combed through his financial records, trying to find any dirt I could to bury him."

She folded her arms tightly, chilled despite the warm fire. "And you found it."

"You could say that. I worked around the clock trying to put the pieces together. It was all I cared about. I was consumed with it. All I could think about was vengeance. I wanted him to pay. No, I wanted to bleed him dry."

How could this man talking about her father in such a harsh way be the same man who had held her so sweetly just fifteen minutes before?

"I had to take everything I found to the county attorney. When they finally filed charges and I was able to arrest him, it was the greatest day of my life, like finding the Holy Grail, Eldorado and the lost city of Atlantis, all rolled into one."

That nausea churned again in her stomach at his words.

"I destroyed your father, Lauren. It was calculated and deliberate and driven by my thirst for revenge. I set out to bring him down any way I could and I succeeded beyond my wildest dreams."

He reached for her hand. "I was looking for financial irregularities. That's all. You have to believe me. I never expected the rest of it, about his bigamy and his other family. That only came out during questioning after he was arrested."

He paused and squeezed her trembling fingers. "And I certainly never expected things to end the way they did."

She slid her hand away and folded her fingers together. "You were on duty at the jail the day my father killed himself," she suddenly remembered out loud.

"Yeah. I was the deputy who found him."

She stared at him, this man she loved, as a horrible suspicion took root. She didn't want to believe it of him, but she felt as if her whole world had been turned upside down and she had to ask.

"Did you have anything to do with it?"

He reeled back as if she picked up the fireplace poker and shoved it into his gut. She saw shock and hurt cross his features—and then she saw something else. Guilt.

"Not directly," he finally said.

She rose, desperate for air, for space. "Directly or indirectly. What difference do semantics make?"

"You're right. Absolutely right." He sighed heavily. "I have lived with this for five years, Lauren, wondering

what I might have done differently. Should I have guessed
R.J. would take that way out after he was arrested? I don't
know. I knew your father, both personally and from the
profile I created while running the investigation. I worked
for him for three summers and my dad was an employee
of Maxwell Construction my whole life. I knew the kind
of man R.J. was and how important his image, his standing, were to him around here."

Her father loved being addressed as Mayor, even of a
little town like Moose Springs. He had loved being the
most important man in town, the wealthiest, the most
powerful.

"I never expected him to end things the way he did,"
Daniel went on slowly. "But in retrospect, I should have
taken better precautions. Put him on suicide watch."

"I'm sure you didn't exactly cry over his grave."

"Believe it or not, I found no satisfaction that he killed
himself. Absolutely none. I wanted a trial. A public venue
where all his wrongdoings could be aired for the whole
world to know."

She drew in a ragged breath. "You hated me so much?
Hated my *mother* so much?"

"Of course not! You and your mother were innocent
of everything. That was clear from the beginning and
I was sorry you were hurt peripherally by everything.
What choice did I have, though? Once I started to discover the magnitude of what your father had done, his
years of corruption and greed, I had to follow through. I
was an officer of the law, Lauren. I couldn't let him get
away with it."

"Of course you couldn't."

She was suddenly exhausted, utterly wrung out. The
emotional roller coaster of the evening had taken a grim
turn and she wanted the hell off.

She rose, desperate for space and distance. "You were wrong. I didn't need to know this. I could have lived quite well the rest of my life without knowing that the man I'm…that I have feelings for is the same man who destroyed my family."

His features twisted with pain. "Lauren—"

"Good night, Daniel."

She walked to her bedroom and closed the door gently, though it took every ounce of self-control not to slam the thing over and over to vent some of this consuming pain.

She sank down onto the bed—the very same bed where he had just touched her, caressed her—and buried her face in her hands.

She heard the echo of the harsh words he had said. *I wanted him to pay. No, I wanted to bleed him dry.*

All these years, she had assumed correctly the awkwardness between her and Daniel had something to do with her father's sins. She just never imagined what was beneath it all.

Would her father's crimes haunt her for the rest of her life? She thought tonight when she was in Daniel's arms that she might just have a chance at happiness. Once more, like that imagery Daniel had used, the dead giant of the past was crushing her, smothering her, sucking any trace of joy from her present.

Daniel had been the one to shine a magnifying glass onto R.J.'s actions, the catalyst to everything that came after. If he hadn't come home motivated by vengeance, perhaps none of the rest of it would have happened.

She pressed a hand to her mouth to hold back the sob there. The man who had kissed her with such aching tenderness seemed a different individual from the hard-eyed stranger in her living room who had spoken of revenge and hatred.

Intellectually, she knew she couldn't really blame Daniel for her father's death and for the circumstances leading up to it. R.J. had made his own choices, had created his own destiny with his arrogance and his greed.

He couldn't honestly have thought he could get away with stealing so much money forever, it was only a matter of time—and a dogged investigator—before he would be caught.

R.J. had made his bed and lined it with stolen taxpayer funds. He had lied and cheated and stolen his way to a fortune. The sheer breadth of his wrongdoing still took her breath away.

Circumstances had put Daniel in the role of that investigator. She understood he had been doing his job. And if not him, it would have been someone else on the police force or an auditor somewhere or another elected official with sharp eyes.

But it had been Daniel. He had known, all these years, that he had set the wheels in motion that had crushed her mother and her. His investigation had resulted in her father's last, horribly selfish act—leaving them behind to face the shambles he had created.

Lauren curled up on her bed, hugging her arms tightly around herself. She had given her heart to the man who had destroyed her father and her family.

She couldn't snatch it back. It was entirely too late for that. She loved him and she couldn't just stuff all those feelings back into her subconscious now that they had been set free to soar through her.

She loved him. Now she just had to figure out how she could get past the brutal truth.

And how she could spend another day trapped in this house with him, pretending her heart wasn't broken.

Chapter 13

She finally fell into a restless sleep shortly before dawn. When she woke gritty-eyed and achy a few hours later, her first instinct was to cower in her bedroom all day, just drag the blankets over her head and hide away from the world.

Or at least from Daniel.

She knew she couldn't. She had a guest in her home, a young, frightened girl who needed her. Lauren knew she couldn't abandon her—for Rosa's sake, she would have to walk out there and face him, no matter how much she dreaded it.

She didn't know what she could possibly say to him. She wasn't angry with him. Somehow in the night, the worst of her betrayal had faded and she was left with only this deep sadness in her heart.

Most of all, she hated that five years after his suicide,

her father's legacy was still tainting everything good and wonderful she wanted. She loved Daniel. Nothing had changed that.

She loved him and as she had tossed and turned the night before, her mind raced through their interactions the last few days and she was fairly certain she saw signs that he might care for her in return.

Could she move beyond his revelation? she wondered. Or every time she looked at his strong, beautiful features, would she see his hunger for vengeance and the chain reaction of calamities it had wrought in her life?

She didn't know. She hated thinking about him toiling away, digging through her family's dirty laundry, and wondering at all the soiled linens he might have uncovered there.

She was quite sure she still didn't know the full story of all that her father had done. She didn't really *want* to know, but she hated thinking Daniel might have all that information.

Lauren pushed the blankets away. She wasn't a coward. She never would have survived the rigors of med school and a grueling residency if she had been. She was strong enough to walk out there and pretend all was fine, even though she hated knowing she and Daniel would return to the tension that had marked their relationship before these last few days.

She took a long, hot shower and spent longer than usual getting dressed, driven to take extra pains with her hair and makeup as armor against the day and the awkwardness she knew waited for her.

Even with blush and more eye makeup than usual, she still looked haggard and worn-out, but at least her hair looked good, falling in soft waves around her face.

She supposed a girl had to take what she could get.

Filling her lungs with a deep, cleansing breath, she pushed open her bedroom door and prepared to spend the day with a polite smile stuck to her face, as if she had taken a staple gun to it.

She followed the low murmur of voices and found Rosa in the kitchen talking comfortably in Spanish to another woman, with Daniel nowhere in sight.

Rosa smiled a welcome when she saw her, as did Teresa Hendricks, the only female deputy in the sheriff's office.

"Hi, Teresa," Lauren said. "This is a surprise."

"Morning." Teresa gave her wide, friendly smile that made everyone trust her, good guys and bad guys alike. "The sheriff had some business in the office that couldn't wait and asked me to come spell him for the morning. He should be back this afternoon. Hope you don't mind that I grabbed some cocoa out of the cupboard. You've got quite a collection."

"I…no. Of course not. Do you want coffee?"

"No. Cocoa will do me. I'm a bit of a fanatic, too."

That was Lauren. The crazy doctor who self-medicated with chocolate to heal all wounds.

She had a feeling she better stock up in the coming months.

She forced a smile for Teresa and joined them at the table. "So how are you? How are John and the kids?"

"Great. Just great. They keep me running every minute."

Lauren treated Teresa's two children at her clinic. They were great kids—Casey was ten and Mia was twelve and Lauren had been their primary care physician since she moved here five years earlier.

Envious of Teresa's fluency with the language, Lauren hauled out her halting Spanish to ask Rosa how she was feeling. She didn't need to hear the girl's answer to see that every day she seemed better.

Something was different about her today. Her bruises were fading, but that was only part of the conversion in her. Lauren tilted her head, studying the girl. There was a new light in her eyes, something that hadn't been there before.

Hope, Lauren realized with a little catch in her throat. Rosa no longer wore that lost, disillusioned look in her eyes. For the first time since Rosa opened her eyes in the bed of Dale Richins's pickup truck, she looked as if she was happy to be alive, as if she believed in a future.

She had a long, arduous journey ahead of her, Lauren knew. But she was on her way, and that was the important thing.

Rosa chattered something to Teresa and the deputy answered just as quickly.

"How did you learn Spanish so well?" Lauren asked.

"I spent a couple years in Guatemala on a church mission. I've lost a lot over the last fifteen years but I practice whenever I can."

Rosa said something and Teresa answered her and the two of them chattered away in Spanish for a moment, with Lauren catching one or two words in every sentence.

Though after several days, Rosa seemed comfortable talking to Daniel, Lauren had never seen her talk to him with such animation. She talked to Lauren, but always with Daniel as a go-between.

She must have been desperately missing the freedom of having another woman to converse with, Lauren realized. Had Daniel picked Teresa as his replacement for just that reason? she wondered. Because he wanted Rosa to have Spanish-speaking company to talk to?

"Sorry," Teresa said, making a rueful face after a moment. "Didn't mean to exclude you."

"Not a problem." She smiled. "To be honest, I'm glad you're here to talk to her. I'm sure she's frustrated with having to repeat everything she says to me a hundred times before I get it, or use Daniel as a translator."

With the deputy there and Rosa in such good hands, she could escape the confines of the house for a moment.

The thought whispered through her mind and suddenly she was desperate for a little air and to see something besides her own walls. "In fact, I have some paperwork at the clinic that I've put off longer than I should have. If you don't think it's unforgivably rude for me to leave, I would love the chance to run down there for an hour or so and try to gather some things to work on here at home tonight."

"No problem." Teresa smiled. "We'll just stay here and have a good visit while we dig into your hot chocolate stash."

"*Mi* cocoa *es su* cocoa," Lauren said with a smile.

She grabbed a coat out of the closet and found her keys. Fifteen minutes later, she felt like a prisoner out on work release as she pulled her Volvo into the parking lot of the clinic. She paid a high school student to shovel off her parking lot every time it snowed. Brandon Tanner had a pickup with a plow on the front and took the job seriously, never missing a storm.

Lauren walked through the cleared parking lot and unlocked the door to her clinic. She was here often alone by herself. Usually it didn't bother her, but today the emptiness of it seemed to echo, giving her the creeps.

That's what happened when she was surrounded by people for three days. Rosa and Daniel had been a constant presence and she was just having a tough time adjusting to solitude.

Still, she shivered and headed straight for the thermostat. She had turned it down before she left three days earlier, keeping the temperature just warm enough to keep the water pipes from freezing, but certainly not a comfortable level for anyone but a penguin.

She turned it up, then walked to her office at the end of the hallway.

She was proud of what she had done here. She ran an efficient, effective operation. Though she still had her detractors, many more people in the community trusted her than didn't. She treated their grandchildren, their grandparents, and everyone in between.

She was good at her job and she loved her patients, something most big-city physicians couldn't understand. She was invested in their lives, in their health.

When Karen Elliot's cholesterol level dipped twenty points from her new exercise regimen, Lauren rejoiced as much as she did. When Dallas and Sara Fitzgerald's baby overcame a rough start as a two-pound preemie and learned to walk by eleven months, Lauren had been the first one standing in line to cheer her on.

She worried about them, she grieved with them, she celebrated with them.

This was her town. Her life. She loved it here, warts and all.

If not for her father's actions, she would have missed this. She stared at the closed door of her office, startled by the realization. Before R.J.'s arrest, Lauren had been fielding offers from medical facilities across the U.S. She had most seriously been considering an attending position at the Chicago hospital where she finished her residency.

After her father's suicide and all the horrible revelations began to jumble up one after the other, she had pulled her name from consideration. She had known she must return to Moose Springs. As she had told Daniel, she felt a huge obligation to the people of this community who had, in effect, paid for her education by default.

She had come home to help her mother try to pick up the pieces of their shattered world and face down the stares and whispers. In the process, Lauren had begun to build this clinic. She had created something good here— something that might not have existed if not for the chain reaction Daniel had started in his quest for vengeance.

Daniel. She was still going to have to face him at some point. Could they find their way past the rubble of their shared history?

She shook off the depression suddenly settling over her shoulders and pushed open her office door. Her voicemail light was flashing. Big surprise there. The rest of the world didn't stand still just because she took a few days off.

She keyed through the lengthy list of missed calls on the caller ID menu. Only twelve missed calls—and six of those were from Kendall Fox. She sighed. The man didn't seem to understand the concept of rejection.

She turned on her computer to print out some files and was just about to hit the playback messages button on her phone when it rang, sounding abnormally loud in the empty clinic.

She intended to let it ring, since she absolutely didn't want to talk to a drug company salesman or an insurance rep right now. But out of curiosity, she checked the caller ID and groaned when she saw Kendall's name and mobile number.

This was ridiculous. She thought she had made her feelings clear the other day at the hospital, but apparently she would have to come down harder.

"Hello?"

There was a brief pause, as if he hadn't quite expected her to answer. "Lauren! I've been trying to reach you for days."

"I've been off. I just came into the office to catch up on some paperwork and saw that you had called."

"Only a half-dozen times. I would have called your home or cell but I couldn't seem to track down those numbers. Can it really be possible that I have failed to get the personal contact numbers of the most gorgeous doctor with privileges at my hospital?"

If she weren't so tired, she could no doubt come up with some brilliantly concise reply that would discourage him once and for all without being rude. But with her brain sluggish and slow, nothing came to mind.

"You found me now. What did you need?"

"Aren't you even going to ask me how the Sundance after-party went?"

"How did it go?" she asked automatically, hoping her complete disinterest didn't filter through her voice.

"Miserable. I was lonely and bored and missed you every second."

Which meant he probably had only one girl on each arm.

"Listen," he went on, "since you've been bragging about the cross-country skiing in your little cow patch, I decided to come up this way and see what you're talking about. I'm just outside town now. I figured I could take you to lunch, then you could show me the trails you're always talking about. What do you say?"

Just what she needed, for Kendall to show up and complicate everything.

She sighed. Last week, she turned him down because she wasn't interested in a flirtation with a coworker. After the last few days spent with Daniel, she knew she could never go out with Dr. Fox, charming though he might be.

How could she even look at another man? She loved Daniel Galvez with all her heart.

"I didn't realize it was within my power to completely wow you into speechlessness."

Heat rose in her cheeks as she realized she had been woolgathering about Daniel instead of responding to Kendall's lunch invitation.

"Sorry. It's been a…strange few days. I'm afraid my mind is running in a hundred different directions. I'm sorry, but today isn't a good day for me."

"Are you saying that because you don't want to go with me or because it really isn't a good day?"

She thought of Rosa at home and the FBI agents who would be on their way to take her with them in a few hours. She should be there with her, she realized, and was ashamed of herself for taking a coward's way out and escaping to the office.

"It's not a good day."

"But if it were, you still wouldn't go, would you?"

She sighed. "I would have no problem showing you the ski trails around here, Kendall. And lunch would probably be fine, as long as you don't consider it a date."

"And if I did?"

"Then I would tell you no. It's nothing personal, I promise. I have the greatest respect for you as a doctor and I enjoy your company, but I just have a strict policy about not hooking up with other doctors I work with. I've had a few bad experiences where things became messy and it's easier all around to keep those parts of my life separate."

She paused. "And to be honest, I'm involved with someone right now."

It wasn't precisely a lie. Her heart was involved with Daniel, even if they had yet to even go on an actual date.

"Let me guess. The big, bad cow-patch sheriff."

She blinked. Were her feelings that obvious? "I...why would you say that?"

"I don't know. A vibe I caught between you two. Am I right?"

She didn't know how to answer that. After a moment, he gave a short laugh. "I'm right. If you ever get tired of the tough jock type, you know where to find me."

"I'll keep that in mind."

"Hey, speaking of the sheriff, what was the deal with that girl we treated last week? I meant to stop by and see how she was doing, but she had more security around her room than a movie star hiding out from the paparazzi. Next I know, she was released. Any word on how she's doing?"

"She and her baby are both fine," Lauren answered. "She's an amazingly resilient young woman."

There was an odd pause on the line and she thought for a moment his cell call had dropped, before he spoke again. "She had some great doctors. Especially the extraordinarily talented one she had in the E.R."

"I'm sure that has had a great deal to do with her rapid recovery," Lauren said dryly.

He laughed, though it sounded oddly strained. "Well,

since I'm already in town, the least you can do is tell me how to get to the ski trail you're always talking about."

"Right." She gave him directions to the trailhead for an easy-to-moderate groomed trail that led past pine and aspen to a frozen waterfall.

"You can just ski there from your house?"

"Right. I'm just a quarter mile down the road," she said absently. "The last house before you get to the trailhead."

"Good to know. Thanks."

He seemed in a hurry to hang up after obtaining the directions.

After she said goodbye and disconnected the call, she spent a fruitless twenty minutes answering email and trying to finish her paperwork. When she realized she had been staring at the same computer screen for ten minutes, she finally gave up, gathering the papers she needed and stuffed them in her briefcase.

She didn't want to be here, she wanted to be home with Daniel and Rosa. The irony didn't escape her—for three days she had balked at being stuck in her house, had felt trapped and isolated and restless, but now she didn't want to be anywhere else.

Would Daniel be back at her house yet? she wondered. And if he had returned, was she ready to face him?

Yes. The knowledge washed through her, warm and sure. She loved him. She loved his laugh, she loved his strength, she loved the deep sense of honor that had compelled him to tell her something painful at a time when any other man would have ignored his conscience and taken what he wanted and she had been more than willing to give.

That he had started the investigation that destroyed her

father didn't matter. She sat up in her office chair, staring unseeing at the sage walls. She loved him. He was a loving son who had been grieving for his father and angry at the mistreatment of his mother. She couldn't blame him for wanting vengeance.

Daniel may have been the catalyst to the finale, but R.J. had been completely responsible for his own downfall.

She thought of the heat of Daniel's kiss, the tenderness of his touch, his kindness with Rosa. That was the man she loved.

She wanted what they had started the night before. No, she wanted more. With a deep, fierce ache, she wanted to see him, to tell him she was sorry for her reaction the night before and the cold words she had uttered.

Despite the anticipation spiraling through her at seeing him again and trying to make things right between them, she couldn't seem to shake a vague sense of unease as she climbed into her Volvo and headed back to her house. She couldn't quite put a finger on it, but something niggled at her, some dissonant tone to the music of her morning.

She was just tired, she assured herself as she neared her house. Exhaustion from her sleepless night was playing tricks on her.

All seemed quiet at her house as she pulled into the driveway. Smoke curled up from the chimney and sunlight glittered off the fresh snow. When she opened the garage door, she saw Daniel hadn't returned. Teresa Hendricks's personal SUV was still parked in the second bay.

She walked into the house and her unease ratcheted up a notch. Something wasn't right. The television was playing in the family room, but neither Rosa nor Teresa were anywhere in sight.

"Teresa? Rosa? Hello?" No one answered.

"Hello?" she called again, only to be met by more silence.

She grabbed her cell phone out of her coat pocket and punched 911. Just as she moved her thumb to hit the send button on her way to check Rosa's bedroom, she heard a low, anguished moan.

Warily, her heart pumping with thick urgency, she followed the sound to the entryway, then shock sucked the air from her lungs at what she found there.

Chapter 14

Daniel perused the duty roster for the week, his second-in-command across the desk.

With a department of only eight full-time officers, including himself, sometimes personnel issues and making sure everybody's schedules worked for the slot they were assigned was his biggest challenge.

"I still don't know what we're going to do about tomorrow night." Kurt Banning shook his head. "I've juggled and juggled but no matter how we shake it, we're still short a deputy and we're completely maxed out on overtime this month."

"Davis and McKinnon said they're coming for our witness this afternoon. That should free me up from guard duty so you can add me back on to the rotation. I can handle the graveyard shift tonight and a double shift tomorrow."

"You sure about that? Maybe you ought to take a few days off after your tough ordeal of sitting around Lauren's place all day drinking tea and watching movies."

"Ha ha. You're hilarious, Banning."

"So they tell me." His lieutenant and good friend grinned. Banning had given him a hard time today about his "easy" guard duty at Lauren's place. They probably would have a tough time believing he would rather have been out in the middle of a blizzard directing traffic than enduring more time in Lauren's company, knowing she despised him now.

"Just put me on the schedule. I don't mind the extra hours."

"Will do. So the feds are coming for the girl today, you said?"

"Right. In a few hours. They're moving her to a safe house in the city so they can start prepping her for grand jury testimony."

The deputy shook his head. "Hell of a case to fall into our lap, wasn't it? My heart just breaks for that little girl and for the others who came over the border with her."

"She's had a tough time of it, but she's hanging in. Tell me what's been going on with the Cole case."

They spent a few more moments discussing progress in some ongoing investigations and were just starting to wrap things up when they heard a shout from outside.

"Sheriff! You need to get in here now!" Peggy yelled from the dispatch desk.

He and Banning shared one quick look and his lieutenant's expression mirrored his own shock. Peggy had been dispatching for thirty years and she never lost her cool. The urgency in her voice moved them both to action and they rushed from the office.

She had put the 911 call on the speaker and his gut tightened with raw fear when he instantly recognized Lauren's voice.

"I need an air ambulance immediately at my house, Peggy. Officer down. Deputy Hendricks has been shot in the stomach. She's bleeding heavily and drifting in and out of consciousness. I need the local paramedics here with oxygen but call LifeFlight first and get them in the air."

"I'm on it."

"Where's Daniel?"

He rushed forward and picked up the mike. "I'm here, Lauren. Are you hurt? Where's Rosa?"

"I'm fine. I don't *know* where Rosa is."

Though he could tell she was trying her best to stay in control, he could hear the anguished panic filter through her voice and it ripped him apart. "I went to the clinic for a while. I was only gone maybe an hour. I just walked in the door and found Teresa on the floor and no sign of Rosa. I think they've got her. Please hurry."

"I'm on my way, sweetheart. Hang on."

He rushed for the door, strapping on his weapon and yelling orders as he went for Banning to let the FBI know, mobilize all deputies and call the county sheriff for re-inforcements.

"We need to establish a search perimeter and block off all exits into and out of town. I don't know who we're looking for or how many suspects, but whoever it is, they're armed and dangerous. Do whatever it takes to protect yourselves and the girl."

Sick with worry and guilt, he rushed to Lauren's house with his lights and sirens blaring. How the hell could this have happened? He should never have left her house.

Skulking away that morning before she woke had been an act of cowardice, borne from a selfish wish to avoid seeing the disgust in her eyes.

As a result, a damn good deputy was injured and Rosa was missing and he didn't know how he would ever live with himself.

For the second time in his life, he had let his own emotions stand in the way of the job.

Put it away, he ordered himself. There would be time for recriminations and blame-slinging later. Now he needed to focus on the situation, on Rosa and Teresa.

He covered the distance between the sheriff's office and her house in record time and jerked his Tahoe to a stop in the driveway. Inside, he found Teresa on the floor of the entryway, with Lauren applying a pressure bandage to her blood-soaked abdomen.

She looked up at him with vast relief. "Daniel!"

"How is she?"

"Stable, for now, but she's losing blood fast. Peggy says LifeFlight is on its way. Our volunteer medics should be bringing oxygen."

Teresa blinked her eyes open when she saw him and struggled to sit up, but Lauren held her fast.

"Sheriff," Teresa mumbled, her eyes glazed. "Sorry. So sorry."

He had a narrow window of opportunity to obtain as much information as he could. Though his instinct was to let her rest and conserve her energy, he had to push. "What happened? Where's Rosa?"

Teresa groaned. "Don't know. She was in the bathroom when the doorbell rang. I told her to stay put there. Lock the door. Through the peephole, I saw a blond guy, looked familiar. Five-ten, five-eleven, maybe. Red SUV in driveway."

She coughed a little and Lauren changed compresses. His gut clenched and he thought of Teresa's two kids and John, her husband. If she didn't make it through this, he would never forgive himself.

"I shouldn't have answered the door," Teresa mumbled. "Rookie mistake. Knew better. Guy asked for Lauren. Said he was a friend. She's not here, I tell him. He says he'll wait and pushes his way inside. Next I know, he's got a weapon out, tells me not to move. Asks me where the girl is. I played dumb, just like we talked about, but he wasn't fooled. Knew she was there, he said. Told me to get her. I tried to draw my weapon, then he…shot me. Everything after that's blurry."

"Did he find Rosa?"

"I don't know, Sheriff. I don't remember. I heard him looking, tearing through the house, but then…the pain. I passed out."

Before he could ask her any more questions, the volunteer paramedics arrived, bringing oxygen and equipment.

Daniel forced himself to step back and let them do their job. His deputy was in good hands. Lauren would do everything possible for her here and that high level of care would continue after the chopper airlifted her to the University of Utah.

He needed to focus on finding Rosa. He headed to the bathroom. According to Teresa, Rosa had been there when everything went down.

The bathroom door had been kicked in, he saw immediately, careful not to disturb any forensics.

That matched Teresa's story. She said she told Rosa to lock the door. The perp would have checked every door, found this one locked and probably known immediately this was where he would find his prey.

Daniel looked around, then his gaze caught on something discordant. The hamper had been moved. He had showered in this bathroom for three days and he absolutely remembered it being against the other wall.

Now it was shoved in an awkward spot by the toilet—and directly under the small, high window.

His heart kicked up a pace as a small glimmer of hope shot through him. Rosa could fit through that window. She was petite, even with her pregnancy. If she heard a gunshot, would she have cowered in here like a frightened rabbit or would she have tried to run? He had to believe the latter. She had already proved her courage and strength. He couldn't imagine her just waiting in here for her fate.

He was convinced when CSU dusted the windowsill, they would find Rosa's prints there. It didn't mean she had escaped, he reminded himself. The shooter easily could have figured out the same thing and followed her. But at least it was something to hang on to.

The hot spurt of adrenaline in treating a trauma victim, especially one she knew and cared about, sustained Lauren through the next fifteen minutes as the air medics arrived and were briefed on Teresa's condition.

She stood back and watched them load the litter into the waiting helicopter for the short flight to the city.

"You riding along, Dr. Maxwell?" Jolie Carr, the flight nurse, asked her.

She thought seriously about it for maybe half a second, then shook her head. "Her condition is stable. You have things under control for the fifteen-minute flight and I know you don't need the extra weight. Since we have a possible kidnap victim out there somewhere, I'd better stick close just in case I'm needed here."

Jolie nodded and strapped down the gurney. "Understandable. We'll take care of her."

"I know you will. Have the attending at the trauma center page me if there are any questions."

"Will do."

She climbed in and closed the door behind her. Lauren stepped back and watched the chopper lift off, swirling the powdery snow in a cloud as it rose into the air.

She pulled her sweater closer around her, chilled to the bone by more than just the temperature and the chopper's vortex. She had done all she could for Teresa. Now she could only trust in the University of Utah trauma team and pray.

She blew out a breath and returned to her house, which bustled with activity. Cops and emergency workers from every nearby jurisdiction had already descended with remarkable speed.

Inside, she saw Daniel giving orders to several other men. He towered over them and even from here she could feel the air of command radiating off him.

When she looked beneath the surface, she had to close her eyes and whisper another prayer, this one for him. Under the layer of control and authority, she could just catch a glimpse of something else, something raw and dark, almost tortured.

Since she returned to town and opened her clinic, she had seen Daniel in action in all kinds of tough circumstances. Bad car accidents, mine rescues, ugly domestic disputes. No matter what the situation, he always seemed to have an air of quiet competence about him. He was a deep pool of calm in a troubled sea.

Right now, despite his thin veneer of control, he looked adrift.

When he seemed to finish talking to the others and they left for their respective duties, she walked to him on impulse and laid a hand on his arm.

His dark eyes seared into hers with a raw emotion and her chest ached with the urge to wrap her arms around his waist and never let go.

"I think she's going to be okay, Daniel. She's tough and help arrived not long after it happened. That's a big plus in her favor."

If she hadn't followed impulse and returned to the house when she did, she feared Teresa would have bled to death right in her entryway, but she didn't tell Daniel that. His eyes burned with too much guilt already.

"This is my fault. I should have been here."

"Then you would have been the one with a bullet in your gut," she pointed out.

"I don't have two kids who need their mother." The anguish in his voice destroyed her. She squeezed his arm again.

"I think she's going to be okay," she repeated. "We just have to wait and see, but she's young and strong and has the thought of those kids to help her hang in."

He nodded, and she thought her words penetrated.

"Any sign of Rosa?" Lauren asked.

"There's a chance she may have gone out the bathroom window." He paused. "You saw her this morning, didn't you? Do you remember what she was wearing?"

She tried to picture Teresa and Rosa as they chattered

around the kitchen table. "Jeans and a sweatshirt. The yellow one."

"What about shoes? I bought her a pair when I picked up the other stuff, but she hasn't worn them except that first day I brought her here."

Lauren shook her head. "I can't say. I didn't notice her feet this morning. I hope so. I hate to think of her out on the run somewhere in the snow with no shoes."

"Sure as hell beats the alternative," he said grimly.

She shivered. "You're right. You're absolutely right."

"If she's out there, we'll find her, Lauren."

"I know you will."

She paused, her mind racing with a hundred things she wanted to say to him. This wasn't the time for any of them. "Be careful," she murmured instead.

He nodded absently but before he could answer, Kurt Banning hurried over to them. "Sheriff, we think we may have something. Joe Pacheco, a mile or so down the road, called Peggy to report some movement in his horse barn. He thought he saw someone sneaking in there. He thought it might be a kid, by the size, but he thought with all the activity down this way, he should let us know."

"If it is Rosa, she's probably terrified out of her mind. We can't just run in there with guns blazing. She doesn't know who the good guys and who the bad guys are here."

"She knows you," Lauren said. "She won't be frightened if she sees you."

"You're right. Kurt, take charge here. I'll take a couple of the county deputies and see if we can roust her out. Lauren, she may need treatment for frostbite and exposure, especially if she ran a mile through the snow without shoes."

"Right. I'll go back to the clinic and meet you there."

He hurried away, that brief glimpse of emotion shielded now. All she could see was a tough, determined male. He would find Rosa, she assured herself. If anyone could bring her back, it was Daniel.

Her car was hemmed in by rescue vehicles so one of the deputies rushed her to the clinic before hurrying off to the roadblocks at the routes leading out of town.

She unlocked the doors and headed immediately to her treatment room to begin prepping it with any items she could think of that might be needed to treat someone with possible exposure.

She was putting clean blankets in the clinic's small warming unit and wishing for one of her nurses to help her with some of these details when she thought she heard the outside door opening.

That was fast, she thought. Amazingly fast! Such speed had to be a good sign, didn't it?

"Daniel?" she called. "I'm in the treatment room. Bring her straight back here."

No one answered, and she frowned. Had she been hearing things? She turned away from the warmer to investigate, then gasped and stumbled backward, just managing to stop before she burned herself.

To her shock, Kendall Fox loomed in the doorway, but this was a far different man than the polished charmer who flirted with every nurse in the hospital. His hair was messy, his clothes disordered, and he looked savagely furious.

Her heartbeat kicked up a notch. "Kendall!" she exclaimed. "What are you doing here?"

Even as she asked the question, somehow she knew.

It wasn't possible, it couldn't be, but she couldn't come up with any other explanation.

Her mind raced, trying to piece together a puzzle that made no sense. Teresa had reported her shooter was a blond white male about five-ten, which described Dr. Fox perfectly.

"Where is she?" he demanded.

She played for time. "Who?"

"You know," he growled. "The stupid little bitch who is ruining my life. Where is she?"

Panic sputtered through her and her eyes darted around the room, frantically looking for some kind of weapon. Warm blankets wouldn't exactly cause lasting harm, she was afraid, and any sharp medical implements were wrapped in sterile packaging.

She had a feeling Kendall wouldn't sit patiently and wait while she peeled back the plastic on a surgical kit for something sharp.

Think, she ordered herself, but she couldn't focus on anything but her shock and fear.

"I don't know what you're talking about," she finally said.

"Don't play stupid. You suck at it. You know. The girl you've got staying at your house. If I'd had any idea she was one of ours the night you brought her in, you can bet she wouldn't have made it out of the E.R."

Icy cold blossomed in her stomach. "You don't mean that," she said, sickened at the blunt claim, especially delivered in such a cold, emotionless voice.

"Don't I? No way am I going to let her testify to some frigging grand jury and destroy everything."

This couldn't be happening. She knew Kendall. She had talked with him—even laughed with him—just a few hours before. Could she really have been so blind as to have missed the darkness skulking inside him?

One of ours, he had said, and the implication behind the words sickened her further.

"You're the fifth man in the smuggling ring."

"I'm not the fifth anything. I'm number one, baby. The whole thing was my idea. You would not believe the kind of money a few stupid whores have put in my pockets."

"They're not whores, they're children! Young girls who had no choice about the things they were forced to do! What you've done is obscene. Despicable."

Rage spasmed over his features and he stepped closer. She had nowhere else to go, with the blanket warmer at her back. "Don't sit in judgment of me, Dr. Self-Righteous. I didn't have a rich, crooked daddy to put me through med school. I had debts. Big ones. I had to do something."

"By kidnapping girls and forcing them into prostitution? How does a med student go from the Hippocratic oath to peddling human flesh?"

"I'm not some kind of monster!"

Could he honestly think what he had done was anything *but* hideously monstrous?

"I went to med school in San Diego and my last year I started working a clinic over the border," Kendall said. "It was a legitimate job. But then I got the brilliant idea to make a little money on the side. I started packing a few things back over each trip I crossed the border. Prescription drugs, Ruffies, that kind of thing. After a while, I thought, why not people? And here we are."

She let out a breath. "Here we are. You've now moved from drug smuggling to kidnapping, enforced prostitution and attempted murder. Nice career move, Dr. Fox."

"Shut up," he snarled. "You don't know anything about this."

"You're the one who sent Gilberto Mata to Rosa's room at the hospital, aren't you? I wondered how he knew where to find her."

"What the hell else was I supposed to do? She was going to ruin everything. She said she was going to go to the police and tell them everything she knew. We couldn't just leave her running loose to flap her gums to anyone who would listen. We were screwed. Gilberto said he could take care of things. My only mistake was in trusting him."

"How did you figure out she was here in Moose Springs?"

"Lucky guess. I saw the way you hovered over her at the hospital. I figured you would at least know where they took her after she was released, all I had to do was charm it out of you. I never imagined she was in your own house until you told me."

She closed her eyes, sick to think she had led him right to Rosa. She had to find some comfort that Rosa was safe from him for now, or he wouldn't be here looking for her.

She, on the other hand, was in serious trouble. So far he hadn't pulled out any kind of weapon, but she knew he must have one, the same weapon he had used to shoot Teresa. He wouldn't be telling her this if he had any intention of leaving her alive here.

She didn't want to die. She needed to get through this, if only to tell Daniel she didn't blame him for her father's sins, that she knew and understood he had done nothing wrong during his investigation of her father.

That she loved him.

She wanted a future—a future with Daniel, if he would give her a chance.

If she could somehow reverse their positions slightly, she might be able to pull the instrument tray behind her to give her enough time to escape. It was a long shot, but she had to do something. She refused to stand here and accept the fate he intended for her.

She shifted slightly, edging in a barely perceptible half circle. "How many girls are we talking about here?" she asked to distract him.

He shrugged. "Enough. We have two houses in Utah, but the real money is in Vegas and Phoenix."

She slid a little more to the left. She started to reach behind her for the instrument tray when she heard the outside door open.

"Lauren?" Daniel's voice called. She and Kendall gazed at each other for half a second, then she opened her mouth to call a warning. Before the words could escape, Kendall moved fast, grabbing her in a choke hold and shoving his hand over her mouth.

Here was the gun, she realized wildly as he pulled it out of his pocket and held it to her head. "Not a word," he hissed. "Or your sheriff is going to have a nice gunshot wound to the chest."

She choked back her tiny sound of distress, fear a hard, vicious ball in her gut. Her brain felt numb, sluggish with sudden dread.

She couldn't bear the idea of something happening to Daniel. If he walked through that door, she had no doubt Kendall would shoot him, just as he had shot Teresa.

She had to protect him. She *had* to, no matter what the cost.

Kendall eased them both behind the door and she felt the slick cold metal pressed against the skin at her temple.

She had one chance only. With a prayer for courage, she drew in a deep breath, then clamped her teeth as hard as she could on the flesh of his palm.

As she hoped, he instinctively moved his hand away, just far away for her to yell, "He's got a gun!"

"You stupid bitch," Kendall growled. He backhanded her exactly where her stitches were from the attack by Gilberto Mata, striking her so hard she whipped back and struck the wall.

For a moment, she was light-headed as pain exploded in her head and cheek. She reeled, her knees suddenly weak, and started to slide to the floor. He grabbed her before she could hit the ground and yanked her in front of him, the gun again at her temple, just as Daniel crashed through the door.

Chapter 15

A smart cop doesn't just run headlong into a room when somebody yells *gun*.

He takes a minute to case the situation, to call for backup, to devise a strategy.

Daniel knew all that, but he didn't give a damn. All he could focus on was the hoarse panic in Lauren's voice and the tiny yelp of pain he heard her utter right after her warning.

Before he had time to even wonder what the threat might be on the other side, he whipped out his weapon and plowed through the door.

What he found was worse than anything he might have imagined. A man had her in a choke hold and had jammed a big, ugly black Glock against her temple.

"Stop right there, Sheriff," the bastard holding her yelled, like something out of a bad Western. It took him only an instant to recognize the smarmy doctor from the emergency room who had been hitting on Lauren the night they took Rosa in, then a few days later in the hospital lobby.

Fox. Kendall Fox.

His mind registered a dozen things simultaneously— among them that she looked dazed, her eyes blurry with pain, and a tiny trickle of blood seeped from the bandage on her cheek.

He died a thousand deaths wondering what Fox might have done to her—and trying to figure out his own next move.

The bastard had already shot one cop. He had to be the one who had wounded Teresa. If Daniel played this wrong, he knew Fox wouldn't hesitate to shoot him, too, and then where would Lauren be?

And Rosa. Damn it all to hell. He should have at least taken the time to make sure she was safe before rushing in here.

"Let's all just take it easy." Daniel infused his voice with every ounce of calm he could muster, not an easy task when he wanted to rip the son of a bitch apart with his bare hands for hurting Lauren.

Fox was sweating, he saw, and the gun in his hand trembled ever so slightly against her head. "Shut up," he barked. "Just shut the hell up and drop your weapon or I'm going to shoot her."

This was the part where a good negotiator would placate the suspect, earn his trust, establish some sort of rapport. Daniel just couldn't do it. Not when Lauren was in danger.

"You hurt her more than you already have and you can be damn sure you won't take another breath," he promised, in that same calm, controlled voice he had to hope cloaked his gut-wrenching fear.

The doctor's hand trembled a little more on the weapon while Daniel forced his own hand to remain perfectly still.

Fox looked trapped, his eyes darting wildly around the room like some kind of wild creature looking for a convenient hole to slink into. It was obvious he was searching for any kind of escape from the mess he had created.

Daniel just had to make sure his way out didn't involve any more harm to Lauren.

He took his eyes off the suspect for half a second, just long enough to reassure himself that she was all right. She still seemed dazed and he saw fear in her eyes. But when she met his gaze, they brimmed with a deep reservoir of trust that humbled him.

"All I want is the little *puta*," Fox growled. "Where is she?"

He assumed the bastard meant Rosa. "I don't know. We haven't found her," he lied. No way in hell was he going to tell the man she was out in his vehicle wrapped in blankets with the heater going full blast.

Daniel had only come in first to make sure Lauren had an exam room ready before he carried Rosa inside to be treated for her mild hypothermia. Now he could only be grateful to whatever instinct had compelled him to leave her in the vehicle.

She was far from safe, though. He knew the dangers. He would rather she were miles away in the FBI safe house with Cale Davis and Gage McKinnon.

Heavy pressure dug into his lungs, the onus of knowing he had to protect two women. He couldn't mess this up.

Fox hissed a pungent oath. "I don't believe you."

Daniel shrugged. "Believe what you want. She's not here. Who knows? She could be halfway to Juarez by now. It's just the three of us. Now why don't you let Lauren go so you and I can figure out a way to work this out. I know you don't want to hurt her."

His arm tightened around her throat and he dug the gun into her temple harder. Daniel's gut clenched. He could see the desperation in Fox's eyes, the grim realization of what he had done already and the implications of those actions.

He had shot a deputy sheriff. He had to be feeling any chance at a future that didn't involve serious prison time slipping away.

"This wasn't supposed to happen. This whole thing has been screwed up from the minute we brought that little bitch over the border. It's all her fault everything is falling apart."

Daniel hitched in a breath as he saw that Glock quiver again. The man was as twitchy as a polecat bedded down with a rattlesnake.

"Look—" he kept his voice slow, even "—let Lauren go and you and I can talk about this. I'm sure if we put our heads together we can figure out what to do from here. She doesn't need to be in the middle of this. I know you don't want to hurt her."

His arm clenched around her throat. Any tighter and he would be cutting off her air supply, Daniel feared.

"Here's a better idea. Drop your weapon nice and slow and Lauren and I will go for a little drive."

No way in hell. Fox wanted to use her as his ticket out of here. As soon as she lost her usefulness as a bargaining chip, Daniel knew the bastard would have no qualms about killing her and dumping her body somewhere along his escape route.

His mind raced through his options. They were terrifyingly limited. Whatever he did, he didn't have much time. Already, Fox was on a knife's-edge of control, not thinking rationally. He had to know he was in far worse shit now than he would have been even if Rosa had testified to the grand jury about the smuggling ring.

The slightest misstep by Daniel would likely send Fox careening over that edge.

Daniel's options were limited and his window of opportunity was narrowing by the second.

"Come on, Sheriff. We can't stand here all day. Sooner or later, one of us is going to blink. You know you can't shoot me or you'll hit Dr. Maxwell here. You want to keep her alive, your best chance is to drop your weapon now and let us out of here."

He released a breath, knowing he had no choice. After a long, painful pause, he bent at the waist and placed his weapon on the floor.

Lauren gave a tiny, anguished whimper, the terror in her eyes ticking up a notch.

Trust me, he mouthed while Fox's attention was glued to his Beretta on the floor tiles between them.

"Good choice," the man said. "Now if you'll just step aside, we'll be on our way."

Adrenaline flowed through him as he tensed, ready to pounce, when suddenly he heard a noise from outside the treatment room. The outside door opening, he realized.

A moment later, he heard a small, concerned voice. "Daniel? Lauren? *Donde éstan?*"

Rosa. *Mierda!*

Kendall Fox froze at the voice, then a dark and ugly satisfaction spread over his too-handsome features.

"Your lover boy is a liar, Lauren," he purred. "Looks like I'll be able to take care of my little problem after all."

He drew the gun away from Lauren's head to aim it at the door and released her slightly. Daniel knew this was his only chance.

He hadn't played college football in more than a decade but he still knew how to take a man down. He used Fox's momentary distraction to charge. In an instant, he pushed Lauren out of the way and plowed into the other man.

They both toppled to the floor and Fox instinctively fired, but the shot went wild. Still, the other man managed to keep hold of his weapon and for what felt like an eternity, they grappled fiercely for it.

Daniel was desperate to wrest it away, but the doctor was just as determined to hang on. Though Daniel outweighed him by at least thirty pounds, the bastard was tougher than he looked, wiry and quick. It didn't help his concentration that he was painfully aware of Lauren and Rosa huddled together in the doorway.

He wanted to yell at both of them to get the hell out of there and call for help but he didn't dare even take his attention off Fox for an instant.

Finally, the tide began to turn. He was able to drive an elbow into the doctor's nose and when his head whipped back, Daniel grabbed hold of his wrist and slammed it with vicious force against the hard tile floor.

The weapon flew free, sliding across the floor. Breathing hard, adrenaline coursing through him like crazy, Daniel dragged them both to their feet and shoved Fox against the concrete wall. His head connected with a loud crack, and with a moan he sagged to the ground.

In seconds, Daniel yanked out his handcuffs and used only a little more force than strictly necessary to drag his arms behind his back.

The bastard had shot one of his deputies, was responsible for all the misery Rosa had endured, and had threatened the woman Daniel loved.

For the first time since he went through police officer training a decade ago, Daniel fiercely wished he wasn't a cop bound by laws and the Bill of Rights. He would give just about anything for the freedom to administer a little frontier justice right about now.

He read the dazed man his rights. Only when he was sure he wasn't going anywhere did Daniel pick up his own Beretta and Fox's weapon and turn to check on Rosa and Lauren.

Rosa was gazing at him with a wide-eyed kind of awe that left him highly uncomfortable. Lauren, on the other hand, looked ready to spit nails.

"Are you both okay?"

"We're fine," Lauren answered, her voice hard and tight. "You're bleeding."

He looked down and saw a red blotch spreading on his sleeve. He hadn't paid any attention to it in the heat of the moment, but now he realized his arm stung like hell.

"Did he shoot you?"

He flexed his arm. "Don't think so. I'm okay. I must have broken through my stitches from the other night when I was subduing him. I'll deal with it after I get Fox into custody."

Her mouth tightened. For a moment, he didn't quite understand the reason for her anger, and then he remembered everything, all he had told her the night before about her father's downfall and his role in it.

Of course. She hated him now. She was probably wishing Fox *had* shot him.

The satisfaction that churned through him at subduing and arresting Fox—at finding the man who had hurt Rosa and shot his deputy—dried up instantly and he was miserable once again.

She had never been so angry in her life.

The fury coursed through her like a thick, torpid creek and she couldn't seem to wade across it.

She managed to contain it while she treated Rosa for mild exposure and tried to follow the girl's story about what had happened earlier, about how she had heard a gunshot and climbed out the bathroom window and slogged through the snow as fast as she could looking for shelter.

She asked questions and made appropriate responses as best she could in Spanish, but the whole time she was afraid her fury would suck her under. The source of her anger was still in her clinic talking to Cale Davis and Gage McKinnon about what had happened.

She would have to give a statement soon, she knew, but right now her patient took precedence.

Rosa yawned suddenly in the middle of her story and Lauren forced her attention back to her patient, tucking the warmed blankets closer around her.

"Rest now," she said. "You can tell me the rest of the story later when Daniel is here."

Daniel was apparently the magic word. Rosa was crazy about him. The events of the last hour only seemed to have solidified the girl's hero worship.

Rosa nodded. Lauren smoothed a hand over her hair and she smiled, closing her eyes. She stayed with her until she fell asleep, then dimmed the lights and slipped out of the room, leaving the door ajar so she could hear if her patient awoke.

Out in the hallway, she finally let down her guard and leaned against the wall, utterly exhausted by the strain of the day and the sleepless night that preceded it. Her cheek and her head both ached where she had slammed against the wall and she closed her eyes, trying to relax the tight grip of tension in her shoulders with a couple of breathing exercises.

They didn't seem to want to be soothed, especially when some sixth sense warned her she wasn't alone.

She jerked her eyes open and found Daniel standing five feet away, watching her out of those intense dark eyes that missed nothing.

He looked so big and comforting and wonderful and she had to grip her hands together to keep from sagging against that hard chest and holding on tight.

Until she remembered how angry she was with him.

"Everything taken care of with Kendall?" she asked, her voice deliberately cool.

"Yeah. Cale and McKinnon will be picking him up at our jail and taking custody. Your Dr. Fox isn't going to be seeing the light of day anytime soon."

"He's not *my* Dr. Fox. I hope he never gets out of prison for what he's done."

He looked a little surprised at her vehemence, which only seemed to make her angrier. Did he honestly think she would have a shred of sympathy for Kendall?

"You need to let me look at your arm."

He glanced down with a distracted look, as if he had forgotten all about it. "I think it's stopped bleeding."

"I still want to check it out. Come in here."

She didn't give him a chance to argue, just headed for the nearest exam room. After a pause, he followed, looking about as thrilled to be there as a two-year-old on the way to a booster shot.

"Would you take off your shirt, please?" she ordered. The words had an oddly familiar ring and she couldn't figure out why until she remembered she had made the same request of him the night Dale Richins found Rosa in the bed of his pickup.

Everything had changed in those few short days. She had kissed him, touched him.

Discovered how very much she loved him.

She huffed out a breath. She wasn't quite ready to surrender her anger yet by giving in to that soft twirl of emotion.

Still, she had to admit her insides shivered when he shrugged out of his uniform, baring that vast expanse of bronze skin and muscle.

She was a professional, she reminded herself. She shouldn't even notice. She stepped closer, and pulled the exam light over so she could look at his injury.

"The stitches still look good," she said after a moment while she rifled through a drawer of the exam table for the necessary supplies to clean off the crusted blood. "You must have just bumped it in a bad spot and started it bleeding again. I'm sure you were too busy being an idiot at the time to notice."

He raised an eyebrow. "Was I?"

"What else would you call it? You could have been

killed, Daniel. He had a gun, in case it escaped your attention."

"I believe I was aware of that."

"What kind of idiot rushes toward a man holding a gun aimed at his chest?"

"It wasn't aimed at my chest when I tackled him, it was aimed at the door. I was well aware of the risks but I had everything under control. I had to take a chance, Lauren. I couldn't let him hurt you or Rosa."

"You were willing to sacrifice yourself for us!"

"It wouldn't have come to that. I wouldn't have let it."

Abruptly, all her anger seeped away, leaving only the echo of that raw, terrible fear she had endured watching him wrestle an armed and desperate man. She swallowed hard, hoping he couldn't see her hands tremble as she wiped gently around the edges of his injury.

"You could have been killed," she said softly. "I have never been so scared in my entire life."

To her horror, her voice broke on the last word. She took a breath, then another, trying to regain control, but it was too late. A sob escaped her and she dropped the gauze on the exam table and buried her face in her hands.

"Lauren," he murmured, then he wrapped those strong, wonderful arms around her and held her against his bare chest while she wept.

Those terrible moments replayed through her mind again and again, her fear and helplessness and the horrible dread when that single shot exploded through the room.

"Everything's all right now," he said. "We're all okay. You and Rosa are safe and that's the important thing."

Her hand curled into a fist and she struck out blindly,

punching him in the chest, even though she was far too upset to put much force behind it.

"Don't you *ever* do that to me again, Daniel Galvez. I died inside when I thought he had shot you."

At her words, he froze, the hard, smooth muscles against her fist suddenly tight. After a charged pause, he covered her hand with his and drew it to his heart, squeezing tightly as if he didn't dare let go.

Her gaze lifted to his and the intense emotion there snatched away her breath.

"You did?" he asked, his voice low, shocked.

Her chin quivered as she nodded and wiped away a tear with her finger. Another one slipped out after it, but he dipped his head and absorbed it with a gentle whisper of a kiss.

"I'm sorry," he murmured, kissing away another and another.

"You'd better be," she replied, then she wrapped her arms tightly around his neck and drew his mouth to hers.

She kissed him fiercely, pouring every ounce of the emotion raging through her heart into her embrace. Love and anger and a deep, cleansing celebration of life.

Several long moments later, he lifted his head slightly, his expression dazed and his breathing ragged.

"You're going to have to take me back a few steps here, Lauren. I must be a little slow this afternoon. I thought you hated me. After what I told you last night, I figured you would never want to talk to me again."

"I could never hate you."

"Ten minutes ago you were furious with me."

"I was angry at you for rushing a man with a gun, for risking your life. I still am."

During those long, terrible moments, all she wanted

was the chance to tell Daniel how she felt about him. Now that she had the opportunity, the words seemed to catch in her throat.

She swallowed hard, then drew a deep breath for courage. "Mostly, I was angry because I couldn't bear thinking you might have died before I could ever tell you I love you."

Had she really just blurted that out? *She* was the idiot here. With her pulse pounding loudly in her ears, she finally lifted her gaze to his and the raw emotion in his eyes sent that pulse racing into what she was sure couldn't be a healthy rate.

He looked thunderstruck at first, completely stunned, then a fierce joy leaped into his eyes.

"Say that again," he ordered, his voice hoarse, stunned.

She managed a watery smile, tenderness soaking through her. She wasn't afraid of this. With everything inside her, she loved this man. Somehow she knew he would never hurt her. He had risked his life for her. Risking her heart was a piece of cake compared to that.

"I love you, Daniel. I think I have for a long time, I just never realized it until these last few days. I love your strength and your courage and your goodness. I love the way you touch me and the way you make me feel inside, like I'm riding a roller coaster without a seat belt, and the amazing way you seem to believe I can do anything I set my mind to do."

Daniel heard her words but he couldn't quite comprehend they were coming out of her mouth. He was afraid to believe it could be real, especially after the long, miserable night he had spent lying awake on her couch watching the flames dip and sway and wishing away the past.

He hated to ask, but couldn't seem to contain the question. "What about your father? About the investigation? You don't blame me for what happened?"

She sighed, looking weary. "How can I blame you for doing your job? My father made his own choices, every step of the way. You had nothing to do with them. I've had to accept that his choices had a ripple effect in many, many lives. I just never realized until today that some of those ripples have helped shape and guide my life into a direction I can't regret. I have a great life here. Good friends, patients I care about, a growing practice. No. I don't blame you."

Relief poured through him and he wrapped her in his arms again, resting his forehead on hers. He was at peace as he hadn't been in a long time and he wanted to hang on to the feeling forever.

"I have one more confession," he murmured.

She looked wary suddenly and he smiled, kissing her hard. "I have to tell you that when I was a kid, you were everything I ever dreamed of, everything I wanted. I think I was in love with you, even back then. Nothing has changed."

He stopped and shook his head slightly. "No, that's not true. *Everything* has changed. Before, I wanted this image I had of you, the perfect house and the pretty girl who went along with it. I didn't know that pretty girl would grow into this smart, incredible woman I love so much, someone who pours her heart and soul into healing others, who has this powerful sense of justice, a bottomless well of compassion in her heart. And a rather terrifying obsession with hot chocolate."

She laughed, though a faint wash of color danced across her cheekbones. He brushed his mouth across her soft, delicate skin. He couldn't believe this was real, that she was in his arms.

She loved him. It seemed a miracle, an incredible gift, and he was fairly certain his heart would burst with happiness. He smiled, not concerned in the least.

At least he would have a good doctor around when it happened.

Epilogue

"If you don't stop sniffling, she's going to hear you."

"I'm trying," Lauren whispered back to Daniel. She pulled out the handkerchief she had at least had the foresight to bring along, dabbed at her teary eyes, then shifted on the hard bleacher seats of the high school gymnasium trying to find a comfortable spot.

It wasn't an easy task for anyone—forget a woman who was six months pregnant.

Beside her, Daniel canted his hips slightly and tugged her against him so she could use his solid bulk as a backrest.

"Better?" he murmured as the commencement speaker talked of lessons learned and the road less traveled.

"Much." She leaned into him gratefully, feeling the tight muscles in her lower back ease. After three years of marriage, she still couldn't understand how he instinctively seemed to know exactly what she needed before she even figured it out herself.

He did this kind of thing all the time, these quiet acts of consideration that always seemed to take her breath away. Her heart bubbling over with emotion, she reached for his hand, linking her fingers through his.

She would never have believed she could come to love him so much. She thought of the aching loneliness in her life before that January that had changed everything, before she acknowledged the feelings that had been growing inside her most of her life. She thought she had been content building her medical practice, living her life as best she could, trying to repair all that her father had done.

The contrast of these last three years to her earlier life only illustrated how starkly empty that world had been. Marriage to Daniel had been filled with everything she might have wished—laughter and joy and the peaceful assurance that this strong, wonderful man was crazy about her.

Not everything had been easy. Their early months together had been tempered by heartache as she had helped Rosa deliver her baby and then a day later handed the beautiful dark-eyed girl to the adoptive couple Rosa had selected.

More tears bubbled out now as she remembered Rosa's courage—and pain. Lauren was a physician, trained to help people heal, and she had hated knowing she couldn't make everything right for Rosa. Giving the child up for adoption had been the right choice. She knew it. But it hadn't been an easy one for any of them.

As an adopted child herself, she knew Rosa had been giving her daughter a better life than she could provide as a fifteen-year-old single mother with little education.

She and Daniel had talked long and hard about the possibility of adopting the girl themselves. In the end, Rosa made the decision for them, with a wisdom and strength that still amazed Lauren.

Here in Moose Springs, Rosa said, there would always be rumors swirling around her daughter. Everyone knew of the trial, of Rosa's violent rape and the attempts on her life. She wanted her child to grow up where she would never have to know the ugly circumstances that had created her, where she could be free to thrive and grow.

"My daughter is innocent of what happened to me and she should not have to live with that burden. No child should," Rosa had said firmly.

As it had been her choice, Daniel and Lauren stood by her and helped her find the right placement for the child. Rosa had finally selected friends of Daniel's sister Anna in Oregon, a wonderful, loving couple who had been childless for eight years.

Seeing their utter joy at their new daughter had eased some of the heartache, but not all. Still, the whole experience had given Lauren a new appreciation—both for the unknown woman who gave birth to her and for her own parents.

As the young speaker finished her speech with an enthusiastic plea to the graduates to grab all life had to offer, Lauren forced her attention away from the past back to the present.

"She's next," she whispered.

She didn't realize she was squeezing Daniel's hand so tightly until he laughed slightly and slid his hand away to cover her fingers with his. "Easy, sweetheart. She'll be great."

Jim Fordham, the principal of the high school, stood

to introduce the next speaker and Lauren's heart kicked up a notch.

"Every year the senior class at Moose Springs High School votes on the most inspirational graduate of the year," the principal began. "It has been a tradition at this school since I attended, back in the Dark Ages. Never before could I say how wholeheartedly I support their unanimous selection."

He smiled as the crowd applauded. "This student exemplifies courage and strength under difficult conditions. She came into this country with barely an elementary school education but in two years, despite her circumstances, she has thrived. She does not have the best grades of anyone in her graduating class, but every teacher she has ever had at this school tells me no one tries harder to succeed. She is never without a smile, she is kind to everyone she meets, and she will be greatly missed by students and faculty alike when she leaves to attend nursing school on a full scholarship in the fall. Your choice as inspirational graduate of the year, Rosa Vallejo."

The graduating seniors jumped up and began clapping. Beside Daniel, Lauren thought her heart would burst with pride as Rosa walked to the microphone, her long dark hair gleaming against the glossy white of her graduation robes.

The frightened, battered girl she and Daniel had found in the back of Dale Richins's pickup was now a strong, beautiful, confident young woman. Rosa smiled at the crowd, though Lauren thought her gaze lingered on them for just a moment as she waited for the applause to fade and the crowd to sit again before she launched into her speech.

As Rosa began speaking in her accented but clear English, Lauren followed along in her head with the speech they had practiced for two weeks. It was a wonderful message and though Lauren had heard it dozens of times, she was still touched as Rosa talked of life's challenges, and how people can choose to wallow along in their adversities or they can reach out to lift others. She talked of the bright future and of possibilities in a speech punctuated several times by applause.

Close to the end, Lauren waited for the big inspirational finish. Instead Rosa's voice faltered. She paused for several seconds, long enough that Lauren began to fear she had forgotten the words they practiced.

"I wish I had better English," Rosa said after a moment. "Maybe then I could find the words to thank the two people who have given me everything. They have given me help and courage, friendship, understanding, love. They have given me a home and they have stood with me through my darkest hours."

Rosa gave a watery smile and Lauren sniffled in response. Beside her, Daniel gripped her hand tightly. "Most of all, they have given me hope. My mother died in Honduras when I was thirteen. I did not know when I came to this country I would find two new parents but I have been so blessed. My heart is full of gratitude and love for them. To Daniel and Lauren Galvez, thank you. From the very, very bottom of my heart, I thank you. Because you reached out to help a stranger when you could have turned away, my future is a bright and wonderful place."

She stepped away from the podium and began to clap. Around them, others stood and clapped as well. This was her town, Lauren thought as she looked around at the smiling faces looking back at her. Her neighbors and friends and patients, and she loved them.

Daniel slid an arm around her and pulled her close and she risked a look at his strong, rugged features. Suspicious moisture leaked from his eyes and she handed the extra tissue she had brought along.

He would be a wonderful father to this child she carried. She had no doubt at all, because she had seen his quiet guidance with Rosa these last few years.

As the principal returned to the podium to begin reading off the names of graduates to hand out diplomas, Lauren touched her abdomen. Rosa was right. The future was a bright and wonderful place.

She couldn't wait.

* * * * *

MATCHED BY MASALA

Mona Shroff

Deven, this one's for you. But let's be real,
none of them would exist without you.

Acknowledgments

Every story needs a village to make it happen,
and this one was no different. Super thanks to
Dr. Anjali Saini, who has been my friend since
before I was born, for her medical information! My
alpha readers/brainstormers Angelina M. Lopez,
Emily Duvall and Shaila Patel are fabulous, and
I couldn't have written Amar and Divya's story
without them.

Waves of gratitude for my agent, Rachel Brooks,
as well as my Harlequin Special Edition editor,
Susan Litman, for their unyielding faith in my
ability to tell a story.

Equal amounts of gratitude for my friends and
family and their support of my efforts, especially
when I'm a bit crazy while on deadline.

Last and never least, my partner in crime, the one
who witnesses the chaos up close, my own personal
hero, Deven. I love you.

Chapter 1

Amar Virani watched with curiosity as an old clunking short school bus rumbled down his narrow suburban street. There were no longer any school-age children living in the ten houses on this cul-de-sac. Which seemed like a good thing, because from his vantage point, smudged though his kitchen window was, the bus was not necessarily fit to hold children.

The iconic yellow-and-black paint was peeling, and the rattling sounds it made suggested that it could just stop running at any moment. When it halted across the street, in front of the Shahs' house, Amar pressed his lips together and shook his head. Of course the bus was hers. Sure enough, the doors opened with a loud screech and a thud, and all five foot two inches of Divya Shah bounded out.

Though Amar tried to control it, his traitorous heart

leaped. She was home. Back from whatever her latest daring adventure had been, in a ridiculous-looking old bus. Perfectly normal for Divya.

"What the hell is that clatter?" Amar's sister, Anita, came up behind him and stood on tiptoe following his gaze out the window. Her amber eyes widened and she broke into a huge grin. "Come on!" his sister squealed. "She's back." Anita bounded toward the front door.

Anita's new husband, Nikhil, cocked an eyebrow at his very excited wife but held back. "Be right there."

Amar absently dried his hands on a kitchen towel, his eyes never leaving the bus. Or rather, never leaving Divya. She was walking around the vehicle, occasionally squatting or standing on tiptoe to check something out. From here, Amar could make out the blond tips she'd added to her short-cropped hair before she left a few weeks ago. She had on denim shorts and a tank top, all of which accentuated her curves in what Amar could only describe as the most perfect way.

"Hmm."

Amar turned at the sound to find his brother-in-law watching him, an annoying smirk on his face.

"What?" Amar snapped. He didn't dislike Nikhil, but he wasn't necessarily fond of him either. Nikhil and Anita had recently remarried after having been divorced for three years. Amar was, to say the least, skeptical.

"You have got it bad." Nikhil chuckled.

"What are you talking about?" Amar stepped past Nikhil, walking toward the door, his irritation with his sister's husband increasing exponentially.

"Divya."

"What about her?" Amar maintained his short of tone, willing this line of conversation to end.

"The way you look at her." Nikhil was undeterred.

"There is no *way* that I look at her." Amar rolled his eyes. "She's my sister's best friend. We grew up together."

"Okay. Whatever you say." Though Nikhil did not sound like he agreed with Amar at all. "But you don't look at her like she's just a friend."

Amar stopped short. Nikhil had no idea what he was talking about.

Whatever. Anita was already across the street.

Nikhil passed Amar as they got to the door. "Come on, man."

Amar shook his head and tossed the towel over his shoulder as he stayed put in the shade of their front porch, though even the shade couldn't cut the thick Maryland humidity in August. He fidgeted with the old leather-strapped watch he'd worn every day for the past eight years, as he leaned against the railing and took in the house across the street. Red brick front, black door and shutters, it looked almost the same as his. As teenagers, he, Anita and Divya had never knocked on any door, simply walking in and out of each other's houses with the knowledge that they belonged wherever they were. It also meant another set of parental eyes watching over them. When he and Anita had lost their parents, Amar had taken great solace knowing that Uncle and Auntie were still there, across the street, watching over them. Like parents.

Now, as he watched, Divya had jumped into Anita's arms.

Amar couldn't help his smile or the warm, fuzzy feeling he got watching the two of them. Peas in a pod. Ride or die. It had been that way since they were freshmen in high school.

Amar held nothing but gratitude in his heart for Divya for that. He and Anita had lost their parents in a car crash almost eight years ago, and Divya had not once left Anita's side. She had seen Anita through her marriage, divorce and remarriage.

The bus was still making all sorts of odd noises—Amar wondered if it wouldn't just die right there. Not to mention that it was in desperate need of a paint job. Why the hell did Divya even have this bus? Not that he should care much what she did. After all, her advice was the reason he'd lost his job.

"Just add whatever you think it needs," Divya had told him on a last-minute catering job they'd done together. *"Why would Ranjit care, if you're actually improving his food?"*

It had made sense at the time, so he'd added a spice mix he'd learned from his mom. The guests raved, Ranjit Kulkarni, owner of Taj Catering, had not. In retaliation, he had let it be known around town that Amar was a difficult chef to work with, temperamental and full of himself, which was ironic, as it actually described Ranjit more than Amar.

The end result was that no one would hire him.

Realistically, he knew it wasn't Divya's fault. No one had forced him to change the recipes. It simply would never have occurred to Amar to do such a bold thing on his own. He should have known better. His name wasn't going on the food, but it just burned him that Ranjit even got those high-end jobs when the man clearly did not know how to cook. He was Bollywood-star handsome. But those good looks did not equal talent in the kitchen.

Divya, on the other hand, was impulsive, excitable

and charming…and a damn good pastry chef. She was also loud. He could hear her from the porch.

"It's a dessert food truck. I'm going to call it For Goodness' Cakes." She was beaming at Anita and Nikhil. "But her name is Lola."

"Wait, what?" Amar could not help himself. He exchanged his house flip-flops for the outside ones and stepped off the porch into the scorching sun. In a few long strides, he closed his distance from the group.

"A dessert food truck." Divya faltered a bit as he approached, but she regrouped in a second. "Want to see?"

Amar nodded vigorously. "Duh."

He hopped onto the bus, expecting to see—well, he had no idea what he expected, given the dilapidated exterior. But the interior was impressive. Double oven, microwave, crepe pans, fridge, area for prep and storage. Utensils, recipe books. He let his gaze slowly take in some of the details. A small Ganesha in one corner made him smile. Of course Divya wanted to be rid of obstacles.

Spotting a picture of Divya and Anita at Divya's cancer-free celebration, he tore his gaze away.

"You don't have a stand mixer?" he asked.

"I still have to pick one," Divya explained.

"How much was all this?" He waved his arm over the area.

She gave him a number.

His eyes bugged out. "What? How did you manage that?"

She shrugged. "I took out a loan. And I helped do the work. I've been working on it for a year. It was the only way I could handle being stuck working at that ridiculous grocery-store bakery. I finished before I left for my trip."

"What's your business plan?" Amar asked, eyeing the interior.

"Not hundred percent sure yet, but I can do almost anything in here." Her voice was slightly scratchy, and in this moment, she had his full attention. "Just need to find my perfect stand mixer."

Amar folded his arms across his chest. He'd never have the nerve to try something so risky without taking time to create a business plan. Budget every purchase. And most especially—for a *baking truck*—*get a mixer*!

"I have three parties, though, in the next couple of weeks."

"Birthday parties?" Amar raised an eyebrow. Kids' birthday cakes would not keep this bus afloat.

"Yes. Adult birthday parties," she said with satisfaction, as if she could read his mind. "Clients want the centerpiece cake, but then they want sweets as well."

"Indian sweets?"

"Some, and some fusion stuff, which you know I am awesome at." She grinned at him with satisfaction.

Divya Shah did not have a self-esteem problem. But she could back it up. Her Indian fusion sweets were like no one else's in town.

"Divya—the engine's bad. Did you even take it to a mechanic?" Amar leaned against a small stainless-steel counter.

"Doing it today."

"Then how do you know it will even run?" he groused as they both stepped out of the sweltering school bus.

"It'll run just fine." Divya squinted in the sunlight.

"You can't just will it to run—" he argued back at her.

"I can and I will, Amar Virani," she snapped.

"If you want to start a business, you need a solid plan,

marketing strategy, social media presence, all that," he continued.

Divya pinned him with a stare. "Do you have all that?"

"As a matter of fact, I do."

"Then why haven't you started your catering business?" She smirked at him. "You've been talking about it forever. Right, Anita?" She nodded at his sister.

"She has a point." His own sister, throwing him under the school bus. "You need to start a business to actually have a business."

Of course Anita would say that. She'd been pushing him to start catering forever. There was just never a good time. Divya pouted at him, a taunt in her eye.

It wasn't the taunt in her eye that froze him, it was those pouted lips. Just once, he'd like to forget that kiss they'd shared over a year ago.

But, Nikhil had it right—though Amar would never admit it to him. He'd loved Divya Shah his whole life, but all he'd ever have was that one errant, slightly drunken kiss. Despite what all those books say, opposites might attract, but they couldn't be together. Especially if that opposite was your sister's best friend.

Chapter 2

Divya wasn't sure why she enjoyed pushing Amar's buttons, but she absolutely did.

"Ranjit has seen to it that no chef will hire me." Amar glared at her. "I took your advice, used Mom's masala mix, and now—no work."

"You're welcome for that, by the way." She grinned widely.

Amar's brown eyes bugged out. "I do not have a job, Divya. I'm hardly appreciative."

"But you have a skill, Hulk." She pointed at the cartoon on his T-shirt. The fact that he was irritated with her for suggesting he change Ranjit's recipes didn't bother her at all. The fact that he was unemployed? A blessing. If she could start her own business, so could he.

He shook his head and walked away from her. He did that a lot. Especially after she'd kissed him last year.

She ignored the pang in her heart that came from being blown off by him. Life was short and unpredictable, so she had simply gone with the moment, without really thinking about what might happen afterward. Of what his reaction to her impulsiveness might be.

Human connection of any sort was invaluable. Interacting with people reminded her that she was alive. That in some small way, she was making an impact on someone's life, and they were making an impact on hers. For as long as she had it anyway. How long was anyone's guess.

Sure, she'd been in remission for a long time, but she didn't trust it. Acute lymphocytic leukemia, while treatable, could come back. At any time, the evil cells could come back and steal her life. She'd discussed it endlessly in therapy, and she'd talked to her doctors, but in the middle of the night, when she was alone with her thoughts, that ever-present fear floated to the surface and reared its slimy head to taunt her. "What if you die," this monster would ask, "before you do everything you want to do?" *What if?*

So she packed her days overly full and fell asleep dead tired. (No pun intended.) It was why she loved being a pastry chef. Sweet things made people happy. Plain and simple. And she wanted to make people happy with whatever time she had left.

That night, about a year ago now, she'd had a few glasses of wine. She really had no idea what had come over her. The idea that Amar might kiss her back hadn't even played into the equation. But then, the look on his face, after. Like he'd won a prize. Like—like she'd meant something to him…

She knew right there she'd messed up, kissing her best

friend's brother. She'd bolted, and things just hadn't been quite the same between them since.

"Climbing Pikes Peak was incredible. Thanks for asking," she called after him.

He turned back to her, his hands on his narrow hips, and sighed. Damn, he was tall, and that T-shirt fit him just so, clinging to nicely defined biceps and shoulders. His faded blue jeans clung to his long legs. "You made it home in one piece, so I assume you enjoyed yourself."

"It was absolutely amazing." She ran her gaze over Nikhil and Anita, so it wasn't like she was only talking to Amar. Even though she was.

"I have dinner on the stove." He pointed his thumb toward his house and turned to go in.

"My parties need food, too," she called out.

He paused for just a microsecond before continuing into the house. He didn't even turn around.

"I guess he's really pissed he listened to you," Anita said, chuckling.

Divya shrugged. "I guess. But I wasn't joking. My parties do need food. They asked me to recommend a caterer for the savory stuff. I really do think Amar would be the best choice for the job, and it would give him great exposure." She paused. "I'd like to make it up to him, if he'll even talk to me."

"Come on, he's cooking something. Let's let him feed us." Anita threaded her arms through Divya's and Nikhil's and marched the three of them into the house. "You sure Sai won't be jealous of Lola?"

Divya laughed. "No chance." Her Indian motorcycle was one of her most prized possessions. "One is work. One is pleasure."

"Okay, Amar. We're here and we're hungry," Anita announced as they entered Amar's pristine kitchen.

The aroma of dhal, rice, shaak and fresh rotli wafted through the air. Divya looked around the kitchen. Used dishes and pots were stacked—neatly—in the sink. Three pots simmered on the stove, with utensils placed on trivets. Amar was rolling out the flatbread and baking them just as quickly. Anita immediately walked over and flipped the rotli over with her fingers, effectively taking over the cooking part.

"Thanks," Amar murmured, his voice rumbling out of him as if words were an effort.

Divya opened the refrigerator to take out the yogurt, and found the light off and the persistent hum of its motor missing. "Um, Amar. Your fridge is dead."

He barely glanced up. "Again?" He looked at Anita. "Here, you got this?" He wiped his hands on the towel that seemed to live on his shoulder. "Let me check the circuit breaker." He went down to the basement.

Divya retrieved a cooler from their garage while he was gone and started emptying the contents.

He returned in minutes. "It's fine."

"Well, then, your fridge is dead," Divya stated.

Amar glared at her as if she had broken it. Whatever. A sudden loud pop and a bang and sparks came from the wall oven, and a small flame ignited. Without missing a beat, Amar grabbed the compact fire extinguisher that was kept on a wall in the kitchen and put out the slight fire.

"What the hell, Amar?" Anita called from the stove, where she was still making the rotli.

He looked sheepishly at his sister. "Yeah. The house has some issues." He nodded at the stove. "Particularly the kitchen. To be honest, that thing is barely functional. I got lucky today."

"Well, that's a problem, then. Since as a caterer, it's nice to have a place to cook," Divya said.

Amar just shook his head at her. "What are you doing with the cooler?"

"I'm filling it with your fridge contents. We can take it across the street and just put it in my fridge for the time being. It's practically empty, since Mom and Dad are getting ready to leave on their four-week cruise in a couple days. And I haven't had a chance to go grocery shopping yet."

Amar softened, which was a rare thing. "Thank you."

"Tell us about Pikes Peak, Div?" Anita asked, her back to her, while still making the rotli.

Nikhil took over cleaning up the mess from the oven, so Amar started helping his sister. He shared a small eye roll with Divya over what they both would have classified as "Nikhil trying too hard."

"It was fabulous, Anita!" She was extra enthusiastic, probably to hide her silent communication with Amar.

"You literally decided one month out that you were going to climb a mountain that is fourteen thousand feet above sea level," Amar said. "Not nearly enough time to prep."

"I had everything I needed," she countered. "I even got to touch a cloud. The views were amazing—I was literally above the tree line. Incredible."

"Sounds wonderful," Anita said. "Next time, we'll go with you. Right, Nikhil?"

"Wouldn't miss it."

"You know me better than that," Divya stated with a

chiding smile. "When you're ready, we'll pick a different mountain—so we can experience it together."

Anita rolled her eyes at her friend. "You could actually do it again. The experience would be different if we were along."

Divya just shook her head. There was no way she was going up that mountain again. There were too many other things to do than repeating something you'd already done. "I'll have to grab another cooler. This one is full." She glanced at Amar. "That first party is thirty people. The two after are bigger."

"I can barely get this stove to work for the families I cook for. Taking on a big catering job right now—"

"Why don't you cook at Divya's?" Nikhil asked.

Anita and Nikhil had only been remarried a few weeks, and Anita seemed happy, but Divya was reserving her full judgment on Nikhil for the time being. Still, his suggestion that Amar use her kitchen was a good one. Especially if it would give her a chance to convince him to take on at least one of her parties. She'd heard that Ranjit was trying to get them all.

"That's not a permanent solution," Amar said as he met her gaze. He clearly didn't think much of the idea.

"It doesn't have to be permanent—it just has to work." Divya grinned.

"Why do you want me to do this so bad?"

"Because if you don't cater, they'll probably hire Ranjit. And I do not want to work with *him*," Divya explained, heading to the garage to find another cooler.

"What if you redid this kitchen?" Nikhil asked. Divya turned to him. That was a fabulous idea. Points for Nikhil.

"Yes! Let's redo this kitchen," she squealed, looking at Anita, who was smiling and nodding. "If you knock out this wall—" Divya indicated the wall between the kitchen and formal dining room "—get rid of that old oven, you can put a double oven here." She walked around the space and out into the current family room. "You don't really use this whole area, so cut the sitting room in half and you'll have more island-slash-counter space. There's room for two refrigerators, a walk-in pantry and plenty of cabinets." Divya's face lit up and she became more animated.

"Absolutely not!"

"Sounds great!"

Brother and sister spoke at the same time. Amar threw Anita a withering look as if she had betrayed him by agreeing to Nikhil's and Divya's suggestions to completely tear apart the house.

"Amar, it's a great idea. You'll need help getting it licensed as a commercial kitchen if you expand the business, but that happens to be Tina's special power," Anita said.

"That's true. My sister is the queen of the loophole," Nikhil added, grinning.

Amar just glared at his brother-in-law, cutting his eyes to Divya. She met his gaze, her mouth twisted.

"No. I'm not changing the house." He turned to his sister. "I can just buy new appliances. Cheaper, anyway, as I don't have the money for a renovation."

"Amar. It's been almost eight years. It's okay to let it go—" Anita started.

"I can rent space." He avoided looking at her.

"You just said you don't have money for a reno, how could you have money to indefinitely rent a commercial space?" Divya asked. "Besides, you can't go to a commercial kitchen in the middle of the night." *Oops.*

Amar snapped his gaze to her and narrowed his eyes. "Sometimes I bake in the middle of the night and I... see your light on." Heat rushed to her face. Why should she be embarrassed because she knew he cooked in the wee hours? It wasn't like she was ogling him. Not really.

Amar turned away from her. "I'll figure it out." He looked at his sister. "And by the way, I can take over your mortgage payment now. You moved out a month ago."

"You don't have a job," Anita shot back at him. "A couple of regular clients aren't enough to cover the payment, Amar. Be reasonable."

"I'm not changing the house." He crossed his arms over his chest.

"If you cater the parties and cook at my house, you can easily take over Anita's share of the mortgage," Divya pointed out quietly. "And seriously—do you want Ranjit to get that business?"

He looked from his sister to her. Divya knew he was at least considering the possibility, from the way his mouth was set in a line. He unfolded his arms and leaned them on the counter. "Fine. In return, I'll cook for you while your parents are gone. I have no idea why a trained chef eats takeout."

Divya raised her eyebrows at him. Apparently, he was as nosy as she was.

"You live across the street," he said, turning away. "I see the delivery vans."

"I like baking. If I cooked for myself, I'd eat nothing but cake all day." She laughed. "Everyday cooking is not my forte." She was unapologetic, while she tried to control her exuberance. "And I would never say no to a h— Um, a guy who wanted to cook for me." She was going to say "hot guy." Quickly, she glanced at Anita to see if her friend had noticed.

"What? He's Amar. He's not *a guy*," said his sister.

"You know I can hear you, right?" Amar shook his head, and Divya caught the hint of a smile. As small as it was, the expression lit up his face.

"You both know what I mean." She cleared her throat, forcing herself to look away from him. "But, sure, it's a deal." Divya looked around again at Amar's neat, organized kitchen.

Oh boy. He was in for a surprise at her house.

Chapter 3

Amar paced the kitchen while his contractor, Michael Young, sat and waited for his employee, Janki Mahadevia, to check out the wiring.

Janki was quite petite, all of maybe five feet tall. But her stature was deceiving. According to Michael, they had hired her in the last few months, and she was the best electrician they had.

"Stop pacing, Mr. Virani. She's great." Michael bit into his breakfast sandwich and settled in.

"Call me Amar." He and Michael seemed about the same age. Besides, *Mr. Virani* reminded him of his dad. He fingered the leather strap on that old watch.

Janki grunted, her ponytail bobbing as she went downstairs to the circuit breaker. Amar started to follow.

"I, uh, wouldn't follow her if I were you," Michael said. "Just enjoy your bagel. She'll be gone for a bit. Have a seat."

Sitting was not an option. Amar grabbed his bagel and wandered out onto the back patio instead. It was early, not much past 8:00 a.m., but the air was already thick with humidity. He took a bite of his bagel and a small whimper caught his attention. He stepped down off the patio and looked behind the firepit. A small dog with matted white-and-brown fur cowered there.

"Hey there, little guy." Amar forgot about the kitchen for a moment. He broke off a piece of his bagel and held it out to the scared animal. The dog eyed the food, clearly hungry, but hesitated.

"That's all right," Amar spoke softly. "I'll just put it down." He set down the small piece of bagel and stepped back. They'd had a dog growing up. Anita had begged until their father relented. Kulfi had been timid at first as well.

The mutt stepped toward the food and sniffed it out before he ate it. Amar dropped another piece. The dog ate that, too. Amar grinned, his kitchen woes forgotten. The dog had a small patch of brown over one eye. "You're a hungry little guy, aren't you, Nick Fury?"

He didn't know what had inspired him to give the stray a name. But with the "patch" over his eye, it was clear that Fury fit.

The dog gobbled the next bite. Bit by bit, Fury ate half of Amar's bagel.

"Hey, Amar," Michael called from the house.

Amar turned to him.

"She's back."

Amar looked back to Fury, but he was gone. Amar sighed, then shook it off. He'd been with the dog for fifteen minutes. Probably shouldn't have named him.

* * *

Janki glanced at her boss before turning to Amar. She laid out the facts. "I think the oven shorted a bunch of stuff out. Or maybe there were a series of shorts leading to the oven fire, and now there are more shorts—in any case, in addition to updating the appliances, you really need to update the electrical work—some of it is barely up to code. This is an older house, and whoever did the wiring to begin with took some shortcuts that I wouldn't necessarily approve. I'm surprised this didn't happen before. Do you lose power occasionally?"

"Occasionally," Amar responded. "More, lately." He almost mumbled.

"Good thing we emptied out the fridge last night." Amar startled at Divya's raspy voice from behind him. She held a thermos and some paper cups. "Chai, anyone? I wasn't sure if your stove would be up for making anything this morning."

How she managed to sass him with a straight face was beyond him. She had on athletic shorts and a tank top, clearly dressed to go running, but had thought to bring him chai beforehand.

"Um, yeah. Sure." Michael turned toward Divya, a huge grin filling his face. "Chai would be amazing. Thanks." He gave Divya an appraising glance. Amar couldn't blame him, but the urge to punch Michael was real.

"Is that your bus across the street?" Michael asked.

"It sure is," Divya claimed proudly as she poured the steaming liquid into four paper cups. The aroma of the cardamom and clove might have calmed Amar if it weren't for how Divya held Michael's gaze for an extra beat.

"Wow, that smells amazing." Michael took what Amar

Matched by Masala

thought was an unnecessarily long inhale of the chai. "Cardamom, cinnamon, clove… What am I missing?"

Was he flirting with Divya over chai spices?

"Black peppercorn, for that hint of heat." Divya cocked a sideways smile at him. "Impressive. Are you a cook?"

"Nah. I just love chai, especially when I can get the real thing." He held up the cup to her. "So what's the deal with the bus?"

Divya explained, and Michael listened like his life depended on it. Amar wanted to roll his eyes. He gulped at his chai and scorched his mouth and throat, causing him to cough.

"You okay?" Divya asked. "The chai is really hot. Take it easy."

His eyes were watering, and he could barely speak, so he just nodded and turned away to gather himself.

"I'd be happy to help you paint it," Michael offered. He grinned widely again as he continued to check Divya out.

"Oh yeah? I'm still considering colors and design," Divya mused.

"I can help you paint," Amar blurted out as he spun back around to face them. What was he doing? He did *not* need to be spending extra time with Divya. It was bad enough he would be sharing a kitchen, however temporarily, cooking right next to her. Painting the bus could easily put a wrinkle in his carefully controlled feelings for her. The list of reasons why Divya was off-limits may not be long, but it was strong.

Basically, he didn't deserve her. She could totally do better than him. He just didn't want to watch it happen.

Divya raised her eyebrows. "Really? You know how to repaint a bus?"

"Sure." Amar shrugged. "How hard could it be?"

"You have to do it right, get the right chemicals and make sure it's all sanded correctly before you paint." Michael sipped his chai as he spoke.

"It sounds like a big job," Divya said, "but with the three of us, it shouldn't be so bad." She grinned at them both.

Fabulous. Now he was going to help her paint that thing and watch her and Michael make eyes at each other. He should back out.

"Sounds good to me," said Michael, finishing up his chai. "What do you think?" He turned to Amar.

"Sure. The more the merrier," he managed to squeak out over his singed throat.

"Okay." Michael stood. "This work is going to take some time. Janki and I need to figure out how to bring everything up to code. In the meantime, I have to shut it all off so you don't end up with another fire. Great chai, Divya. We'll grab some tools and be back in an hour or so."

He and Janki left.

Amar's heart sank. He didn't have the money for all this work plus taking on Anita's half of the mortgage. "So. Ah... You have the contact info for those parties? I guess I'll need to talk to them in order to put together menus."

"Already done. And I called the Aroras and Herreras, too—they have the bigger parties. They all want you to cater. We're meeting with the Raos tomorrow." Divya smiled at him.

"That was fast." One thing about Divya, once she set her mind to something, she followed through. "Thanks... for offering me the jobs. And the kitchen space. Are your parents still around?"

She nodded. "They leave on the red-eye tonight."

"So, I'll cook for them, too. How about khichdi today?"

Divya's eyes widened, and she looked slightly green.

"What? It's comfort food."

"No offense, I swear, but I can't eat khichdi anymore." She spoke softly, and her face actually took on a green tinge.

"I used to make it for you all the time."

She inclined her head. "Yes. And it was great. It was literally the only thing I could keep down after chemo. But now—"

"It reminds you of chemo." Amar did a mental face palm. Of course. His last meal with his parents had been at an Italian restaurant. He couldn't eat fettuccine Alfredo anymore. He didn't even cook it anymore, if he could help it.

"Yes," she said, looking relieved that he had caught on. "All the nausea, everything."

"No problem." He grinned at her. "No khichdi."

"Thanks for understanding." Divya beamed back at him.

"How about the other comfort food of Gujarat?" he suggested.

Her eyes lit up. "You have the millet flour to make rotla?"

"I do. I haven't made them in a while." The thicker flatbread required a different skill than the thinner rotli he typically made. "But I can manage."

"Potato shaak?"

"You got it."

"That totally works." Her eyes lit up in appreciation, dimples in both cheeks.

He was a goner.

Chapter 4

Divya left Amar and went for her run. It was late morning and the Maryland August sun was bearing down, heating the already-sticky air. She ran anyway, because running cleared her mind as well as any therapy, and it was also when she got some of her best recipe ideas.

There had been a time when she could not run, all her body could do was fight cancer—for two years. She won, so now, every day that she could run, she did.

Fatigue had been one of the hallmark signs for her. She found herself unable to keep her eyes open in school. It had angered her, her not being able to control her body. Especially when all she wanted to do when she got home was sleep, eventually blowing off after-school activities she loved. It was then her parents had taken her to the doctor.

Amar's offer to help paint Lola made her disproportionately happy. Plus she'd decided to look for a stand mixer today. Once she bought one, she'd be all set. The thought lightened her mood, and she pounded the pavement a little harder, a little faster.

Feeding people sweet things made them happy, which made her happy. And there should be more happiness in the world.

A couple of miles from home, she stopped to rest on the playground of the middle school and snack on an energy bar. Sweat dripped down her back and off her face, and she reveled in feeling the satisfying ache in her muscles.

After a few minutes she turned to head back when she caught sight of a dog digging through the trash near the dumpster. His white-and-brown fur was matted, and he was so skinny his ribs showed through his skin. He had a small patch of brown around one eye, giving him a pirate look. What he did not seem to have was a collar. Strays were not common in this neighborhood, so this little guy clearly didn't have a home.

There had been a time when Divya had desperately wanted a dog. She'd fantasized about a constant playmate, one who did not care if she was well or not. Her parents, who would have done close to anything for her, had not given in and gotten her one. Their hands were full with her care and treatment. They had also been concerned about germs, despite all the facts that pointed to how animals helped soothe stress.

Even as her heart melted upon seeing this lost little animal, she knew she no longer had the time for a pet. Still, a small voice that sounded very much like her teenage self, made the point that if she had a dog, she wouldn't feel so lonely when her parents traveled.

Divya shook her head and reminded herself of all the adventures she still had to go on, so many experiences to be had. She simply couldn't be tied down.

Divya held out a small piece of her bar to the animal. He eyed her with suspicion, even as his nostrils flared from the scent of the food she offered. She put the piece on the ground and took a few steps back. The dog immediately came close to the morsel and gobbled it up. Divya broke off another small piece and placed it on the ground, stepping back once again.

The dog came and took that bite, too. She did it again, and the third time, the dog looked up at her, waiting for more. She held a tidbit to his nose, and moved it back, until his bottom hit the ground. Divya then let him take the small kernel into his mouth.

She grinned. "Good boy." She continued to break off pieces and feed them to the dog until her bar was gone. By then, the animal had become quite comfortable with her, allowing her to pet him, even.

"Well, Dog, I'll bet you'd have my heart in another few minutes, so I'm going to head on. People to see, places to go and all that. Not to mention, cakes to bake." Oh crap. She was talking to this dog as if he knew what she was saying. Time to leave. She took off running but gave in to the urge to look back just once. The dog was sitting and watching her run away. Divya ignored the pang in her chest. Just because she didn't have time for a dog didn't mean she wouldn't have loved to take this little guy home with her.

Well. She'd have to alert the local shelter as soon as she got home. Hopefully, he'd find his forever family in no time.

She made it back in record time and was just enjoying

the air-conditioning and her protein shake when someone knocked at the door. No one knocked, mostly because the only person who ever really came over was Anita, and she basically let herself in.

She heard her father open the door and speak to someone. Curious, she went to the entry and found Amar's contractor just outside. Martin. No, Matthew. Michael! That was it, right?

Her father raised an eyebrow at her. "This gentleman says he needs to speak to you."

"Sure." She stepped to the door. Her father did not leave.

"Hey! Michael, right?" She smiled. He was classically handsome, if you liked the brown-hair-blue-eyed-square-jaw kind of look.

"Yes." He nodded enthusiastically as if impressed she remembered his name. He flicked his gaze to her dad. "You still live with your parents?"

"Yes." She was unapologetically matter-of-fact. It was no one's business why she still lived with her parents at twenty-eight. Part of it was cultural, the other part was that, quite frankly, she liked her parents. Sure, everybody loved their parents. But she *liked* hers, as in liked talking to them, cooking with them. All of it. She really missed them when they traveled, but she never told them that. They *should* be traveling and doing all those things that they had been unable to do when she was sick.

"I just stopped by to see if this Sunday worked for painting your bus?" Michael's gaze flicked from her to her father and back.

"Yes. That's great."

"Perfect. I'll text you a list of what you need. It should take a few hours. Maybe we can grab a bite after?"

Divya reflexively darted her gaze across the street to the Virani house. Not that she should care what Amar thought. This was her life, and she could do what she wanted.

"Sure." Why not? "Give me your phone." He handed over his phone and she entered her number. "See you Sunday."

She shut the door and nearly bumped into her father. Her father was just a couple inches taller than her, balding, with a slight paunch. "You're going on a date with a guy you met this morning?"

"Dad. I'm twenty-eight years old."

"Veer," her mother called from the kitchen. "Leave her be. She will never get married if she doesn't date."

Divya smiled triumphantly at her father and headed back to the kitchen. He grunted and followed her. "Mom, Amar is making us dinner tonight."

Her mother lit up. "Fantastic! What a good boy."

"Are you finished packing?" Divya asked.

"Yes."

"It's a four-week cruise. Are you sure?"

"It's not the first time I have traveled, beti," her mother answered. Her mother kept her dark hair in a short bob, that frizzed out in humidity, giving her a wild look at the moment.

"Uh-huh." Divya glanced at her father, who rolled his eyes and shrugged. "Are you going to stay the whole time this trip, Mom?"

Her mother suddenly became engrossed in wiping down the countertop.

"Mom?" Divya insisted.

"I have every intention of finishing out this trip," she

said to Divya, flicking a glance at her father. "But I can make no promises."

"Mom!"

"It's the best I can do." She lifted her chin to Divya in defiance. Divya was about an inch taller than her mother's petite five foot one, but when she lifted her chin like that, Divya stepped back. Even Divya saw the resemblance when she did that. People didn't call her her mom's mini-me for nothing—minus the hair. Divya liked knowing that in twenty-five years or so, she'd look like her mom did now.

"You need to stop worrying about me. I'm fine. The chances of me getting sick again are—"

"I know the stats, Divya. Honestly, if you rattle them off to me one more time…" Her mother's dark eyes blazed at her, and twenty-eight years old or not, Divya shut her mouth. "Not to mention, my dear, that you keep going on all these 'adventures' as if there's no—" She turned away without finishing her sentence and started the mountain of dishes that overflowed the sink. She knew what her mother had been going to say.

As if there's no tomorrow.

"Mom, just because I like to try new things—"

"Try new things?" She spun back to face her daughter. "You just got back from hiking a mountain—on a whim. You went scuba diving—on a whim. Flew to Las Vegas to party with people you had known for one week, did a triathlon with no training, swam the bay. You did all that in the last six months. Sweetheart, you act like you're running out of time. I'm worried that you'll miss out on the small miracles. Things like sleeping in, a lazy Sunday morning, falling in love."

Divya said nothing. It was an old argument. She didn't

have the patience to stay in bed once her eyes opened, any more than she could *not* be productive on a Sunday— or any—morning. And falling in love? She didn't think she was capable of entrusting her happiness to another human being. What if it didn't work out? She didn't want to waste time healing a broken heart. Or worse—*what if* she got sick again, and broke someone else's heart? She couldn't be responsible for that. She was compelled to keep moving, keep doing.

"I need to bake." It was the best way to end the discussion.

Her mother went back to the mountain of dishes, her pride and sadness in her daughter clearly written in the stiffness of her back, the vigor of her scrubbing.

Divya found her mixing bowls but had to make space on the counter as all her area was covered with cupcakes and icing and fondant she'd started last night. She just needed to add final touches before she delivered them.

"You need more counter space," her father said.

"Yeah, Dad. I totally do." She looked around the kitchen. It wasn't dirty, just cluttered with her baking pans, cooling cupcakes, icing bags, etcetera.

A knock at the door put a smile on his face. "And here it is."

She looked from her mom to her dad. "What did you guys do?"

She followed her dad to the door just as the delivery person waved, leaving behind a large rectangular package. She glanced at the photo on the front. "A movable island?"

He shrugged. "Well, you need counter space. So this was the easiest way to create more."

She dragged the box inside to the formal dining room,

all thoughts of baking forgotten for the moment. There wasn't any furniture in that room, as it had basically become a storage place for all her random baking supplies over the years.

When they moved to Columbia to be closer to Hopkins for her treatments, furnishing a formal dining room had not been a priority. Dilip and Varsha Virani, their neighbors from across the street, quickly became their closest friends, so formal dining was never necessary. The room had always stayed relatively empty.

"Let's do this, then." Divya opened the box and started assembling it, already thinking about where everything would fit on it. Before she knew it, she had a fully constructed movable island. More storage, more surface area.

"I have so much more room for prep, cake decoration, everything."

Her father grinned. "Kalpana. Return it—she doesn't like it."

Her mother's laughter rang loud, their previous disagreement locked away for the moment. It was a sound Divya felt she didn't hear enough. "I'll get right on it."

Whenever young Divya had had a tough day—at the hospital, or at school—it didn't matter, her mother and father would pull out ingredients and they would bake or make sweets together. Because a little something sweet would wipe out the taste of anything bad, her mother always said.

As she got older and decided to make it her career, her parents had never been anything less than completely enthusiastic. Divya knew it was those afternoons and evenings spent baking with them that formed her into the pastry chef she was today.

Divya laughed at their silly antics and hugged them

both. She caught sight of Lola outside, taking up the whole driveway. Her parents hadn't even mentioned how much space Lola required. Divya knew they never would.

Lola might need some paint and a bit more TLC in a few places, but the old bus was the embodiment of her dreams coming true.

The thing about the actual act of baking was that Divya could completely lose herself to it. Her thoughts were focused on the mix of flavors and textures that she was creating, not only for the mouth but for the eye. Once she got caught up in a project, time had no meaning.

Today she was practicing for the Rao birthday cake that she'd be making in two weeks. One layer of chocolate cake, one layer of dark chocolate brownie separated by a layer of mint ganache, all covered with a coat of mirrored chocolate. She made a series of small cakes, experimenting with the different layers, different cake and brownie recipes, different textures of the ganache, until she landed the perfect combination.

Her kitchen was still a disaster when Amar walked in with dinner. He had changed into a Hawkeye T-shirt, and his hair appeared damp with the ends curling ever so slightly. Seeing him brought a sense of calm to her, just as it always did. Maybe she simply associated his presence with good food, which quite frankly, was more than enough to calm her.

"Hey." He grinned at her as he took in the kitchen. "You figure it out?"

"Figure what out?" she asked as she washed her hands and got to work on the dishes.

"The cake?"

"Oh yeah. That. How'd you know?"

"I know things." He shrugged and quirked a smile. "And you have five little cakes scattered around here, so…" He came up close to where she was standing and made room for the food he'd brought.

"You smell good," she said without thinking. What?

"What did you say?" He snapped his head to her.

"Uh, the food—the food smells good." Whatever he'd brought did smell delicious. But so did he. She went back to scrubbing her cake pans. "Want to try the cake?"

"Hmm?"

She looked at him over her shoulder. His eyes were closed and he was chewing slowly, a chocolate-tinged fork in his hand. She could have sworn he moaned, because she felt that sound through her entire body. She stole the moment to watch how he savored the bite of cake, how his enviable lashes lay thick and dark against his brown skin. She was mesmerized by the movement of his jaw and what she was now noticing was the perfect shape of his mouth. And she flashed back to that kiss.

No. Nope. Uh-uh.

She watched him swallow, then quickly turned back to her dishes before he opened his eyes.

"That's the winner, Div. It's fantastic. Rishi Rao won't know what hit him."

"Amar Virani." She turned off the water with a snap and turned around to face him, her lips pursed. "Did you just give me a compliment about my baking?"

Amar turned all the way around and leaned against the counter, one eyebrow raised. "Don't act like I have never given you a compliment."

"Um, you have never given me a compliment."

He stared at her a beat. Then he broke out into a wide

smile, and a hint of mischief glinted in his dark eyes. "Well, maybe you never made anything I liked before."

She narrowed her eyes and threw the sponge at him. He cleanly dodged it, which gave her a chance to get close enough to smack his shoulder.

"Ow." He laughed and mock-rubbed his shoulder.

"Amar Virani, you are a royal pain in my ass." She set her jaw and flared her eyes as she made to smack his other shoulder, but he caught her hand.

"Okay. Okay. Mercy. I'm sorry." He held on to her hand and placed it on his chest. "If I complimented everything that you made that I loved, it would take forever for me to finish. If I've never said it before, I'll say it now. You are, hands down, the best pastry chef I know."

Divya was speechless. It wasn't just his words—but oh my god—did he just say that? It was the intensity in his gaze, the closeness of his body, the rapid beat of his heart underneath her hand. "Oh."

Is that what she'd just said? *Oh?* But her brain wasn't functioning. She couldn't even step back from him. Or maybe she didn't want to.

"Divya?" Her mother's voice broke Amar's spell and Divya moved away from him, shaking her head as if she really had been under the influence of some kind of Confundus charm.

Amar released her hand and stood straight, clearing his throat and shoving his hands in his shorts pockets. He was flushed, too, as if he'd revealed more to her than he'd intended.

"Yeah, Mom," Divya called back.

"Can you come grab these bags? I don't want your dad trying to bring them down."

Before Divya could answer, Amar passed her. "I'll

get them, Auntie. No problem." She had never seen him move so fast.

Divya took a moment to breathe and went back to her dishes.

Amar was back in minutes.

"You can go ahead and set out the food," she said when she heard him return.

"Where?" He looked around.

"Just move stuff."

He sighed and did so, just as her parents came down. Her mother pulled Amar into an embrace. "Beta. Your hair is wet."

"Michael turned off the electricity, so there's no AC. I took a quick shower before I came over."

"Michael—the guy who came over today and asked you on a date?" her father asked her. Amar snapped his gaze up to her.

"He did not ask me on a date. He was setting up a time to paint Lola." She turned to Amar. "He wants to do it this Sunday." There was no reason to add that she was going out with him afterward.

Amar froze for a moment, then shrugged. "Yeah. I'll be there."

"Then he asked her to join him for food after." Her father was just a fount of information. "A guy she met today." Her father shook his head. "Can you believe it?"

"Uncle, I'm sure Divya can handle herself." Was it her imagination, or was the previous joviality gone from Amar's voice?

"Beta. If your AC isn't working, just stay here. The spare bedroom is ready. It must be too hot over there," her mother said as Amar took out the food and began to serve them.

"Auntie, I'll be fine—"

"Amar Virani, I do not care how old you are. You listen to your auntie." Her mother was generally a sweetheart, but she could bring the Bossy Auntie in the blink of an eye. "Divya. You make sure he stays here."

"Mom." Divya shot her mother a look.

"Okay. Got it," Amar said at the same time.

"Come, you two. We'll eat together," her father said. "Then you can drop us to the airport. I want to start my vacation with my wife."

Chapter 5

Amar tossed and turned in the very comfortable queen bed in the Shahs' spare bedroom. How was he supposed to get any real sleep when he knew Divya was just two doors down? He was probably better off in the sweltering heat of his own home. When the sun finally infiltrated the blinds in his room, Amar was groggy from his sleepless night.

He stumbled down to the kitchen to find that Divya had made a pot of coffee and left him the address to the Rao home. Amar went for a quick run, then took his car to meet Divya at the Raos'.

Amar was early.

Divya was late.

He waited in his car until it was time, then looked around one more time for Divya before grabbing his backpack and getting out of the car. He tugged on the bottom of his chef's whites before ringing the bell. He had exactly one pristinely snowy chef's jacket, and he used it for meeting clients. Waiting for someone to come to the door, he glanced around one more time. Still no Divya.

He didn't understand. How could she be late to a meeting like this?

A petite, well-dressed woman opened the door. She could easily have been his mother's age. This was how he saw people sometimes. Older or younger than what his parents might be had they lived. He was sure it wasn't healthy, so he didn't share these thoughts with anyone. "Mrs. Rao? I'm Amar Virani, a friend of Divya Shah? I'll be working with her on your party."

"Of course." Mrs. Rao's smile was warm and genuine. "Come in. Is she here?"

"No." He plastered a grin on his face. "She's just running a bit behind, but if you like, we can get started in the meantime."

"Of course."

Mrs. Rao led him to her spacious kitchen—which was the entire size of his first floor. He tried to avoid staring enviously at her eight-burner stove and her nearly commercial-sized fridge as he pulled out his tablet and pulled up his sample menu for her event. He had gone over the few options he and Divya had prepared when she stopped him.

"I like this one." She pointed to the most expensive option. "Your biryani sounds fabulous."

"I'd be happy to set up a tasting. I realize time is short right now, as the party is in just over two weeks, so we could do that as early as tomorrow, if that's convenient for you," Amar suggested as per his discussion with Divya.

She had banked on the client wanting to try his biryani, so he had already started the prep for tomorrow.

Mrs. Rao's eyes lit up. "Oh—" The doorbell interrupted her. She stood to answer it, and Amar glanced at the time. Divya was twenty minutes late. He grimaced and shook his head. Unbelievable. This was not the way to run a business.

The raspy sound of Divya's laughter mingled with the dainty chime of Mrs. Rao's nervous giggle as they entered the kitchen, and Amar caught his breath. Though to be honest, he caught his breath every time he saw Divya. Her inner glow captivated him despite his frustration, and he struggled to figure out how to describe the light within her. A light that she seemed to be completely unaware of. Whatever it was, Divya was exquisite, even in unprofessional cropped leggings and a T-shirt, carrying her motorcycle helmet and laughing with the client, who did not appear to be one bit put out that Divya was late.

Amar raised an eyebrow at her.

She simply dipped her chin at him and turned on her full smile to Mrs. Rao. "So sorry I'm running a bit late, I simply did not judge traffic and distance…"

"Not a problem, beta," Mrs. Rao answered, beaming.

Everyone was taken in by Divya's charm. Amar simply nodded, his lips pressed together in a forced smile as he attempted to hide his irritation.

"Auntie." Divya dipped her chin at their client, before glancing quickly at him. "Amar."

Auntie? Was that professional?

"I had the most amazing idea on my ride over here. Why not do a dessert truck? I'll do made-to-order sweet crepes and you can do the savory. That is, if Auntie doesn't mind that the paint job may not be done by then?"

Exuding her irresistible charisma, Divya turned to Mrs. Rao, and Amar instantly knew they were doing made-to-order crepes. Forget that they had already discussed the menu at length—and that he'd just spent nearly half an hour going over options with the client.

He inhaled deeply for a count of four, then held his breath before slowly exhaling. "Mrs. Rao," he emphasized with a raised eyebrow to Divya, "was interested in the biryani."

"Oh yes, Rishi needs that biryani!" Mrs. Rao stated. She nodded at Amar. "Call me Auntie, beta."

Divya half smiled her satisfaction at him. "Of course we'll keep the biryani, *Auntie*. It's one of Amar's specialties." Divya sat down at the island. "Let's just tweak the rest of the menu a bit."

Tweaking the menu "a bit" basically involved changing everything they had already discussed. Except for the biryani—Auntie was insistent that they include it, and for that, Amar was glad, as he knew it was one of his best dishes.

By the time he got back to his house, he was beyond irritated. Michael and Janki were back in the basement, working on the wiring. Anita and Nikhil were talking to them, grim expressions on all their faces.

"What?" Amar asked without preamble. Whatever it was, he just needed to know so he could deal with it.

"This job is going to be more complicated than we expected. We may need to take out some of the wiring in places, not to mention adding additional circuitry," Michael said matter-of-factly.

"That's just the beginning," Janki said, going into extensive detail about what she would be doing.

"That's a lot," Amar said as he unbuttoned his chef's

whites. In fact, it was overwhelming. There was still no AC in the house. He took off the jacket.

"Just do it," Divya called from the doorway. She carried her helmet and set it down on his island. "That way you can just redo the kitchen at the same time."

"Exactly," Anita agreed. Amar scowled at his sister.

"Hey, Divya." Michael greeted Divya with a smile and a lingering look.

Seriously? He was going to have to watch this flirtation now, too?

"I'm not redoing the kitchen." He turned away from her.

"How many times over the years have you actually drawn up the plans for a whole new kitchen?" Divya was irritatingly calm right now.

Amar spun around. He had, many times, but he'd had no idea she was paying attention. "That wasn't real. I was just messing around. Besides, I barely have the money for new appliances and the basic work Michael wants to do."

"Take out a loan." Divya shrugged. "Consider it an investment in your own business. That's how I got Lola."

"You don't just renovate a house on a whim." Amar folded his arms across his chest.

"It actually sounds like a fabulous idea," Nikhil added.

Amar fixed a glare on him. Who had asked Nikhil for his opinion?

Nikhil either ignored his expression or didn't care. "I mean, you clearly hang on to all this because of your mom and dad—"

"What exactly would you know about it?" Amar growled.

"I, uh, lost my dad when I was a kid. It's not the

same, but I understand not wanting to let go," Nikhil said quietly.

Amar softened, chastised. "Right. I'm sorry I forgot."

Nikhil waved off his apology. "The point is that it can be difficult to take those first few steps, but you can do it. And you'll be better off for it."

Amar did not really believe him, but he kept his mouth shut.

Anita walked over to him. "You are stagnating. Come on, Bhaiya, take a leap." His sister put her arms around him. "They were my parents, too. I cooked with them in this same kitchen. I would think that by now, you'd be eager to move on. Maybe get a new look, at least."

Amar hugged his sister close, then pulled back so he could look at her. She was the perfect combination of their parents' physical traits. There was nothing but love and concern in her eyes, which were exactly like their mother's. Determination exuded from the set of her mouth, which was the same as their father's. They had looked out for each other with fierce intensity for the past eight years. Maybe she was right.

A glint of light behind her caught his eye. His mom's favorite rotli pan caught the sun as it leaned in the drying rack. His mind was flooded with images of their family cooking in this kitchen. Doing homework, arguing, singing and dancing badly. Living life. And his heart ached again.

"Well, then you'd be thinking wrong." What he wanted was to go back in time and undo what he had done that led to their accident in the first place.

Divya watched Amar for a moment, then shook her head in disappointment. "You're making a mistake." She wasn't sure why she was fighting him on this. It was his life. If he wanted to live it hiding behind his grief and never realizing his full potential, that was his business.

Except that she hated watching people she cared about waste the perfectly healthy lives that were given to them.

"No. I'm not."

"Yes, you are. If you decide to redo later, it'll cost you more. And by then you'll be super busy, and a big renovation could slow you down. Right now, you're just getting started—"

"I'm not redoing the kitchen, ever." Amar nearly snapped at her. In all the years she'd known him, he had never so much as raised his voice. Whatever. She was undeterred. Though this was a huge turnaround from their interaction yesterday.

"Why not? It's your house. *Your* kitchen." She had to push him.

Amar stared at her. "I'm getting the repairs done and keeping it as it is."

"It's a waste."

"It's my money to waste."

"Not the money." She moved closer to him. "You. You are wasting you." She poked his Ant-Man T-shirt. Her finger bumped against hard muscle, but she refused to be distracted. "You could turn this into an amazing commercial kitchen. Your catering business will know no bounds. If you simply redo what's here, it's clumsy and inefficient, and you know that. You're choosing to wallow—"

"I am not wallowing." He barely moved his lips as he shot the words out at her.

"You most certainly are." She grimaced at him. Wallowing was not a pretty sight. She would know.

Amar stepped away as if to dismiss her. "You have always been a fighter, you never—"

"Felt sorry for myself? Of course I did. In the privacy of my room. And then I got over myself and moved on."

Amar just stared at her for a moment, then something about him softened. "I'm sorry for all you went through. I'm happy that you've gotten through it all. But I'm not changing my mind."

Divya forced herself to shut up. "It's your life." *To waste.*

"Damn straight."

"It doesn't matter what he wants," Anita spoke up. Amar turned his focus to his sister.

"Neets…" Nikhil spoke softly and made eye contact with her. "There's no need to—"

Nikhil was taking his side?

"It's true. I can decide." Anita pressed her lips together, and Nikhil shook his head.

Divya questioned him with her eyes, but Amar couldn't respond.

His sister was about to turn on him. She was going to do the one thing they had decided they would not do.

Divya's brow furrowed in confusion as she turned to her friend. "Anita, what are you talking about?"

"I own fifty-one percent of the house." Anita let her bomb settle for a moment. "So what I say goes."

"We promised we wouldn't do this…" Amar glared at his sister, even as acid filled his stomach. She was planning to do it. She would destroy this kitchen. Their parents' kitchen. The last thing he'd done with his parents, was to argue about this kitchen. It was his last connection to them as well as a daily reminder of what his last words had been to them. The leather band from his father's watch itched his wrist, reminding him once again of the result of that conversation. He was not capable of changing this kitchen. He'd lose them all over again.

His sister's eyes filled with tears. Her husband rested his hand on her back. "I know what we said...at that time... Amar... I don't want to pull that string, but I will. Divya is right. You're wasting your life. If Ranjit hadn't bad-mouthed you, you'd still be working for him or for someone else who wouldn't appreciate your talent. You would never let yourself shine."

"Anita." His voice shook, his stomach burned. She couldn't do this to him.

"Amar." She came over and tried to touch him, but he stepped away from her, shaking his head.

She straightened and swallowed, fisting her hands by her side. For a quick second, she looked like their mother when he'd screwed up. He half expected to see her waving a belan at him, threatening to strike him. His mother never had, but his sister was about to tear up his world.

"Amar, I love you. So much. That's why I have to do this." She lifted her chin, and Amar knew there was no changing her mind. He couldn't count the number of times he'd seen her do that over the years. It was the point of no turning back. "You're an amazing chef. It's time to let the world know."

Pain and anger bubbled inside him. "There are other ways. I'll rent commercial space. I'll—"

"You do what you want. This kitchen is being renovated whether you agree to it or not. Now, if you want to have things your way, I suggest you work with Michael. If not, I'll give him my own suggestions."

"You have the new floor plan already in your head," Divya said softly.

Amar had envisioned this kitchen a million different ways. Not just new appliances, but a new flow, more efficiency. He had tried to explain this to his father. More than once. He sighed heavily.

"Well, as I apparently have no choice—" Amar turned to Michael, passing a hard gaze over his sister. "I'll send you the floor plan."

Chapter 6

Later that evening, Amar walked into the dining room of the Shah house, carrying his most important kitchen tools, expecting to have to make room in the cluttered space he remembered. Instead, he found a large island on wheels awaiting him. "How long have you had this?"

Divya shrugged. "Since yesterday. Dad and Mom got it for me. Didn't you see it in the morning?" She looked around her kitchen. "They figured I needed more counter space." Every surface was covered with some step of Divya's baking process. As well as, it seemed, every spatula she'd ever owned. The tools actually spilled over into the family room, but the dining room island was empty.

He hadn't seen it. "So why aren't you using it?"

She flicked her gaze away from him. "I left it for you."

"Oh. You didn't have to do—"

"No. It's fine. You need some space if you're going

to cook here." She nodded at the boxes he'd brought with him.

"Thanks." He swept his gaze over the area and started mentally organizing.

She stopped and watched him unload. "You know, Anita is doing the right thing."

Amar stiffened. "Just like she did the right thing re-marrying Nikhil?"

"Well, he does love her."

"So now you're on board with that?" It had been the one thing they'd agreed upon.

Divya shrugged. "I'm not saying that, yet. But she's really happy. He's obviously good to her. I want to support my friend in her happiness."

"And if it doesn't work out?" Amar spoke from behind the island cupboard door where he was storing a few of his sauté pans.

"Then you and I will help her through it." She touched his shoulder and he turned to look at her. "Although, to be honest, I don't think that's going to happen. They are both in it for the long haul."

Amar grunted.

"In any case, that has nothing to do with the fact that she's doing the right thing by renovating the kitchen."

Amar shrugged. "She thinks she is. But I disagree. Although clearly, I have no power here." He blew out a frustrated breath. "I have no idea why my parents split the house fifty-one to forty-nine. It makes no sense to me."

Divya chuckled. "It makes perfect sense. Your parents knew you. They may not have been thinking about the kitchen per se, but they knew you would be more likely to cling to the status quo than Anita. They gave her the power to force you out of your comfort zone. Pretty good parenting, actually."

"Am I that obvious?"

"Nothing wrong with that. Everyone has feelings— why hide them?"

Amar felt himself flush. She couldn't possibly know how he felt about her, could she?

"I'll tell you what I do not understand," she continued. "You're a professional chef, and I've always known you to be practical. A new kitchen would be a dream come true for a chef." Divya jutted a hip out and leaned against the wall.

Amar just stared at her. The words simply would not come. It was easier to be angry with his sister. They stared at each other in silence until it got uncomfortable, at which point, Divya spoke. "Well, in any case, it's a relief to not watch your potential go to waste."

"My potential was not going to waste." Or was it? No. The thought of changing the kitchen opened a pit of grief in his stomach. It had nothing to do with his potential.

"Uh-huh. You think about that." She nodded at the island. "Consider that island your space while you're here." Divya's tone cooled. Clearly, she realized she'd overstepped in some way, and she was pulling back.

"Thank you," he said, equally aloof. Maybe it was better to keep things professional between them instead of…personal.

"Have you picked out a name for your business?"

"What do you mean?" Though he knew exactly what she meant.

She grimaced. "You know you have a name picked out already. We all do."

He turned away from her and began to set things up.

"Ginger and Cardamom," he mumbled, quickly glancing at her. He caught her smiling and nodding her approval.

A bit lighter and happier, he began working on the dinners for his daily customers. Made the dough for the flatbread, chopped up veggies, roasted and blended spices. Before he knew it, the dhal was boiling, the shaak was simmering, his rotli were done and the summer sun still burned bright, despite the early evening hour. He had an hour before he had to deliver the food.

Divya was finishing up her truffles and decorating cookies. "The gulab jamun are done and soaking. Truffles are ready."

The sound of barking caught his attention. "What is that?" He went to the door and opened it. "Hey, Fury. How did you know I was here?"

"Who are you talking to?" Divya came up behind him. "Hey—what's he doing here? How did he find me?"

"Um. Oh. I found him yesterday, lurking in my backyard. I fed him a bit, but then he took off." As Amar spoke, the dog began to nuzzle Divya. *Lucky dog.* "Wait, what? How do you know Fury?"

She stared at him as the dog snuggled against her ankles. "Fury? You named this dog after Nick Fury?"

"The patch," Amar explained sheepishly, though it seemed obvious.

Divya rolled her eyes, but she had a smile on her face. "I found him in the playground by the middle school the other day, when I was on my run. I guess I'm a sucker just like you, because I fed him a bit, too. He must've followed me home from the playground." She looked around outside. "I wonder if he was hiding in the yard somewhere, because I haven't seen him since then."

Fury nuzzled closer to her. "I guess we might as well

clean him up." Divya picked up the dog and took him upstairs. Amar followed.

Fury squirmed in Divya's arms, but she held him easily. The poor guy was underfed and quite thin. At the top of the steps, Amar stepped in front of Divya to get to the bathroom and run the water. He grabbed towels from the hall closet. Sometimes it amazed him that he knew this house almost as well as his own.

As he ran the warm water, Divya lowered Fury into the tub. Amar used a small plastic cup to pour water gently over the shivering pup as Divya retrieved baby shampoo from somewhere.

"It's all I have." She shrugged. "We never had a dog, so no dog shampoo." She lathered it up in her hands and started scrubbing Fury. The dog was not having it and began to squirm and try to get out of the tub.

Amar laughed. "Hold him still a minute. Anita and I had this issue with Kulfi."

Divya held him in her arms. Amar quickly removed his shirt and watch and got in the tub in just his shorts. He held his hands out to her and wiggled his fingers.

Divya did not move at first. Her mouth was open and she just stared at him.

"Div. Hand me Fury." Amar watched her. She wasn't... checking him out, was she? In the next instant, all thought left his mind as Divya handed him the wet and wiggly dog. It was Amar's turn to stare. Divya's tank top was soaked through.

He forced his attention to the task at hand.

"I'll soap, you hold," Divya said. She knelt by the tub and scooted down closer to him, so she could reach Fury.

She scrubbed his fur with her hands. Every so often,

her hands would graze his, and it was as if electricity zinged through him in that instant.

Her face was close to his and he could not tear his gaze away from the smoothness of her bronze skin and the discovery of the faintest sprinkling of freckles across her nose.

"You have freckles." He spoke softly as she was near to him. "I guess I've never—" He was going to say "been this close," but that wasn't true. He had been, he simply had been too busy kissing her to notice.

"Never?" She raised an eyebrow, but did not turn to him, her full focus seemingly on the task at hand.

"Never noticed."

Her dimple made an appearance as she smiled. "Not so observant, are you?"

Actually, he noticed everything about her. Like how she was currently soaking wet and soapy, scrubbing the dog he held in his lap. He grunted.

"You really wanted a dog when you were growing up, didn't you." A change of subject was needed.

She sighed as she poured clean water over Fury. "I really did." She shrugged. "It was too much for my mom and dad. Taking care of me, when I was sick. Plus they were afraid of the germs. They didn't even like me playing with Kulfi."

Amar chuckled. "But you did."

"Well, don't tell them." She turned her face to him and widened her eyes.

"Cross my heart." He used one hand to cross his heart, and Fury took advantage and tried to make a break for it. The dog launched himself from Amar's lap, and as Divya grabbed for the sopping wet animal with one hand, so did Amar, and all three of them fell backward. Amar splashed against the inside of the tub, with Divya's back pressed against his chest and Fury in her arms. She smelled of sugar and baby shampoo.

"Nice catch," he said, laughing.

"Thanks." She laughed. Amar could not remember the last time he'd felt as light as he did right now, with Divya practically in his arms, the two of them laughing and trying to hold the fidgety wet dog.

They stopped laughing and suddenly Divya was scrambling to get up. "Oh. I'm sorry. I was literally on top— I mean, I fell back—" He'd never seen her so flustered.

His eyes met hers. "Just hand me the dog, and take your time getting out of the tub."

"Yeah. Okay." Her voice was suddenly breathy, but she nodded and handed him the dog. It was all Amar could do to not stare at how her wet clothes clung to her body as she wrapped Fury in a towel.

"You good?" she asked as she exited the bathroom.

"I'm fine. I'll…um…be down in a minute." He rested his head back against the tile to gather his thoughts.

Why was he sleeping here?

"You think someone lost him?" asked Amar as he rifled through the fridge for something to feed Fury. He made scrambled eggs and rice while Divya played with him.

Divya shrugged. "No idea. There's no collar. And you must have seen how scruffy he looked, and he was so hungry…" Her voice trailed off, and for once he saw a vulnerability in her expression as she looked at the dog. Something she rarely revealed.

She must have realized he was watching her because she quickly glanced away.

"I'll take him to the vet tomorrow," said Amar, bringing the puppy's meal over. Fury tucked into the food as soon as Amar put the bowl on the ground. "See if he's chipped." Amar grinned at Fury. "I have to go deliver the food to my clients. You got him?"

Divya cuddled Fury, and a smile spread across her face. A smile of pure unadulterated joy. Damn, but she was beautiful. He stood. "And my AC should be up and running tomorrow."

She looked up at him. "I've been thinking. Why not just stay here until the kitchen is done? I mean, why should you stay there with all the dust and everything? Besides, this way you'll have full access to this kitchen at all hours." She shrugged like it was no big deal.

The thought of living in the same house with Divya was at once enticing—and petrifying. He'd hardly been able to sleep last night.

"You're afraid I won't be able to handle the demolition."

"Well…" She hesitated. "You're very attached to that kitchen, Amar. To the past. So yes. I am concerned."

Amar tried not to focus on the fact that maybe her gaze had lingered longer than necessary. And that maybe that gaze was because she was worried about him, because she remembered that when push came to shove and he'd had to deal with difficult things, he'd been unable to. She remembered that he was weak.

Chapter 7

"What's all this?" Amar entered the kitchen yawning, his hair still sleep tousled, a light scruff on his chin. Seeing the counters and table covered in cooling racks, filled with sugar cookies, he broke into a huge smile that made Divya stop for just a split second in her tracks. He had on shorts and a worn Spider-Man T-shirt. Damn, but he looked amazing first thing in the morning.

Why had she never noticed that before? Why was she noticing *now*? Who was she kidding? She'd been noticing his fitted T-shirts, taunting eyes and perfect mouth for a couple of years now. Definitely since that body-liquefying kiss last year.

What the hell was going on in her brain? Not that it was only her brain that was reacting to Amar this morning.

Fury ran to him, tail wagging. "Well, hey, little guy."

The pure adoration in Amar's eyes as he bent down to pet the dog was the last straw. There were officially parts of her that were melting. They were different than the parts of her that had reacted to him yesterday while they'd bathed Fury. The casual way he had taken off his shirt and displayed his muscled abs, as if he had no idea how attractive he was. Which was most likely the case. Which just made him more attractive.

She sipped her coffee to try to distract herself. It did not work.

He poured himself coffee in the Avengers mug that he had brought over.

"So." She cleared her throat and forced herself to look away from him. Gesturing to the racks, she said, "*These* are *cookies*."

Her sass won her that half grin of amusement that she rarely got to see but was quickly starting to crave. "I can see that." He added cream and sugar to his coffee. So, he liked it sweet. "But none of our parties have ordered sugar cookies, and these aren't even decorated."

"That's because I'm taking them to the ward for the kids to decorate."

Amar carefully sipped his coffee. "The ward?"

"Pediatric oncology." She tried to say the words clinically, as if they had no effect on her, when the opposite was true. "Once a month, I take cookies or cupcakes for the kids to decorate. The other weeks, I just take books, or crafts."

Amar drank more coffee as he looked at her. "You visit every week?"

"Every other for sure. More if things are slow."

Amar curled his bottom lip. "Impressive."

That single word sent a zing through her. It was the

second time in a week that Amar had said he was impressed by her. He nodded at the leaf-shaped cookies. "Fall theme?"

"It's almost September. Next time, I'll do Halloween, maybe Diwali." She continued moving cookies from the baking sheet to the cooling racks.

"Can I come?"

"What?" She almost dropped one.

"I don't have much going on today after I take Fury to the vet. I can spare a few hours. Sounds like fun."

"Um, yeah, sure. Courtney—you know, she worked with me at the grocery store? She usually comes as well."

"Great." Amar glanced at the microwave. "I better change or I'll be late." He quickly finished his coffee and ran upstairs to change. When he returned, Divya noted he'd changed into a Dr. Strange tee, which also fit him quite nicely. Though the image of him without the shirt popped right into her mind.

Honestly, what was happening here? She'd missed a lot of school, and Anita had been her lifeline. When she was well enough, she would go to Anita's, and Amar would sometimes hang out with them. He'd bring her food when she was ill from chemo treatments, too. But she'd never really considered Amar a *guy* until their ill-fated drunken kiss.

Since then, she kept herself busy and willed the feelings away whenever they would come up.

But now, he was sleeping in her house.

She shook her head. *Cut it out*, she told herself.

"Shouldn't be long at the vet," Amar said as he gently picked up Fury and held him close, absently scratching behind his ears. "I have an old leash and collar from Kulfi at the house that I'll grab."

Divya nodded and then proceeded to watch Amar cross the street before getting back to her cookies. She colored her icing and put it in piping bags and packed it for the hospital before taking her shower.

She was just running her fingers through her hair to style it when the doorbell rang. Short hair was fabulous, she marveled happily. No fuss, no muss.

No problem if it fell out.

Shaking off the haunting thought, she ran downstairs to answer the door. It was Michael. "Hey."

"Good morning." He smiled at her. "Is Amar here?"

"He's at the vet—oh, here he is." Divya indicated behind Michael as Amar pulled up in her driveway and got out of the minivan. Fury trotted alongside him on the leash like he'd always been there.

Her initial excitement at seeing them—seeing Fury—dissipated as Amar walked up, a grim look on his face. Instead, a knot formed in her belly. She realized that she hoped Fury did not have a family so they could keep him. Which was ridiculous since Fury had spent exactly one night in her house.

"What?" she asked him as she knelt to greet Fury.

"He's a bit malnourished, but he's chipped. Someone must be looking for him," Amar said. He was trying to sound matter-of-fact, but a bit of sadness in his voice told her he'd had the same thoughts as her. "What's up, Michael?"

"Just wanted to let you know that Janki has the electrical working, so the AC is good to go if you want to move back home. We'll fix the drywall during the reno. The appliances we talked about are on back order. I'll have our architect take a look and come by the house before we finalize the plans. But based on the designs we discussed, it'll take us at least a few months to do the renovation anyway."

"Thanks, Michael. I'm going to stay here while we do the renovation. I need easy kitchen access, and besides, with all the demolition that will be happening, it's not safe for Fury."

Michael furrowed his brow. "Of course."

Divya was still cuddling Fury, but at Amar's answer, a zing of happiness flashed through her. She tried to convince herself she just liked the company, but deep down, there was a part of her that was excited to have Amar in close proximity. No matter how many times she pushed the thought aside it kept floating to the surface.

"We'll start the demo as soon as the architect gives us the go ahead. I'm hoping next week," Michael said.

"I'll start emptying the kitchen this afternoon." Amar nodded at him.

"Great! We're painting this weekend, right, Divya?" Michael grinned at her.

"Looking forward to it," she said.

"I'll be there," chimed in Amar.

Michael's grin faltered just the tiniest bit. "Fabulous. The more the merrier." He turned to leave. "I better get back to work."

Divya secured Fury in the mudroom and they headed for the hospital in Amar's minivan. "I thought you wanted to go back to your house."

Amar shrugged. "That was before Fury. It's easier if we're both with him, don't you think?"

Of course Amar would only want to stay for Fury's sake. "Yes, makes perfect sense."

Amar turned to her, confusion on his face. "That's

okay, right? I mean, I can go home and leave Fury with you, but—"

"No." Divya shook her head. "I'm happy for the company. And besides, I think he's already really attached to you." Now she was talking too fast.

Amar pulled his minivan into the visitors' lot. He held the box of undecorated cookies while Divya rolled in the remaining supplies in her suitcase carrier. They headed for the main building in the hospital complex, which was the tallest, looming large and intimidating over the other buildings.

Divya looked up at it, her heart rate quickening as it did every time she came here. She thought after the first few times that she would get used to it, but she had not. She practiced her 4-7-8 breathing to calm her heart rate as they entered the hospital. Inhale for four counts, hold for seven, exhale for eight. Walk. Repeat.

She plastered a smile on her face, and all the normal niceties emerged from her mouth as she ran into people she knew, even as she continued to flex her free hand. She squeezed her fingers into a fist as the doors to the pediatric oncology ward opened.

The odor of sickness and cleaning supplies filled her nostrils, along with the artificial lavender scent that was pumped out in an attempt to calm the patients and parents. It all nauseated her. She stretched her fingers and fisted them again. In a moment, she would adapt, as her focus became the children on the ward as opposed to the memory of her own trauma. It was the same every time she came.

She stretched her fingers out again but, this time, was

met with the warmth and strength of another set of fingers intertwining with hers.

She closed her fingers around Amar's and literally siphoned calm and strength from him. Her heart rate slowed, the smells became part of the background and, in a rush of beeps and hellos, the surrounding world came back to her.

"On your left," Amar mumbled.

Divya looked at him, but he was focused ahead.

The nurse's station was in the middle, patient rooms arranged in a U shape around it. Baskets of lollipops were scattered at the nurse's station. Divya led Amar to the small activity room and quickly learned that having Amar along was a fabulous idea, and not just for his ability to calm her. He quickly organized the cookies and supplies, leaving aside the ones that needed to be taken to the children too ill to join the group in the activity room.

"Hi, Divya." One of the newer nurses, Megan, greeted her with a smile. "Who is this?" She nodded at Amar as her smile widened, and Divya could have sworn she batted her eyelashes. A new sensation stirred inside Divya as she envisioned Megan suddenly melting into the ground.

"This is—"

"Amar Virani." Amar grinned, extra big, Divya was sure, and held out his hand. "Nice to meet you…"

"Megan," the young nurse said as she shook Amar's hand and gave him an appraising once-over. "Nice to meet you, too."

The handshake lingered exceedingly longer than Divya thought was necessary, and she could have sworn that Amar did not seem to mind. *Ew!*

"So nice of you both to come and hang out with the children. Please let me know if you need anything."

"She seemed nice," Amar commented after she left.

"Eh. If you like that sort of thing," Divya answered.

"You mean the sweet, friendly kind of thing?" Amar asked.

"Whatever."

Amar shook his head and finished setting up. Divya followed his lead, trying to make sense of why Megan had bothered her so much. She had never had that kind of reaction to her before.

Was she jealous? Maybe. But she had no reason to be jealous. There was no part of Amar that was hers.

Courtney Stone arrived in a whirlwind of energy and provided a welcome distraction from her wayward thoughts. "Sorry I'm a bit late. Last-minute cake personalization at the bakery." Courtney had worked in the grocery store since she and Divya had graduated from culinary school, but she seemed to enjoy it, and the steady paycheck, whereas Divya had felt it was some kind of slow-motion living hell with overly sweet icing. "Wow. This looks great, Div. Nice."

"It was actually Amar. He's the organizational master." She caught his eye. Now that she thought about it, he always had been. "Did they teach you how to decorate cookies at that fancy chef school you went to?"

"I can manage." He gave her that side smile that always sent a spark through her body.

"Perfect. Courtney can handle the kids in here. Amar and I will hit the ward." Divya inhaled and looked around. Amar rested his hand on her shoulder, and it was like a cloak of calm came over her. Amar Virani had a superpower.

The first room had two children, aged eight and twelve. Amar grabbed a cookie and some icing and made a beeline for the older one. He arranged everything on the child's tray while introducing himself. The preteen girl flushed and could barely make eye contact with him. Divya could totally relate.

If Amar noticed, he didn't show it. He simply sat down next to her bed and showed her how to use the piping bag and various sprinkles. When he handed her the bag, she sat up and eagerly got started, glancing at Amar from time to time. He gently guided her through the project. Within a few moments, the young patient was relaxed and giggling and decorating her cookie.

Divya did the same with the eight-year-old. He had been here before and already knew how to use the supplies. So Divya simply chatted with him while he worked. When they finished, Amar and Divya gathered their supplies and headed for the next room.

"You decorate a decent cookie," Divya commented to Amar.

"High praise from a pastry chef." Amar laughed.

Divya led the way into the next room. This one also had two patients in it, teenagers. Parul and Ethan. Parul had been in and out of the ward for a year, so Divya knew her. Ethan was new. Divya caught Amar's eye and he went to Ethan.

Divya had had a hard time getting through to Parul. Fourteen years old when she was diagnosed, the young girl's brown skin was sallow and yellowish. She wore thick black eyeliner. Her wig of straight hair was pure black. She topped the look with black lipstick and black nail polish. Divya knew her look was as much about fighting her cancer, as the chemo that had taken her beautiful hair. Divya absently ran her fingers through her own hair.

Initially, Parul had tried to act like everything Divya had to offer was beneath her. It wasn't until Divya told Parul that she'd been sick as well that Parul even listened to her. But once the teen found out that Divya had a sweet tooth, the two became thick as thieves. Decorating and eating cookies was her thing, so Divya always brought Parul an extra.

Amar and Ethan were doing fine, so she turned her attention to Parul.

"Hey! I made cinnamon-sugar cookies today, your favorite." Divya pulled up a chair next to Parul's bed.

"Thanks, Divya." Parul sounded tired. Not unusual.

"And I brought those silver pearl balls you love. Aaaand pink icing." She presented the tube with great flourish.

"Great." Parul still sounded off. "But pink isn't a fall color."

"But it is your favorite color." Divya grinned. "Tell me about that cute guy two doors down. Fernando? Did you ever talk to him?" This elicited a small flush and a mini eye roll accompanied by a shy grin. For all her bluster, Divya had found Parul was actually a very shy girl.

"I did. I said hi."

Divya widened her eyes. "Oh my god! What did he say?"

"He said hi back." The teen giggled.

"Good start." Divya put the setup in front of Parul and they started decorating the cookies.

Parul shrugged.

"What? It *is* a good start. Talking to boys can be nerve-racking. Especially the ones you think are cute."

"But what's the point?" Parul effortlessly made a pink skull and crossbones on a leaf cookie.

"The point is that it's fun, and it's good practice for when you go back to school." Divya never commented on any child's choice of decor. This was art and it was an outlet for them.

"Yeah, but it's not like I'm going to fall in love." She carefully placed silver pearl balls where the skull's eye sockets were.

"You never know," Divya said, watching the young girl place more candy pearls along the edge of the cookie with professional flair. This girl should totally go to pastry school.

"You think I could fall in love? That someone would love me?" Parul seemed absorbed in her work, but Divya knew that was only partly a ruse. She was afraid of the question she'd asked.

"Of course." Divya did not miss a beat. "*Someone* would be lucky to love you. And to have you love them."

"You think so?" Parul was fighting a real smile and looked up from her second cookie.

She touched the girl's chin, and held her gaze. "I do not lie, Parul. You *are* beautiful, inside and out."

"What's it like? Being in love?" Parul asked as she worked.

Divya shot a quick glance at Amar. "I don't know, exactly. Can't say I've actually been in love."

"But you're so old!" Parul said and immediately started laughing.

"Thanks for that." Divya laughed with her.

"What about him?" Parul jutted her chin out to Amar.

"What about him?" Divya cleared her throat.

"Um, *hello*. He's totally hot. And he's here with you, in the middle of the week, teaching cancer kids how to decorate cookies." Parul rolled her eyes and shook her head like Divya was an idiot.

Divya kept her focus on Parul's work and shrugged. "He's a good guy. Plus he's a chef."

Parul leaned toward her and whispered, "He keeps looking at you."

Divya dared a glance in Amar's direction and caught him looking away as she turned to him, and her heart thudded.

"He's just checking to see when we need to go to the next room. Besides, he's my best friend's brother."

"What? Whoa!" Parul delighted in this info as if it were scandalous. "But your best friend, she wouldn't stand in your way to happiness if it turned out you and Hot Chef over there got together?"

"We're not getting together." They were too different.

"But you want to," Parul teased.

"I don't know what I want. Besides, I'm busy with my dessert truck, Lola. She needs a lot of redecorating." Time for a topic change.

"Change the topic all you want, Divya, but Hot Chef is still looking at you."

Divya sighed as heat ran all through her body.

After the last cookie was decorated, Courtney helped them pack up before she rushed back to her late shift at the store. Amar took Divya's hand as they exited the building. Once outside and on the way to the car, Amar turned to her. "You okay?"

"Oh yes. I'm fine." She made to drop his hand. He held on.

"It's okay, Div. You can hold on as long as you want. I know it's not easy for you, coming here."

He was holding her hand simply for support. She should let go. She really should. But she didn't want to. She finally had to once they got to the car.

They packed the car and got in. "I have to ask—why do you come here, if it stresses you out?"

Divya inhaled and relaxed as they pulled out of the parking lot. "It used to be the highlight of my week when I was…in treatment." She glanced at Amar quickly. "Visitors who weren't your parents were fun and exciting." She didn't really talk much about her treatments and that time in her life, but with Amar, she didn't have to, since he had been there. She stared out the window as the trees and cars passed in a blur. "There was this one volunteer, Margot. She would come each week with different crafts and projects to work on. She was maybe twenty-three, but she seemed so much older and very sophisticated. She was an art major at the University of Maryland. She was amazing."

"She sounds amazing. What happened to her?" Amar asked.

"I don't know. I went into remission and was released. She had an end-of-treatment party for me—we did it for all the kids when they finished chemo." Divya stared out the window. She had come home and had not had to go back. She never saw Margot again, but she never forgot how Margot had made her feel seen. It wasn't the arts and crafts she'd brought for them, it was the feeling of being a normal kid that was important. It was the ability to forget she was sick—even for a short time—to feel like she was just another kid, coloring and gluing, like all kids did.

"Well, Parul definitely looks up to you," Amar said, his eyes on the road.

"You think?"

"Oh yeah. One hundred percent. She looked at you with complete adoration." Amar smiled at her, then turned back to his driving.

Divya bit her bottom lip, her heart warm. It felt good to make a difference, to make someone else happy. Especially Parul.

"What was that you said before? When you took my hand, you mumbled something about *left*?"

"Oh." Amar flushed. "You know in *Avengers: Endgame*, at the end, right before the big battle, when all seems lost? 'On your left' was a joke between Sam and Steve, because Steve said 'on your left' every time he passed Sam on the track. When Sam is getting ready to come to Steve's aid right before the big battle, he says 'on your left.' Some think it's a friendly joke, but I also think it's his way of saying 'I'm here, I've got your back.'"

Divya just stared at him, speechless. "Well, thank you for that. It, um, was…very helpful."

Amar shrugged. "Mind if I join you next time? Maybe we could take Fury? Some of the kids might enjoy playing with him."

Divya turned to Amar. He was serious. "Sure, I'd love the help. And we can check and see if Fury is allowed to come onto the ward."

Amar's face lit up. "It's a date."

Chapter 8

"You need to cook, not watch all this," Divya said. She handed him a glass of something cold.

He was standing over Divya's sink, looking out the window at workers doing the demolition across the street at his house. "Huh? What? I'm cooking." He took a sip from the glass and turned to her, the tart sweetness still on his tongue. "This is amazing mango lassi."

"Well, at least it got your attention. Something your biryani could use." She raised her eyebrows at him.

"I'm cooking. See?" He looked around but realized all he had done was chop some vegetables and herbs.

Divya pursed her lips at him. "You've been distracted all afternoon, staring across the street. How do you think playing amateur spy is going to get your dishes prepped on time?"

"I have to make sure they do it right," he insisted as

he took another sip of her mango lassi. Or nectar of the gods, either one, it was that good. Perfect blend of tart and sweet.

"This is their job. Michael is one of the best. I'm sure he only hires the best. They will do it right." Her hand squeezed his bicep in reassurance.

"How do you know he's one of the best?" Amar knew that, but he was irritated by the fact that Divya had gone out with Michael after they'd worked on stripping the paint off Lola last Sunday.

"You hired him. You're paying him big money to do this job. That's how."

Amar grunted.

"What's your problem with him, anyway? He's good at his job and he's a nice person."

Fury barked at Amar's feet. Amar smiled down at the dog. "Fury doesn't like him."

It was true. Fury growled every time Michael came over. So now Michael simply texted Amar when he had a question. Amar covered up a grin. He'd known right away he liked this dog.

Divya bent down to cuddle Fury as she shook her head. "Any word?"

"Nope. The vet has not had any luck reaching his owner. She's left a few voice mails, but nothing." Fury belonged to someone in Ellicott City, which was a good seven or eight miles from where they lived. How he had traveled so far from home and why the owners weren't frantic was beyond him. Meanwhile, both he and Divya enjoyed having Fury around.

Amar glanced out the window again, the lassi raised to his mouth, but what he saw two of the workers carrying curdled his stomach. He put the glass down and started for the door, Fury at his heels.

"What? What is it now?" called Divya as she followed him out.

"They're—" He couldn't even get the words out. He was breathless without having exerted himself. "They're getting rid of Mom's stove." Divya caught up with him as he walked out the door. She squeezed his shoulder to hold him back.

"What's the plan here, huh?" She spoke quietly, calmly.

"That's the stove Mom taught me on."

"Yeah, but it's a gas stove that potentially leaks gas. It's a hazard, as is the wiring in that house."

He turned back to her. She wasn't understanding. "I learned how to cook on that stove."

"I know." Her eyes went sad for a moment. "So did I."

He stared at her. He had been so wrapped up in himself, he'd forgotten how close their families were, how much time Divya had spent at their house, and vice versa. "Yeah. Right." He shook his head. "I'm basically an idiot."

"Well, maybe most of the time." He looked at her, a little surprised, and she smirked at him. "But right now, that might be a little harsh. Amar, everything you learned is not in that stove. It's in you." She pressed her hand against his chest.

He just stared at her, squinting in the sun at him, not letting him wallow in his own thoughts.

"What are you going to do?" she challenged him. "Tell them not to take the potentially explosive stove?"

"I didn't want them to take anything. I didn't want—"

He felt frustrated beyond words. This was his sister's doing.

"You shouldn't be out here, Amar." She applied firm pressure to his bicep, nudging him to go back in. Her expression was soft; her eyes were knowing.

He turned back to the street. The movers were putting the stove into the truck. He could not tear himself away. Even though he knew deep down he was being unreasonable—it was just a stove. Wasn't it? He almost felt as though he was being forced to confront the loss of his mother all over again.

Divya stood next to him, her hand still on his arm, her body soft against his. He drew strength from her presence as he watched the truck drive away. When the truck was out of sight, Divya turned to face him again.

"Listen, I know this isn't easy for you, but consider what it'll be like to be back in your new kitchen, using all the lessons you learned." She nodded at his house. "That's the point, right? To continue your parents' legacy?"

He stared at her as she spoke. She was right, of course. If he didn't move forward, it wouldn't matter what he had learned or where.

She just didn't know the whole story.

"Enough." She fixed him with those dark eyes. "Rishi Rao is turning forty today, and your biryani and cholay poori for thirty of his best friends will make the party perfect. Time to put all your skills to the test. Plus we're doing the made-to-order crepes on Lola."

He just needed to work. It's why her mother would bake with her after a doctor's appointment when she was sick. Divya had enjoyed it, so now baking was her distraction, her therapy and her job. Hence her flared hips and generous thighs.

Amar finally looked at her. Like, *really* looked at her. She was dusted from head to toe with flour and cocoa powder.

"Oh my god, Divya. Look at you!" He burst out laughing.

"I've been *working*!"

He followed her inside, downed his lassi and got down to business.

Divya was right. *Enough is enough.*

He opened a drawer to grab his spoons, but they weren't there. "Seriously, Div. How hard is it to put the stuff back where you found it?" He opened a few more drawers before he located his spoons. "It's literally a waste of time looking for things."

Divya shrugged. "I'm not used to sharing space."

Amar grumbled and went back to work. It was cramped, and work space was hard to come by.

Even though he did most of his prep on the movable island, he still needed the stove. Divya's stove behaved differently than his, but he adjusted. But the space was small for two people, and more than once, Amar found himself grazing against Divya's body as he moved around the area. Not that he minded, but the jolt he experienced each time was akin to a drug and he found it addictive and distracting.

He gave the cholay one last taste before pouring it into a serving dish. He and Divya reached for the poori dough at the same, their hands crashing against each other in their haste. Divya flushed and stepped back.

They packed up Lola, and Divya drove them to the Rao home to set up. They'd stripped Lola of her paint and had managed one coat of primer. She wasn't completely presentable, as in Divya's mind, Lola was only wearing her underwear, but she wasn't completely naked either.

Divya had changed the menu to fresh dessert crepes and cholay with fresh fried pooris to order. Amar's biryani was on the side. It wasn't a traditional menu, by any means, but it had all the elements that the customer wanted. Ranjit never would have done a menu like this. He would have found it blasphemous. Ranjit had been all about classical Indian cooking. Amar liked to mix things up. Everything did not have to be standard dhal, rotli, shaak and rice. And though he was nervous about the execution of the made-to-order crepes, he knew Divya was correct in her assessment that different was better sometimes. Amar might not have thought of it, but he was willing to see how it all went down.

While things did not go completely smoothly—he was constantly bumping into various parts of Lola—and Divya—the food and service was a hit. Rishi was properly surprised and impressed, recommending them both to all his friends.

At the end of the night, Divya drove Lola, while Amar sat behind her. He took off his chef's whites and sat in his Black Panther T-shirt.

"My shins will never be the same." He'd banged them more than once on containers holding supplies. "But your menu was a hit. I didn't think we'd be able to pull it off."

"I didn't know if we could either. But there was only one way to find out." Divya grinned at him in the rear-view mirror.

"What do you mean, you didn't know? You told Mrs. Rao you had colleagues who did this all the time, and it worked."

"Well, I have a friend who tried it and it worked."

"One friend?" He narrowed his eyes at her in the rearview mirror. "How many guests?"

"Ten."

"Are you serious? You took that big a gamble with our first event?" Even though the job was done, Amar's stomach went into knots at the possibility that it might not have worked at all, based on what he was hearing now.

Divya shrugged. "Kind of. I was hoping."

"Hoping?" He shook his head. "Unreal. What if it hadn't worked? And we lost business, and no one wanted to hire us again?"

"That wouldn't happen. We both make great food. It was just a logistics thing—"

"Logistics can break an event—and you know it." Amar's great mood from the party was gone, overtaken by frustration with Divya's casual demeanor. He just didn't understand her. How could she build a business like this?

"But it didn't." Divya stood her ground.

"We got lucky. This time."

"We need to take some risks," she insisted. "Be different than everyone else."

Amar stayed silent. "You should have been honest with me."

"Would you have gone along with it, if I had?" Divya glanced at him in the rearview mirror.

"No. Of course not."

She grinned, her expression laced with the unspoken "see how well I know you?"

"Admit it." She smirked at him. "That was a rush."

He was pissed that she had misled him. But despite that, he felt a smile quirk at his mouth. Encouraging her was a bad idea. "Maybe." If he was honest, it had been a huge rush, cooking against the demand of people, and their satisfied expressions when they realized the wait was worth it. "But you can't keep secrets if you want us to work together, Divya."

She smiled broadly at him. "Never again. I promise." Then she cackled, as if she'd pulled off some kind of heist. Her laughter was contagious and pure and though he tried to fight it, Amar found himself laughing along with her. He should know better than to fight Divya Shah.

Chapter 9

Amar fed Fury a gourmet dinner of scrambled eggs with chicken broth and rice.

"You're spoiling him," Divya chided.

Amar shrugged. He was a chef. He cooked. That was his thing. "I'll walk him, then I'll—" *Spoil you.* He stopped himself. "Then I'll cook us dinner." This was a free evening, nothing to practice, no clients to cook for. It was their first day off since the Rao party a few days ago. They had worked a bit on Lola's paint job, but tonight was just the two of them.

Fury looked back at Divya as Amar leashed him and walked out of the house. "Fine." Divya made a show of dragging out the word as she smiled at Fury. "I'll come, too."

Fury trotted happily alongside him as he and Divya walked the neighborhood they had both grown up in. The sun was still high in the sky, despite the fact that it was early September. The air had cooled a bit, taking some of the stickiness out of the air, making the walk more pleasant. They ran into neighbors, stopped to chat. People asked about his sister and her new married life. They asked about Divya's parents' travel and downsizing plans.

Amar shot a look at Divya. *Downsizing?* She shrugged it off.

"Your parents want to move?" Amar pressed.

"They were always going to move." Divya wouldn't make eye contact with him.

"What, Div? Spill it."

She stopped walking and turned to him. "Some... time ago, my parents and...your parents had decided to look for smaller places. Together. I guess they were used to living near each other after so many years. They were interested in condos in the same neighborhood. But then..." She pressed her lips together, and met his eyes with apology.

"The car accident," Amar finished for her, but not without a pang in his heart, the watch heavy on his wrist.

She nodded. The Shahs had taken the loss of their friends hard.

"So why didn't they move anyway, after a while?" Amar started walking slowly.

"Because—" Divya started walking beside him "—they wanted to make sure you and Anita were okay. Now Anita is settled, and you're finally starting your own business—"

"They're ready to move on." He shook his head. He couldn't believe it... And yet, was it really so hard to see? Veer Uncle and Kalpana Auntie had been like parents to him and Anita for as long as he could remember. "They didn't have to hang on for almost eight years."

"Amar, seriously? They're parents. That is what they do."

"So, when?"

"Not for a few more months. They found a place, but the owners won't move until after Christmas."

"What about you? Would you keep the house?" Amar couldn't imagine Divya not living across the street. Obviously, she wouldn't have lived there forever, but the idea that he would be the last one standing on the block, out of their once close-knit group, was suddenly getting real. He would be alone.

She frowned, shook her head. "I'll get an apartment. Too much space for me by myself."

"But what about a kitchen? You've always had that fabulous kitchen," Amar asked.

"I'll rent—"

"Or you could use mine." The idea sprang into his head and out his mouth before he had a chance to think about it. "I'll have plenty of space after the renovation is done. There's an area I can set up just for you. A true baker's kitchen."

"I'd pay you rent," Divya quipped.

"Not if we become partners."

Wait a minute. *What am I saying?*

"Seriously?" Her face lit up with the possibility. "Partners?"

Amar looked nonchalant. "Maybe."

"Yeah." She grinned. "Maybe."

Fury continued to draw quite a bit of attention, and he ate it up. Wherever this little guy came from, it did not seem as though he cared to go back.

Amar caught Divya's eye a few times, and he was visited by the thought of how comfortable they were together. How great it might be to see her at work every day. Or even, just to be with her every day.

Just quit it. They'd drive each other nuts.

They went around the block and arrived back in front of his house. From out here, it looked the same.

"Let's take a look inside," Divya said as she walked up the driveway. Amar followed behind her, a little uneasily. Though part of him had always wanted the space altered, he wasn't sure how he would feel about the changes. Not now.

Inside, he really began to worry that this might have been a mistake. Walls had been taken down, all the appliances removed. The area was more like one giant great room. The space was hollow, a shell of what it had been.

Divya beamed as she walked around. "This is amazing. You get to start all over."

Amar looked around through her eyes. Maybe she was right. The floor was just being put in. He had picked a ceramic tile that looked like hardwood, and it was starting to come together quite nicely. The space was large and open. The setting sun filtered light in from all the windows, adding a warm glow to the room. The design he'd gone with included a large work space, with plenty of room for two or three people to be chopping, blending, decorating, whatever. Michael had marked in chalk where the new appliances would go. A small area just to the left of the door, away from the cooking, would be where he met with clients, so customers could come to him for consultation or just to pick up their prepared food. All in all, it looked like it was going to be a beautiful place.

He grinned at her. "You know—"

"Oh hey! Divya. Great to see you," Michael's voice called from behind them.

Amar stifled a groan but stepped away from Divya all the same.

"Michael." Divya glanced at Amar. "Hey."

Fury began a low growl, and Amar bit away a smile. "Michael."

"Amar." Michael eyed Fury and kept his distance. "I'm just finishing up for the day. There's a box of stuff we found behind the old fridge and that countertop. I left it on your desk."

"Thanks." Amar took Fury and went to his dad's office. This was the one place they had left the same, in terms of renovation. Just a bit of drywall repair was needed from the rewiring. It currently housed much of what was in the kitchen that didn't need to be used or tossed.

Michael had stepped closer to Divya as Amar left the room, and he could hear them talking softly.

Amar walked into the study and saw the small cardboard box on top of the desk. He could swear traces of his father's cologne still wafted in the air, mixed with the lingering scent of incense. This study also housed the small family mandhir. Amar hadn't prayed at it in a long time, so he knew the scent of incense was as much in his head as his father's cologne. Memories flashed before him: he and Anita reading books in here while their father paid the bills, praying at the mandhir each morning with their mother, trying to write down "recipes" of dishes he had made with them, while both his parents shook their heads at him. *"Cook from your heart and taste, not a piece of paper,"* both would say.

It was too much. He turned and left the office as sadness overtook him. He didn't really want to see what had been behind his refrigerator all these years. Amar had a sudden urge to cook. He walked right past Michael and Divya and out the front door, Fury by his side.

"Amar?" Divya called out.

He stopped. Divya caught up to him, rested her hand on his arm. "What happened? What was in the box?"

"I have no idea. I just need to get out of there." He glanced behind her at Michael. "I'll catch up with you later." He continued for the door and heard Divya calling out to Michael.

"See you around nine?"

So, they were going on another date? Now he really needed to lose himself in the kitchen, more than anything. The repetition of chopping and mixing, the aroma of spices tempering that focused him on what was going on in the pan, the complete immersion of his thoughts and emotions into the dish he was making—there was no therapy quite like cooking. They crossed the street together and went into the house, and he went straight into Divya's kitchen, Fury and Divya beside him.

"What do you feel like?" he asked Divya as he unleashed Fury.

"Well, how about some basics? Dhal, shaak rotli. I'll help." She looked around the kitchen. "Although I'm still not used to these changes."

Amar shrugged as he removed some okra from the fridge. He had stayed up last night and reorganized the whole kitchen. Everything had a spot, and it all flowed better. "Here, start chopping these up." He nodded at the okra. "I'll find you some wine to take the edge off the shock of an organized kitchen." And the edge off whatever was in that box and the fact that Divya was going on another date with Michael.

Divya stood in the middle of the kitchen. "I literally can't find anything. Even a knife to cut vegetables."

Amar poured them each a glass of a crisp white wine as he jutted his chin in the direction of the very obviously positioned knife block. Divya sighed and took a knife and started cutting the okra.

Amar started the dough for the rotli. "Everything you need is in this kitchen, but I have watched you spend ten minutes looking for a spatula and walking back and forth across the kitchen unnecessarily. So I streamlined it." There was now space to chop or knead, and her pans were all together and easily located, as were her various pots and baking sheets.

"It's so...clean." She said this like it was a bad thing. "I don't know where anything is." She finished the okra and moved it closer to the stove, pulling out a frying pan to cook it in.

"Yes, you do." He made eye contact with her as he kneaded the dough. "Say you want to make a cake, what's the first thing you need?"

"Mixing bowl."

"Get it out."

She ran her gaze over the kitchen, then opened one of the cupboard doors near the pantry. Mixing bowls. She turned her head to him with chagrin. She opened the pantry door and there was the flour.

"See?" He brightened up. "You can grab flour at the same time. Faster."

"I like having stuff out where I can see it." Divya almost pouted but took another sip of her wine, but he could see she was impressed.

"Space is at a premium here, Div. Especially while we're sharing. You'll get the layout once you start working." He covered the dough with a bowl. "Trust me." He sipped his wine, then poured oil into the frying pan that Divya had taken out and turned on the gas. He added mustard seeds and curry leaves. Soon enough, the aroma of warm spices filled the kitchen. He added the cut okra to the pan with a satisfying sizzle.

Divya sipped her wine, then inhaled. "My favorite." She sighed with contentment. "You all can have khichdi as your comfort food, I'll take bhinda nu shaak any day of the week." She pulled out a tiny pot that was used solely for the purpose of tempering spices.

Amar grinned. "You found that, no problem."

"Okay. Maybe I can get used to organization. But I'll definitely need you around to help me if I get lost in my own kitchen." She poured more wine into his glass. "You're not measuring anything."

"Seriously, Divya? When have we ever measured while cooking? I used to try to when I was cooking with my mom." He flashed to that memory that his father's office had revealed. He had started writing down her "recipes" when he was a teenager so he could duplicate them. "But now I wing it." He heated oil in a small pan, and then added cinnamon and clove for the dhal.

Divya giggled. "Baking requires measuring, even the Indian stuff. The proportions of things to each other have to be right." She poured more wine for herself. "You know, I like having a colleague to work with. It's the only thing I miss from the grocery store. I'm really glad you're living here. It gets lonely when Mom and Dad travel. And now we have Fury."

"Well, maybe just for a bit." He had made one rotli.

He spread some butter on it and rolled it up and held it out to her.

"Butter? Not ghee?"

"My mom used a stick of butter for rotli. She claimed it was faster than using ghee. So when I do home cooking, I use butter."

Divya leaned in and took a bite, moaning in pleasure. Amar froze for a moment.

"This is just heaven," she proclaimed.

"Um… Div. I need to cook."

She opened her eyes and gave a small shrug as she realized that she had essentially had him feed her. She took the rotli and sampled a couple more bites, savoring the flavor, then spoke up again. "Speaking of… Do you remember that kiss?"

He nearly dropped the spatula. Did he remember that kiss? The safe answer here would be a flat-out *no*! Because he wished more than anything that he could get over it. What he wouldn't give to forget how her lips and mouth had felt against his. It had been over a year ago, and neither one had ever mentioned it. He had simply assumed the kiss hadn't really meant much to her, so he had put the episode behind him. Or tried to anyway. And he'd assumed she had done the same—until now. He was shocked she had mentioned it.

Though her question was probably the wine talking.

Amar cleared his throat and tried to sound matter-of-fact. "We had been drinking, Divya. We weren't ourselves."

"Right. Of course. A mistake. Never to happen again," Divya stated and cleared her throat.

"Why would it happen again?" Amar asked.

"It wouldn't," Divya stated again. "That kiss never

should have happened to begin with." She glanced over at him.

"Right," he agreed, nodding his head emphatically. He was trying to convince himself.

"We're too different." They spoke together. And then laughed, and tension in the air evaporated.

"Right," Divya continued. "You and I have teased each other the whole time we've known each other."

"True." He grinned at her. "Although, full disclosure, I did that in high school because I didn't know how to interact with girls."

"Um, yeah." She quirked a smile. "You were totally Anita's dorky older brother."

Amar shrugged. "Eh, I'm okay with that. Popularity is overrated. Dorky is real."

"I didn't think you were dorky." Divya flushed and drank some wine.

"What? You were constantly arguing with me. About everything." Amar paused in his cooking to look at her.

"You argued back."

"Yeah. That's the fun of it." Amar smiled as he wiped his hands on a towel and tossed it aside. "Stir the shaak. I'll make more rotli quick."

Divya did as he asked. They stood side by side at the stove, and her voice softened as she reached to the back burner and stirred the dhal, as well. "It really was fun. I loved that you argued with me at every turn, because you didn't treat me like I was sick. You and Anita treated me like I was any other kid."

"Well." He grinned at her as he started baking the rotli. "You were annoying."

She widened her beautiful eyes in mock indignation. "You were irritating." She moved closer to him, taking over the baking so he could do the rolling. They were in complete sync. Her face, that beautiful, sassy mouth were only inches from him.

Amar could see how dark brown her eyes were. They almost melted into the black of her pupils. He was getting pulled in to her gaze...

He shook himself. This was what had happened with that last kiss. They had been at some party. There was a lot of wine, and they'd ended up alone in a corner, talking intently about something—possibly having one of their disagreements—and the next thing Amar knew, her mouth had been on his and he was, yeah, in heaven.

If they moved any closer, he'd be close enough to kiss her again.

Divya's eyes were slightly glazed from the wine. Her voice softened. "You know, that kiss was pretty amazing. As kisses go."

He caught the photo of his sister and Divya on her fridge and stepped back. This could never happen. If things went south, he couldn't do that to his sister. He owed Anita that much after all that she had been through. Amar stepped back from Divya, and he could almost hear the moment snap away from him.

"Div. It's burning."

She turned toward the rotli, which was now black. "Oh no! I'm sorry."

"It's okay," Amar assured her. "Why don't you sit and I'll feed you? You know. Your dream come true." He tried to lighten the moment.

"Yeah, okay." She filled her empty wineglass with water and sat down at the island.

Amar made her a plate with fresh rotli, the crunchiest pieces of okra (which he knew were her favorite) and a bowl of dhal. She grinned with pure joy as he set it down in front of her. "Aren't you eating?"

"Sure." Amar made himself a plate as well and was just about to sit down next to her when his phone buzzed. It was the nurse from the hospital, Megan. She sent pictures of the finished cookies from the ward. He smiled, typed a quick response and took a seat next to Divya to eat.

"Who was that?" Divya asked.

"Megan?" Amar shrugged and tucked into his rotli. "From the ward? You introduced us. She must have gotten my number from the sign-in."

"I did not introduce you to her." She seemed a bit put out.

"Yes. You did." Amar wrapped a small piece of rotli around a few pieces of okra and scooped them into his mouth. "You said 'Megan, this is Amar. Amar, meet Megan.'"

"Yes. I made introductions, but I did not *introduce you* introduce you."

Amar narrowed his eyes as he ate and shook his head again. "I feel like you're saying something, but I'm not getting it."

Divya rolled her eyes like he was an idiot. "What did she want?"

"Just sent some pictures of the finished cookies. I'm sure she texted you, too."

Divya pursed her lips. "She did not."

"Oh. Here, you want to see?" He reached for his phone.

"No." She continued to eat. They dined in silence for a moment or two. "All I am saying is that you need to watch out for her."

"Divya. I am no longer the dorky kid I was in high school. I can take care of myself."

She stared at him a moment before going back to her dinner. "That. Is true."

"Hey." He cleared his throat. "I forgot to mention we're meeting with Anita's mother-in-law, Seema Auntie, tomorrow for some event they want to hire us for. She had texted earlier."

"You're telling me now?" Divya snapped at him.

"I just found out a couple hours ago." Amar became defensive. "You were busy making dates with my contractor. It slipped my mind."

"I can make dates with whoever I want," Divya said.

"I'm not stopping you." Though the thought had crossed his mind more than once.

"And you can make dates with whoever you want." She finished her plate and took it to the sink.

"I know that. Not that I was looking to make dates with anyone, but I'm glad I have your permission," he shot back.

"Great." She started clearing up. "Speaking of dates, what are you doing tonight?"

"I guess we're done," Amar murmured as he stood and took his plate to the sink. "Nothing that would interest the adventurer in you. Fury and I are going to make masala popcorn and rewatch *Endgame*."

Divya paused in her filling of the dishwasher. "Sounds fun."

"Really?" Amar eyed her with suspicion. "Miss I-never-watch-a-movie-twice-it's-a-waste-of-time thinks rewatching *Endgame* might be fun?"

"I was talking about masala popcorn, duh." She rolled her eyes. "Besides, I have a date in fifteen minutes,"

Divya stated as she continued to fill the dishwasher and Amar emptied the pots.

"Do you want to go to the Joshis together in the minivan?" Amar asked.

"Nope. I will meet you there." She was curt with him, and he suddenly felt as though he had done something wrong.

"Divya, have I done something to upset you?"

"Nope." But the way she said nope meant yes. That much he could tell.

Whatever. If she didn't tell him, he couldn't fix it. No matter how much he wanted to.

"Great. Have fun with Michael, then." He leashed Fury for a walk.

"I will," she snapped, but then she knelt down to cuddle Fury.

"Fine," Amar snapped back. "Have fun."

"I intend to." She nearly smirked at him, but her fingers lingered on Fury even as she stood up.

For the life of her, Divya could not concentrate on what Michael was saying. She had a mild buzz going from sharing that bottle of wine with Amar. They had been having such a lovely evening, she had been getting ready to cancel her date with Michael because, quite frankly, hanging out with Amar and Fury at home had an appeal to it that Divya didn't understand. Maybe her mom was finally rubbing off on her.

But then Amar had received that text from Megan and he'd been...so happy about it. As if girls didn't text him all the time. Which was ridiculous. Even twelve-year-old girls got all flustered around him.

The question bugging Divya was, when had he

stopped being simply her best friend's dorky brother, and started being the hot guy who she loved arguing with all the time?

And maybe fantasized about kissing.

"Divya?"

A hand was waving in front of her face. Crap. *Michael. Focus!* What had he just been saying?

"Yes. Michael." The bartender was standing in front of them, holding up a bottle. Divya took a wild guess at the question she'd missed. "Yes. I'd love another glass. This pinot is fabulous." She grinned.

Michael shook his head. She looked in front of her; her glass was still full. She had barely sipped from it. She dropped her head, then quickly raised it to look at him.

"I'm sorry. Amar and I split a bottle of wine at dinner before I came out with you tonight." She laughed. "We were just, you know, celebrating the success of our first event as partners." It was a lame excuse, though, and they both knew it.

"I don't think it's the wine, Divya."

"Of course it is." It had to be the wine. Any other explanation was unacceptable.

"You're here. But you're not really here, Divya."

Divya eyed him. "What do you mean? I'm here. We're having wine and snacks." She gestured at the charcuterie platter, which she hadn't noticed before.

"All true." Michael nodded. He took a sip of his wine and looked Divya in the eye. "The Virani kitchen is coming along nicely."

"It really is. Your team is doing an excellent job." Divya beamed. "I know Amar didn't seem into it at first, but I think the whole concept is growing on him. He's going to end up loving it."

Michael dipped his gaze, a slight sadness coming over his blue eyes. "That's the most excited you've been all night. Talking about the chef."

Divya flushed as she gulped at her wine. "That's not true. We work together, kind of. That's all. We usually end up yelling at each other."

"And why do you think that is?"

"Because we're complete opposites. He's too…safe, too organized for someone like me. I like to take chances. Besides, there could never be anything between us. He's my best friend's brother," Divya insisted, ignoring the fact that she had just spent the last hour focused almost entirely on her jealousy over the text Amar had received from another woman instead of enjoying the company of the fabulous man in front of her.

Michael looked at her like she was lost. He motioned for the check. "You may not want something to be going on between you two, but there is."

Chapter 10

Amar was relieved to see Divya pull up just as he did in the circular driveway of the Joshi mansion. Seema Auntie had invited them to meet at her home, but honestly, *mansion* was the only way to describe it.

At least Divya had made it on time for a change. Last evening, he had cleaned up after she'd left with Michael. He hadn't heard her come home, so it was possible that she'd never come home. His stomach filled with acid at the thought. But she had her bike. Huh.

He exited his car just as Divya removed her helmet.

"Amar." She nodded at him, her tone a little stiffer than usual.

He glanced at her clothes and realized she was wearing the same outfit she'd worn on her date. More acid in his stomach as he realized she had spent the night with Michael.

None of his business. Why did he care, anyway?

"You have on yesterday's clothes." Did he just say that out loud?

"Where I spend the night is none of your business," she snapped as she rang the doorbell. "But I am on time for the meeting."

"I'm not—" Amar started his denial of the truth, but the door opened before he could respond.

Seema Joshi, Anita's mother-in-law, greeted them at the door. "Amar, Divya. So good to see you." She stepped aside and hugged as they entered. A Joshi family event was usually a big deal, so both of them plastered huge smiles on their faces, tabled their discussion and hugged her back.

Auntie was impeccably dressed in a midlength summer salwar kameez in a blue floral pattern. She chattered about how much she loved what they had done with Ranjit at her daughter Tina's wedding as she guided them to her spacious kitchen.

"This is my eldest sister, Neepa Parikh," Seema Auntie introduced them. Whereas Seema Auntie appeared ageless, Neepa Auntie was clearly the older sibling. She was also dressed quite nicely in a simple cotton salwar kameez. The physical resemblance was strong, but Amar couldn't help noticing that Neepa Auntie's smile never really reached her eyes.

Amar offered his hand. "Amar Virani."

"Divya Shah." Divya offered her hand as well.

"Can I get you some chai?" Seema Auntie offered.

"No, thank you, Auntie, we're good—" Amar started.

"I'd love some, Auntie—especially if you're using Nikhil's chai masala," Divya cut him off.

"In that case, sounds great," Amar said. He rolled his eyes ever so slightly at Divya.

"Life's too short not to enjoy the best chai ever," she murmured to him. Then out loud she said, "You know, Auntie, Amar makes excellent chai, too."

"That's a fabulous idea, Seema. Allow the young man to make it," Neepa Auntie spoke up.

"I'd be happy to." Amar shot Divya a questioning look, but after Seema Auntie showed him where things were, he got to work putting water to boil. Seema Auntie set out a plate of biscuits to accompany the chai.

"Well, I suppose you're wondering why I asked you here," Seema Auntie stated. "Neepa can explain."

"My son Hiral is getting married in three months, but the caterer they had hired a year ago has just backed out of the contract." Neepa Auntie pressed her lips together. "You can imagine that my daughter-in-law to be is beside herself, as all these plans had already been made. We have a large traditional wedding planned, and Seema mentioned that you two helped out, quite successfully, with Tina's wedding a few months ago." Neepa Auntie inhaled. "That chai smells divine, Amar."

Amar had added the chai spice and a few fresh mint leaves to the simmering water, and the fresh aroma of the mint with cardamom and cinnamon was indeed heavenly.

"Thank you, Auntie. Just a few more minutes." He added the milk and allowed the mixture to come to a boil.

"You are starting your own business? Together?" Neepa Auntie asked.

Amar placed steaming mugs of chai in front of the Aunties, and handed one to Divya.

"I told you, Neepa," Seema Auntie said as she blew on her chai. "Our law firm is drawing up their agreement.

But this is Anita's brother and best friend. Their word is golden." Seema Auntie seemed exasperated.

"Thank you, Seema Auntie, to Joshi Family Law for handling that." Divya turned to Neepa Auntie. "I do desserts. Amar does savory dishes. I should mention that I also have a dessert food truck and that we can do made-to-order crepes, which have been a huge hit at the events we've done so far."

Amar froze for a second with his mug halfway to his mouth. This promised to be a large wedding—there would surely be a couple of hundred people there, at least. They had only done one event together—for thirty. He took a sip and set his mug down, nudging Divya's knee with his under the table. *What the hell?*

"You can do crepes for four hundred people?" Neepa Auntie seemed skeptical. With reason.

"Well…" started Amar, but Divya flat-out kicked him under the table. He stifled a curse.

"Of course. Like I said, they've proven very popular so far, though the crepes option comes at a premium, considering all the fresh ingredients and staff involved."

"Cost is no problem. I just want it to be amazing. Poor Meeta is beside herself."

"Perfect. Let's talk menus, and I'm sure we can make it happen," continued Divya.

"Auntie." Amar had finally found his voice, though he was sure his shin was bruised. "When exactly is this wedding? And how many events?"

"The wedding is in two and a half months, the weekend before Thanksgiving. It will be two hundred and fifty for dinner the night before. Four hundred for lunch after the wedding. Just a simple cocktail hour and then, of course, the reception."

Amar stared at her. This was way out of their league. They could never handle this on their own. They'd need a team of people to help prep, not to mention access to a full commercial kitchen. It would be a great opportunity—they could get a lot of business if they pulled it off—but—

"What about servers?" Amar asked.

"The hotel staff will be there for that. Meeta's family has business contacts with the hotel. They are more than happy to oblige," Neepa Auntie answered.

"Sounds great." Divya nodded at Neepa Auntie. "We may need to hire some extra cooking staff, given the numbers."

"As I said, cost is not an issue. Hire who you need."

"We'll need access to a catering kitchen as well," Amar said.

Neepa Auntie nodded. "You will have it. Can you make traditional Indian sweets, as well, Divya? Koprapak, jalebi, penda?"

"I learned from my parents." She grinned.

"Where is this wedding?" Amar asked.

"Virginia."

"We need hotel rooms," Divya said. "In the venue hotel. One each for us and then for our staff. And we would need to be there at least two to three days before. And a full kitchen off-site with access to the hotel kitchen and staff."

"I'll get you access to cook in the hotel kitchen—"

"Sold." Divya held out her hand and Neepa Auntie shook it.

Amar was slightly nauseous. "Doing made-to-order for four hundred people is a difficult feat to pull off."

"Are you saying that you can't manage it?" asked Neepa Auntie sharply.

"Of course not," Divya spoke quickly, and Amar received another sharp jab to his shin. In the same spot. "We have experience. We can do this."

They finished their chai and biscuits, and worked out the details, which included the wedding dessert truck.

Amar basically limped to his car without a word. Leave it to Divya to get them in over their heads again. He drove straight to the house, knowing she'd meet him there.

He didn't even wait for her to get off her bike. "Are you insane?"

"You're welcome," she shot back as she removed her helmet and got off her bike. "I just got us one of the biggest parties of the year. All the guests will have as much money, if not more, than the Joshi or Parikh family. You'll be able to easily cover Anita's half of the mortgage, not to mention paying back the loan you took out for the renovation."

"Not if we can't deliver," Amar growled. "Four hundred people for made-to-order crepes? We barely did thirty." He raised his hands and dropped them. "You're setting us up to fail."

"You do dosa. It's almost the same thing," she said, entering the house.

"Yeah, and the line gets ridiculous, and I'm not doing it for four hundred. We would need four people doing two at a time to even get close." Amar let Fury out of the mudroom and leashed him. They both walked outside and waited for Fury to do his business.

"So, we'll get staff," Divya explained. "Courtney's

always up to make more money. What about that guy Sonny who helped at Tina's wedding? Maybe Anita—"

"Anita's a guest at that wedding. Besides, you and I don't count. We have other things to do."

Divya pursed her lips and nodded. "True. But if we can get even two or three more people, and you and I can jump in—"

"Experienced people, not just bodies," insisted Amar. "They need to know how to make a thin crepe. It's an art."

Divya grimaced at him. "Fine, if I get two or three *experienced* people, we do the crepes."

He counted to ten before responding. "We have to pay them, Divya. Be practical."

"Neepa Auntie's paying. Weren't you listening?" Divya's voice raised in her irritation. "She's desperate and she has money. Two things that work in our favor. This wedding could be great for our future."

Amar narrowed his eyes at her. "*Our* future?"

"Our business future. People will like us together. We still have the Arora party this weekend and Herreras coming up. We know our menus are good."

"Hmm." Amar grunted at her.

"You came to *me* when you needed help for Tina's wedding. Remember?" Divya set her jaw. "We can do this, Amar. You know we can. We're a great team. At least, we are in the kitchen."

They walked back in the house once Fury was done and let him off the leash. He immediately brought Amar a ball. "So… How was your date last night?"

Damn it. Why did he ask questions he didn't really want the answers to?

"It was good." Her gaze faltered. "Michael's a great guy."

"Good."

"Did Megan send any more cookie pictures?" Divya asked with a one-shouldered shrug. "If any are good, I'd like to post them on my Instagram."

"Actually, she sent quite a few," Amar answered.

"Great." Divya held her hand out for his phone.

"I'll just send them to you." He opened up his phone and smiled at a text from Megan before sending the pictures over.

"Thanks." She quickly checked for the photos, then shoved her phone back into her pocket. "Are we on the same page with this wedding?" Divya asked.

He hesitated. "I guess you're right. If we can pull it off, it'll be fantastic for us."

"Then let's do it, Amar. You know we can," Divya insisted.

He wasn't 100 percent sure she was right, but he'd be an idiot if he turned down a wedding. Especially one like this.

Maybe, once and for all, he just needed to trust her. "Okay." He sighed. "Let's finalize their menu. We don't have a lot of time."

Chapter 11

It had only been a few days since they had decided to go full speed ahead for the Parikh wedding, and Amar was fuming. Again.

"I can't believe I let you convince me that we could do a made-to-order crepes station for sixty people! Not to mention promising fresh warm jalebi, in addition to all the food." He had been silent the whole way home from the Arora party, which had been a total disaster, not speaking until the moment they'd pulled into the driveway. Now, though, he wasn't holding back.

Divya gave him the side-eye. "We had to practice for the wedding." Amar was talented and competent. She had to push him. "If you don't challenge yourself, how will you know what you're capable of?"

"What?" They'd gotten out of the bus and were unloading all their supplies. The night was thick and sticky, and Divya was grateful for the darkness so she didn't have to see the disappointment on Amar's face. "You told the client—and me—that you could handle it with extra people and supplies."

She had. Because in theory, her plan should have worked. Her theory had, in fact, *not* worked tonight. It had been only the two of them. Courtney had called out sick at the last minute, and then Mrs. Arora was so excited about the crepes, she had Divya start earlier than she had expected, so Divya was left to manage those as well as fry and soak the warm jalebi in sugar syrup. She became royally backed up, burning some of the crepes and serving the jalebi too soon.

Amar had hopped onto Lola to help as soon as he could, but by then, the hostess was grumbling about everything. Including Amar's food, which Divya knew was spot-on and flawless. The woman was just out of sorts, since her guests were still waiting for the desserts she had hyped. Divya would have thought that the free-flowing alcohol would distract people, but unfortunately, they'd all wanted sugar…and for the first time in a long time, she'd failed. And though she couldn't bear to acknowledge it to Amar, it stung more than she wanted to admit.

"Well, I thought it would be good practice."

"How'd that turn out?" Amar grumbled as he placed the stands in a corner of her garage they were using for storage.

"We just…need to work at it," she insisted, the words sounding hollow even to her own ears. "To coordinate better."

"You think?" Amar sighed. "If we don't get the flow right, we have to tell Neepa Auntie we can't do the made-to-order stuff."

"We'll figure it out." She sighed, too. She hated to admit it, but he had a point. She just did not want to back down. They would make it work. They had to.

"We also lost a bunch of potential business tonight."

"My theory was sound," Divya defended herself. Once they'd emptied the van, they went inside and let Fury out of the mudroom.

"Maybe you should have told me this was a practice run?" Amar fired off at her. "Then I could have planned for it." Fury acknowledged Divya but made a beeline for Amar, who was already on his knees, waiting to greet the dog.

"Well, if you weren't such a grump, maybe I would have!" she shot back.

"Grump? Are you kidding me? This has nothing to do with me being a grump and everything to do with the fact that you always have to prove that you can do things on your own. You've been like that all the time I've known you, which is fine when it's just you." He cuddled a very happy Fury, and the puppy seemed to soften him. "We're in this together, now. If either of us screws up, we both go down. If we want to be true partners, you have to at least tell me what we're up against."

Amar took a breath and spoke in calmer tones. "You don't have to prove anything to me. I already *know* you can do whatever you decide to do. I wouldn't have agreed to partner up with you if I didn't think you were capable."

She raised an eyebrow and gave him a half smile. So, he did believe in her. The idea made her slightly giddy. "You admit you're a grump?"

"Fine, I'm a grump." He leashed Fury and stood to take him out.

Divya joined them. It was late, and a sliver of moon

hung brilliant in a navy sky. The night was warm despite the lack of humidity, typical for September in Maryland. There was less autumn every year. Sometimes they just jumped from summer to winter.

Amar turned to her. "I… I'm sorry for going off like that. I just can't fail at this, Div. The renovation, the mortgage…" He trailed off, staring straight ahead. "Next time, keep me in the loop so I'm not blindsided. It's part of a partnership."

Did he just admit to her that he was afraid of failing? Divya nodded her agreement. "Will do. I…uh… Well, I don't like failing either."

She felt Amar's gaze on her. "I know, I know—hard to believe, but true." She held up her hands in surrender without looking at him. "We just need another practice." Divya stopped short, grabbing Amar's arm. Fury kept going, his leash getting taut as Amar stopped.

"Of course. We'll have a Diwali party." Divya kept hold of his arm as she turned to him, nearly skipping with excitement. "You call Sonny, I'll call Courtney. It's a little early, but what's a few weeks? Like your parents used to have."

Amar's face froze, and instantly, she felt sorry, knowing she'd brought up a difficult memory.

"Oh sorry. We don't have to call it that," Divya backtracked. "I wasn't thinking, Amar—"

He shook his head firmly. "No, Divya, that's fine."

"You sure?" For once, she looked uncertain. "I mean, if it's going to be painful for you—"

He smiled, but she could see the shadow of grief in his eyes. Still, there was determination in his tone. "No, you're right. We need to test it. And not on real clients, again. I have an idea—we'll get Anita to invite all of the Joshis over."

"Yes! And our friends. Your parents used to host the best Diwali parties." Divya lost herself in the memory for a moment.

"We used to prep for days. Anita and I made the menu and as we got older, we would help cook it, until we were teenagers and then we cooked the whole thing." Amar looked off into the darkness. "I haven't thought about those celebrations in a long time. Diwali just came and went these past few years. Anita and I never even acknowledge it."

"Your mom always had some kind of do-it-yourself dessert. Remember?" Divya had been all about skipping over the meal and going right to decorating cookies shaped like diyas. "It's part of what made me become a pastry chef."

"That's so cool." Warmth filled his voice. "I didn't know that. Mom would've been thrilled to know she had even a small part in inspiring you." Amar turned to her in the scant moonlight, a true smile on his face. "Let's do it. She would probably love that you were testing out made-to-order crepes at an iteration of her party."

Divya jumped in excitement. "We'll have it at my house, since your kitchen—"

Amar glanced across the street at his house, and his eyes clouded over. "Yeah. Okay."

She didn't say anything, she was still holding his arm, so she simply wrapped her arm around his to try to offer some comfort. Clearly, all that dough kneading paid off, because now she was distracted by his muscles.

After Fury did his business, they made their way back to the house, letting the dog off the leash in the kitchen.

"Come on, Falcon." She nodded at his T-shirt. "It's been a long night. We need to get to bed."

She knew it was wrong the instant she said it. "I meant sleep. We need to get to sleep." But now her head filled with thoughts of what it would be like to lie next to Amar.

In her bed.

She shook her head of the thought. Not going there. Amar was off-limits.

"Yeah," Amar agreed. "It has been a long—" Just then, he was interrupted as Fury barked at a sudden ruckus in the foyer.

"Hey! We're back!" her mother's voice called from the front door.

Divya inhaled and exhaled deeply to release her disappointment that they hadn't stayed for the whole vacation. Again.

Amar looked at her, a sympathetic grin on his face. "At least they made it three weeks into the trip this time."

Divya went to the door to greet her parents, Amar right behind her. Her parents were fairly laid-back about most things. They'd never cared what career she chose, as long as she loved it. They'd encouraged her to date— her mom had even handed her condoms when she was seventeen. No need for Divya to get an STD, her mother had said. Divya remembered being mortified.

They were, however, slightly overprotective about her health. It was smothering, even if it was understandable.

"When did you get this dog?" Her father bent down to cuddle Fury, who was apparently irresistible to everyone.

"Amar found him and fed him." She caught Amar's eye and shrugged.

Her mother's eyes widened. "Divya, the germs!" She stepped back from Fury.

"Mom. Seriously. I am not sick anymore." Divya was more than a little irritated. It was one thing that they came home early, but to be concerned about Fury's presence? "And I always wanted a dog."

"Yes. When you were little. I thought you had outgrown that." She dropped her gaze on Amar. "Good to see you, beta. Mind making some chai? It was a long flight."

Amar hugged her. "Of course." It was midnight, but chai was chai. "Also, Fury is technically mine."

"We're just keeping him until his real owner claims him." *But maybe they won't!* "You've been gone three weeks," Divya continued. "And you're home early."

"Your father was worried about you." The withering look from her father told Divya who was really worried about who.

"You promised, Mom." Divya nearly let her emotions overtake her usual control. "You promised you would stay for the whole vacation this time. Four weeks in the Mediterranean. Eating pasta and olives and gelato and drinking fabulous wine."

"What can I say? I wanted my chai." She smiled at Amar.

Divya rolled her eyes.

They had walked into the kitchen as they spoke. Amar had a pot of water heating and was pulling out the loose tea and the chai masala as well as the milk.

"How's the kitchen coming along?" Her mother settled herself at the island while her father brought the last bag in.

"Great. It'll still be a few months of work, and the appliances are slightly delayed."

"Well, I hope you're staying regardless. Divya could use the company," her mother said.

"I know I feel better knowing my little girl isn't alone in the house." Her father squeezed her in a tight hug.

She groaned but hugged him back. "Dad, I'm hardly a little girl."

"You know what I mean."

She did. It was the same reason her mom never finished a vacation. The same reason they were surprised that she had a dog.

Her mother took her first sip, and her eyes popped open. "This is delicious, beta. You have outdone yourself this time."

Amar flicked his gaze to Divya. "I'm actually using chai masala that my brother-in-law makes."

"Nikhil?"

Amar nodded.

"That's fantastic. They're doing well?" Divya's mom was as concerned about Anita and Nikhil's well-being as she was about Divya's.

"Yeah. Second time around seems to be the charm," Amar said dryly.

"You don't sound convinced." She raised an eyebrow at him. "In this, my daughter agrees with you."

Amar glanced at Divya. They did agree.

"As long as she is happy." She grinned at them both. "Now, we just need to get you settled, and then Divya, and we will have done our jobs as parents."

Amar and Divya stared at her, actively not looking at each other. "So…we're throwing a Diwali party. You're home just in time." Divya spoke first.

Her mother clapped her hands together. "How fabulous. See, it's a good thing we came home. We would have missed it."

"How about some of your cinnamon rolls, Divya, for the morning?" her father asked.

"Sure, Dad." Divya pulled out the flour and other ingredients to make the dough so it could rise overnight. She backed into Amar getting the mixer out.

He grabbed her arms from behind her to steady them both.

"Sorry."

"No problem."

They both spoke together, she turned to face him. A slow smile came over his face, and he did not let go of her right away.

"It does get tight in here, doesn't it?" her father said.

Amar stepped back from her and released her arms. "It can."

"We manage."

They both spoke at the same time again, grinning like teenagers as they made eye contact.

"Hmph," her father grunted, looking from her to Amar and back.

Chapter 12

Amar had to hand it to Divya, she put the Diwali party together in a week. Clear skies and cooler temperatures more typical of mid-September were promised for the party tonight. He thought about teasing Divya about it, but figured she'd be impossible to work with if he even hinted that she could control the weather.

His friend and fellow culinary school graduate, Sonny Pandya, would be over later after he closed his new Indian comfort food restaurant. He wouldn't be able to make it to the Parikh wedding in Virginia, since the restaurant was still so new, but he was capable and would serve to help their practice run.

Courtney had agreed to come as well, so that was four of them, with four crepe pans. They set everything up. Amar cooked up a meal worthy of his parents. Anita came early to help decorate, and was in the backyard and house, putting up lights and lighting diya like they did when they were kids.

"How long are you going to stay mad at me, Amar?" Anita asked, her voice hesitant.

"I haven't decided." He came off more flippant than he'd intended.

"Stay as mad as you want." She was fired up. "I did the right thing."

"Your sister-in-law, Tina, is a genius," Amar offered calmly, almost in apology for his earlier tone. "She's going to have the licensing set up."

"Is that excitement I hear in your voice?" Anita's voice relaxed, too.

"No. It's resignation," he quipped.

"Oh my god. You two," Divya groaned. She had just entered the room wearing a beautiful light green sari that hugged her gorgeous curves in the most perfect manner. She had pulled it across and draped it over her left shoulder, letting the material flow, leaving parts of her midriff and back exposed. Amar was so captivated by her, he barely even registered the mini lecture she was giving him and Anita about getting along.

"Amar?" Anita nudged his elbow.

"What?" He looked down at his sister, who was currently wearing an annoying smirk, looking from him to Divya and back.

"Didn't you hear me?" Anita asked innocently. "I mean, I'm standing right here. Unless your mind wandered off somewhere." She narrowed her gaze at him.

"Neets," her husband whispered on the other side of her. "Leave him be."

"I'm right here, Anita. You were saying how we get along just fine, weren't you?"

Anita seemed surprised he'd heard her, but the suspicious look did not leave her face. "Go light more diya." He turned away from her because the last thing he needed was for Anita to think he had a crush on Divya.

"Dude. Stop staring," Nikhil murmured.

Amar cleared his throat and forced his gaze away from Divya, shrugging at Nikhil. "I'm good."

Nikhil gave him the same knowing smile that his sister had. "Why haven't you made your move yet? You've been living in this house a month."

Amar deflated. "She's dating my contractor."

Nikhil's eyes flashed open. "Seriously? That's what's in your way? She went on, like, one date with him."

"Two. And I don't think she came home after the last one. And when I asked her about it, she got all defensive." Not to mention, it was too risky for him to date Divya. How could she possibly ever want him?

"The date lasted two hours. They had nothing in common. She drank wine with Anita and slept on my sofa. Anita dropped her off early so she could get her bike and meet you at my mom's."

Amar just stared at his brother-in-law.

"She was super worried about showing up late for that meeting." Nikhil punched his bicep. "She didn't want to disappoint you."

"Or she didn't want to lose the job." He shook his head.

"Amar, listen to me. It wasn't the job she was afraid of losing." His brother-in-law touched his shoulder to make sure he was listening. "It was you. Not once did she mention that she was afraid you wouldn't get the work."

Amar looked at Nikhil. "I… I'm going to change." He turned away and headed upstairs, where he quickly changed into a jabo and matching bottoms, the golden silk tunic reaching his knees. This one was old, but he hadn't made the time to hunt down a new one.

When he came down, both Divya and his sister had lit all the diya, enveloping the house in a golden-orange glow. Divya turned to him as he descended the stairs, a huge smile on her face, and he understood completely in that moment why her parents had given her the name. She was divine—and she lit up whatever room she was in.

Nikhil came up to him and handed him a beer. "Seriously. It's like you've never seen a woman in a sari," he mumbled.

"No woman wears a sari like Divya," Amar let slip.

"Uh-huh. Good thing you're not attracted to her." Nikhil smirked.

He turned to Nikhil and shrugged. "Are you denying she's attractive?"

Nikhil frowned over his beer. "As the man who is married to your sister, there is actually no good way for me to answer that question."

Amar frowned. "Humph." He side-eyed Nikhil and walked away, bumping into Divya's parents in the next room.

"Kalpana Auntie, Veer Uncle. Happy Diwali." Amar clasped his hands together and bowed before them. They stopped his bow and pulled him into a hug instead.

"Happy Diwali, beta," Uncle said. He looked around. "Your sister has done an amazing job with the lights, and the food smells wonderful." He raised his hand to wave at someone. "Kalpana, Anita's mother-in-law is here. Come." They went to greet Seema Auntie.

"The kitchen really is the heart of any household, isn't it?" said Divya, coming up beside him. She was holding a glass of prosecco. He tapped his bottle to her glass and they each took a sip. Her gaze swept the area, taking in the setup they'd done earlier. He followed suit. Plates of appetizers were arranged on the rolling island, which they'd moved out to the great room. The dinner he'd prepared was on the stove, keeping warm. They'd loaded all the stuff for the crepes onto Lola before the party, too.

He raked his gaze over Nikhil and Anita. Nikhil's brow was furrowed and Anita's mouth was pressed into a line. Anita turned to her husband and said something, Nikhil shook his head.

"What the hell is going on over there, do you think?" murmured Divya, turning to him.

"No idea," Amar grumbled. "But she doesn't look happy."

"Trouble in paradise," Divya mumbled.

Amar felt the tension rise in his stomach. They had barely been remarried for a few months. He had half a mind to give Nikhil a piece of his.

Guests had already arrived, and even though the entire house was decorated and made inviting to all, everyone hung out in the kitchen. It was, indeed, the heart of the home. They ate and drank and caught up with friends they hadn't seen in ages. When darkness fell, they went outside for dessert and fireworks.

"Alright, everyone. We have a little something different for your Diwali dessert tonight. Made-to-order crepes," Divya announced as everyone gathered outside near Lola. "We have mango, strawberry and banana, which can be mixed with hazelnut chocolate or white chocolate with powdered sugar on top. Anita will take orders, and the four of us will be making them fresh, right here." She gestured to the bus behind her, where

Amar and Sonny, and Courtney were ready to go. "Any combo you want."

There was general nodding and a murmur of excitement as people lined up for dessert.

Divya had had the small windows on one side of Lola replaced by one long service window and a small counter that could be pulled back into the truck after service. During service, four could work side by side, though it was tight.

After making her announcement, Divya pulled the long hanging part of her sari around her waist and tucked it into her skirt. She tied an apron over her sari and quickly climbed into the truck with her team. She passed him as he pushed up the sleeves of his jabo. She stopped.

"They'll just come down again," she said as she quickly folded his sleeves up his forearms, securing them behind his elbow. Her touch on his arms was gentle, and he was sure she dragged her fingers slightly slower than necessary over his bare forearms.

"Thanks," he said as they heated up the four crepe pans and the guests began to give their orders to Anita— and crowd around Lola to watch the cooking action, too.

Amar looked at Divya and grinned. This *was* going to work. He knew it. He was going to have to admit she was right and thank her for not letting him give up. She was going to gloat, but it was totally worth it.

Divya worked fast. The only thing that held her up was the actual time it took to cook the crepes. Anita was quick with the orders, and Sonny's experience with dosa at his restaurant ensured that he was as quick as Divya.

Amar was good at making dosa, but crepe batter was thinner, and he was in the zone. Within an hour and a half, everyone had their orders and was enjoying their dessert.

They made each other crepes and, exhausted but excited, sat down inside with the family to enjoy them. Divya sat down next to Amar and elbowed him. "How many did you make, Chef?"

Amar shook his head and chuckled. "I managed about twenty."

Divya nodded at Sonny, who sat on the other side of Amar. "How about you?"

"Nineteen." He pushed his glasses up. "I would recommend wearing contact lenses." He grinned.

Amar eyed her. "What about you, pastry chef?"

"Courtney made around twelve, and I made twenty-one. At the wedding, we'll have one more pan. I'll bring an electric griddle that we can just plug in outside of Lola. So we'll have five of us." She looked at Sonny. "Sure you can't join us for that wedding?"

"I'd love to, but I can't leave the restaurant for a whole week."

Amar shrugged. "We'll miss you. It was fun working together tonight, man. We'll have to—"

Amar stopped abruptly as Sonny groaned and jutted his chin forward.

Nikhil was walking toward them, a woman by his side who looked vaguely familiar.

"Hi, everyone! This is my cousin Sangeeta Parikh, she's the groom's sister." Nikhil wrapped an arm around her shoulders and squeezed her close. "She's my favorite cousin." The woman rolled her eyes but smiled.

Sonny had clenched his jaw, his body tense. Amar side-eyed his friend.

"That's her. That's the girl from the *date*," Sonny

grumbled, not even moving his mouth, his gaze fixed on Sangeeta.

"Hi, everyone." She waved, passing her gaze over the group. When her eyes found Sonny, her smile briefly faltered, but she continued on, focusing on Divya. "The food was amazing! I know you're doing my brother's wedding, so if that goes well, I'd love to have you do mine."

"What?" Sonny burst out.

All eyes turned to Sonny.

Sangeeta continued as if he hadn't spoken, though her voice shook just a bit. "I just got engaged. The wedding is in May."

A round of hearty congratulations followed, everyone standing to hug and congratulate her. Amar turned to Sonny. "That's the girl? That's the one you thought—"

Sonny stood. "Clearly I was wrong." He flicked his gaze to where Sangeeta stood. "I need to leave. Say bye to Divya for me, huh?"

"Yeah. Sure." Amar furrowed his brow. "You okay?"

Sonny nodded. "Just as well. I'm busy with the restaurant. Let me know if you need anything for the business." Sonny skirted the crowd around Sangeeta and bolted out the door. Amar noticed Sangeeta watching Sonny leave.

Huh.

"What was that?" Divya came close and whispered to him.

Amar shook his head. "Not really sure." He tipped his head in Sangeeta's direction. "You know what that means."

Divya grinned. "We kick butt at Hiral's wedding, we get to do Sangeeta's."

Amar chuckled. "So let's make it a wedding to re-member, then."

The remaining guests slowly filtered out over the next hour or so. Divya's parents eventually said their good-nights. "Anita, you and Nikhil should just stay over."

"Thanks, Auntie," Anita called up.

"Come on, Div." A slightly tipsy Anita threw her arm around her friend. "Bed. Like when we were kids."

"Five minutes, Anita. Let me clean up," Divya answered.

"We got it," Nikhil said. He was already packing up some of the sweets. "You two go ahead."

Anita grinned and kissed her husband. Divya exchanged a look with Amar. "Take my sister to bed."

"You heard the man. Come on, Divya." Anita linked her arm in Divya's, and the two friends headed up the stairs in a fit of giggles that took Amar back to their teen-age days. A smile spread across his face.

"Don't let anyone catch you smiling, Amar. They might think you're in a good mood," Nikhil said.

"What?" Amar's happy state came crashing down.

"You heard me. You're in kind of a mood."

"Whatever." Amar shook his head and continued col-lecting dirty glasses, putting them on a tray to take to the kitchen. "You're welcome to go to bed as well. I can handle this."

"What exactly is your problem with me?" Nikhil was getting fired up.

Amar stared at him. "I don't know what you're talk-ing about, Nikhil." He picked up the tray of glasses and went into the kitchen, his brother-in-law on his heels.

"Huh? Really? That's rich. If you don't want to talk

about it, say so, but don't lie to me." Nikhil rolled up his sleeves and started washing dishes.

"You want the truth?" Amar gathered empty plates from the living room and stacked them near the sink.

"It would be a refreshing change from the cold shoulder," Nikhil snapped.

Amar started filling containers with leftovers. "You want to do this right now, fine." He took a deep breath. "When you divorced my sister, she was crushed. Now the two of you have remarried, and I'm not convinced that was the best course of action. I saw you two over there—you looked pretty unhappy."

"Couples argue sometimes. We disagree. It's normal." Nikhil calmed down a bit as he loaded the dishwasher. "And if you want the truth, we were arguing about you."

Amar snapped his head up to Nikhil. "Me?"

"Yes. Your sister wants to know why I bother trying to build a relationship with you, when you clearly aren't interested."

Amar placed the top onto a yogurt container that was filled with shaak and turned to Nikhil. "Why do you?"

"Because," he picked up the empty fry pan and scrubbed, "you are Anita's only family. She loves you with her whole heart. Why wouldn't I want you in my life? But you keep shooting me down, and she told me to just forget it. That you were too stubborn and it wasn't worth it. I disagreed, so she was mad at me."

"She was mad at you for continuously taking my abuse?" Amar had to smile. "Sounds like her. She hates a bully."

"Why *are* you so mad at me all the time?" Nikhil asked. "You *can* talk to me, you know. We're family, Amar."

Amar sighed as he and Nikhil finished drying the pots and pans that Nikhil had just washed. Nikhil wiped down the counters while Amar pulled out Uncle's good bourbon and two glasses. He found the last two large spherical ice balls and clunked them into the glasses, then poured bourbon over the ice and handed one glass to Nikhil. They tapped glasses, and Amar took a long sip, trying to figure out how to explain.

"Anita is all I have. Ever since our parents…" Amar raised his glass to them. Nikhil followed suit. They both sipped from their glasses. "We're supposed to look out for each other." Amar pulled out a chair at the kitchen table and sat down. He waved his glass at the empty chair beside him and Nikhil joined him.

"But the reality is…" His voice shook slightly, and he hesitated, forcing himself to keep control. "The reality is…that when Anita needed me the most, I wasn't there. One of those times was when she married you the first time."

Nikhil frowned.

"That didn't come out right. I should have just asked her to wait and not jump into something so fast. She wasn't ready. She was still mourning, looking for that solid foundation our parents had given us. So was I. If I had been more solid for her, been more *present*, maybe she wouldn't have rushed into marriage, and could have been spared the pain of divorce. I let her down." Amar sighed. "And it wasn't the only time. The night my parents died, I…" He trailed off.

"What happened?"

Amar fiddled with the leather strap of the watch and shook his head.

"What's with the old watch?"

"It was my dad's." Amar paused, then picked up his drink, refocusing on Nikhil. "I guess I'm just trying to make up for not being there...so I just come down hard on what looks like any potential threat to her happiness."

Nikhil swirled his glass, the ice ball clinking the sides. He took a sip. "Your sister is the key to my happiness. I screwed up the first time, that's true, but I can guarantee that I will spend the rest of my life making that up to her. We both want the same thing here. We want Anita to be happy."

Amar studied the man in front of him. Nikhil was for real. He loved his sister. Amar was the one causing her pain right now. "And what would make her happy is for us to get along."

Nikhil nodded. "Wouldn't hurt if you could put in a good word with Divya as well. I'm pretty sure she's still mad at me, too."

Amar chuckled. "I do not have that kind of power over Divya. She has a mind of her own."

"You have more influence with Divya than you think."

"Whatever that means." Amar frowned and shook his head. Denial was the best strategy here. He couldn't risk admitting to Nikhil that he had feelings for Divya.

It didn't matter, though, because his brother-in-law saw right through him. "Listen, Amar. It's all over your face. The way you look at her—and not just tonight. You're not fooling anyone. Except maybe the girl herself. Make your move. You might be pleasantly surprised." Nikhil finished his drink. Amar poured them both another.

"You haven't been listening. I will never again do anything to get in the way of my sister's happiness. Especially acting on any feelings I may or may not have for her best friend." Amar gulped at his drink again. "Because the reality is, Divya deserves infinitely better than me. The night of my parents' accident proves it."

Chapter 13

Divya and Amar parked Lola in the hospital parking lot and got out. No Fury. Any animal they brought with them would need to be specially trained. Maybe if Fury became theirs, they could get him training. Until then, Fury was at home, being spoiled by her parents.

Lola's paint job was slowly coming along. The pastel pink-and-blue background was nearly set, with some of the artwork slowly taking form. After their failed dates, Divya had let Michael off the hook for helping with the paint job, so it was Amar working with her now. Which she did not mind at all.

Divya rolled her suitcase of art supplies. As she focused on the entrance doors, the familiar knots formed in her stomach, her heart pounded in her chest. Amar moved closer to her as they entered the hospital and all the smells and sounds consumed her. She was flexing and fisting her hand when, just like the last time, Amar took it and threaded his strong fingers with hers. She immediately exhaled and relaxed into his grip. She looked at him, a small smile finding its way onto her face as she registered his Dr. Strange T-shirt.

Amar glanced at her, no sign of pity or anything on his face. Just encouragement. She was suddenly aware that his hair was slightly longer, with the hint of a wave, and if she leaned just an inch or two toward him, he smelled of spices and soap. A different kind of fluttering went through her. She inhaled to quiet it and nodded to Amar as she exhaled and squeezed his hand.

"You got this," he whispered to her. "Plus, we have Fury waiting at home for us."

That picture he painted was warm and comforting. Waiting. Home.

Us.

She murmured agreement and slowed her breathing. Megan ventured by, all smiles.

"Hey, Amar. How's it going? Hey, Divya."

Divya narrowed her eyes. "Megan." She squeezed Amar's hand tighter, and he turned to her before addressing Megan.

"Hi, Megan," Amar greeted the young nurse warmly.

Megan sauntered closer to Amar, a crooked smile on her face. "I get a break in about half an hour. Care to join me for coffee, Amar?"

Divya dropped his hand and bolted for the craft room. She didn't need to watch this flirtation. She arrived in the activity area to find Amar at her heels.

"Why did you take off like that?"

"Oh! I, uh, didn't need you, and you were setting up

a date, so you know I thought I'd just set up on my own. No big deal." She was blabbering and she could not stop.

"I was not setting up a date. We're here for the kids." He looked at her curiously.

Divya inhaled. Of course. Amar wouldn't abandon the kids. "Right."

"You okay? I mean, with being here? I know it takes a few minutes—"

"I'm good." Warmth flooded through her at the knowledge that Amar seemed to know what she needed. "Thanks. It helps…having you here."

"Of course." Amar nodded. "What are friends for?"

Right. They were just friends. She turned to go to Parul's room, while Amar and Courtney handled the craft room. She walked past a few rooms with children lying in bed, sucking on lollipops, a clear indication that they'd just got done with chemo.

Divya hadn't visited for a couple weeks, having been busy with all the new catering jobs and the Diwali party, but she kept in touch with Parul via text. Parul had spoken to the boy she was smitten with, beyond the initial "hi" of last time. Divya wanted to chat with her in person to see how that was going. Not to mention, she just found out that Parul had never read the *Harry Potter* series. So Divya had brought her personal copy of the first book, to lend to the teenager.

She finally made it to Parul's room, only to find someone else in Parul's bed. Which was odd, since Parul had said she would be in this week for treatment. Divya inhaled and calmly walked to the nurses' station, though her head felt light and her heart pounded in her chest. There was only one reason for a child to leave in the middle of treatment. Divya didn't want to even consider that reason.

"Shanaya?" Divya's voice shook despite her efforts to keep it steady. Shanaya had been a seasoned nurse back when Divya was a patient.

The older nurse turned to her, her glasses propped on the end of her nose. "Divya. Hi, honey. I didn't see you come in."

"Shanaya, where is she? Where's...Parul?" Tears prickled at her eyes as the truth became apparent on the older woman's face.

Shanaya's expression softened. "Oh, Divya. They were supposed to call and let you know. I'm sorry, honey. Parul's case was one of the tough ones. Her body did not respond—"

The book slipped from Divya's hand, landing on the floor with a thud. Her fingers stiffened and her stomach churned. Shanaya's eyes filled with mild alarm and she came around the nurses' desk.

"Divya, hon," Shanaya said softly. "Sit down. You look pale." But Shanaya's voice was far away. She could hardly hear it over the gushing of her own blood through her vessels. The sound got louder and faster.

She turned and ran down the hall until she found the stairs. The sterile stench of the ward choked her. The lavender that was supposed to be so calming nauseated her. As she passed the children sucking on lollipops, she could almost taste the thick sugary confection in her mouth that used to make her gag. She had to leave the building. She registered a male voice calling to her, but she forged ahead.

Divya ran down the steps until she could go no more. She flung herself out of the cold hospital and into the tepid warmth of the late-September afternoon. She ran to Lola.

Lola, which smelled like sugar and cinnamon and vanilla. Which looked like joy and felt like triumph. She inhaled the sweet aroma and curled herself into a ball on the floor, her eyes squeezed tight against the tears that wanted to fall.

She wasn't sure how much time had passed before she heard knocking on the side of the bus. "Divya? You in there?" Amar's normally soothing tone was tinged with concern. "I'm coming in." Divya was unable to respond.

The door opened with a whoosh and a screech, followed by footsteps. If she opened her eyes, it would all be too real and she would lose it. Amar sat down next to her, the heat from his body comforting. He smelled like soap and summer, and he draped his arm around her and gently scooted closer to her so their bodies were touching. Still, she resisted the temptation to melt into him and fall apart. "Divya," he whispered, his mouth right next to her ear, "it's okay."

She snapped her eyes open and flipped her head to face him, anger rising like a volcano. "It's okay? It's *okay* that a fifteen-year-old girl has died despite her strength and fight and all the so-called medical miracles out there? Is that the definition of *okay* these days?" Divya was shouting now.

Tears were somehow streaming down her cheeks, though she did not remember releasing them. Sobs choked her, making it hard to breathe. Still, Amar simply tightened his arm around her, pulling her even closer.

"No. It's not okay," he said softly, his voice gruff with his own sadness. "That will never be okay. But it is okay for you to let her go." She was powerless against the strength he was giving, especially since she had none of her own.

"I don't want to let her go." She finally turned to him, burying her face in his chest, sobbing and clinging to his T-shirt. "She never even read *Harry Potter*! She never knew what it felt like to fall in love." It wasn't fair. It just wasn't fair.

Amar just held her and said nothing, letting her cry until she had nothing left inside to give. He handed her a tissue from a box he'd apparently grabbed from the nurses' station—and she wiped her eyes.

"Parul was special to you," he finally said.

Divya nodded as she blew her nose. "She was a tough cookie. When I first met her she never used to participate in the crafts or games. The other kids thought she was stuck-up, but she was just shy. She was diagnosed at the start of her freshman year of high school—"

"Like you," Amar murmured.

"Yes. But she didn't have Anita, like I did." Divya looked at Amar. "She didn't have a friend to stand by her."

"She had you," Amar said softly. "You were her Anita, Div. That girl lit up around you."

Tears burned again at her eyes. "What?"

"You were her friend. You had been through all this, and she knew it. That's why she loved you. That's why she connected with you. Because your mere existence gave her hope and you did not bullshit her."

"A lot of good it did her." Divya shook her head.

"Yes, it did do her a lot of good. Without you, she wouldn't have been able to experience the things that she did. She never would have talked to her crush. Maybe she never fell in love, but she put herself out there to try."

Amar looked her in the eyes. No BS there. "And because of you, she actually experienced true friendship as well."

Fresh tears burned behind her eyes, but she felt somewhat lighter. "Thanks," she croaked out. "It's still not fair."

"No, it's not." Amar smiled at her, but there was a sadness in his smile that reached his eyes. He understood what she was feeling on a level no one else could.

Amar still had one arm around her. She felt safe, secure. Parul's teenage observations from their last visit came to her. Just because they were teenage observations did not make them poor observations.

Amar's face was mere inches from hers. It would be so easy to just lean in and press her lips against his. As the thought crossed her mind, she felt herself moving into him and he tightened his arm around her, drawing her close. She needed this. Needed him. This proof that there was good and love in the world.

Their lips just grazed, barely a touch, hardly a taste. So tempting. She inched closer, anticipating the kiss that she only now realized she had been craving since that night at the party last year. She hadn't been quite as drunk as she had let on back then. Hadn't been as immune to the effect of that kiss as she'd tried to pretend. But since neither of them knew what to make of it, she'd stuck with her story of inebriation.

He pressed his mouth to hers, deepening the kiss, and she responded hungrily, savoring the feel of his lips on hers, the gentle scratch of his beard scruff on her face.

It was the most intimate moment she'd ever shared, and it was pure bliss for as long as it lasted. Her heart thudded in her chest, and she knew there was good in the world, and that good came from Amar Virani.

But then, his hold on her loosened and he drew back. Instinctively, she drew back as well.

"I'm sorry, Div." Amar looked awkward. "I shouldn't have— I just can't."

"What?" She was still a bit dazed from their kiss.

"This." He shook his head. "Us. It should not happen."

For the first time, Divya had no idea what to say. His kiss had calmed her, soothed her. She wanted more. She didn't understand why he was rejecting her. "What do you mean, 'should not'?"

"I mean—" He took her face into his hands and looked at her with such longing, she was convinced he would kiss her again. But instead, he sighed, and sadness filled his eyes. "I mean, I can't. I'm not…" He dropped his hands. "I should get back." He stood and walked to the door of the bus, then turned back to her. "You coming?"

She did not understand Amar Virani. Whatsoever. He couldn't kiss her—*like that*—and then just up and leave and act like nothing had happened. But that was exactly what he was doing. Divya gathered herself, confused by everything he'd said as he left. But she knew better. If he did not want her, she wasn't one to chase anyone. Life was too short to be with someone who didn't need her.

Except…the sense of grounding she got when she was with him was like nothing she'd ever felt. For all their bickering, she felt safe and whole in his presence. She didn't have to pretend to be strong when she didn't feel it. She could be scared and sad, and Amar didn't judge her. He didn't think she had to be anything that she didn't want to be. Just like his sister, Amar did not define Divya by her illness.

But this was the second time that Amar had pulled

away from her. And it would be the last—she would make sure of it. She inhaled and looked around her.

"Div?" The man in question waited for her at the door. "You coming?"

"Yes. Of course I'm coming." She lightened her voice, tingeing it with irritation, to hide her disappointment. If he was going to walk away from *that kiss*, then she would have to just move on. Divya walked beside him in silence, folding her arms across her chest so he wouldn't feel obligated to hold her hand. They reached the ward and made their way to the children who were waiting to show off their artwork.

Divya was hyperaware of Amar's presence, even when he wasn't beside her. He may not want to be with her, but that kiss had changed them. They spent a couple of hours working on projects with the kids and were just finishing up when she caught sight of Parul's parents at the nurses' station.

"Auntie, Uncle." Divya had often spent some time with Parul's parents, and she found them to be loving, if slightly overprotective, very similar to her own parents, even though she was a grown adult and ten years cancer-free. She hugged them, offering what little comfort she could. Their eyes were swollen and red-rimmed, with a glassy look that indicated they were still not quite sure how they had gotten to this place in their lives.

"I'm so sorry," Divya said, her voice filling with emotion.

Parul's mother nodded, but her father could barely make eye contact with her.

"We forgot something of Parul's, so we came to get it," explained her mother.

Shanaya reached under the nurses' desk and pulled

up a well-loved pink teddy bear. Parul's father burst into tears upon seeing it. Her mother expressed her thanks to Shanaya and took the toy. "This was her favorite. She'd had it since she was six months old and she never went anywhere without it." She managed a watery smile at Divya. "Parul had requested your cookies at her…funeral. She said no one could be sad when they ate those."

Divya's heart broke and lightened all at the same time. "It would be my pleasure," she managed to croak out.

Parul's mother hugged her and left.

A teenage boy—the boy that Parul liked, Fernando, approached Divya. "It's true, then? Parul's gone?"

"Hey." Divya looked at him. He was too thin, his skin sallow, but his amber eyes were bright. "Um, yeah." She swallowed her own tears. "She's gone."

His face fell and he dipped his head. "She was really cool."

Divya tilted her head to see his face. "She really liked you."

He pressed his mouth together, clearly saddened. "I really liked her. Even though I met her here." He waved to indicate the ward. "Sometimes when we talked, I forgot we were sick. She acted all tough, but inside, I could tell she was really nice." The boy's eyes watered.

Divya swallowed, tears burning her throat. "She was special that way."

The boy walked away, and Amar leaned toward her ear. "She knew what it felt like to fall in love."

Divya nodded without looking up at him. His breath on her ear was torture. She wanted to melt into him and forget that all of this was going on in the world. Instead, she focused on watching Fernando go back to his room, his head down.

Amar left her side to clean up. It was just as well that he'd pulled back from her and broken the kiss. The last thing she wanted to do was cause him more pain than he'd already endured after losing his parents so tragically. No, Amar was off-limits.

She could still see Parul's parents leaving the ward. Auntie thanking every nurse she saw, Uncle standing stiffly beside her, moving only what was necessary, lest he fall apart.

This, right here, had always been her worst fear. She wasn't afraid to die, she was more afraid for the people she'd leave behind. Her parents, her friends.

She turned back and found Amar kneeling on the ground gushing over the art creation of a little boy who was too thin, with sunken eyes and messy hair. Amar's smile was broad, and his words were earnest and soon enough, the little boy broke into laughter.

People she loved.

Chapter 14

He should *not* have kissed her. He never should have kissed her last year; he already knew that. But then he had to go and kiss her again. And it had been nothing short of incredible. Years of distracting himself—or trying to—of avoiding her, dating other women. All for nothing, because he'd kissed the one woman he could never allow himself to have. Because she deserved better than him.

And now, his mind was so cluttered with trying to find his belan and not think about how it had felt to kiss Divya, that he hadn't even realized she had entered the kitchen.

"You know you're muttering to yourself, Thor." She pointed to his T-shirt, which today, sported the Norse god of lightning.

Still drowsy, she squinted with sleep as she poured herself some of the coffee he had made and hopped up onto the counter. He gritted his teeth. She was beautiful. Eventually, he'd learn to live with his denial of his feelings.

"I can't find my belan," he barked. "How am I supposed to roll out rotli without it? I'm cooking for clients who need to pick up their dinner early. I can never find anything in this place. I organized everything, and I still can't find it. It's always such a mess in here. How hard is it to put it all back where it was found?"

"I never use that belan. It's too thin for my purposes." Her eyes lit up, and she raised an eyebrow at him. "You're the only one who uses it, so don't yell at me."

Her coolness only frustrated him more. He needed a reason to be irritated with her, because it was the only way he could think of to keep from kissing her again. Amar glared at her, searched all the drawers and cabinets. Nothing was as he had put it. He started reorganizing the shelves to soothe his nerves.

"I got another email from the Kantharias about the seventieth birthday party for their mom?" Divya announced between sips of coffee.

Something in her voice made him stop and look at her.

Divya pressed her gorgeous lips together and she widened her eyes. He knew that look. He shook his head at her. "You changed the *whole* menu? Not just the desserts—but my food, too! Without consulting me or my schedule."

"It's a party for one hundred and fifty—it'll be great for business," Divya insisted.

"Div, I have two other fifty-person parties that same weekend. I don't know how I can possibly be at two places at one time to do what you promised." He ran a hand through his hair. "You should have talked to me before making these arrangements."

She sipped her coffee calmly. "We'll figure it out."

"*We?* There's no *we* here. There's Divya and all her ideas," *and her amazing lips and kissing*, "and then there's me." He glanced behind her and walked over. He reached around her, careful not to touch her, but unable to avoid the heat coming from her body or to ignore the flowery scent of her hair. He grabbed his belan from the utensil container that was marked *Divya's Tools* and showed it to her.

She forced a huge smile, invoking her one dimple, which Amar had always thought was the cutest thing. Having her this close was intoxicating. "See? You found it."

He shook his head and stepped back from her, careful not to breathe in her scent.

He walked over to the dining room area—his area—and brought out the dough he had made for the flatbread. "I, uh, need the stove for a bit."

"Sure." She hopped down and stepped aside. She pulled out flour and chocolate chips from the pantry. She grabbed butter and eggs and set about making her chocolate-chip cookie dough.

Amar had to reclean the area she had been sitting on. He murmured his irritation to himself.

"What's that?" she called from behind him.

"You cannot sit on the countertops we're going to be working on. Didn't they teach you that in culinary school?" he barked.

"Oh yeah." She shrugged. "Sorry about that. But you're so tall, it's easier to talk to you that way." She gave him a smile. She seemed relaxed and unbothered by his presence, while her presence was unraveling him. He needed to get a grip.

He was rolling out the flatbread when he felt Divya's hand at his hip, tapping him to move aside. It was their normal nonverbal communication, but today her touch zinged through him and he tensed.

"Sorry, I need to get into this drawer. It's where you put my measuring spoons," she snarked at him as he stepped aside.

"It's the most logical place for them."

"I still can't find my stuff. It may have looked disorganized to you, but I knew where everything was," she snapped.

"It was madness and mayhem, and we'll never get licensed like that." He continued making little balls of the rotli dough.

"We're not trying to license my kitchen." Divya threw up her hands. "So maybe don't mess with my equipment."

"Maybe consult me before you make major menu changes!" he shot back.

"That is called building a business." She spoke slowly as if he were daft.

"Putting things back in an orderly manner is called consideration."

"Whatever." She turned on the stand mixer.

"You didn't even use the measuring spoons." He motioned to the set lying next to the salt.

Divya's eyes widened, and she quickly shut off the mixer. She looked in and shook her head, scowling. She grabbed the mixing bowl and dumped its contents. "I have to start over," she snapped at Amar as if he had done something.

"You're welcome." Amar shrugged as if he couldn't care less and went back to making rotli.

They worked in silence and moved about the kitchen, being extremely careful not to accidentally bump or touch each other. It was exhausting. He was hyperaware of every move she made, in a way he hadn't been before they kissed. She was pulling her first batch of cookies out of the oven as Amar finished the last rotli. The silence between them was deafening. He'd much rather be bickering with her, but they'd crossed some kind of line and they could not return.

He stored his rotli in a container that would keep it warm. The aroma of fresh rotli mingled with the aroma of freshly baked cookies was truly heaven, but today, even that did not improve his mood.

"I can't do this, Divya." He said these words so softly, it scared him.

"Do what?" She moved each cookie to the cooling rack with exaggerated care.

"I can't work side by side with you."

"Because you couldn't find your belan?" She looked up at him, a taunt in her eyes.

"Last week, it was my entire spatula set. And the week before, all my ladles." He sighed and looked at her and softened into his angst. "It's not the stuff. I just can't— We never should have— It's just too hard to work next to you now."

"If you're talking about that kiss, I'm over it," Divya said, still racking her cookies.

"You're over it?"

"Yes. You said you didn't want to be with me. I moved on. It was one kiss—"

"Two."

"Two—whatever. But it didn't mean anything, it's not like you and I are going to date—we're too different and there's Anita to consider."

"Exactly." He said the word, but he was reeling. The kiss did not mean anything to her. Only to him. So he was doing the right thing, pulling away from her. Made sense. Divya was a free spirit. She didn't waste time.

So how come he wanted to call her out for dismissing that kiss? There was no way that could have only meant something to him. And her expression afterward... She'd looked so dazed. If he hadn't been so intent on pushing her away, he might have relished the fact that he could kiss that dazed look onto her face, that he could set her off balance the way she did him, just by existing.

But he couldn't—wouldn't—do that. Especially when he understood he couldn't be with her anyway. He couldn't have it both ways, and he knew it.

They continued working in silence. Amar made dhal and shaak to go with the rotli. He set some aside for Divya's parents. The rest he would deliver to his client.

Divya continued making her cookies in silence.

When her parents finally returned home, it was close to lunch. It was as if there was finally air to breathe.

"Good morning, children," her father said. "Something smells great. Good thing we're famished."

Amar made a pot of chai, put together plates of food for them, while Divya set out a few cookies.

Her parents sat down to eat and stopped and looked at Amar after a few bites.

"What?" Amar asked. He hadn't tasted the food today—he'd been so distracted trying to ignore the fact that Divya was in the kitchen. He went over and tasted the shaak and dhal. Bland. Tasteless. He picked up a spoon and stirred. He hadn't added any garlic or salt.

"Your cookies, too, Divya," her mother said, making a face and spitting one out. "Salt."

"What?" Divya's eyes bugged as she grabbed a cookie and took a bite, promptly spitting it out.

Amar grabbed one and took a bite. Unbelievable. She'd used salt instead of sugar!

Raising his head, he met Divya's gaze. Shaking his head at her as he pulled out vegetables and dhal to re-make everything.

"You two okay?" Auntie asked. "I mean, aren't you supposed to be professionals?"

"Didn't you go to school for this?" Uncle joked.

Neither one of them spoke as they made eye contact. Divya sliced some bread she had baked two days ago. Amar dug into the fridge and found the cilantro chutney he had made. He sliced some onions and cucumber, and in complete silence, the two of them whipped up a couple chutney sandwiches for her parents.

"Here you go, Mom." Divya handed two fresh plates to her mother, while her parents just looked knowingly from Amar to Divya.

"We'll just take this out on the deck, while you two… cook."

"This isn't working, Divya," Amar said once they'd left. He knew he was revealing how he felt, but he couldn't afford to make mistakes with his food. Clearly Divya was at least somewhat affected, given how her cookies had turned out.

Divya nodded. He took it as agreement.

"We'll do the Parikh wedding. By the time that's done,

my kitchen should be ready. We'll be truly separate entities. In the meantime, I'll rent space."

"You can use this kitchen until yours is ready. We'll work up a schedule so we're not together."

"I can rent space for five weeks. The Kantharia party is the only other thing we have together, and it's in three weeks. We'll manage." Amar fought to keep the resignation from his voice.

"What about Fury?" Divya sounded defeated. He'd never heard that before.

"You keep him. He's used to this house."

Divya shook her head. "He'll miss you too much."

"He'll be fine. Besides, my house isn't safe for him with the renovation ongoing. I'll stop by in the mornings and walk him. Since he's used to that." Amar absently pet Fury's head.

Divya faced him, a challenge in her tone. "Answer me this, before you go. I know you feel something for me. Two people cannot share a kiss like that and not have something between them. So why are you pushing me away? Don't say it's because of my friendship with Anita, because you and I both know your sister is as tough as they come."

Amar sighed and stared at her. This beautiful, strong woman who he had been in love with since he was just a boy and she was just a girl. "Divya…" How could he make her understand? "The truth is…" He sighed at the look of complete innocence—and hurt—on her face. "The truth is that you deserve better than what I have to offer." His shoulders sagged and he suddenly felt very much weighed down. "You deserve someone equal to you. And that is not me. It won't ever be me."

Divya's mouth dropped open. "But Anita said…"

"It doesn't matter what Anita said. What I'm saying is that I—" He stopped again. Keep it simple. "You deserve someone better."

Better than him? What the hell did that mean? She was frozen to her spot. The night of the Diwali party, Anita had drunkenly told her that Amar was in love with her, and had been forever. Divya had not known what to make of that information until they'd kissed on Lola. And he had kissed her back, with intent. With desire…

But then he'd pulled back, and today he'd pushed her away. Well, she did not need to be told again. If he wanted to move out and rent space and not work together, that was fine by her. She had things to do.

She turned off her oven and grabbed the keys to her bike. She needed to ride. She automatically headed for Anita's.

But as she idled at a light, she realized that was the one place she couldn't go. Her heart hurt. Eventually, she rode around town until she cooled off and was thinking clearly.

What had she been thinking when she kissed him? Obviously, that she was falling for him. She wiped the thought from her mind.

She drove out toward the highway, and north and east past Ellicott City. She took a random exit and found herself in some older neighborhoods. She'd stopped to get her bearings when a familiar photo caught her eye. She got off her bike and went closer. She studied the picture and there was no doubt. It was Fury. His family was looking for him. She was amazed, because she had to be over ten miles from home. She ripped the picture from the telephone pole and ran back to her bike.

She pulled into her driveway and raced into the house, flinging her helmet in the garage on her way. "Amar! Amar!" She waved the picture as she ran to the kitchen, catching her breath. Right now, she did not care about how awkward things were between them. "I found something." She rounded the corner and nearly bumped into him. He looked even sadder than when she had left. "What's wrong?"

"Divya. I've been calling you."

"I can't hear my phone when I'm riding." Butterflies took up space in her stomach as she continued to look at him. "But I found this. Past Ellicott City." She shoved the paper at him.

He glanced at it and turned back to her. "I know. The vet called. They found Fury's owner."

The next day, Divya and Amar drove Fury, whose real name was Milo—what kind of name was that, anyway?—to the vet where the "real" owners were going to come get him—after over a month. All Divya could think was it better be a cute kid or a little old lady. A minivan pulled up and sure enough, the cutest three-year-old twins popped out of the van along with an older woman. So it was both. Great.

Fury whined and wagged his tail and ran to them. The little traitor. The children cuddled the dog, and Fury/Milo ate up the attention. The little old lady, it turned out, was their grandmother, and Fury/Milo was her dog. He had gotten away, and all their attempts to find him hadn't resulted in anything. When the vet had called, she had been away on vacation. The older woman was close to tears in being reunited with her companion.

Fury came back to Amar and Divya for a snuggle, and Amar bent down to him. He ruffled the hair on his head. "You be good and don't run away from this nice family again."

Divya bent down and gave Fury a hug, too.

"Thank you both for taking such good care of him," the woman said. She tried to pay them for their troubles, but both Divya and Amar refused.

They stood next to each other, not touching but close, as the minivan drove away with Fury/Milo.

"Well, I guess that's that," Amar said, getting into his car. "One less thing to worry about."

"Amar." She wanted him to hold her, to be sad with her. After all, they had both fallen for that stupid dog.

"Yes?" His answer was clipped, guarded and distant. He wore no expression, no sign that he was upset that Fury was gone.

Anger welled inside her. Fine. She didn't have time to chase someone who didn't want her anyway. "Make sure you get your stuff out of my kitchen."

His face hardened. "Consider it done."

They were never even together as a couple. So why did it feel like they were breaking up?

Chapter 15

"Hey."

"Hey," Amar responded without turning around. He knew his sister's voice and was busy taking in the vast open space of his house, now that the walls were down. "What's up?"

"Kitchen is coming along nicely," Anita said.

Amar nodded. The new counters and island were being installed, and the appliances were on the way. "Slowly."

"What's up with you and Divya?" Anita never wasted time. Just got right to the point.

The entire month of October and then some had passed since he and Divya had parted ways. In a way, Amar felt he should be grateful his sister had waited this long to confront him.

Amar flicked his gaze to Nikhil. Nikhil shook his head. "Nothing. We're leaving for the wedding tomor-row—"

"Tina told me that you both put a halt to your partnership paperwork." Now Anita sounded bossy.

"That's true."

"Why? And why are you renting kitchen space?"

He shrugged. "Divya and I cannot work together." Stick to the facts.

Anita narrowed her eyes at him. "That's exactly what she said."

"Then maybe it's true."

"No." Anita shook her head. "Something is up. You two never agree on anything." Anita turned away from him and headed for the study. "I need some of my school records and things. I know Mom kept all that stuff. And I have to get some jewelry for the wedding. I'll be out of here before you know it. You didn't change the combo on the safe, did you?"

"No. Your jewelry is still here?"

Anita pressed her lips together and gave a one-shoulder shrug. "I never took it with me. No safe." She turned away and then back to him. "I guess I liked the idea that I was 'borrowing' from her, like other daughters did." Her half smile was filled with chagrin. "I guess you're not the only one who needs to hold on to things."

"Yeah, well…" Amar shrugged and passed his gaze over the kitchen. "Take your time." He started to follow her when Nikhil motioned for him to stay back.

"What's going on with you and Divya?" Nikhil whispered.

"Same answer I gave my sister. Nothing."

"Come on, Amar. I know you don't want to involve Anita, but I promise—if you want to talk to me, whatever you say stays between us." Nikhil looked at him. "I think you need to talk to someone."

Amar shook his head. "Look, I said what I had to say. It's never going to work for us. Trust me." Amar followed Anita into the study.

It was still cluttered with all the miscellaneous items from the kitchen that he hadn't tossed when he emptied it. And that box. The box of things Michael had found when he had removed the existing appliances and cabinets.

Amar sighed and glanced in the box while Anita rummaged through the file cabinet. There were some old photos of the four them. A couple of Divya and Anita as teenagers. His high school portrait in wallet size.

A few random papers he sifted through, but a couple caught his eye and gripped his heart.

The first was a note from Anita when they were children. It was a letter she had written for him on Raksha Bandhan. That particular year, he was ten, she was nine, and they had spent the day picking on each other, arguing and fighting. This was the one holiday of the year that celebrated their sibling bond, and neither of them could be bothered to be nice to one another for even five minutes to tie rakhi on each other's wrists.

Their mother was livid. She gave them a verbal thrashing and then sent them to their rooms with her final words. "If something should happen to me and your father, you are all you two have. Just the two of you."

They had heard that so many times, it hardly even registered. They had stomped to their rooms, full of the righteous indignation of siblings who had determined that everything was the other person's fault. They even managed to give each other the evil eye, while hardly even looking at each other.

About an hour or so into their solitary banishment, a folded-up piece of paper was shoved under his door, followed by the rapid scurrying of Anita's feet. He unfolded it and found that it was a note from his sister, and she had included his rakhi. The note read:

Dear Bhaiya,

(She must have been really sorry because she almost always called him Amar.)

I am sorry we fought all day. If it ever was just the two of us, I am glad that you are the other one of the two. I love you. Happy Raksha Bandhan (well, what's left anyway).

She had signed it *The Other One of the Two, Your sister, Anita.* She had drawn and colored in flowers all over the letter.

Amar had crept out of his room and knocked softly on Anita's door. When she opened it, he apologized for fighting with her all day, as well, and asked her to tie his rakhi. She obliged, and they had their own Raksha Bandhan quietly in the hallway between their rooms, without even the sweets (which they had always agreed was the best part). Amar gave her a gift, but for the life of him, he could not remember what it was.

Shortly thereafter, their mother called them down for dinner. She noticed the rakhi on Amar's wrist, but said nothing, short of a small harrumph.

Amar smiled at the letter, his heart heavy.

He missed the closeness he used to share with his sister. And even though she was married, in a way it was just the two of them, wasn't it? He glanced across the room at her. "Hey. Look what I found." He grinned at her and handed over the letter.

Her face lit up as she took it. "Oh my god. I had no idea you kept this."

"I didn't. It was behind the fridge or something. I mean, I had kept it, but then I lost it and didn't know where it was."

She handed it back to him. He hated fighting with her. "I'm sorry, Anita. I am so sorry for being such an ass about this whole kitchen thing." He walked around the desk to where she was and opened his arms to hug her.

Anita squeezed him tight, and he realized she had missed him as much as he had missed her. She pulled back and punched his arm. "Damn straight, you were an ass!" But her eyes glistened with unspent tears that made him feel like a horrible brother.

"I'm apologizing. Please don't cry."

"I had to do it, Amar. I'm not sure what's going on with you, but that kitchen was a mess."

"You're right. It's just—"

"Aw. Look at you two, finally making up." Divya stood in the doorway of the study. She typed something into her phone and put it down on a shelf by the door. Amar's heart raced at the sound of her voice. Except for the Kantharia party three weeks ago, he hadn't seen Divya since he moved out of her kitchen and her house. They communicated via text or email, and only about work. The party had been a huge success, but it had been exhausting pretending that he and Divya were still partners.

Anita beamed at her friend. "It was just a matter of time until my brother saw the light of day."

Divya passed her gaze casually over him and addressed Anita. "I saw your car and came over to see you. It's been forever."

She had had the same look about her at the party. Closed. All business.

"Yeah, I'm sorry. Law school is rough and you two have been plenty busy." Anita smirked.

He glanced at Divya. She shrugged. "This wedding requires a bunch of prep."

"The Kantharias raved about you two," said Anita. "They usually go with Ranjit at Taj, but they tried you and were impressed. Nikhil heard that Ranjit is pissed he let Amar go."

"Well, he should be," Divya said as she glanced in boxes and around the room. "Amar is one of the best."

Her compliment was like the warmth of sunshine on him. Honestly, he needed to get a grip.

Divya reached into the box and pulled out a piece of paper. She glanced at it and had started to put it away when she drew it close and studied it. "Hey. What's this?" She sounded almost accusatory as she handed the paper to Amar.

Amar took the paper and looked. What he saw made him light-headed. He stared at Anita. "Is this a joke?"

"What are you talking about?" She grabbed the paper. Her eyes widened. "This is Dad's writing, not mine."

Amar's stomach hollowed out. "Dad drew that?"

Divya looked over Anita's shoulder. "Yes. And the date is—"

"A week before the accident."

"No!" Amar was going to be sick. Why? Why would his father argue with him? Amar felt the blood rush from his head and was forced to sit down. The watch on his wrist suddenly felt tight.

It was Divya who was at his side first, laying her hand on his shoulder. It was the first time she had touched him since that kiss. He hadn't realized how much he craved her touch until he felt the strength and the warmth of her hand on him.

"Amar? You okay?"

"Amar." Panic filled his sister's voice. "What's the matter?"

"It's a sketch. Of a new kitchen." Amar forced out the words.

Why hadn't his father said anything about this drawing? Why had he let Amar keep trying to convince him to redo the space—and yet, he kept refusing?

"I... I had been talking to him about renovating—just a bit. New counters, new oven, etcetera. Nothing major like what we're doing now."

"Isn't that a good thing?"

He sighed. "No. Maybe. It is a good thing. But he never told me that he was thinking along those lines. He simply kept putting me off. It pissed me off, to be honest." His sister's eyes were huge and her face was pale. His heart and stomach ached.

"You argued that night." Divya's voice was somber.

Amar nodded. "We—or at least—I did. It was bad." His last words to his father were inexcusable. "I said horrible things—"

"Like?" Divya nudged him.

"I said he was stuck in the past. That he couldn't understand progress. Then he drove off." Tears burned at his eyes. He looked away.

"He didn't say anything back to you?"

Amar shook his head. "But my ideas—they're in that sketch."

"It was like getting Kulfi," Anita said.

"What?" Amar snapped his head to her.

"Remember? He said no, but he wanted something from me first. When I behaved responsibly, he got me the dog." She looked at the paper. "Read the top."

It was written in Gujarati. Amar made out his name and read the second word, deciphering as he went along. "Grad-u-a-tion."

"He was going to show this to you when you finished culinary school." Anita tipped her chin at him.

"It doesn't change what I said—"

"No, but you need to forgive yourself for that. You said things out of frustration. You had no idea that someone was going to swerve their car that night." His sister held him tight. "We all say things we don't mean. He was probably chuckling to himself and Mom about how he got you all riled up and how great the surprise was going to be. That's what he loved."

"It's why I didn't take the call," Amar confessed.

"Because it came from Dad's phone and you were still upset." Anita nodded her head in understanding.

"I just needed time to cool off." He looked from Anita to Divya and back. He could not look at Divya. "But it was too late."

His sister hugged him. "Why didn't you ever say anything? Why did you carry this with you all these years? You know what? It doesn't matter. What does matter is that Mom and Dad would not want you to carry this around. Time to let it go." Anita was as bossy as ever—but maybe she was right.

Amar looked at the drawing, choked with emotion. His father *had* been listening. Amar had been heard by the man he loved and respected. His heart felt a little bit lighter.

He squeezed Anita's hand. "These are my ideas."

"See? Dad knew how smart you were."

Maybe. But what haunted Amar wasn't just the last things he'd said to his father. It was what happened after his parents' accident that kept him up at night. That kept him from Divya.

Amar was holding something back. There was more to the story. Divya could tell.

Whatever. It was no longer her problem. In fact, it had never been her problem to begin with. Or so she told herself.

Her heart thudded in her chest and all she wanted to do was hold Amar and tell him it would be all right. Instead, she watched while his sister comforted him. As far as the thudding in her chest and the pit in her stomach, there was nothing for it.

Her phone rang, Nikhil was closest, so he grabbed it, glancing at it as he handed it to her. He froze as he saw the screen, looking at her in shock. Anita did not miss his expression.

"What?" She turned to Divya. "Who is it?"

Divya, for once, had nothing to say. Nikhil shook his head.

Anita turned back to him. "Nicky, who is calling Divya that made you look at her like that?"

Nikhil couldn't stop looking at her, his mouth pressed in a line, his eyes filled with accusation. She flicked her gaze away from him. She couldn't face the accusation in his eyes. No matter how deserved.

"It's Ranjit," Divya finally said. All eyes turned to

her, but the only ones she was paying attention to were the darkest brown of them all. The only ones that mattered. Amar's.

He narrowed his eyes as he looked at her. "Why is Ranjit calling you?"

Divya swallowed as heat rose to her face. "He needs a pastry chef for a party." She jutted her chin out toward Amar, even as anger and betrayal filled his eyes. *If looks could kill, as they say.*

"You're working with Ranjit?" Amar's lips barely moved as he spoke. "You said you weren't going to call him back."

"And I didn't, until you left. Until we decided not to work together. My best option is to pair with caterers. Even you said that," Divya spat out.

"But this is *Ranjit*." Amar said the man's name like it was a four-letter word.

"I need income. My parents are downsizing. They're going to sell the house, so I'm getting my own place. Every referral we have wants the both of us, even whatever we get from this wedding. Since we clearly cannot work together, I figured I'd work a couple of parties with Ranjit to make some money. I have to look out for myself."

"But Div—" Anita was shaking her head at her.

"Don't *but Div*, me!" She turned on her friend, tears spilling from her eyes. "I should have known that when push came to shove, you'd side with your brother."

"No. That's not—" Anita reached for her friend. "There has to be another caterer—"

Divya stepped out of her reach. "Not with Ranjit's connections." She couldn't tear her gaze from Amar.

The look of hurt and betrayal on his face would haunt her forever.

"You could have worked with anyone. But you chose Ranjit." His tone was steel, but she heard the shock beneath.

"No. I chose *you*." Divya grabbed her phone. "But you won't work with me."

Chapter 16

Amar was waiting outside Lola with his duffel bag an hour before they needed to depart. It was early, still, so the moon would rule the sky for a few more minutes. It was only a half-moon, but it shone bright, giving just enough light to see by.

He leaned against the bus in the early morning November chill and took in the house he had watched from across the street for most of his life.

Uncle and Auntie were moving. He would no longer have the eyes of parents watching over him. Divya would be leaving as well. The thought was like a knife edge against his heart. Even though they hadn't spoken since their argument, close to six weeks ago, Divya was as much a fixture in his life as her parents, or his sister, or even his kitchen.

They needed to load up the refrigerated things at the

last minute. He waited for Divya to come out—he could no longer simply walk into that house anymore. Things had changed—he and Divya had changed—and there was no going back. The weight of the difference settled heavily in his heart, and it almost felt like grief.

As the sun began to peek over the horizon, the garage door rose open, and like a glutton for punishment, Amar turned to watch Divya come out. But it wasn't Divya who walked out into the breaking dawn, it was her father.

"Uncle." Amar's voice echoed in the still navy blue darkness.

"Amar." Uncle approached and looked Amar up and down. Amar towered a head over Uncle, but Amar remembered looking up at Uncle as a young teen, wondering if he would ever be as tall as him. "Beta. Why are you waiting outside in the cold?"

Amar frowned as if that was a ridiculous question. "I didn't want to disturb you. Divya will come out when she is ready."

"Ah." The older man grunted, still eyeing Amar with a scrutinizing gaze. "You didn't want to disturb... Since when is it disturbing for parents to see their children?"

"Uncle, it's early. I didn't want to wake—"

"You think it matters whether Divya wakes me or you or Anita?"

Chastised, Amar looked at his feet. Why, he had no idea. He was a grown man, for god's sake. "No."

"What is going on, beta? Talk to your uncle. What has happened between you three?"

Amar sighed. "Anita forced me to gut the kitchen. Divya agreed with her. It...changed things between all of us."

Uncle pressed his lips together and leaned against

Lola, looking across at Amar's house. The sun was making a slow and lazy appearance, turning the sky a brighter blue with shades of orange and pink as it made its entrance. "You are connected to your parents in that kitchen."

"Everything of value that I learned, I learned in that kitchen, watching the two of them."

"You went to that fancy culinary school."

"I didn't only learn how to cook. I learned…" Amar stopped, not sure if the words would come.

Uncle waited patiently.

"I learned…how much they loved each other. It wasn't that they never fought or bickered, they absolutely did. It was how they always came back together. They came back together over how much marcha to add to a dish, whether fresh lemon juice was required, or the bottle would do. They mended their hurt feelings and wounded egos while choosing the best vegetables, experimenting with prep and grinding out new spices. The way my dad looked at my mom, and the way she looked at him… They were solid. I didn't know it when I was growing up, but I look back at it now, and I know that is what I want." He flicked a look at Uncle. "And I'll never have it, because…"

"Because what, beta?"

Amar glanced at Uncle. Veer Uncle was watching him intently. The sun continued to bring light into the day. "You know. You were there."

"I know I have watched you take care of Anita all your life—she is, after all, your sister. You have also taken care of Divya. And don't even try to tell me that my daughter is like a sister to you. I'm her father and I see how you treat her." He cleared his throat and raised an eyebrow. "Not to mention how you look at her."

Amar flushed, grateful that they were in shadow from the rising sun. Apparently, he was more transparent than he'd thought. "Well, you were there, with Divya and Anita when—the night of the accident. You saw me." Amar stopped and met Uncle's eyes.

Uncle furrowed his brow. "What did I see?"

Amar swallowed against the rising emotion that threatened to choke him. "I was weak." He had never uttered those words out loud. Heat rose to his face at his admission.

"Weak?" Uncle seemed to be searching his memory. "I saw no such thing. I saw a young man lose both of his parents in one night. In a tragic, horrible accident." He reached out and placed a warm hand on Amar's arm. "You were in shock."

"Anita experienced the same loss. She managed."

"Did she?" Uncle shook his head. "She married too quickly, then divorced just as quickly, looking for that same stability. It's grief, beta, and it is a process. It never shows up the same way in different people."

"Divya was there. She saw how I fell apart, how I was unable to function. How my sister was forced to carry the burden all alone." Amar kicked at the ground, unable to look at Uncle.

"Anita was not alone. She had us. She had you. Divya never left her side."

"Uncle." Amar shook his head. "Divya needs someone solid. Someone she can count on when she needs them. I'm not that person. She deserves better."

"What Divya deserves is not for you to decide. She can make her own choices. You have to decide what *you* want." Uncle raised an eyebrow. "Everything you learned, cooking and otherwise, is not in that kitchen, Amar. It is in *you*. You can redo that kitchen ten times, and the lessons you learned from your parents will never leave you. How they looked at each other, what they taught you about love, that will always be with you."

The sun was properly up now. They would have to leave in thirty minutes to get to the site of the Parikh wedding in time to begin prepping. "Dad?" Divya called as she walked out in leggings and a sweatshirt, pulling a cooler behind her.

"Huh, beti?"

"What are you doing— Oh." She stopped when she saw Amar.

Amar stepped up. "Here, I'll get that."

"You're here," Divya said.

"I'm here." He took the cooler from her. "You can get the other stuff while I play Tetris out here, trying to get all of this—" he motioned at the boxes he had brought from his house "—in the bus."

"Um, yeah. Sure." Divya looked at him and her father and went back in to get the other perishables they needed.

Amar packed what he could into the onboard freezer and fridge and the other things stayed in the cooler.

"Amar." Uncle laid his hand on Amar's shoulder as he knelt in front of the small freezer. He waited until Amar turned to look at him. "Forgive yourself. This is no way to live. Life—" he sighed and looked toward the house "—is too precious."

"Dad," Divya called from outside the bus. "We have to go."

Uncle squeezed Amar's shoulder. "Kicking the old man out, huh?" he said as he exited the bus.

"Dad." Divya giggled, and Amar could imagine her eye roll. "You're not old."

"All set back here," called Amar as he sat down in the seat behind the driver. Divya had started to teach him to drive this thing, but he hadn't changed his license yet to ensure he had legal permission.

They waved to Uncle as they drove off.

Divya looked at him in the rearview. "Coffee?"

He held up his to-go cup. "Chai."

Something flickered in her eyes, but she quickly hardened her gaze, and with a sharp nod, she turned back to the road.

They rode in silence for about twenty minutes.

"How was that last party you did with Ranjit?" Amar had to ask.

"It was fine." Divya kept her concentration on the road.

"Really? That's all?"

"What do you want me to say? That Ranjit makes boring food?" Divya snapped.

Amar suppressed a smile. "If that's the truth."

Divya made a noncommittal noise.

"How is Lola working out?" They had finished the paint job together, if not at the same time.

He caught her smile in the rearview.

"She's great. I'm thinking about taking her to the hospital parking lot once a month or so, to sell cupcakes, cookies, that kind of thing."

"That's fabulous," Amar agreed. "You may not need to work with Ranjit anymore."

"Maybe." She shrugged. "The parties are more lucrative though."

"But if you set up Lola in different areas, like a moving bakeshop—"

"You just don't want me to work with Ranjit."

"I don't. You're right, but you have options."

"Not the options I want." She met his eyes in the rearview.

"What do you mean, there's only one room?" Amar demanded. He hiked his backpack higher onto his back as he shifted his weight and leaned on the counter. "Two rooms were booked for me and my—partner. As well as rooms for our staff."

They'd arrived at the five-star hotel, with a glamorous lobby, large open veranda, high-end athletic center and gorgeous outdoor pool, on schedule. Even though it wasn't quite Thanksgiving, various iterations of Christmas trees dotted the lobby, leading to one massive tree in the center of the veranda. Christmas music played softly in the background.

Divya was parking Lola while Amar checked them in. Their first event of the three-day wedding celebrations was the 250-person prewedding dinner, the night before the wedding, tomorrow night. They had made decent time, considering the bus didn't really go that fast, arriving in just over two hours. This gave them all of today and tomorrow to prep once they got settled. But first they needed to check in to their rooms.

Amar desperately checked his email. Sure enough, they had confirmations for two rooms. This was the biggest event he'd had on his own, and doing it well meant more business from the Parikhs and Joshis, as well as their friends and family.

Now it seemed the only thing threatening his focus

would be having to share a room with Divya. The drive down was painful enough, even after that talk with Uncle. Amar had not ever really admitted his feelings of failure out loud, and right now, he was raw.

"I'm sorry, sir." The hotel employee checked her computer again. "This wedding block is full, and I have only the one room under your name. Two queen beds, non-smoking."

"Try Divya Shah."

The employee, Rosa, squinted at her computer again. She shook her head. "Nothing at all under that name."

"Okay, I'd like another room, then," Amar insisted.

"Sorry, we are fully booked. Between this wedding and the optometry convention, we are at capacity."

He sighed. "Fine. Can you just send an extra pillow and blanket to the room?" He would just take that and sleep on the bus. He caught Divya's eye as she entered the lobby. Even with her mouth set and that invisible but effective wall up, she made his heart melt. He stiffened his back and set his jaw. *Fake it till you make it.* He inhaled deeply and approached her. "They only have one room for us. I got an extra pillow and blanket. I'll sleep on the bus."

Divya stared at him. He literally could not read her face right now.

"How many beds?" she asked.

"Two."

"So, we'll share. We each get a bed." She shrugged, but did not meet his eyes.

"No. That's okay—"

"Amar Virani. I do not have cooties. We are grown adults. While we're at it, this whole silent treatment thing that's been going on since you kissed me—"

"What? *You* kissed *me*."

Her eyes bugged open. "Um, no, that is not how it went down."

"Well, however it went down, I didn't hear you complaining."

"No. My only complaint is—" She stopped herself and stepped back from him and inhaled deeply as if she'd been about to say something she would regret. "Actually, you know what? I can manage to keep my hands to myself, so we can share that room. Can you?"

"Absolutely. No problem," Amar lied.

"Glad to hear it. Good to know you can act like an adult." Divya grabbed the handle of her roller bag.

"Fine." Amar pressed the elevator button.

"Fine."

They entered the elevator to Christmas music and headed up to their room to get settled.

"We should drop off our stuff and unload Lola. It'll give us a chance to check out the kitchen," Amar said as they entered their room. "Unless you want a nap."

"Napping is never an option. Waste of time."

He rolled his eyes. A nap was never a waste of time. He rolled his bag to a corner of the room and stopped. In the center of the tiny room was one large king bed. No. No no *no*. He picked up the phone and called the front desk. Rosa picked up.

"There is only one bed in this room." The words zipped out of his mouth, his voice tighter than normal in his desperation. "You said it had two beds."

"I'm sorry, Mr.…Virani—our system had it wrong."

"But you said *two beds*." He was frantic. "Can you send up a cot?"

"I'm sorry, sir. But we only have a limited number of cots, and they are all currently in use."

Amar hung up.

Crap. This was not good.

"No cot." He met Divya's eyes and looked from her to the bed.

Her face revealed nothing. "Whatever. We'll make it work."

"Sure," Amar lied again. Maybe if he kept saying it, it would end up being true. "Let's go find the kitchen and unload Lola."

They checked out the hotel kitchen, and true to her word, Neepa Auntie had arranged for them to have access starting tomorrow. In the meantime, tomorrow night's dinner and any other prep would take place at the nearby home that Neepa Auntie had rented for the family. All the prewedding groom's ceremonies would be happening there.

They drove Lola to the address they had been given and parked in the driveway, stunned. This house rivaled the Joshi mansion in size and elegance. Amar looked at Divya, a large grin on his face. This kitchen would be amazing. He couldn't wait to get in there. Divya nodded as they took in the massive exterior.

They worked together to unload what they needed from Lola and then found the kitchen. It was a dream. Two commercial-sized refrigerators, a full eight-burner stove, a farm kitchen sink and a small bar sink in the island. Three dishwashers and counter space for ages. Amar and Divya grinned at each other like children in a candy shop, then quickly got to work.

They worked on what they needed tomorrow night,

as well as some early prep for the wedding lunch. Just easy things that could be easily moved.

They worked in silence. Divya would start the wedding cake and the ice cream for tonight's dinner. She had already made some of the Indian sweets that would be needed for the wedding lunch and dinner. Amar was prepping for the meal tomorrow night. It would be easier to do all the wedding day prep at the venue kitchen.

"What did my dad want this morning?" Divya asked, breaking the silence.

Amar frowned as he continued chopping and shook his head. "Just chatting."

"Looked pretty intense."

Amar smiled to himself a bit. "He was just…being a dad."

"He's really good at that." Divya gave a small chuckle.

Amar looked up at her and grinned. "Yes, he is." They were making great progress. Courtney would arrive in a few hours, as well as Anjali and Anand, the two culinary school students he had hired to help out this weekend. They were a brother-and-sister team, and Amar had been impressed by their work ethic. Amar relaxed into his work. This was going to be okay. The wedding would go smoothly, and they would get more contracts.

Neepa Auntie came bustling into the kitchen. "Oh. Great, you are here. Did you settle in okay?"

"The hotel is beautiful, but they only had one room for the both of us."

"Tsk. I am very sorry. I'll do what I can to fix that." She flicked a wide-eyed gaze between the two of them. "In the meantime, I have had a small change of plans, and I will make it worth your while if you can help me out. I have seventy-five people that I need to feed tonight.

I was not expecting it, but don't worry, something simple should be fine. Like naan pizza or something." She looked at Amar. "Maybe some of those mini cupcakes we thought we wouldn't need?" She grinned at Divya.

"Auntie. This is short notice—" Divya started.

"I will make it worth your while. Guaranteed."

"We need a car," Amar said. This was added work, but they could manage.

"I thought so." She dangled the keys and set them on the counter. "Thank you!" She waved as she left the kitchen.

Amar and Divya simply stared after her, frozen. Then, as if they had choreographed it, they both moved. Amar went to the fridge, Divya to the pantry.

"More flour," Divya stated. She spoke into her phone to make a list.

"Eggs. Yogurt. Butter," Amar called out.

"Sugar. Vanilla. Cardamom," Divya continued. "I assume you'll need garlic, onion?"

"Yes. Tomatoes. Cheese. Assorted vegetables. You'll need more milk than this half gallon?"

Divya nodded. She grabbed the keys. "Grocery store is five minutes away. It'll be faster if we both go."

Chapter 17

Divya was just putting finishing touches on the night's
mini chai cupcakes. After that, she'd be free to continue
baking the various layers of the wedding cake. She was
a bit behind due to Auntie's last-minute demands, but
she'd manage. Assembly of the cake would happen tomorrow on-site. Final decoration would be day of. But
everything had to be ready to go.

Amar pounded into the kitchen, his face a mask. But
after having worked in close quarters with him, Divya
could tell from the set of his mouth and the way he moved
his body that something was amiss. Rather than the normal easy flow of his arms and hands as he worked, his
moves were rough and agitated. Not to mention that when
something was really off, he would worry the end of the
leather strap of his dad's watch. She smiled to herself.
For all his secret ways, Amar was an open book to any-

one really paying attention. And clearly, she had been paying attention.

Amar started pulling flour from the pantry.

"What's up?" she asked as she put away the cupcakes and cleaned her work area.

"I have to start the naan over. We bought a bad batch of yeast. The dough did not rise."

"Don't you normally bloom the yeast—"

"I did. No idea." He shook his head.

"I can go—"

"Already got it." He held up a new jar. "I still need to make sauce, chop toppings."

Divya grabbed the yogurt from the fridge. "So have Anand and Anjali work on it."

"Anjali never made it. She has a fever and stayed home. Anand brought another classmate, but I don't know anything about— Here they are." Amar plastered on a smile. Another thing she had noticed. The difference in Amar's expressions. This current one was meant to greet someone, but really he wanted them to just get to work already.

"Hey, Anand, and you must be Mohit." The young men nodded. "You can start over there, chopping whatever vegetables you see." He instructed them as to the kind of cuts he needed, which dishes the vegetables were going into, and then turned his attention back to the naan.

"Let me make the naan dough. You start your sauce." Divya took the yeast from him. "Don't worry, Amar. I make dough like this all the time."

"What about the wedding cake?"

"I'll figure it out. Right now, we need to feed seventy-five people naan pizza and salad. Besides, Courtney is only ten minutes away."

"Yeah. Okay." Amar gathered canned tomato sauce, fresh tomatoes and garlic and got to work. His voice was steady and even. His movements became fluid again. He was in the zone. One thing about Amar, he did not panic once he hit the zone. He was always calm, cool, focused. Even with the crepe fiasco, he'd never lost it while cooking.

Divya made the dough by hand. The stand mixer never quite got the naan dough the way she liked it. It was gentler, and naan did not require rough kneading.

Amar was completely focused on the sauce while Divya made the dough. She did it in three batches, to be sure of the proper texture. Her cake needed baking, but tonight's dinner took priority over dessert. Neither of them would sleep much this weekend anyway. And that had nothing to do with the fact that they were sharing a bed.

Nothing at all.

Divya set the dough aside to rise and went back to her desserts.

Sometime later, Amar glanced away from his sauce to check on the students and see how Divya was faring. She was rolling out naan. She had flour on her arms and a smudge of it on her cheek, but she looked adorable. His pulse raced as he watched her turn out perfect naan, over and over. He imagined walking over and gently brushing the flour off her cheek. Pulling her to him in a kiss…that one big bed in the hotel…

He truly needed to let go of *that* line of thinking.

He wanted to tell her he could take over so she could work on her desserts and the cake, but a glance at the time told him he needed every bit of help he could get. He checked on the students and was slightly disappointed. They were slower than he had anticipated. "You're both culinary students?" he asked. Mohit looked a bit young to be in school.

"Well, I am," said Anand. "But I couldn't find anyone on such short notice, so I brought my cousin. But Mo has been helping us cook forever."

Amar sighed. Whatever. He needed the help. He stirred his simmering sauce and checked on the items he had started for tomorrow.

"You've been holding out on me, Div." Amar inhaled the fabulous aroma of fresh-baked naan.

"What do you mean?" She didn't look up. Kept rolling.

Amar grabbed a rolling pin and joined her. "Your naan are gorgeous."

She stopped for a second to look at him, her beautiful face the picture of shock. "Well, they should be. Don't you remember?"

He furrowed his brow. "Remember what?"

"Whenever I was well enough, I would sleep over at your house with Anita. We always cooked together, you, Anita, your parents. More often than not, we made some kind of bread. I learned naan from the same place you did."

Amar froze as his heart was gripped, and tears suddenly threatened his eyes. He snapped his head toward her. "My dad."

She looked up at him, and her smile fell seeing his face. "His were the best."

He sighed. "I had forgotten. It's nice to remember that." He smiled at her. "And I'm glad you learned from him, it's a huge help. I know you have your cake and those gum paste flowers to do."

"How do you know about the flowers?" Divya seemed surprised.

"I saw your cake design." Amar shrugged and looked away.

Divya smirked. "Oh, you're doing flowers with me tomorrow. Don't you worry."

"I don't know how to make those."

"No problem. I learned how to make naan from the best. You will learn how to make gum paste flowers from the best." She cocked a smile at him and nodded at his naan. "Don't overwork that dough."

"How are we going to keep these pizzas warm?" Amar pulled out another pan from the oven.

Divya grinned. "On Lola. We'll use the crepe pans."

Amar raised an eyebrow.

"People can just get the pizzas from there. We'll cook the remaining ones in Lola's ovens."

Amar's mouth quirked and he looked around. "We have a good start. Set up Lola in the back, next to the outdoor kitchen. We'll have to use those ovens, too. If it gets too cold, we'll have Auntie turn on the firepit."

Divya smiled as she grabbed the keys to Lola. "Anand, Mohit. Meet me around back with whatever Chef gives you. Courtney, come help me set up."

Amar was already in motion. Divya's heart lifted. This was going to be okay.

They served up fresh hot pizza from the bus, to moans and groans of satisfaction. Dinner service went off with minimal delays. Divya's cupcakes were the perfect ending to the last-minute dinner.

"Nicely done, Chef," Divya said to Amar as she wiped down the crepe pans later that night. Amar was cleaning the prep area. She had hardly even felt the tension between them while they were so busy, and it was a welcome relief. It was unnatural watching her words around Amar after so many years of just...*being*.

"You, too, Chef." He grinned at her, relaxed and smiling. He had rolled up the sleeves of his whites to clean up, brazenly displaying his strong corded forearms. Divya forced herself to look away from him. He patted the countertop while still looking at her. "Could not have done it without Lola. She really came through today."

"She really did." Warm, fuzzy thoughts about Amar's arms were starting to invade her brain. She shook her head to clear the feeling, just as a familiar voice reached her from Lola's door.

"Hey!" Anita hopped on, grinning from ear to ear. "You two are a hit!" A young woman stood right behind her, her eyes wide and mouth open.

"This is so cool!" the woman said, smiling at them.

"Divya, Amar, you remember Sangeeta, Hiral's sister? She's getting married in May."

Sangeeta waved to them. "So great to see you both again—and eat more of your food! I love, love this food truck! I cannot wait to see what you have in store for the rest of my brother's wedding." She paused. "I hope my mom dropping last-minute dinners on you doesn't scare you away from my wedding. I'd love to hire you."

"We would love to do your wedding, Sangeeta." Amar grinned at her, flicking his gaze to Divya. Did that mean they were working together again? Divya wasn't sure. "Divya is the pastry chef, and I do the food. We can arrange a time to sit down and see what your ideas are. Make sure that what each of us offers appeals to you."

Hmm. He'd left it open for her to reject one of them.

Or for one of them to reject her. Just when she thought they were moving past all the tension.

"Fabulous!" She took their information and left, taking Anita with her.

Divya grabbed some decorating supplies and moved back into the house to prep for the next day. She still needed to get the cake started, not to mention coloring the icing and the gum paste. Amar joined her inside and brought with him all the angst that they had put aside. Anand, Mohit and Courtney went back to the hotel to get some rest, while Divya and Amar worked late. There wouldn't be much sleep tonight.

After several hours of prep, they were finally done. Divya packed up her cakes. Meeta had only wanted three tiers, and they were fully cooled and ready to be stacked and decorated. The gum paste flowers would have to wait until tomorrow—she could barely keep her eyes open.

"Come on," Amar said softly, as he packed up what he needed. "Let's get some sleep. It's going to be a long weekend."

Yawning, she put her things together and followed him out to the driveway. As they left the kitchen, some of the tension seemed to disappear.

"Let me drive." Amar held his hand out for the keys.

"You don't have your bus license yet." Divya yawned.

"You can't seem to keep your eyes open." He chuckled. "I like my odds better."

Divya hit the jump seat, and Amar pulled Lola around. They drove in silence. Divya suspected Amar was concentrating hard so he wouldn't get pulled over. They got to the hotel and parked Lola in the back. After securing their things in the hotel kitchen, they dragged themselves to their room.

They both headed for the bathroom at the same time.

"You go." Amar stood back and motioned toward the door.

"Thanks." Divya changed for bed, donning long pajama bottoms and a tank top, and washed her face.

When she came out, Amar was just pulling an old T-shirt over his head, his naked chest in full view. She swallowed hard and then cursed the Spider-Man T-shirt for covering his glorious muscles.

"Oh, hey…" Amar stared at her, cleared his throat. "I…uh… I didn't hear you come out…"

They stared at each other while the silence thickened. "You done?" Amar narrowed his eyes at her. "Div?"

"Hm?" She snapped out of it. "Oh yeah." She stepped away from the bathroom and went toward the bed.

Amar washed up and settled down next to her on his side, bringing with him his clean masculine scent. There was maybe two feet between them, but it might as well have been a mile—or two inches. He was too close and too far all at the same time.

"I'm aiming for five hours, so we can get a jump on things in the morning," Amar said.

"I'll take it," she said as she lay back on her side of the bed.

"A little dicey today." The deep rumble of Amar's voice was a balm to her ears, and his words eased the tension that was flowing through her.

She turned her head to him. A sliver of light from the street peeked through the hotel room drapes, backlighting Amar's form on the bed next to hers. While she could appreciate that he was much closer than she'd thought, she couldn't make out the expression on his face.

"Yes." She paused. "We made it work."

"We did."

"You know, you made it sound like we didn't have to work together for Sangeeta's wedding."

"It's business. I want her to choose each of us if that's who she wants. I don't want her to be saddled with me just because she wants you. That's all. Get the account first, deal with the details later." Amar spoke softly, as if he were falling asleep.

"Now you sound like me." She smiled into the darkness.

He was quiet for a moment. "You're rubbing off."

"Right." She glanced at Amar quickly. His eyes were shut, and his breathing was even. Fine. She closed her eyes and willed sleep to come.

Chapter 18

The sharp beeping of his alarm roused Amar from fitful slumber. How was he supposed to sleep with Divya breathing softly next to him? Before he even opened his eyes, he was immediately aware of Divya's warm, soft body barely inches from his. She smelled like burnt sugar. Professional hazard, he supposed. But not one he'd ever want her to fix. Not that he had anything to say about it. She was turned away from him. The sliver of light from the window behind him cast a golden glow over her silken skin. She slept in pajama pants and a tank top, which he already knew, but he didn't know that she slept curled up in ball. If he wrapped his arm around her and pulled her to him, closing that space, her curves would fit perfectly with his body.

"You going to make that stop?" Divya mumbled without opening her eyes.

"Oh. Yeah." He turned and reached for his phone to silence the incessant beeping, and he tore himself out of the bed and headed for the bathroom.

He hadn't even touched her, yet his body was cold and lonely from the loss of her. He showered and changed and tried to focus on his strategy for the day, but all he could think about was getting back in that bed with Divya.

What was he thinking? That was a terrible idea. These thoughts only proved to him that he should not be working with Divya moving forward.

He focused on his plan for the day, which instantly melted away when he came out of the bathroom. Divya was in tree pose, her eyes closed, perfectly balanced on one foot, and any other thought he'd had was washed out of his mind by her completely serene presence.

Amar did not move.

"I can hear you breathing. You can move," Divya said softly. She stretched her arms up and over and opened her eyes. She beamed at him. "Good morning. Ready for the day?"

All he could do was nod.

They were scheduled to be back at the rental house later that afternoon for the dinner service of 250 people for the prewedding dinner. Today they had some limited access to the hotel kitchen, which they would use to prep for tomorrow's postwedding events.

Once Divya was ready, they went straight to work in the hotel kitchen. Amar had things to soak, chop, knead. They each pretty much kept in their own lanes, focused on the work—deliberately trying to avoid each other. Amar was hyperaware of Divya's presence, whether she was behind him or next to him or not even in the kitchen.

The intensity of focusing on the work, while still having complete awareness of the woman he loved but wouldn't have drained him.

Divya appeared fully focused on the cake and the desserts needed for tonight and tomorrow's events. Plus the crepes for tomorrow night...

He hoped they could handle it all.

"How's the cake coming?" he asked.

"The cake is fine. The icing is driving me nuts. And I have over one hundred gum paste flowers to make. Courtney is working on the ice cream and cookies for tonight." She sighed. "How's the food?"

"So far, so good." He grinned. "I left most of the spices I roasted on the bus. Remind me to grab them on the way to the house."

"It'll be easier if we take Lola," Divya said.

"True. And I did like driving that bus."

Divya's gaze lingered on him for a moment.

"What?" He looked down at himself to see what he had spilled on himself, then back at her. She was looking at him, at his face. "Do I have spices on me? What?"

She frown-smiled and shook her head. "No. Nothing." She cleared her throat and went back to her work.

"After dinner's over, you can show me how to do the flowers," Amar reminded her.

She snapped her gaze back to him. "You sure? I was just kidding."

"I'm sure. The work has to get done, unless you want Courtney to—"

"No, Courtney is handling other things and I need her to sleep so she can manage the servers." She eyed him, eyebrow raised. "Have you ever worked with gum paste?"

"In school. I just need a refresher and any tips you

might have." The fact that he would be helping her, learning from her, not to mention he'd get to be near her made him feel light and happy.

Ugh. No. Not supposed to go there.

Divya nodded her agreement. "Okay, but I'm warning you, I am very particular about how the flowers look. Only perfection."

Amar chuckled. "I'll do my best." He was grateful for the easy banter with her. That was fine. Easy banter was good. Maybe they could go back to the way things were. Maybe they could even work together.

They were suddenly interrupted by the sound of screeching brakes and crashing metal from outside. Amar ran toward the back exit door in a flash. He barely registered Divya behind him. The rear doors opened to the service area parking lot where they'd parked Lola last night.

"Oh god, Div. Don't look," Amar gasped.

Divya pushed past him. "What the…? What happened?" she screamed.

A white delivery van sat with its right front corner wedged into Lola's side, just below the long service window. The window was shattered and bent above the van.

The driver of the van got out, apparently unharmed but obviously confused as to what had occurred. Anand came barreling out of the kitchen behind Divya.

"Anand, call 9-1-1," Amar barked at him as he followed Divya toward Lola.

"What happened?" Divya yelled at the man.

"I…don't know. Honestly." The man seemed dazed. "I was coming around the corner. I saw the bus, but I lost control." He was shaking his head in disbelief.

Amar approached the man. "Are you okay?"

The man sat down on the curb heavily. "I'm not sure."

"Anand, tell them to send the ambulance, too," Amar called out. He glanced at Divya. Tears swam in her eyes as she took in the damage to Lola.

"You okay for a minute?" He looked at the man. He nodded.

"Div." Amar stood and put a hand on Divya's shoulder. "Div. It'll be—"

"Don't you dare say it'll be okay," she barked, turning to him, tears escaping from her lids. "I don't have the money to fix this. I put everything I have into this bus." Tears just streamed down her face. "This bus was my whole life."

Amar put his arms around her and pulled her close. She let him, turned into his chest and melted into him.

Sirens wailed in the distance, getting closer and closer, until a police car pulled up, followed by an ambulance. Amar held Divya's hand while the paramedics took an assessment of the driver. They ended up taking him to the hospital. She continued to hold his hand as the police took information from them. Finally, they were allowed to get onto the bus to see what else had been damaged.

Internal damage was structural. But the appliances, including the crepe pans, were in good shape. All the spices that Amar had roasted and blended were spilled and mixed and unusable.

Divya had calmed down after the initial shock and now observed with a critical eye. "We have work to do."

Amar nodded agreement. "I can roast and blend new spices now. And I believe we can still do the crepes..." He studied the four crepe pans, two of which were built into Lola.

"Those pans come off," Divya said. "So I guess we're not completely out of commission for later."

"Right," Amar said as he removed the pan. "We can use propane tanks—"

"And gas burners outside, in that open area," Divya finished, ending her sentence in a sigh.

"We can set up a table for toppings."

"And pretty much do exactly what we had planned, just not on Lola." Her voice cracked on *Lola*, and Amar went to her.

"Hey," he said softly. "It will be okay. *Lola* will be okay."

She scanned the area again, her eyes wet with tears. "Amar," she called to him, her voice small and pained. She reached out her hands to him as if he were her lifeline. He was at her side, holding her hands in an instant.

"Div." He tugged on her hands and pulled her to him.

She looked at him, trying and failing to swallow her tears, and his heart ached for her. In that moment, he knew he would do whatever it took to help her keep her dream alive.

She squeezed his hands tight as if siphoning all her angst into him. She looked him in the eye. "I'm scared." Her voice was barely a whisper.

He nodded at her, and moved one hand to her face, wiping away her tears. In all the years he'd known her, even during her illness, he'd never seen her this vulnerable. "I know. But you're not alone. I'll be here. I promise."

Her grip on him relaxed. She bit her bottom lip and nodded.

"Listen. You have insurance, so all we have to do is

get through this wedding. When we get home, we'll figure it out together. Okay?"

Divya nodded, a small smile coming back to her face.
"Thank you."

"I called a mechanic." Amar and Divya heard Nikhil's
voice behind them and turned to find him standing there
with his phone as Anita ran to Divya. Amar stepped away
to make room for his sister.

"Someone local who can come out and take a look
and make sure Lola can make the two-hour drive home,"
Nikhil continued.

"Thanks," Amar said to his brother-in-law, a foreign
feeling of affection for him settling in. Weird.

Anita and Divya talked quietly for a moment, Divya's
gaze flitting to him every few seconds.

"Listen," Nikhil continued, "you two have work to do.
I can wait for the mechanic."

"But it's your cousin's wedding."

"Yeah, and if you two don't get back to work, there
won't be any food." Nikhil chuckled. "Go."

"I'll clean up Lola for you, so you don't have to worry
about all that," Anita said.

"You guys are the best," Amar told them as he and
Divya headed back inside to the kitchen.

Amar threaded his fingers through hers. "It's going
to be okay."

"Duh." She squeezed his hand, a watery smile breaking across her face.

Once in the kitchen, Amar immediately started on
roasting the spices again. Divya got to work with kopra-
pak. Once the spice combinations were cooled, they
needed to be ground. The only thing Amar could find,

though, was a very small coffee-bean grinder. He sighed as he looked at it. It was going to be a very long night.

Divya disappeared for a few minutes then returned with two brand-new electric coffee grinders, still in their packaging, and a set of small Ball jars. "I had these stowed on Lola. For backup, if I ran out of powdered sugar, or whatever, or needed to store something. I'll help you."

"What about—"

"We're a team. We'll get it done. Besides, you said you'd help with the flowers." She was smirking at him, but when he looked at her, her mouth formed a huge smile, invoking that dimple.

He'd do anything for that dimple. "You got it. Let's do this."

Over the course of the next few hours, they ground spices, with Divya smelling and tasting them all. "Hmph," she said, leaning against the counter while he filled the last Ball jar.

"What?"

"I was right about you starting your own business."

"Why do you say that?"

"Because, Amar." She leaned in and inhaled the aroma of the spice mix he was filling. "These spices are amazing. You're not simply talented, it's in your blood."

He stared down at her, eyes closed, inhaling, an expression of pure contentment on her face.

"Are you complimenting me?" he asked. He'd meant for it to sound like a taunt, like a tease of their conversation in her house weeks ago, but instead, his voice came out low and rough, a result of him watching her.

She opened her eyes, catching him in the act, but he

didn't move. He couldn't. "Have I never given you a compliment before?"

He shook his head.

She took his hand and pressed it against her heart. She spoke softly, her eyes never leaving his. "You are, hands down, the best chef I know."

Her heart thumped against his hand making him forget why it was that he could not be with her. He was going to kiss her. He was going to kiss her and tell her he loved her, consequences be damned. He leaned down close enough to feel her breath on his lips. She wasn't moving away.

"Guys! Good news. I just spoke with the mechanic—" Divya turned as Nikhil's voice reached them, and the moment was gone.

Amar backed up.

Nikhil froze and glanced between them, clearly realizing too late what he had interrupted. Amar waved off his look of apology. "The mechanic said Lola is drivable, but to drive her only if necessary. Anita and I can drive you two, Anand, Mo and Courtney to the rental house."

"Sounds good," Amar said. "We'll be out with the spices we need in a minute."

"I'll get everyone else in the car," Nikhil said as he left.

"Good news," Amar said, watching Divya.

She met his eyes briefly. "Yeah. At least we can get home and I can fix her."

Their almost-kiss floated in the thick silence between them.

"Two hundred and fifty people need to eat tonight." Anita's voice floated to them.

"Right," Divya called. They quickly gathered what they needed and got into the car.

Once there, Nikhil and Anita offered to help them, but Amar and Divya insisted the five of them were fine and they should go back to being guests.

The five of them got dinner and sweets together in no time.

They worked in sync and in time with each other. Amar barely had to have a thought before it was addressed by Divya, and he found himself easily able to anticipate her needs and wants.

At least, in the kitchen.

All that time cooking together, they had found a rhythm with each other they hadn't even been aware of, and when push came to shove, they were completely of one mind.

Divya was exhausted. Even with the accident, dinner had been a hit, and none of the guests were the wiser. It was after midnight when the seven of them drove back to the hotel.

Courtney, Anand and Mohit exited the car and immediately headed for the elevators and up to bed. It was all hands on deck bright and early tomorrow.

Anita side-hugged her as they entered the building. "Nice job, you two." She looked at her brother, then at Nikhil. "Time for bed. Unless you two need help."

"No. You both really were awesome today. We're good," Divya insisted. She'd figure this out herself. Anita and Nikhil were tired, too.

"You sure?" Anita asked.

"Yes." Divya turned to Nikhil. "Take your wife to bed."

Nikhil draped an arm around Anita and looked at her like she was his whole world. It warmed Divya's heart. She must be getting soft. But there was no denying the unabashed love on Nikhil's face as he looked at Anita.

"Fine," Nikhil said. "If you insist."

"Just go, before I think about it too long," Amar said with mock disgust.

Nikhil and Anita left for the elevator while Divya headed for the kitchen. Amar followed behind her.

"That was adorable." Divya smiled to herself.

"He was pretty amazing today." Amar poorly suppressed a smile.

"You should get some sleep, too," Divya said as she took out the colored gum paste and her tools.

Meeta had wanted a smooth, white three-tier cake with red roses cascading in a downward spiral. The roses and the vine would all be edible, but it was a lot of roses. Divya wasn't slow, but the process had to be done right since the roses were the center of attention. She plopped herself on a stool and got to work. She hadn't been working for more than twenty minutes when she felt Amar come up beside her. This had been happening more frequently. Her being able to sense where he was without having to use her eyes. Especially when he was near her.

"What's up?" she asked without looking up.

"I'm ready for my lesson." Amar stood in front of her station.

She turned to stare at him. "Are you serious?"

"Yes. You helped me. It's only fair." There were dark circles forming under his eyes, his hair was tousled, but he was smiling, and despite the circles, his gorgeous dark eyes were alert.

"Well, okay, then. I really could use the help." She

handed him a set of tools and took a few minutes to show him her technique. "Courtney offered, but I need one of us to be alert tomorrow."

Still, Amar was a quick study as she knew he would be and while he wasn't as fast as her, his roses looked wonderful. In fact, she could barely tell his apart from hers, which was saying something.

An hour into working, Divya stopped to stretch and do a few easy yoga poses. This always refreshed her, and she could go back to work alert.

"Wow, this feels great," she said from her downward dog position. "Yoga is a lifesaver. You should join me."

In a few seconds, Amar was next to her in the same position.

"Amar?"

"Yes?"

"Thanks. For today. With Lola."

"I know how much she means to you. She's your dream come true. I understand that."

He really did. Divya smiled to herself and turned to look at him. Amar in downward dog was a sight.

"So, how long do we have to stay like this?" Amar asked.

Chapter 19

They finished the roses in a few hours. Amar got faster the more he practiced. They had alternated between working in comfortable silence, talking about the bride and groom, laughing at the antics of the guests, and marveling at how Neepa Auntie was growing on them despite how demanding she seemed. They cleaned up and set things up for the next morning.

Divya needed a few things from Lola so they went out together to get them. The November chill, even in Virginia, made them both shiver. She stopped as they approached the bus in the moonlight. Lola's beautiful paint job that they had painstakingly finished was ruined. The window would need to be redone, as would the body beneath it. Nikhil had said the awning might be salvageable, but it was hard to say right now.

She sighed deeply. He wrapped his arm around her shoulders and pulled her close.

"Lola does not own my dreams," she said. "My dreams are with me. Lola is just an old school bus, metal and parts. I put my heart and soul into her, but I still have my heart and soul. I'll figure this out."

Amar leaned toward her and kissed her temple. He hadn't even realized what he was doing until it was done. But Divya did not pull away from him. She took his hand and they walked into the bus.

Anita had done an amazing job of cleaning. There was no evidence of the spice spill. The internal damage was much less than the external, so from this perspective, Lola seemed completely repairable.

Divya found the containers she was looking for, and a few other tools she would need for assembly tomorrow. Then she stilled and just looked around. "Do you mind if we just stay here for a few minutes?"

"Sure." It was dark inside the bus, the moon provided just a tiny bit of light. Amar leaned against the small work space, opposite Divya. She shivered and started to reach over him to grab the warm fuzzy blanket she kept there.

"I'll get it." Amar turned and easily opened the sliding cabinet door and grabbed the blanket. He wrapped it around her shoulders and leaned back against the work space again.

"You still wear that watch." She jutted her chin at the leather-strapped watch Amar wore every day. "Even though it's cracked and doesn't keep time."

Amar nodded. "It's a reminder."

"Of what? The car crash?"

"Not really. It's a reminder to me that things can change in an instant. It's a reminder that I need to be… present." Amar spoke softly, saying words he hadn't ever thought he would utter out loud, and then least of all to Divya.

"Present?"

He looked away.

"Is that what you were talking to my dad about?" She shrugged as he raised his eyebrows. "I heard some of it."

Amar lifted his chin. *Crap.* "What did you hear?"

"Just the tail end. Something about…feeling weak."

"It doesn't matter." He really hadn't wanted Divya to hear any of that.

"Amar, it matters to me." She took a step closer to him, and even in the darkened bus, he could make out the concern in her eyes. "It matters because even if you won't be with me for whatever reason you have, I know you care about me. And I care about you."

Amar remained silent for a moment. She had no idea how much he cared about her. But it didn't matter. He was never going to be with her, so he might as well tell her the truth. Then at least she would know and could move on.

"My dad had this watch on—" he cleared his throat "—when the accident happened. I'm not even sure when it found its way to me, because I was… Well, I was kind of out of it for a while afterward."

"I remember."

"Do you?" Amar's stomach fell. There had been a small hope in him that somehow Divya had not registered or at least not remembered his moments of weakness.

"Yes. You were kind of out of it. Like your brain didn't want to register that your parents were gone, so it just… shut down. I'd seen it in the hospital when I was sick. Parents, siblings, unable to process, they shut down." She shrugged. "I knew you'd be back."

"You did?"

"Of course. You would never leave Anita alone. Your mind just needed to catch up to your heart. Or the other way around, I'm not sure. You needed a bit of time." Divya said these words as if what had happened was normal, as if the fact that he had literally checked out for a week was an acceptable way of processing grief. She pulled the blanket around her. "In fact, now that you told us you had an argument with your dad that night, it just makes more sense." She nodded at him. "Anita put that watch on you, and the next day, you kind of woke up."

Amar furrowed his brow and looked at the watch. He had woken up in his bed, one morning about a week after the crash. The funeral was over, people had returned to their homes. The first thing he had realized was that his father's watch was on his wrist. And everything had come flooding back to him. He had called out for his sister and finally acknowledged his grief.

"I've always felt like I'm weak because I fell apart. Because Anita had to handle all the arrangements herself."

"That's what you've been carrying with you?"

Amar nodded.

"Is that why you pull away? Why you never let yourself be happy?"

"I let myself be happy," Amar pushed back. It was a reflex.

"When?"

He had no answer.

Finally, understanding dawned on her. "So, it's not me that you're rejecting, is it? You are literally rejecting happiness for yourself."

"I guess so."

"That doesn't seem fair...to me." She inched closer to

his side of the aisle, which quite literally was only two more steps.

"To you?" Amar furrowed his brow again.

"Yes. To me. Because I believe that us being together would make you happy as well as make me happy. So by withholding your happiness, you are withholding mine. Pretty selfish if you ask me." She grinned at him.

"So you're saying…"

She placed her hand on his chest. "I'm saying that I want you, Amar. I know you want me, too. I couldn't understand why you kept walking away from me, but now I do. No one but *you* blames you for how you handled your grief. Talk to me, Amar. Tell me what happened."

Amar looked down at her, so close to him right now. She was an open book and she wanted to know what happened. Suddenly, all he wanted was to share those days with someone who would understand. And here she was. Ready to understand.

"My mom and dad had come into the city that night for dinner." The words came out like glass shards on his throat. Divya watched him, patiently waiting. He swallowed and cleared his throat before continuing. "I was excited to take them to a restaurant in town where I knew the chef, so I could show them the kitchen. Even then, I knew I wanted to live back at the house, have my own catering business from home." He shrugged. "It was what I always wanted.

"Dad thought changing the kitchen at home was a bad idea. He told me to just rent commercial space. We argued."

They went back and forth for a bit, Amar getting increasingly irritated as the argument continued. His father remained calm, however, and this only frustrated

Amar further as they got into the car after dinner to go back to his apartment. His father was no longer listening. He had said his piece and he was done. Amar had gotten out of the car and accused his father of being backward and living in the past. Those were the last words he said to his father before he stormed into his building. He had said nothing to his mother.

"He simply would not budge." Amar shook his head. "I wish I'd— Anyway, I ignored the initial call from the police—it had come from Dad's phone—so it was Anita who talked to the police and then called me. She was a mess." He turned away from Divya. "You remember."

Divya placed her hands on his face and turned him to her. "Yes."

"I don't really know how I got to the hospital. I just remember seeing you, then Anita and she was telling me…that they were…gone." Tears burned behind his eyes as images from that moment swirled in his mind. Disjointed conversations, the feeling of losing the ground beneath his feet.

He had assumed he heard her wrong, or that she was somehow misinformed. He had looked to Divya for confirmation. When Divya nodded her head at him, her own shoulders trembling with sobs, something inside him snapped.

Because there was no way that his parents could be gone. They'd just had dinner together. They'd had an argument. His last words to his father had been horrible, and he hadn't even said goodbye to his mother. So they couldn't be dead. He was going to call them in the morning, apologize and tell them how much he loved them. That was how it worked in real life. Right?

"There was a buzzing." He waved his hands next to

his ear. "And my body felt weak, everything was moving so fast. Anita was screaming at me. I tried—" He looked at Divya, imploring her to believe him. "I tried to talk to her, comfort her, that's what she needed—" He shook his head. "But I was frozen."

"You were in shock." Divya spoke quietly.

Divya had wrapped her arms around Anita, like a sibling, and Amar had had the errant thought that maybe Divya and Anita should have exchanged rakhis because he was turning out to be an awful brother. But he couldn't move, couldn't feel anything.

"You took care of her."

Divya nodded. "We had a doctor come look at you. She said you'd be fine once you had some time. We took you home."

"I was at the funeral, the cremation." He nodded at Divya for confirmation.

"Yes," she answered.

"I didn't speak."

She pressed her lips together. "No. You were processing."

"But my sister, my sister needed her brother..." Tears sprang to his eyes. He blinked them away.

"That morning, I woke up to the smell of chai, and the fog lifted. I saw this watch on my wrist, cracked and broken, and everything came flooding back."

"Anita?" he called as he came downstairs. His voice croaked as if he hadn't used it. Maybe he hadn't. The aroma of chai reached him, swirling him in memories of his father making chai every morning. It was the aroma of comfort. It was why Anita had made it, even though they were coffee drinkers.

He heard footsteps running toward him. "Amar? Did you call me?"

He swallowed hard. "They're gone?" He sounded like a child, even to himself.

Anita nodded, tears filling her eyes.

"I'm so sorry." Tears burned and he let them fall. "I'm so sorry I wasn't there for you. It's all my fault."

Anita pulled him into a hug. "No. It's no one's fault. People react differently—I'm just so relieved to have you back. I was so scared. I was afraid I might lose you, too."

"I'm so sorry. It was my fault." He sobbed to his sister, and she held him. She never realized that he meant he was responsible for their parents' accident. His father must have been angry with him, or so hurt by his words, that maybe he hadn't paid attention to the road.

That was on Amar.

He was responsible. He knew it.

Divya's voice was full of sadness—but not pity, he realized. "Amar. You blamed yourself, all these years?"

He nodded. "It wasn't until I saw those drawings the other day that I realized that the accident wasn't my fault. That it was solely the fault of the drunk driver."

"Do you get it now?"

"I do."

Divya stepped close enough to him that their bodies touched.

"Div—"

"I was there. I saw everything. What I saw were my friends grieving over their parents. I did not see weakness, only strength. And you're talking to someone who has seen a lot of death. Do you remember what happened after you 'woke up'?"

Amar shook his head.

"You took care of your sister and the house, and you both found a way to finish college. You were there when she was divorced and when she decided to go to law school. You put off your dreams and worked for the likes of Ranjit for years—wasting your talents—so that Anita could have her dreams."

Divya reached up and touched his face. "That takes strength. And you did it all quietly, asking nothing in return. I don't know anyone stronger than that. Nikhil broke your little sister's heart, and if you can forgive him, you can forgive yourself. If he gets a chance to be happy, then so do you."

Amar could hardly process what Divya was saying. "Why do you care so much about me forgiving myself?"

"Because you have so much to offer, Amar." She stepped back, and the cold air between them was jarring. "Because blaming yourself for something you cannot undo is a waste of the life you have." She grabbed his arms with her hands as if to drive home her point. "And I cannot stand around and watch people I love waste their lives."

"You love me?" He raised an eyebrow.

She leaned back against the small counter and pursed her lips at him. "Both times we kissed, I kissed you." She quirked a smile. "Your turn."

Amar placed his hands on the counter behind her, caging her in between his arms. *This woman.* This woman who drove him out of his mind. This woman who mesmerized him with everything she did, who got under his skin and inside his head. This woman who fought death and won.

He wasn't weak.

He was an idiot.

Amar had intended on gently kissing her, easing them into it, but somewhere between his intention and her lips everything changed. He took her mouth with a hunger that had gone unsated for half his life. She responded immediately, moaning deeply as she closed the scant inches between their bodies and kissed him back.

He wrapped his arms around her, and lifted her up, his hands on her glorious bottom. She wrapped her legs around his waist, and he kissed her like he'd loved her forever—because he had. She would know he loved her, because he didn't want to hide it from her anymore.

The proper, responsible voice in his head that guided him to always do the right thing was promptly silenced by a much stronger voice that she had kissed him twice and he had turned her away. That if he wasn't careful, this might be his last chance to have her.

Divya pushed off Amar's chef's jacket and then gripped the bottom of the Superman T-shirt he'd worn underneath. She tugged upward, to take it off him.

Holy crap. Had she wrapped her legs around his waist? She thought she might have, but coherent thought was near impossible right now. The way Amar looked without that T-shirt, combined with the way he was looking at her right now, made her feel special. No—treasured. Like she was the only woman he'd ever wanted and now he had her.

"Superman, huh?" she teased.

"Manage your expectations. I am human." Amar's soft rumbling voice vibrated in her core.

She cocked an eyebrow at him.

"Although humans don't disappoint." He quirked a

mischievous grin at her, the tip of his tongue peeking through his teeth, and she melted right there.

He slowly unbuttoned her whites, his eyes never leaving hers, as if he was waiting for her to stop him, to say she didn't want him. His fingers shook a little, which was only fair, because her entire body was vibrating. He removed her jacket, revealing the tank top beneath. He stepped toward her, lifting her onto the counter. He gripped the bottom of her tank top to take it off, meeting her gaze in a question. She nodded, and he slowly obliged. She wasn't shy about her body, she simply appreciated being healthy. She'd been naked with men before, but she'd never felt this deliciously exposed, so vulnerable, yet so in control. She shivered and he wrapped the blanket around them both. She wrapped her legs around him again and finally felt his mouth on hers again. This, she decided, right here, her body enveloped by his, skin to skin, was her new favorite place in the world.

To say she hadn't ever felt this way before seemed cliché, but it was true. Amar had fallen asleep on the floor next to her, his magnificent bronze back on display. They were still in the truck. Divya did not want to move, just in case the moment was lost.

So much for not fooling around with her best friend's brother or even her work colleague. But they weren't fooling around. She hadn't planned on it, but she had fallen for him. Amar Virani had stolen her heart.

She ran a finger down Amar's spine and he stirred, turning to face her.

He reached for her, pulling her on top of him, wrapping the blanket around her shoulders to ward off the chill. Not that she was in the least bit cold, considering the heat that was coming off him.

"Hey, you." His gravel-tinged voice had never sounded so good.

"Hey, yourself. You fell asleep." She grinned, making circles on his shoulder.

"You exhausted me." He chuckled, a rare, deep throaty thing that she immediately dubbed her favorite sound.

She snuggled closer to him. "Right back at you." She caught his eye. "Maybe we should get back to the room, get some sleep? Tomorrow's a busy day."

He nodded. "Maybe." He drew the very tips of his fingers lightly down her spine, a small promise of things to come. His eyes glistened with mischief. "Or maybe not."

"Maybe not." She kissed him.

Chapter 20

The cold eventually forced them back to their room and they caught a couple hours of sleep. Amar was convinced that there was nothing quite as amazing as waking up in the morning with Divya in his arms.

"Div, we're going to be late." Amar nudged her with no intention of actually getting out of bed.

"Mmm. I need a shower," Divya said without opening her eyes.

Amar's eyes snapped open. "Oh yeah?" He sat up. "Come on, then."

They were surprisingly only a few minutes late to the kitchen. Courtney was already working and the aroma of fresh coffee greeted them and set them straight to work.

"You're late," Courtney said to Amar.

"Ten minutes," he answered.

"You're never late." Courtney looked at Divya. "And you're early."

"We got here the same time. How can he be late and I'm early?"

"Because you're usually thirty minutes late," Courtney quipped.

Divya rolled her eyes and Amar turned away from her lest Courtney figure out why they had come down together.

"Just start the syrup," Divya said to her, starting work on her penda dough.

Amar immediately started to prep for snacks and lunch. His two assistants showed up right on time, and he gave them their prep lists and got them started on their dishes before turning to his own list.

He got lost in his work, as he usually did. But not so lost that he wasn't aware of Divya, working with her usual intensity. He caught her eye every so often and was treated to a smile or a mischievous smirk.

He wasn't so naive as to think that last night meant the same to her as it did to him. The reality of it was that he had given in to a lifetime of feelings for her. He had walked away in an effort to keep things uncomplicated. But he'd had no idea how deliciously wonderful the complication would be.

It took every bit of discipline he had to not go over and pull her into the hall and kiss her. But there had seemed to be an unspoken understanding between them that they would keep this to themselves.

No one needed to know.

Especially Anita.

Divya's focus was solely on the cake in front of her. Always the centerpiece of any wedding, no matter how simple the design. It had to be perfect.

Except thoughts of Amar kept interrupting her, in the most delectable way.

"What are you smiling at, Chef?" Courtney asked as she helped place and secure the gum paste flowers that Amar had helped Divya make.

"I'm not smiling," she insisted as she smiled.

Courtney gasped. "You hooked up!"

She had known Courtney since their culinary institute days. They had worked together and played together. Courtney knew her. "You think everyone hooks up."

Courtney pursed her lips and shook her head. "No. You're different. Blushing and crap that you don't do."

"Um, yeah. No." Divya pressed her lips together and waved a hand at her friend in dismissal. Denial was the best approach.

"You are totally blushing." Courtney shrugged. "What's the big deal? Weddings are all about the hookup, girl." She nodded approvingly. "Who was it? The best man? Or the bride's man of honor—because he is—"

"Courtney. The cake." Divya widened her eyes.

Courtney went back to her job. "Fine, don't tell."

"I won't."

Courtney grinned and pointed a finger at her. "Ha! So there was someone last night!"

Divya clamped her mouth shut.

"Divya Shah! Did you hook up last night and not tell me?" Anita's voice came from behind her. Divya snapped her head around, nearly squishing the flower in her hand.

"Anita!"

Anita was decked out in a sequined soft pink sari and Nikhil was in a matching sherwani. They were ready to dance in the groom's procession.

She dropped the ruined flower and turned to her

friend. "Oh! You two look amazing. That jaan is going to be so amazing. I heard that he's coming in on—get this—a fire engine."

"I know—it'll be awesome." Anita dismissed the distraction with a wave of her hand. "Answer the question. Did you hook up last night? Although I'm not sure how you had the time. My brother has obviously kept you completely occupied." She looked around at the obvious chaos of the kitchen.

Divya froze and felt the blood rush from her head to her stomach. "What?" She glanced at the stove behind Anita, but Amar seemed to have left the kitchen.

"Hey, Div." Nikhil seemed to be hiding a smile as he followed her gaze to the empty stove.

"I mean, you obviously helped him make more spice blends." She nodded at the shelf where all the spices were lined up. Anita raised an eyebrow at her. "Although if you had time for a hookup, then maybe you have more energy than I ever could have imagined."

"Hey, sis." Amar's voice came from behind Divya, the richness reverberating through her body. People needed to stop showing up behind her.

He had to pass Divya to get to his sister. Divya could have sworn even the air that passed between them was full of sparks. It was certainly full of his masculine scent and warmth. She swallowed hard and hoped her face stayed masked.

"What's this about a hookup?" He turned and met Divya's eyes, his face the picture of innocence.

"Nothing." Divya grinned and shook her head but felt the heat crawl up her face all the same.

Anita had her arm around her brother's waist. "She's

clearly not working hard enough if she has time to meet someone."

Amar gaped. "All I care about is that she makes great sweets. Which she does. In fact, her jalebi are amazing."

Anita narrowed her eyes at him. "How do you know?"

Divya bit the inside of her cheek to keep the smile off her face.

"Well, I've had a taste." That glimmer of mischief he shot at her before masking it, heated her core and she felt herself flush again, so she looked back down at the penda she was making.

"So...you're not curious about her mysterious hookup?" Nikhil asked, an annoying grin of satisfaction on his face.

"Not even a little bit. It's her life." Amar shrugged. "I have to get back to the stove." He hugged his sister. "I'll see you at home tomorrow sometime."

"Home? What about tonight?"

"Tonight?"

"Yes, Neepa Masi had extended the invite for the reception to you and a plus-one if you wanted to join the party."

He flicked a quick glance at Divya. "Oh right. You know, it's been a crazy few days. I haven't really slept much. I may just crash."

"Why, um, aren't you sleeping well, Amar? I'd think, with all this work, you'd hit the bed dead tired," Nikhil deadpanned.

"Can't turn my brain off, I guess." Amar shuffled his feet, pointedly making eye contact with Nikhil.

"Uh-huh." Nikhil paused. "Yeah, of course. That makes sense." But he did not sound convinced. "How about you, Div? Mr. Discipline can go to bed early, but you can come party with us." Nikhil made eye contact with her.

He knew.

She wasn't sure why they didn't want to tell anyone, but she and Amar seemed to have an understanding that whatever was going on was going to go on just between them, at least for now.

Divya nodded. "Um, sure. Let me see how things work out. You know the pastry chef always works the latest, because dessert is last." She forced a laugh, glancing at Amar.

Anita sighed. "Sure. Though you probably want to find your hookup again."

"I have to get back to this cake," Divya stated, widening her eyes at her friend and avoiding Nikhil's gaze.

Anita held up her hands in surrender. "Whatever. But you've never been this secretive about a hookup before. It's weird."

Divya waved to Anita. "I'll see you later."

Anita stepped toward the stoves with Amar, but Divya heard her ask, "Is Div okay? She's acting weird."

"She's fine. It's a big wedding and there's a lot riding on this. Plus there was the crash," Amar told his sister gently. "I think there's just a lot going on. We're all a little on edge in here."

Anita nodded. "Makes sense." She looked at her brother. "Actually, you seem strangely relaxed, considering."

"I'm focused, Anita. I'm always focused at the event," Divya heard Amar insist. She smiled to herself. Always focused on the task at hand, that was for sure.

Anita furrowed her brow. "Seems like more than just focus to me, but okay. It's way better than grumpy Amar."

She side-hugged her brother, careful of her sari. "We should go. Jaan is starting soon. Don't want to miss any of that."

Amar leaned down and whispered something in his sister's ear. Anita's eyes popped open and she smiled at her brother, nodding vigorously. She beckoned Nikhil over with a toss of her head. "Consider it done," Divya heard her say as they left.

Divya had no idea what brother and sister were whispering about, and she did not care. Her attention was on Amar. She waved at her friend as she left. She passed her gaze over the fine man that Amar was and returned her focus to the cake.

There'd be plenty of time to ogle him in private later.

Amar continued his focus on the food as the day progressed. Nikhil popped into the kitchen after lunch to tell them that everyone was raving over the pav bhaji. His brother-in-law hung out in the kitchen for a bit too long, as if he had something to say. Amar knew what it was and simply ignored him. He wasn't ready to tell anyone about him and Divya. Besides, it had only been the one night. So far.

Luckily, dinner was a buffet, so he was able to leave the kitchen and join Divya on Lola to prep for the crepes when she told him she was ready. He wanted to get there when Divya did, so when it was almost time for dessert, he donned fresh whites and ran out to Lola.

Fairy lights were strung from the bus out to the building, casting a warm glow in the area. Small round café tables were scattered underneath them. Music from inside played in small speakers out here. Flowerpots dotted the area, and many heaters would keep people warm while they waited in line.

Anita and Nikhil had come through.

Divya was alone on Lola when he got there, and his heart leaped.

"Hey." He went up behind her and placed his hands on her waist.

Divya turned around to him, tears in her eyes. "This is beautiful. It's just…" She shook her head in disbelief. "Is this what you and Anita were whispering about?"

Amar chuckled. "You don't miss much, do you?"

"Well, I was just watching you." Divya flushed.

"Yeah?"

"Yeah." She settled into his arms. "What about it?"

"Fine by me." Amar grinned at her.

"Do you think they know?" Divya asked.

"I don't know. Nikhil seems like he does." His brother-in-law was turning out to be more observant than he'd thought. May be the writer in him.

"Whatever. Just hope he doesn't tell Anita." She leaned into him and kissed him.

And just like that, everything around them vanished. There was no wedding, no Lola, no nothing. Just Divya kissing him.

Laughter from the hotel jarred them from bliss, forcing them apart. "Um, maybe you should prep." Amar stepped back from her, a bit dazed.

Divya nodded at him, her eyes still glazed over. She shook her head. "Yeah."

"I'll be back in a minute."

When Amar returned a few minutes later, she was in her zone, prepping filling for each of the four stations, as well as crepe batter and utensils. He wanted to put his hands on her waist and kiss her neck while she chopped the strawberries.

Instead, he went to his station and prepped his ingredients. Courtney and Anand were right behind him, so he assigned them stations and gave them directions.

Divya went to each station and checked the temperature of each pan, making sure everyone had enough of the fillings. She stopped by his station and pointed to his opened whites. "Button up, Iron Man." Damn, but she was going to enjoy unbuttoning him later.

Amar and Divya moved like well-choreographed dancers. The practice on Diwali had helped them figure out how to move quickly in the small amount of space, so out in the open, they were fine. Courtney and Anand were efficient, and Mohit turned out to be quite entertaining as well as effective in taking orders. He kept the crowd occupied while they waited, so everyone was happy. Anita and Nikhil popped by for their crepes, Anita light and laughing, Nikhil eyeing Divya and Amar.

They ignored him.

Amar and Divya had numerous people taking their information for future events, not the least of which was their present host, Neepa Auntie, who officially asked them to cook for Sangeeta's wedding in six months.

"Sure, Auntie!" Divya gushed as she made them their crepes. "That would be great." She turned to Sangeeta. "Reach out to me in a week. We can talk cake details and all that."

Amar nodded at Auntie and Sangeeta. "I'll send you sample menus, but we can…" He looked at Divya. "We can do anything."

Neepa Auntie and Sangeeta both beamed. Sangeeta entered their information into her phone and went off to join the party.

Amar's phone buzzed. He almost ignored it, thinking it was either Nikhil or Anita. But it was Michael. He read the text and called out, "Hey, Div! Michael says he has good news."

"Oh yeah?" Divya glanced up from her crepe. "What's up?"

"All of the appliances are in. Michael set up delivery for Tuesday, so with final touches, the kitchen will be ready for us to move in, in a week."

"Us?" Divya spared him a look.

"Well, yes. If you want. You don't have to. But your parents are moving soon, you need a kitchen…"

"Even if I'm working with Ranjit?"

Amar clenched and then unclenched his jaw. "You have to do what works and what is right for your business. If that means working with Ranjit, then so be it. It's your business, not mine. I really have no say in that."

"Then why the clenched jaw?"

"Because Ranjit's food is subpar, and I don't like him. I think you can do better than hooking your wagon to his."

"I'm not hooking my wagon to his—we just have a couple of the same parties."

"Like I said. You do you." He wanted to pull her close, but there were literally hundreds of people around.

"What about us?" she murmured softly.

"What about us?"

"How do you feel about working together?" Divya asked.

"Well, I have been told that I can be overly structured and rigid." Amar grinned.

"I've been told I'm flighty and too spontaneous," Divya said.

"Sounds perfect to me."

"Me, too."

Chapter 21

Divya, Amar and their small staff cleaned up after the crepes were finished. The bride and groom had been hauled off for their after-party, and the remaining guests filtered up to their rooms. After they tidied up in and around Lola, they did the kitchen.

She and Amar bid good-night to Courtney, Anand and Mohit and headed up to their room together.

No sooner did the elevator doors shut than Amar pulled her close and kissed her senseless. "I've been wanting to do that all day," he murmured in her ear, sending shivers up her spine.

"About time," she teased.

The elevator doors opened to their floor and it was devoid of people. Amar kissed her the two doors down to their room. Once inside, Divya wasted no time ripping off his Iron Man T-shirt and pulling him to bed.

They were exhausted, but they'd sleep later.

She woke to a sliver of sunrise poking through the curtains. She got out of bed and shut the curtains tighter before climbing back into bed.

"You're coming back to bed?" Amar said, his voice thick with sleep.

"Yes."

"That's a first. Divya Shah sleeping in."

She grinned and snuggled closer to him. He was so warm. "I'm trying new things. Doesn't seem like a waste of time anymore."

"Hey! What's the emergency?" Divya ran into Amar's house. They'd been home for a couple weeks, and Amar had been getting his new kitchen in order for most of that time.

She had gotten a text from Amar to meet him across the street ASAP. His face lit up when she walked in. He was practically bouncing off the walls, and he was completely adorable in his *Guardians of the Galaxy* T-shirt.

"I want to show you something." Amar pulled her into the house, stopping before the kitchen. "Close your eyes."

"Okay." She closed her eyes.

Amar took her hand and led her forward, somewhere into the kitchen. "Okay. Open."

She opened her eyes and found herself staring at a giant stand mixer. "What—"

"Just look." Amar started opening drawers and cabinets that had some of her pastry-making things in them. He had her spin a circle, and she saw that she was in a section of the kitchen that appeared to be dedicated to desserts.

"It's just an idea I had. This could be your work space.

We would still have our own separate businesses—
so we're free to work with whoever we like. And of
course you have Lola—but we could physically work
together in the same location." He was talking very fast,
which was very un-Amar, but he must have been really
excited about all this. "We're good together." He stopped
to take her into his arms. "This space is way bigger than
yours across the street. Besides, your parents are sell-
ing, so you would have a place to work and not have to
pay rent. You have your own area, we wouldn't have to
share so much as a spatula." Amar kissed her, light and
gentle. "I won't even organize it if you don't want me to."

Divya was stunned. Floored. Speechless. That Amar
would give her needs this much thought.

"If you hate it, I'll put it all back—no harm done."
Amar looked at her, dark eyes wide with expectation.
"I did kind of buy the mixer, but I suppose I could learn
to use it."

"I love it. Really, truly love it." She stood there, scan-
ning the area, unable to comprehend what he was saying. They could work side by side.

"Really?" Cautious relief exuded from him.

"Yes, really. I love it, and I can't wait to work here
with you. I have ideas popping into my head for both
our menus."

"Of course you do." Amar grinned again. "But, wait,
there's more." He held up a finger for her to stay where
she was, and he went into the office. He emerged a few
minutes later with a bundle of moving black fur.

Divya went to him, her arms out. "You got a puppy?"
She took the puppy from Amar's arms and held him close.
The dog was all black, with a white patch over one eye.
"I suppose you'll name this one Fury as well."

"You would think, because of the eye patch. But no, this one seems like more of a Coulson to me."

Divya laughed. "Of course he does. He's yours?"

Amar met her eyes. "Um, well, he could be *ours*."

"He could?"

"If you want." Amar's eyes reflected a vulnerability she didn't think she'd ever seen.

Divya snuggled little Coulson, letting him lick her face. "Can I take him home?"

"Sure."

She looked into the office and saw Coulson's crate. "Maybe it's better if he stays here."

"You can stay here, too," Amar said. "I mean, we did live at your place for a bit."

"Well, not exactly together-together."

He grinned. "So let's make the change. We've wasted enough time as it is."

"You sound like me again." She laughed.

"We must be rubbing off on each other, then. You're sleeping in, rewatching movies."

"And you're worried about wasting time."

"Take your time. Wait until the house sells, then you can move in here. Or get your own place."

"You're serious."

"Divya, I love you. Maybe all this is too soon, too fast, and if that's the case, I understand. But I have loved you since like the second time I saw you, and I do not want to waste any more time."

She stared at him. Here was the wonderful side of Amar she always knew was there but he had been hiding from her. Her heart swelled.

She reached over and ruffled the puppy's fur. "I guess

we should really think about what's best for Coulson, here."

"Absolutely. It's all about this puppy here." Amar half smiled, that vulnerability still in his eyes.

She kissed him and then laughed. "Imagine, soon I'll be asking you to organize my part of the kitchen."

"What's going on with you, beti?" her mother asked. "You're more 'Divya' than ever."

"I'm just excited the wedding went so well and Amar's kitchen is done." Divya threw more of Amar's cooking supplies into a box to take across the street. She'd take her stuff over slowly. No need to alert her parents right now.

"Oh." Her mother turned to her, a knowing grin on her face. "Amar."

"Yes, Amar's kitchen. The one that is finally done." Divya did not make eye contact with her mother. Kalpana Shah could give a government interrogator a run for their money.

"No, beti. It's Amar." Her voice had a knowing finality to it that Divya did not like.

"What's Amar?" Her father came into the kitchen, holding another box full of Amar's stuff.

"Amar and Divya are dating," her mother answered.

"Mom! I said no such thing."

"You don't have to—it's all over your face," her mother said with a smile.

"There is nothing on my face."

"You and Amar are dating?" her father asked, his eyes widening. "Where is he?"

"Across the street. And it's fine, Dad. You don't need to go barreling over there, just because we're dating."

"Ha! See? I was right," her mother said, victorious.

"Oh. I am going over there," her father said and stomped out the door. Divya and her mother looked at each other and followed.

"Dad! Seriously! I am twenty-eight years old," Divya said, running across their lawn and into the street to catch up with her father. Honestly, who knew he could move this fast.

"I know!" he said and kept walking. He stopped at the door and turned to Divya. "Are you happy with him?"

"Of course I'm happy with him. But we just started dating—it's been like two weeks."

"It was a long time coming, Divya," her mother quipped.

Divya turned back to her mother, who had also crossed the street very fast. Out of the three of them, only Divya was out of breath.

Her father opened the door and marched right in. With the majority of the first floor as the kitchen, there wasn't really a large foyer anymore. The door opened to the large stainless-steel island. Divya and her mother were right behind him. Amar, Anita and Nikhil were cleaning and organizing.

The kitchen was beautiful. Stainless-steel finish to everything, deep triple sink. The walls to the dining room and sitting room were gone, opening up the first floor to accommodate this dream of Amar's. Every time Divya saw it, it took her breath away. Much like the tall guy in the corner, currently wiping down counters. Honestly, was there anything sexier than Amar cleaning?

Maybe if he took off that *Guardians of the Galaxy* T-shirt. But kept cleaning.

"Amar," her father called out as he entered the kitchen. Nikhil grabbed the box from him. "I got that, Uncle."

"Uncle." Amar stood and grinned at her father. "Auntie." He cut his eyes to her. "Div."

"Amar, answer me one question." Divya's father sounded stern.

"Of course, Uncle, anything." Amar was relaxed.

Divya tried to convey her apologies to Amar through her eyes, but she could see he was confused by her. Anita and Nikhil also looked confused. Oh no! Anita and Nikhil!

"Maybe you want to talk in the office, Dad?" Divya suggested.

"Why would I do that? Amar is like a son to me. I can ask what I want."

Amar smiled, gracious and innocent as ever. "What's up, Uncle?"

"Are you in love with my daughter?"

Silence filled the space for what felt like an eternity. Whatever Divya had been afraid would happen, it wasn't this. Amar's smile widened, a pleasant flush reaching his face, and he nodded at her father and did not miss a beat.

"Yes, Uncle. I am."

"But everybody knows that," piped up Anita. "Amar has had a crush on Divya for years."

Did they? Clearly Divya was the last to know. Both Divya and Amar snapped their gazes to Anita.

"Good point," said Uncle. "So then, are you also dating my daughter?"

"Dating?" Anita turned to face Divya. Her hand flew to her mouth as understanding hit her. She removed her hand for a moment to mouth "the wedding" to Divya. Divya bit her bottom lip and gave her friend a small smile and an abashed shrug. She turned to catch Amar's eyes flick over hers.

Amar met Divya's gaze with acknowledgment. Too late he figured out what was going on here.

"Yes, Uncle. Divya and I are together, and I am very much in love with her." Amar was focused on her father, not even looking his sister's way.

Her father walked up to Amar and grabbed him in an embrace. "It's about time."

Divya's father turned back to her. "What about you, beti?" His voice took on that gentle tone he had always used with her.

"What about me?"

"Are you in love with him?" her father asked.

Everything around Divya fell away. Her parents, her best friends. All she saw was Amar watching her, that adorable half smile on his face. "I am. I am totally completely head over heels in love with Amar Virani."

Chapter 22

Amar watched Veer Uncle and Kalpana Auntie leave and waited until the door clicked shut before facing his sister.

"You're in love with my *brother*?" Anita stated. And then turned to Amar. "And you're in love with my *best friend*?" Her voice was stoic, lawyerlike. He couldn't decipher her feelings. "My brother. And my best friend." She shook her head, frowning.

They both nodded and watched Anita. Honestly, this was scarier than Divya's father marching over here. Probably because Anita *was* scarier.

His sister turned to her husband. "Can you believe this? My brother. And my best friend."

Amar saw Nikhil break out into a smile, just as his sister did. "Well, it's about damn time! You two have been dancing around this forever!"

"Seriously? You're okay with this?" Divya spoke first, releasing her breath.

"Okay with it? I'm thrilled. My best friend and my brother. Two people I love? I couldn't have picked better people for either of you." She gathered up Divya in a hug and then pulled back. "I knew you were acting weird at that wedding."

Anita then walked over to Amar and shook her head at him. "About stinking time," she said, smacking his arm. "Don't hurt her."

"What?" He rubbed his arm. "She gets a hug, and I get a smack and warning?"

"Sounds about right." She grinned at him and walked out of the house, arm in arm with Divya.

Nikhil shook his head at him and started putting things away. "I figured it out in Virginia."

"Yeah. I was afraid of that."

Nikhil gave him a deadpan look. "It was all over you. Anita just wasn't paying attention to you. She was trying to figure out why Divya wouldn't share with her."

"You didn't say anything."

Nikhil shrugged. "Not really my place to say anything." He pulled out a few loose-leaf binders. "Where do you want this?"

"In Dad's study. I'll come with you."

They went to the office, and Amar indicated the shelf where he wanted the binders. He then proceeded to clear out some of the other kitchen items they had stored in here. He filled a couple boxes and turned to Nikhil. "Hey. Give me a hand?"

Nikhil was engrossed in reading something. He looked up at Amar. "What's this?" He was holding an old three-ring binder with wrinkled pages, papers falling out of it.

Amar walked over. "Those are Mom's recipes." He waited for the usual dread and sadness to overcome him. But it didn't. "I had started writing down proportions of spices, trying to get measurements." He chuckled. "It drove her crazy, the measurements thing." He took the notebook from Nikhil and paged through it, Nikhil still looking over his shoulder. "I just didn't want to forget how to make food. How to make *her* food."

He had handwritten everything. The pages were wrinkled from spilled water, chai, coffee. But this was what he and his mom had worked on before he went to culinary school.

"What are these notes in the margins?" Nikhil pointed.

"Those were just reminders of when we ate it, how everyone liked it. Variations that worked. Sometimes a story Mom and Dad would tell us about a particular dish. Like this." He pointed. "Khaman. This was what my mom made when Dad and his parents came to see her for the first time. Dad said he was in love when he saw her, but that the khaman sealed the deal." He recalled his father saying that no one made the light fluffy lentil cakes quite as light and fluffy as hers.

"Some of the details are hard to read," Nikhil observed. "I could type it up, save it in a document, if you want."

Amar looked at Nikhil. "You would do that?"

"Yes. Do you know how much family history is in here? You can give me stories to go along with these recipes, and it's something the family will always have. You pass down your history this way. You and Anita can share your parents with your children."

Amar clapped his hand on Nikhil's shoulder. "That sounds fabulous. Let's do it."

* * *

Divya stepped out of the shower and glanced at herself in the full-length mirror on the door. Two more new bruises. One on her shoulder and one on her bum. She didn't remember hitting or bumping anything in those areas, any more than the bruises she had found last week on the back of her arm and shins.

Then there were the bloody noses. Or just the one, so far, when they were driving Lola back from the wedding. Random trickle of blood. She hadn't had a nosebleed in over ten years. Or bruises, quite frankly. Okay, fine. She was athletic. She ran, did yoga and was generally active. So sure, she'd had the occasional bruise, here and there, but one bruise was never cause for alarm. But more than one, and new ones all the time?

Divya froze in front of the mirror. No. It couldn't be. She'd been cancer-free for ten years. How was that even possible? Tears sprang to her eyes. She toweled off and hastily dressed, her heart squeezing at the sight of the boxes in her bedroom. She was getting ready to move on to the next phase of her life. She had just let her guard down, sleeping in, taking life a bit slower and enjoying the simpler points of happiness.

Like being with Amar.

Like how Amar looked first thing in the morning. The feel of his skin against hers. How soft the sheets felt when she slept in. Being snuggled by Coulson. That first sip of the perfect chai. Anything Amar cooked. The way Amar held her hand.

Being able to lean into that feeling of security, knowing Amar was always there.

Being in love.

Suddenly gripped by panic, she picked up her phone and called her doctor. The receptionist answered and she gave her name. "I'd like to speak with Dr. O'Bryan, please."

Chapter 23

Before he was even fully awake, Amar knew what day it was. The heaviness settled almost automatically in every cell, his body aware of the significance of this day before he was even conscious.

Coulson nuzzled him, licking his face until Amar finally stirred. He cracked open his eyes, one hand resting on the puppy, as he tried to determine the time. Probably close to 6:00 a.m., since Coulson was whining to go out. Amar sat up and felt the weight of his father's watch on his wrist. He rested his still-sleepy gaze on his bedside table, where the kitchen plans in his father's writing lay.

Eight years ago today, there had been an argument and then an accident. Today felt different, though. Because today, Amar knew the argument hadn't led to the accident.

Amar stood and looked at Coulson. "Give me a minute to put on clothes. It's cold outside. Do not pee on my carpet. Again."

Amar threw on some sweats and a hoodie as, yes, Coulson peed on the carpet. Amar sighed and picked up the puppy and took him out anyway, all the while murmuring idle threats about homelessness to the dog. Coulson simply wagged his tail.

Tradition dictated that every year on the anniversary of the death of a loved one, the family members shared a meal consisting of the favorite items of the deceased. On the first anniversary, Anita had cooked and they shared it with Divya's family. On the second, Anita had asked him to cook. He had started the process but then been unable to complete the task. Amar had felt almost hypocritical making his parents' favorite dishes when he felt partly responsible. If he hadn't argued with his father, his father wouldn't have been angry and he might have been paying closer attention to his driving.

Anita had simply assumed it was too much for him, so she cooked a small meal every year in their house. Amar usually spent the day in a surly mood, avoiding people. He would choke down the meal in silence and then go to bed, willing the day to be over.

Amar walked Coulson, who peed a rather large quantity given that he just soiled Amar's carpet. He returned to the house right as the sun came up. He cleaned up Coulson's mess and grabbed the plans from the bedside table before hurrying down to the kitchen.

No more. Today would be different. He taped the plans to the rack that hung over his stainless-steel island, his mind racing a mile a minute. No sooner had he sent out a text than Nikhil and Anita sauntered in.

Anita set down the bag of groceries she was holding.

Nikhil was holding the binder that held all the recipes. "Listen, I may be out of line, Anita says she usually cooks today and you basically hide from the world."

"Well—"

"Just listen. This binder. Is. Amazing." Nikhil was bouncing with excitement.

Amar nodded and opened his mouth.

"Hear me out. The recipes are one thing. But the stories are fabulous. And your notes, teenage Amar's notes, are entertaining and incredible. Let me clean it up, just because over time, ink will fade, etcetera, and then the family will have this forever."

Silence.

"Can I talk now?"

"Yeah, yeah. Go ahead. Please."

Amar showed Nikhil his phone, where he had texted Nikhil to come by with the recipe book.

Nikhil seemed confused.

"I want to cook from it today."

"You want to cook. Today," Anita finally spoke. "From that?"

Amar grinned at his sister. "I do."

Anita smiled at him. "Okay. Good," she said as she put down the groceries and hugged her brother.

"I thought it would be the perfect first meal for this kitchen." Amar squeezed his sister tight.

"I agree," she said. She pulled back. "Well, in that case, I have to study. I will see you at six."

"Perfect." Amar let go of his sister. "I'm going to ask Divya to make the gulab jamun, though."

"Duh. Hers are the best." She looked at her husband. "Ready? Our work here is done."

"Uh, well, actually, I'd like to stay and help." He glanced at Amar. "If that's okay with you."

Amar teased Nikhil, "About time you offered your cooking skills. I've heard about them, but I have yet to see what you can do."

Nikhil smiled at Anita and rolled up his sleeves. "I'll see you later. Apparently I have work to do."

Amar found a small Ganesha statue in the mandhir in his father's office and placed it on the windowsill in his new kitchen. As The Remover of Obstacles, Ganesha was always invited first to anything.

He and Nikhil went all the way through the recipe book before finalizing the menu for that evening. The crowd would be bigger tonight, as Amar insisted on inviting Nikhil's mother and siblings as well.

They settled on a few items that may not really go together, but that Amar knew his dad had been partial to. Cauliflower stuffed paratha. Cilantro chutney. Dhal. Rice. Spinach and peas. Okra. Simple food, but delicious.

It was still early, so Nikhil insisted on making a quick brunch for Amar. Nikhil whipped up eggs with Indian spices in a rotli that was so tasty, Amar wrote it down in the recipe book, with a note. "First time Nikhil cooked for me."

The two men spent the day organizing the kitchen, buying more groceries and basically getting everything going. Amar didn't hear back from Divya until late afternoon when he and Nikhil had started cooking. She simply texted that she would come by with the gulab jamun at dinner time.

That was odd. Amar had thought she would make them here in his kitchen. He shrugged it off, thinking that she had all of her stuff still over there, and it would be easier for her in her own. He sent her a kissing emoji and went back to work.

Dinner was ready before he knew it.

"Anytime you decide you're done with writing, I'd love to have you join Ginger and Cardamom. You have some mad skills in the kitchen," Amar said as he turned on the oven to keep the paratha warm and wiped down all the counters.

Nikhil grabbed two beers from the fridge and handed one to Amar. "Good to know I have a backup. But I doubt you could afford me."

Amar chuckled as he popped the top off his beer. "Oh, there's no pay. You're married to my sister." He looked Nikhil in the eye, as they clinked bottles. "You're family."

They would be eating at the island tonight, so he took out everything they would need for that. Amar went upstairs to wash up, and Nikhil did the same. Coulson followed, promptly curling himself into his doggy donut on Amar's bed.

He took off his father's watch as he always did before he showered, placing it on the nightstand next to his bed. He showered and dressed for dinner, forgoing his usual superhero T-shirt in favor of a dress shirt and jeans.

He eyed the watch from the corner of his eye as he dressed. It used to loom large and foreboding to him, but not today. He went over to the bedside table and picked it up. It was not a fancy watch, analog, because well, his dad liked that. The glass was cracked, and the time read 11:14. Amar assumed this was the time of the collision, but it occurred to him that he didn't really know. It might just be the time at which the battery died.

He lay it on his wrist and started to fasten it but

changed his mind. He opened the drawer to his night-stand and carefully placed the watch in there. "I don't need to wear it every day, Dad. I have other ways of re-membering you now."

Chapter 24

Divya sat with her back perfectly straight, on the edge of the chair. Her puffy coat was neatly folded in her lap, her gloves delicately placed on top. She should be comfortably warm as she watched the first flakes of snow fall through the window. But as she was seated in front of her oncologist's desk, she shivered as if she were standing outside in the cold.

While she had known that there was always a small possibility that she would find herself here, she had thought about it less and less as time wore on. The more distance she had put between her life now and her life as a cancer patient, the healthier she'd felt, the more she'd become convinced that she could lead a normal life.

Letting herself fall in love with Amar had been proof. Although there was no "letting" involved. She'd fallen in love with Amar despite her best efforts not to. How could she not? She smiled as she thought about him. And then she chided herself for being one of those women who smiled when she thought about her boyfriend. Huh. Maybe she had been too hard on those women.

She checked the time again. Three minutes had passed since she'd sat down. This was why she never came early to anything. She couldn't stomach the waiting.

She hadn't even told her parents. They had been through so much with her. Plus they were excited to be traveling, and if she told them, they would cancel all their vacation plans. She was a grown woman. She did not need her parents to go with her to the doctor.

The door opened behind her, but Divya did not turn around. She knew from the light floral scent that her oncologist, Dr. O'Bryan, had entered. She checked her watch. Precisely on time. This was the woman who had told her she was cancer-free nearly eleven years ago, when Divya had been all of seventeen. She was also the woman who had told them Divya had cancer in the first place. Divya did not envy this woman her job.

Right now, Divya's concern was the bruising that was popping up all over her body. She'd also had a couple more nosebleeds and she was always tired. This had been how it had started in the first place. She'd had bruises, nosebleeds, always wanted to sleep. Divya was an adult now, with a business and boyfriend. She smiled again at the thought of Amar. (Damn, she was a sap.) So she didn't randomly fall asleep, but she was always tired, it seemed.

When she was fourteen, the bruises had shown up. She had run more than once to the school bathrooms for a nosebleed. But when her parents had taken her to the doctor, she had found herself in this very room, with her parents, listening to Dr. O'Bryan diagnose her with cancer.

Divya sat ramrod straight in the middle chair. The chairs on either side of her, empty.

Dr. O'Bryan had agreed to meet with her against her better judgment. "I'm a pediatric oncologist," she had said over the phone. "You are an adult."

"But I know you," insisted Divya. "Just this one time."

Dr. O'Bryan had relented and now they sat across from each other. "Divya. Yes, your legs are showing some bruising, as do your shoulders and elbows. Nothing you did not already know. In addition to that is your feeling of chronic fatigue. I am referring you to a colleague of mine who treats adults, Dr. Hoang. She's wonderful and her office is just two doors down the hall. The front desk has already made an appointment for you to meet with her in two days."

"So, you agree that I need a specialist?" Divya's heart hammered in her chest and she leaned toward the doctor, though she fought to stay calm. Maybe if she did, there would be nothing wrong with her.

"I agree that you need to see an *adult* oncologist, to have blood work." Dr. O'Bryan was very firm yet always kind. Divya stared at the woman, who was not even as old as her mother, and noticed for the first time, the gray hairs at her temples as well as the wrinkles at her eyes and her drawn complexion. This was not an easy job.

"I will add, however, that just because you are an adult does not mean you have to do even the blood work alone. You can and should bring your parents with you or a friend."

Divya pressed her mouth together. "I'll be fine." She stood and put on her coat and gloves. "I have baking to do." It was what Divya's mother had always said when they left here. They would go home and practice some sweet recipe. By the time they had finished their baking project, Divya would have mostly forgotten the conversation with the doctor, the sweets putting a smile on her face.

"Thank you for your help," Divya managed to say. She hesitated but then reached out and hugged Dr. O'Bryan with unsure hands. "Thank you for everything."

"Of course."

Divya stepped back and walked out the door, her stomach aflutter with nerves. She passed Dr. Hoang's office on the way to the elevator. Two days until the appointment, two more days for blood results. Four days. But Divya didn't need results. She knew her body. It was obvious.

She was sick again. Why else refer her to the adult oncologist?

Divya exited the building to a cold rush of wind and made a beeline for her bike. The snowflakes were sparse and not sticking. Sai was her best source of comfort. Second best. Her heart literally ached for Amar to be at her side. For his warmth in the sudden cold that had nothing to do with the weather.

But right now, she needed to clear her head. Right now, she needed to ride. Sai would give her courage to do what she had to do.

She fastened her helmet and started her bike, the thrum of the throttle empowering her to do what she knew was right.

Chapter 25

Amar recognized the roar of the Indian motorcycle as it pulled into the driveway. He associated that sound with the woman he loved, and it was simultaneously the sweetest and hottest sound on earth.

Divya had been acting strangely lately. He'd sent her some texts about future jobs and she had not responded. She'd also seemed preoccupied, even evasive when they discussed signing contracts for eventual work. True, they were separate entities, but they worked well together, and people were requesting them as a team. Especially for the Parikh/Sheth wedding, the one where the bride was Nikhil's cousin Sangeeta. As far as Amar knew, Divya still had not returned Sangeeta's calls and texts about setting up a cake tasting.

At the sound of the bike, Amar quickly turned off the stove and went to the door to greet her. He hadn't even seen her since he'd cooked the remembrance dinner three days ago. She was busy helping her parents get the house ready to sell as well as getting Lola fixed, and her parents were making travel plans. He had been swamped with luncheons and smaller dinner parties, mostly from Seema Joshi's friends. He had recommended Sonny Pandya's restaurant to some people who had also enjoyed that.

Despite the flakes of snow in the air and the freezing temperature, Amar flung open the door, just as the bike turned off. It seemed that she took forever securing Sai before approaching the house. He threw his arms around her, gathered her up in a kiss that was guaranteed to show her how much he'd missed her.

He felt her melt into him, and his heart went light with joy. He shut the door with his foot once she was in, then leaned her against the door as he removed her coat, his mouth never leaving her skin.

She began peeling off his clothing, not even commenting on his Black Widow T-shirt.

A flurry of small, high-pitched barks came rushing toward them.

"Coulson missed you," he murmured between kisses as he led her to the sofa.

"Uh-huh," she grunted. "All I want right now is you." There was a sadness in her eyes that he hadn't seen before. "You should always be shirtless," she pronounced as she lifted his shirt off.

"Uh-huh. You, too." He kissed her again. Food could wait.

She closed the blinds.

He moved to turn on the lights.

"No lights," she commanded.

"You're the boss." He went to her, kissing her as he

pulled her down to the sofa with him. She ran her hands over his bare shoulders, alternating kissing him and staring at him, as if trying to memorize him.

"I missed you," she whispered as she ran her hands over him, her fingers stopping on his jeans button.

There was something...different about her. A desperation in her voice and movements, the way she was looking at him. Something was wrong.

He reached behind him and turned on the small lamp beside the sofa.

"No lights, Amar. Please," she murmured and reached over him to turn off the light. He gently caught her hand and wrapped his other arm around her bare waist.

"Wait. Div, something's up." He sat up and pulled her onto his lap. "You're different."

"Can't a girl just have sex with her boyfriend?" She threw the words at him, clearly annoyed.

"Divya." His voice was gentle as he searched her face for clues. Brow furrowed, pouting, she was chewing the inside of her cheek. "What's going on?"

"What's going on?" she started in the same annoyed tone as she climbed out of his lap. "What's going on? I'll tell you what's going on." Her voice faltered, the annoyance leaving it, only to be replaced by desperation. He reached for her, but she stepped away. "I just want to make love to the man I love one more time." Her voice cracked as tears appeared in her eyes.

"Div." Amar knelt on the sofa, reaching out to her again. Whatever was happening, he needed her close. "What do you mean 'one more time'? I'm not going anywhere."

She came closer to him, allowing him to hold her hands. Just touching her skin calmed the fear in him. She lifted her chin, fire lighting the tears he had just seen. "I'm saying that I have cancer again. I'm saying that I will be sick and that it may not end well. So this will be the last time we do this." She motioned to the sofa. "Because after today, I won't be coming around anymore. You'll also need to find a new pastry chef."

Amar's stomach fell. He searched her face, her skin and eyes. She didn't look sick, but he knew that could be deceiving. "How…? What…?"

"Yeah, when you're done with that, you'll be where I am right now."

Her lips trembled, and he pulled her close, wrapping his arms around her as if he could shield her from all harm with just his will and two arms. "We'll get through it."

"There's no 'we.'" She pushed back from him and grabbed her top.

He ignored the words he didn't want to hear. "We'll go to the doctor together, figure out a plan."

"Amar." She raised her voice and put on her clothes. "No. *We* will not be doing any such thing." Tears escaped her lids and streamed down her face. "I will deal with this. But you will not. I cannot and will not put you through this. I couldn't bear for you—" A small sob escaped her and instinct had him moving toward her. She put up a hand at arms-length. "I tried to end this on a good note, but that is not possible. This is over. Trust me, it's for the best."

"Are you saying that you're breaking up with me because you think you're sick?" Disbelief over the whole thing hit him in the gut.

"I *am* sick."

"That's what the doctor said?"

"I have an appointment for blood tests in two days. Then I'll have proof."

"So…"

"I can't make myself clearer." She let out a shuddering breath. "I came here to say goodbye because… Amar, look. I have bruises all over my body. This is how it starts."

"That's why you suddenly never wanted the lights on?" Facts. Stick to the facts.

"It takes you a minute, but you catch on."

Wow. That hurt more than anything else she'd ever said to him.

"I know I'm sick. I can feel it." She brushed past him.

"Can we wait and see what the blood test says?"

"You know what? I know. I don't need a blood test to tell me I'm sick. I was always afraid this would happen, and now it has. I know my body. And I know betrayal. And my body is betraying me." She sniffed.

She was really breaking up with him. Funny, he'd never thought that if they actually got together, they would ever break up. But here she was, emphatically telling him that what they had was over before it ever really started.

It was incredible to him that he was still able to even breathe. He was numb. She wanted to break up because she thought she was sick. She was trying to protect him.

"Divya." He finally stood and faced her. "Have you talked to Anita?"

She froze. "I came here first. I'll call her."

"Divya, it doesn't have—"

"Yes. It does have to be this way." She turned to face him. "I never should have let it go past that first night. But I've been cancer-free for so long, I thought what the hell. I can be like other people and fall in love…sleep in late…linger."

"Div—" He reached for her. She backed away as if he could burn her with his touch.

"Don't. This—" she waved a finger between them "—was a risk I should never have taken. A mistake. I'm done. I'm so sorry. I really do love you, or I wouldn't be able to do this." She turned on her heel, and without another word, she stomped out the door, slamming it shut behind her.

Amar stood there, shocked. The sound of her motorcycle revving up startled him into movement. She was really leaving.

He ran to the door and opened it, ready to run after her. The air, frigid on his body, was the only reminder that he was still shirtless. Coulson came bolting out and ran out ahead of him and headed for the street. Amar ran after him, to save the dog from oncoming traffic, and the bike disappeared.

Divya was gone.

Chapter 26

Divya had considered ghosting Amar. Just never answering his calls or going to work. But that seemed cowardly. Divya Shah might be many things, but she was not a coward. It had seemed easy enough in her head. Go over there, tell him she was dying and leave.

But then he'd kissed her before she even entered the house. That really messed things up. She was going to be rational, logical. But who could be rational after being kissed like that? He'd kissed her like she was the most important thing in the world. Like kissing her was all he ever needed. She was powerless against that. She'd gone for a ride, because he simply would have followed her into her house, and she still needed to deal with her parents.

She pulled into her driveway and screwed up her face to be casual about her visit with the doctor, for her parents' sake. She might not be able to cut them out of her life like Amar, but she could minimize their stress.

"Hey!" She fixed her face into an expression that she believed was calm and not freaked out.

"Hi, beti," her father called from the kitchen. Something smelled amazing, sweet and warm, a hint of saffron, nutty with cardamom.

"You're making sheero?"

"You always loved my sheero." He scooped a bit onto a plate for her.

She did love his sheero. Cream of wheat, sugar, milk, plump raisins, nuts. What was not to like? This sweet dish was a must for new beginnings as well. She didn't even bother with a spoon. She took her first bite like she did when she was little, with her finger. The sweet creaminess hit her mouth like a cozy blanket, enveloping her in comfort, shielding her from the world.

She burst into tears.

Her father was at her side in an instant. "I knew something was wrong with you," he mumbled as he wrapped her in his arms.

Divya took a minute to revel in that security, before pulling back from him. She should get a grip—she was a grown woman after all.

"What happened? Did you fight with Amar?"

"I broke up with him." She tried to swallow the sob and failed.

"What?" Her father looked at her like she had just said he was blue.

"She thinks she is sick." Her mother's voice was calm as she walked into the kitchen and kissed the top of her head.

"Eh? You're sick?" Her father pulled back as if to examine her.

Divya nodded. No sense in hiding it. Her father's face

fell, but her mother went about pouring herself chai and serving herself some sheero. Her mother raised an eyebrow at her as she sipped her chai.

"Did you see a doctor?" she asked.

"I saw Dr. O'Bryan. She is sending me to an adult doctor for blood work. I see her in two days."

Her father looked from her mother to her. "You don't have test results yet?"

"It doesn't matter. I know I'm sick." Divya was firm.

"How do you—"

"Because I have bruising all over my body, and I've had a few bloody noses. And I'm tired. This is how it started last time." There. It should be clear to them.

"You haven't even had blood drawn yet," her father said. He shared a look with her mother.

"I will. And it will confirm what I already know." Why didn't they get this?

"Beti." Her mother looked at her, her tone gentle. "It's presumptuous. Let's see what the tests say."

"And why would you break up with Amar?" her father added.

"It's not presumptuous. I know my body." She fired up. "Amar does not need to be tied to me for all of this. Quite frankly, neither do you two. I'm not a child this time. I can manage."

"Did Amar say he did not want to be involved?" Her mother eyed her over her chai mug.

"It's not his decision!" Divya snapped. "He says he loves me. And he's a good man." The best, in fact, that she knew. Her voice broke. "Which means he will suffer through all the chemo, the vomiting and all that. He doesn't need that."

"Did he go along with this?" her father asked.

"I did not give him a choice."

"Beti…"

"Let's make something." She hustled to the pantry. She needed something to get her mind off the fact that all she wanted to do was run across the street and fall into Amar's arms and forget about doctors and cancer and chemo. She wanted to lose herself in him. But that was no longer available to her. Baking was. Baking did not fail her—ever. "Let's do kopra-pak."

She opened the walk-in pantry and grabbed the shredded coconut. It wasn't fresh, but it would do. She also grabbed the sugar container and the cardamom jar. Lastly, she picked up the small saffron tin with her pointer and middle fingers. She hated going back and forth to the pantry for things, and her parents always chastised her for grabbing too much, sure that she would drop something.

She came out of the pantry with her hands and arms full.

"You will drop something," her father stated blandly, as he always did.

"I can handle it, Dad," she said. And just then the cardamom jar slipped a bit. She shifted her arm to save it, but lost her hold on the sugar container, and it fell from her arms, landed on the ceramic tile with a crack and a thud, sugar spilling out everywhere.

She looked down at the mess she'd made, and moans erupted from her stomach. She knelt down in the sugar, unable to keep the sobs from coming. In an instant, her parents were by her side, her mother cradling her head in her arms, her father rubbing her back. No one cared about the spilled sugar.

"It's not fair!" she sobbed, sounding every bit the twelve-year-old spoiled brat who wasn't allowed to have whatever fancy item her friends had. Except the item she wanted was her health. If she had that, she could have Amar and everything that that meant. A future with him. Working side by side, maybe even getting married and having children. Her parents would not have to go to her funeral.

"I know, beti," her mother murmured, still holding her while the sobs subsided.

Once she quieted, she nodded at her mother and began cleaning the mess. Her parents did not try to stop her, they simply helped her. She took her time cleaning the spilled sugar, her mind clearing, and rational thought returning.

Of course it wasn't fair. Nothing ever was. She had seen many of her friends with cancer die, their parents, good people, grieving. That had scared her the most—the impact on the people she'd leave behind if she died. For a long time, she'd kept her relationships to her parents. The less people who loved her, the less who had to mourn her.

Until she'd met the girl across the street. Anita had walked by her side when she finally started school, and had never left. Anita was so full of life and so fun and smart, Divya had taken to her almost immediately. Anita knew from the get-go that Divya was sick, but she didn't care. They talked about school, classes, boys, cooking and so many other things. When Divya was feeling well enough, they even went to the mall together or the movies, but Divya's favorite thing had been cooking with Anita's family.

Amar had always been reserved on those nights, though Divya couldn't remember a time growing up where he wasn't reserved. It was only after having gotten to know him now, that she realized he had another playful side to him. Though she suspected not many people saw that.

Her heart ached when she thought of him. He had been so thoroughly confused by her behavior. Better now than later, but the thought brought forth a fresh wave of tears.

"Enough." Her father spoke firmly and she looked at him. The floor was clean, not a single grain of sugar remained as evidence of her mishap. She was extremely thorough. She left nothing behind. Or at least, she tried not to.

"Come, sit." He walked over to the end of the island. Divya followed her father and sat down, her mother next to him.

She felt drained—and all she wanted was more. More energy. More time. She had so much left she wanted to do. Sitting around being sick from chemo was not one of them.

"Beti, since when do you think like this? You never did this before." Her father studied her.

"Before, I was fighting—I had no choice."

"And now?"

"Now I'm tired of fighting. Me being sick, it's like I never actually won. What's the point in fighting now, if it's just going to come back again when I least expect it?" Divya's logic made sense to her. What was the point of beating cancer again and again, and putting her loved ones through this?

How could she put Amar through this? He'd lost so much already.

"We don't even know if it's back yet, beti." Her mother insisted on not believing her.

"*I* know."

"But, beti—"

She stood and shook her head. "Amar and I are done. I won't put him through this. I wish I didn't even have to put you two through it, but… I'm going to my room." She was suddenly very exhausted. More proof she had cancer. "I'm taking a nap." Her parents exchanged a look, but Divya was too tired, too heartbroken to try to figure out what it meant.

Chapter 27

"Hey, what smells so good?" Anita startled him and he jumped, spilling masala all over the place.

"Jeez. Why are you sneaking up on me?"

"Sorry." Anita came around to the stove and peeked in the pots. "Ohh... urad-style dhal, jeera rice, bhinda. What party is this?"

"No party, just the families I cook for," Amar mumbled as he rolled out the paratha that would finish off the meal.

"Where's Coulson?"

A small bark was her answer. "Behind you."

Anita turned and knelt down to pet the puppy. "I can't believe you got a dog."

"Well, we really miss Fury, so I thought why not?"

"Wait, aren't these Divya's favorites?" Anita scooped a little bit of each onto a plate.

Amar grunted at her. They were her favorites. He hadn't realized that he had made her preferences. The families always wanted him to decide the menu, so he usually made whatever vegetable he found fresh.

He knew why his sister was here. She'd get to it eventually. She grabbed a fresh paratha and sat down at the island. He continued to roll and cook the paratha.

She took a spoonful of dhal and wrinkled her nose. He froze. "What? What's that face?"

"You forgot the salt."

"Seriously?" He stopped his paratha and took the spoon to taste it himself. She was right. He grabbed the salt and added some to the dhal. It was a little late to add salt, but it would do. As he stirred the pot, a burning smell came to him. He turned to see his last paratha had blackened on the bottom, charring the pan.

"Damn it." He grabbed the pan and tossed it in the sink, then rummaged through his cabinets, looking for his backup pan.

His sister simply sat at the island and watched. "You want help?" She cocked an eyebrow.

"Yes, duh. This order is due in an hour."

She sighed and shooed him aside while she opened a lower cabinet producing his backup paratha pan. "You roll. I'll bake."

It's what they used to do when they cooked together. "Fine." He picked up his belan and got back to it while the pan heated.

"So, why so distracted?" Anita asked.

"I'm fine."

"Liar." She looked at him. "You forgot salt in the dhal. Didn't you taste it while you were cooking?"

He had not.

"I talked to Divya yesterday." Anita was watching him closely.

His heart skipped a beat, but he tried to play it cool. "Oh yeah?"

"She's a mess."

"She's sick." He continued to abuse the paratha dough, forcing it into a circle.

"Yeah." Anita pressed her mouth into a line.

Amar stopped what he was doing and pulled her into a hug.

Anita held him for a minute, then pulled back. "She told me she broke up with you."

"Sounds about right," Amar mumbled. He didn't want to think about it. He had no idea how to convince her that he did not care if she was sick. He loved her. That should be enough.

"That's all you have to say?" Anita flipped over the paratha and drizzled oil around its edges. The oil sizzled as it cooked the bread. The comforting aroma of fresh paratha filled the kitchen.

It did nothing to comfort him now.

"Anita." He stopped rolling and turned to her. "She won't see me. I texted her, called her and went over there and stood outside her bedroom door. I even found Mom and Dad's old boom box and was ready to go blast it outside her window, like in that '80s movie you two used to watch all the time, but it's broken and I haven't had time to fix it. So whatever you came here to say, just say it."

"Fine." She flipped another paratha. "You should go see her."

"Did you not hear what I just said?"

"Of course. But she's being tough and independent, trying to cut collateral damage. I was there the last time—this is not something anyone should do alone—even Divya."

"I'm aware." He ripped a small piece of dough from the larger ball and worked it into a smaller ball. "Did you see her?"

"No. She won't see me either."

Amar stopped working and turned to his sister again. "What? You're her best friend."

"And you are the man she loves," his little sister shot back. "You should go see her."

His heart broke and tears burned behind his eyes. "You're not listening."

"I am listening, and that is bull. You love her and she's—"

"Sick. Anita. She's sick and she doesn't want me around to see it."

"Do you care that she told you she's sick?" Anita challenged him.

"Of course not."

Anita pressed her lips together. "All she does is bake. Auntie gave me kopra-pak and cupcakes and truffles."

"So she's getting her work done?"

"Sort of. She skipped her first party with Ranjit last night. She sent Courtney with the sweets. Courtney had to make the cake. Ranjit was pissed. Accused her of agreeing to work with him and then flaking on purpose."

Amar furrowed his brow. Divya did not blow off clients. "When is the next one?"

"Tomorrow night. Gulab jamun and her rose truffles, forty people."

Amar's brain started churning. "Can you finish these paratha?" He scooped some of the okra and some of the dhal into plastic containers and wrapped up a few paratha. "The families come here to pick up. They'll Venmo."

"Um, I have to study—"

"Please? I'll owe you."

Anita feigned a huge sigh of resignation. "You owe me big."

Amar showed up at the Shah residence, carrying a box, his heart pounding and sweat beading at his forehead, despite the cold. Coulson trailed behind him.

Divya's father answered the door. "Hi, Uncle. How is...everyone today?"

"Same, beta. You?" The older man stepped aside.

"I've got an idea," Amar said.

"Let's try it." He looked at the puppy, a small smile coming to his face.

Amar entered, heading straight for the kitchen, and emptied the contents of the box. Auntie was at the computer.

"Amar, beta." She shook her head. "She hardly eats. She only came out today to go to the doctor and give her blood sample. Then she came back and locked herself in her room." Auntie's voice shook. "I'm at a loss..."

Amar leaned over and hugged her close. "Mind if I cook, Auntie?"

"Of course not."

"Coulson." Amar gestured at the puppy. "Go to Auntie." Amar gathered the ingredients, setting aside the food he'd brought from home. Auntie and Uncle watched him closely.

"Amar...what are you are making?"

Auntie looked over his shoulder. "It looks like khadi, rice, rotli and potatoes."

Amar nodded. This better work. "Yes."

"But, Amar... She hates khadi. And she's not really a fan of potatoes." Auntie looked at him like he might have lost his mind.

"I know." Amar continued to cook despite the looks that Divya's parents were giving each other. "But you both love khadi, don't you? You never make it. Because she doesn't like it."

"True."

"Well, you deserve to have your favorites, too."

"But, Amar—" her mother started.

"It's okay, Auntie." Amar smiled at her.

She shrugged and went back to her computer. Uncle sat back, watching him while he played with Coulson.

Soon, Amar had filled the kitchen with the enticing aroma of roasted, spiced potatoes and the yogurt-based soup, khadi. The rice was just about finished as Amar started rolling out the rotli and baking it on a pan next to him.

He had done this at his mother's side until Anita was tall enough to reach the stove and help him. His parents had always loved getting fresh, hot rotli with their dinner. Though, who didn't?

"Uncle, Auntie. Sit down. I'll make you garam-garam rotli," Amar called out.

"You don't have to tell us twice," Uncle said as he gathered plates and bowls. Auntie filled their plates and Amar put fresh, hot rotli dripping in butter on them as they sat down.

"What is that smell?" They heard her voice first, and then Divya appeared in the kitchen, her mouth curled in distaste. "Is that khadi?"

Amar's heart raced. *She came out of her room.* She

looked tired, disheveled in her oversize sweatpants and T-shirt. But other than that, she looked fine. No. She looked amazing. He hadn't realized exactly how much he had missed her until he saw her just now. It took everything he had to not scoop her up in his arms and kiss her senseless.

Coulson got to her first anyway.

She knelt to greet the puppy. "Oh! Hey, Coulson." Divya's eyes brightened a bit as she sat down next to the animal. She giggled as Coulson jumped into her lap and licked her face.

"He missed you," Amar said softly.

Uncle and Auntie had frozen with food in their fingers to stare at the two of them.

Auntie finally glanced at Amar, a look of pure gratitude on her face.

Finally, Coulson had had enough—though, Amar could never imagine having enough Divya—and he was content to curl up at her feet.

Divya stood. "What are you doing here?" She wrinkled her nose. "And why are you making khadi?"

"I'm having dinner with my in-laws." He nodded at Uncle and Auntie. Uncle raised his eyebrows, and Auntie grinned, but neither of them corrected him.

"They're not your in-laws." Divya stated the obvious with the compulsory eye roll.

So Divya. Amar bit the inside of his cheek to squash his grin. "Not yet."

"I'm not marrying you." Divya furrowed her brow. "Besides, did you even ask me?"

"Well, that may not be up to you." Amar continued making rotli, his voice light with innocence. He pulled a fresh one off the stove and slathered it in butter. "Want one?"

"No." Divya appeared thoroughly annoyed. "Whether or not I marry you is up to me."

"Oh, is it?" Amar exaggerated a frown and a shrug. "Because I thought we were making decisions for each other."

"What are you talking about?"

"I'm talking about how you broke up with me because you're sick." He continued making rotli as if they were simply talking about the weather.

"That's different. Breaking up is different."

"Is it, though?" Amar smirked at her. "I never agreed to a breakup. You didn't *ask* if I wanted to break up. You just did it. *You* decided that I should not be around while you were sick." Amar put another fresh rotli on Uncle's plate. "So, I decided that I would make your parents my in-laws. You and I are getting married regardless of how sick you are."

"I am not marrying you."

"I am not breaking up with you."

"You didn't even ask me."

"Neither did you."

"And why are you making the food I hate?" Divya folded her arms across her chest.

"Because if I'd made your favorites, you never would have come down to see what was going on." Amar's voice softened as he buttered a fresh rotli, rolled it up and handed it to her. She absently took it. "Sick or not, I want us to have whatever time we have. I love you, Divya, and I want to be with you, by your side, no matter what."

Divya just stared at him, shaking her head.

"You're afraid, Div." Amar took her hands in his. "You

are the toughest person I know, but it's okay to be afraid. And more importantly, it's okay to lean on the people who love you. Your parents. Anita." He smiled. "Me and Coulson."

Divya was still shaking her head, but a small smile started to appear.

Amar was buoyed by this. "You can shake your head at me all you want, Divya Shah. But I am here to stay." He led her to the table and sat her down. "Wait here."

He went back and filled a plate and bowl with the dhal and the bhinda and the paratha he had brought with him and then placed it in front of her.

She looked at the plate, then him, tears in her eyes. "I can't let you—"

"How many ways do you need to hear that you are not the boss of me? We're a team. Now, eat up. Then we have gulab jamun and truffles to make."

"What?"

"You can help me if you want, but you've already pissed off Ranjit. Do you really want him giving you the treatment he gave me? Your business and my business are linked. You have sweets due in a couple days. I'll make them if you won't, but you know how my gulab jamun are." He shrugged.

Divya simply looked at him, sadness still in her eyes. She looked longingly at the plate he had made her, and Amar thought he was in. But just as quickly, Divya's eyes hardened and she stood up from the table and stepped away from him, the food on her plate, as well as the rotli in her hand, untouched.

She might as well have built a physical wall between them. "No. You need to go." She pressed her lips together.

"I'll do my job, don't worry, but we *are* breaking up. I'm not putting you through cancer."

Amar's heart fell into his stomach. He'd lost. And she didn't even know if she was sick. He nodded and headed for the door, Coulson at his heels. "Coulson, stay with Divya," Amar ordered.

The puppy followed him. Amar stopped by the door and turned around. "You forget I was there the whole time you fought that disease as a teenager. So, I've already been through cancer with you. The only difference was that back then, it was my choice to love you from afar. This time, you're forcing me to do so."

"You should move on. I don't think— I don't really love you." Divya threw out her last hope at getting rid of him.

Amar just looked at her, sadness on his face. Then without another word, he turned and left.

Chapter 28

Divya nearly crumpled when Amar walked out. She should be relieved. She'd gotten what she wanted. But instead, she was heartbroken. She wanted nothing more than to sit at this table, eat the food he'd made her and joke about him becoming her parents' son-in-law. She wanted to run after him and melt into those arms of his and have him hold her and tell her that everything would be okay.

But she couldn't. She wouldn't. Because she would not take Amar down with her. He deserved better than having to care for a girlfriend—or a wife—who was sick.

Who might not survive.

He'd already lost his parents. How could she risk making him a widower?

"Divya! What did you do?" Her mother came to her, shock and horror on her face.

"What I had to." The words felt like marbles in her mouth.

"Beti, no. Call him back." Her father had never sounded so sad.

"For what?"

"He loves you. And you love him."

"That is why I let him go."

"You don't even have test results."

"I don't need them." She turned to the food on the table that had tempted her just moments ago, and her stomach turned. "I know the truth."

Her parents looked at each other, and she knew they pitied her.

"When do you get the results?"

"Two days."

This time the look they shared, Divya hadn't seen before. "What?"

They both shook their heads. "Nothing."

"No, what?"

"We were debating whether or not to change our travel plans. But we'll wait until you get your results."

"You should go on your trip. I'm grown up now, I can handle this." She glanced out the window at Amar's house. The car was gone.

Turning to the pantry, she wiped away a tear and got to work on her desserts.

Divya did not hate the hospital.

She stood in the parking lot bundled from head to toe, staring at the top of the hospital building. She imagined she could see the ward from down here.

Her heart rate increased, and her anger boiled at the sheer injustice of the disease, the absolute randomness with which it chose its victims. The illogical manner in which survivors were chosen.

No. She did not hate the hospital. She was afraid of it. Today was arts and crafts day on the ward. After completely breaking it off with Amar yesterday and her parents constantly giving each other looks that Divya could not decipher, she'd decided that keeping this appointment with the kids was something she needed to do.

She shifted her gaze to the entrance door. Her hands automatically flexed and fisted, her fingers stretching out and curling in, as if they were pumping courage into her heart to allow her to walk in the door. She half expected to feel familiar, warm, strong fingers thread in between hers, securing that last piece of strength she needed to move forward. Of course, it wouldn't come.

No worries. She had done this without him before— she could do it again, couldn't she? She tilted her chin up and stepped toward the entrance doors. The doors slid open, and Divya walked through. She was immediately assaulted by the sterile odor of hospital-grade cleaner mixed with sickness.

She took a second and walked past the Christmas tree to the elevator. She took off her hat and gloves as she entered the ward and the lavender scent filled her nostrils.

Doing this, coming here, had been easier with Amar by her side. His silent, loving support had made her experience with the children that much better. She tried to shake her head free of those thoughts. Instead, she recalled how Amar would cook for her when she was sick, even bringing food to the hospital himself. He had always been a constant quiet presence, even when she hadn't really been paying attention.

And she'd rejected him.

She heard the buzz among the children before she even saw them. They were always excited by a visitor, and word traveled fast. Soon enough, she was immersed in glue and paint and gossip. It seemed the big news was that Fernando, the boy that Parul had liked, had gotten better and gone home just before Thanksgiving, and he was coming to visit. Good news like this always lifted Divya, and she couldn't wait to tell Amar.

Oh. Wait. She would not be telling Amar.

"Divya, why do you look so sad?" Shanaya asked.

"What? Oh no. I'm fine. Really."

"Where is that handsome man?"

"He, uh… Well. We're not together anymore." There, she'd said it out loud. But saying the words drained her.

"Sorry to hear it." Shanaya frowned at Divya. "Kids, I have another surprise visitor for you," Shanaya sing-songed for them.

Their faces lit up as Fernando walked into the room. He was followed by a lovely young girl. Fernando was attacked by the children who knew him, and his smile said everything. He was still thin from being sick and the treatment, but the color was back in his face and he looked much stronger. Divya could now see that he was a bit older than he had originally seemed. Closer to maybe seventeen or eighteen.

Once the initial excitement had passed, Divya went over to hug him.

"Hi, Divya." His voice was stronger, his smile brighter. Divya's heart was full. "This is my girlfriend, Hannah."

Divya widened her eyes but quickly extended her hand to Hannah. "So nice to meet you." She turned to the young man. "You look great." This was the first smile all day that she had not had to force.

"I'm coming along. I've been home for about a month. Hannah and I met just a few weeks ago." Fernando looked Divya in the eye. "I didn't want you to think that I was with Hannah when Parul…"

It had been close to three months since losing her, but the pang in Divya's heart at the mention of Parul was fresh.

Divya shook her head. "Of course. No such thought had crossed my mind." What had crossed her mind was that Hannah did not appear to be at all sick, while Fernando was still at that iffy time.

"Hannah and I like to hang out," Fernando explained, as if reading Divya's mind. "She knows I'm sick and what that means. She doesn't care." The young man smiled at Hannah as if she were the sun and the moon.

Hannah returned that look in spades. "He's so funny and caring and optimistic and real. You don't really see all that a lot in guys our age."

Tears burned behind Divya's eyes. They were tears of joy, she lied to herself. Not regret.

"I know what might happen. We try to focus on now." Hannah looked at Fernando with so much love, it almost felt invasive for Divya to watch. "He needs me. And I need him."

Fernando kissed Hannah's hand. "I'd be an idiot to turn down that kind of love and support." He grinned at Divya. "Just like you and Amar. Although you aren't sick anymore."

"Right." Divya nodded, doing her best to swallow those tears, but she failed.

"Divya? You okay?" Fernando asked.

"I'm fine." She wiped away her tears. "You two want to stay and help out with the craft today?"

"That would be great." Hannah smiled. "We'd love to."

Chapter 29

"Amar. Amar! AMAR!"

Someone was calling him from very far away. But all he wanted to do was stay asleep. He'd been having a phenomenal dream about Divya. It was one in which she didn't actually push him away. She was in his arms, her dark eyes looking at him with love.

There were no doctors. No tests. No cancer.

The voice was male, and it was irritating.

"What?" he managed.

It was Nikhil. *Jeez. Call a guy* family *one time, he thinks he's your brother.* "Today's the day. Divya is getting test results."

Amar opened his eyes.

Divya leaned against Sai outside the hospital building. She was chilled to the bone despite her motorcycle boots and favorite fluffy white winter coat. Her follow-up appointment with Dr. Hoang was in thirty minutes. Dr. Hoang had been kind and patient when she'd seen her the day before yesterday for the tests.

Today was the day she got her results. She had come early because she didn't know what else to do, but now she couldn't go in the building.

Funny. Yesterday, she'd at least been able to get out of the car. Though the same hospital looked completely different to her today. If Amar were here, he'd hold her hand and pull her close and warm her from the inside out.

She shook her head. She was stronger than this. She did not need Amar or anyone else to lean on. She was perfectly capable of getting her results, though she knew it was not good news.

Amar hadn't called or texted since she kicked him out of her house two days ago. Tears threatened to spill from her eyes. He'd never have a chance to be her parents' son-in-law. She chided herself for wasting so much time. Time she could have had with him. Why had it taken her so long to see what had been in front of her the whole time?

She tried to move her feet toward the building. She'd done this countless times, but today she was frozen. Couldn't move. She flashed back to Fernando and Hannah. It wasn't just that Hannah was so brave, so young. It was Fernando. Fernando who was willing to live even though he might be dying. Fernando who seemed to know the meaning of love.

She grabbed her phone and tapped Amar's name. He picked up right away. "Divya."

The rumble of her name in his voice was so warm, so comforting, so filled with love. Tears burned. "Amar. My appointment is now. I know you're at home. But I can't—I can't move. I'm standing next to Sai and I can't… I know it's selfish and I don't want to be selfish, but I can't walk in there alone." She let the tears out. "Please come."

"On your left." His reply was instantaneous, his voice clear. That rumble reverberating through her body was not from the phone. She turned to her left, and there he was. Standing there like he'd been there forever, and she just hadn't seen him. She had pushed him away, even said she didn't love him, but yet, here he was because she needed him. Her own personal hero in dark jeans and an unzipped winter coat.

"You've been here the whole time." Despite the reason she was here, Divya's heart filled with light as realization set in. He had come here because he knew she would need him, even though she had said she didn't. That was Amar Virani's superpower. All those other superheroes had nothing on him.

Her hero nodded. Divya fell into him, and when his arms went around her, she knew no matter what happened in that doctor's office, this safe place would always be here for her. She breathed in his familiar scent and her heart rate calmed. She was warm and comforted and loved.

"I didn't mean it when I said I didn't love you." Tears burned her eyes. "I love you. I was wrong to push you away and I want every single last minute with you that I can get, if you still want me. I don't want to do this without you."

"I know," Amar whispered into her hair.

She pulled back so she could look up at him. He wiped the tears from her face. "I don't want to waste another minute of our time together."

He cocked that sexy side smile she adored. "Damn. Divya Shah, I think we actually agree on something for a change."

"Hmm. You going to kiss me or what?"

"I'm definitely going to kiss you."

When Amar's mouth met hers, it was a kiss of promise, of things to come. He was her future, and she was his. She pulled back and just looked at him.

"Should we go in?" he asked.

"Probably."

"Are you scared?"

She smiled at him, this incredible man she loved. "Not anymore."

He wiped away her tears and looked at her like she held his life in her hands. He squeezed her hand and they walked toward the entrance.

"Wonder Woman T-shirt?" she asked.

"We need the big guns today, Div." Amar grinned.

Why were the doctors' offices she had to go to always in the part of the hospital that tried to use disinfectant to hide the smell of reheated hospital food and stale coffee? At least Dr. Hoang made an attempt at making her office feel homey. She had plants, carpet covering the linoleum floor, and pictures of the beach and mountains hung on neutral-colored walls.

There was definitely a diffuser somewhere, too, because the hospital smell evaporated once she walked in there, to be replaced by the scent of lavender. A scent that Divya had long associated with having cancer.

She sighed. There really was no winning. Cancer ruined everything. Even lavender. The difference today was that Amar was here. He looked down at her and smiled.

Damn, but the man was handsome. How had she not noticed that all these years?

He squeezed her hand and waited for her to enter Dr. Hoang's lavender-scented purgatory.

She wasn't quite ready. She pulled him aside. "Are you sure you want to be part of this?"

"I love you. I told you. I'm all in. I've always been, Divya." He waited for her to lead the way.

She squeezed his hand, then knocked, and from within, Dr. Hoang beckoned her to enter.

She opened the door and braced herself for the wave of lavender that assaulted her.

In her ear, Amar whispered, "That's enough lavender to make you vomit."

She bit her bottom lip to suppress her smirk. If she hadn't loved him before, that last line cinched it. She was desperately in love with Amar Virani. That thought was her focus as she entered the lavender-infused room. She was desperately in love with Amar and she would fight for every last second.

She sat down in front of Dr. Hoang. Amar stood behind her, his hands gently resting on her shoulders. She allowed herself to feel the warmth and strength of his touch. She allowed herself to lean into him.

Dr. Hoang looked at them and nodded her head. "I asked you to come to the office because I like to give good news in person whenever I can."

Divya's heart pounded in her chest.

"The test results were negative. Divya, you are clear. The bruises are just that—bruises. The nosebleeds are possibly due to dryness or allergy. The fatigue seems to be due to low iron, so let's set you up with some iron infusions." Dr. Hoang smiled at them.

Divya was numb as Dr. Hoang's words washed over her. She had been completely convinced that she was sick. That she would die young. And here she was, being told that wasn't true.

"There is always a small chance of recurrence, but the further away you get from that previous diagnosis, the less likely that becomes."

Amar's hands never left her. The doctor said some things about following up, but it was just checkups. She was fine. She was still cancer-free. And most likely would remain so.

"Div. Div." Amar kneeled in front of her, concern on his face. "You okay?"

She nodded.

"You're crying. Did you hear the doctor?"

She wiped her face. "Yes."

"Want to go?" Amar raised his eyebrows with his fabulous half smile.

She stood, still unable to trust her voice completely. Amar did not let go of her hand. They left Sai in the parking lot—she'd pick the bike up later—and got into his car. "Where should we go?"

She took his hand and smiled at him, aware that she was still crying. "Home."

"Whatever you say." Amar wiped away her tears and drove.

They called her parents and then Anita from the car. Amar drove them to Golden Oak Court and parked in her driveway.

"No. Our home." She squeezed his hand. He backed out and pulled into the driveway across the street. He turned off the car and opened her door and held her hand as they walked into the house.

"Come." She led him to the small sitting room sofa.

She sat down next to him and curled up in his arms. "Amar. I want to stay right here, always. I love you. I need you. I never want to be without you." She pulled back and looked at him, this incredible man who would move heaven and earth for her, who knew her almost better than she knew herself.

"Divya, you've been my family, my other half, for as long as I can remember. It has always been you."

She snuggled closer to him. "You're going to have to marry me."

He cocked that half smile she melted for and held out a ring. Platinum band, single diamond solitaire. "I thought you'd never ask."

Epilogue

Divya dropped her backpack in the small entranceway next to Amar's, then collapsed on the sofa. "That was amazing!" But it did feel good to be back on this sofa.

Amar collapsed next to her. "It really was. See, it can be fun climbing the same mountain twice."

Divya curled up next to him. "Couldn't think of a better way to celebrate our second anniversary, husband."

Amar shook his head at her. "You said that when we went skiing on our first anniversary, and also when we went surfing on our honeymoon."

"All great celebrations."

Amar leaned over and kissed her. "I might be able to come up with a couple more ways."

Divya kissed him back and then pushed him against the cushions, straddling him. "But are they better?"

Her husband put his hand on her waist under her T-shirt. "We'll have to find out."

She melted into his touch. "Although, not going to lie, watching Avengers movies right here on this sofa with you sounds pretty darn fabulous."

Amar pulled her closer to him and kissed her again. "Maybe later."

Divya melted into him, his kiss knocking all thought of anything else from her mind. Three years and she still got lost in him. She was just reaching down to remove his Captain America T-shirt when she was hit with a wave of nausea. She put her hand to her mouth, climbed off his lap and bolted for the bathroom.

"Again?" Amar called as she shut the door.

Amar stood and went straight for the electric hot pot. He quickly boiled water, and made a simple tea of ginger, turmeric and honey with just a pinch of black pepper. Divya had been nauseous the entire flight back from Colorado, where they'd summited Pikes Peak together. Maybe she'd picked up something on the hike—he couldn't be sure. He looked at the bathroom door. She was still in there.

He opened the freezer and started pulling out the okra and paratha he had frozen before they left. His fridge was stocked, thanks to Anita. He glanced down the hall. Divya still wasn't out. He started for the bathroom when his phone rang. Anita.

"Hey, sis." He talked while he made his way to the bathroom. "How's Coulson?"

"You're back! How was it? Why haven't you called?"

Anita nearly screeched. "And your dog is fine, feel free to come and get him, he chewed up like half my shoes."

Amar chuckled. *Good dog!* "It was fabulous. I've been back for a total of ten minutes," Amar groused at her. "How are you feeling anyway?"

"Much better. Second trimester is way better than the first. Way more energy, no more nausea, no more throwing up—"

No more nausea. No more throwing up… Amar was barely listening to his sister, his entire focus on the bathroom door. "I gotta go, Anita. Call you later!" He hung up while she was still talking, his heart racing.

"Div?" He pressed his ear to the door. Nothing. "Divya. Open the door."

It seemed a year before he saw the handle turn and Divya's dark eyes were in front of him again. She was pale and her eyes were glassy. She was chewing her bottom lip.

"Div? You okay?" Amar opened the door all the way. Divya stood in the frame.

"Um, yeah. I think so." She looked down at her hand where she held a white stick.

Amar smiled, his heart light. "Is that what I think—"

Divya nodded, finally focusing on him, a smile coming to her face, bright tears in her eyes. "I… I…um." She raised the stick to show him the plus sign.

Tears of complete joy blurred his vision. He pulled Divya into his arms and kissed her. "Looks like we've got another adventure."

* * * * *

Get 3 FREE REWARDS!

We'll send you 2 FREE Books plus a FREE Mystery Gift.

FREE
Value Over
$20

Both the **Romance** and **Suspense** collections feature compelling novels written by many of today's bestselling authors.

YES! Please send me 2 FREE novels from the Essential Romance or Essential Suspense Collection and my FREE gift (gift is worth about $10 retail). After receiving them, if I don't wish to receive any more books, I can return the shipping statement marked "cancel." If I don't cancel, I will receive 4 brand-new novels every month and be billed just $7.49 each in the U.S. or $7.74 each in Canada. That's a savings of at least 17% off the cover price. It's quite a bargain! Shipping and handling is just 50¢ per book in the U.S. and $1.25 per book in Canada.* I understand that accepting the 2 free books and gift places me under no obligation to buy anything. I can always return a shipment and cancel at any time by calling the number below. The free books and gift are mine to keep no matter what I decide.

Choose one:
- ☐ **Essential Romance**
  (194/394 BPA GRNM)
- ☐ **Essential Suspense**
  (191/391 BPA GRNM)
- ☐ **Or Try Both!**
  (194/394 & 191/391 BPA GRQZ)

Name (please print)

Address   Apt. #

City   State/Province   Zip/Postal Code

Email: Please check this box ☐ if you would like to receive newsletters and promotional emails from Harlequin Enterprises ULC and its affiliates. You can unsubscribe anytime.

Mail to the **Harlequin Reader Service:**
IN U.S.A.: P.O. Box 1341, Buffalo, NY 14240-8531
IN CANADA: P.O. Box 603, Fort Erie, Ontario L2A 5X3

Want to try 2 free books from another series! Call 1-800-873-8635 or visit www.ReaderService.com.

*Terms and prices subject to change without notice. Prices do not include sales taxes, which will be charged (if applicable) based on your state or country of residence. Canadian residents will be charged applicable taxes. Offer not valid in Quebec. This offer is limited to one order per household. Books received may not be as shown. Not valid for current subscribers to the Essential Romance or Essential Suspense Collection. All orders subject to approval. Credit or debit balances in a customer's account(s) may be offset by any other outstanding balance owed by or to the customer. Please allow 4 to 6 weeks for delivery. Offer available while quantities last.

Your Privacy—Your information is being collected by Harlequin Enterprises ULC, operating as Harlequin Reader Service. For a complete summary of the information we collect, how we use this information and to whom it is disclosed, please visit our privacy notice located at corporate.harlequin.com/privacy-notice. From time to time we may also exchange your personal information with reputable third parties. If you wish to opt out of this sharing of your personal information, please visit readerservice.com/consumerschoice or call 1-800-873-8635. **Notice to California Residents**—Under California law, you have specific rights to control and access your data. For more information on these rights and how to exercise them, visit corporate.harlequin.com/california-privacy.

STRS23